Wood Rangers
The Trappers of Sonora

by

Captain Mayne Reid

Double 9
BOOKS

Wood Rangers
The Trappers of Sonora
by Captain Mayne Reid

ISBN: 978-93-61156-76-2

Published by

DOUBLE 9 BOOKS
2/13-B, Ansari Road
Daryaganj, New Delhi – 110002
info@double9books.com
www.double9books.com
Tel. 011-40042856

ABOUT THE AUTHOR

Thomas Mayne Reid, an Irish-American novelist, participated in the Mexican–American War. His numerous books on American life discuss colonial policy in the American colonies, the horrors of slave labor, and the lifestyles of American Indians. "Captain" Reid created adventure stories similar to those of Frederick Marryat and Robert Louis Stevenson. They were primarily situated in the American West, Mexico, South Africa, the Himalayas, and Jamaica. He admired Lord Byron. Dion Boucicault turned his anti-slavery novel Quadroon (1856) into a drama called The Octoroon (1859), which was staged in New York. Reid was born in Ballyroney, a hamlet near Katesbridge in County Down, Northern Ireland, as the son of Rev. Thomas Mayne Reid Sr., a senior clerk of the General Assembly of the Presbyterian Church in Ireland, and his wife. Reid's father intended him to become a Presbyterian pastor, so he enrolled at the Royal Belfast Academical Institution in September 1834. He stayed for four years, but lacked the ambition to finish his studies and graduate. He returned to Ballyroney to teach at a school.

CONTENTS

Chapter One
Pepé, The Sleeper

No landscape on the Biscayan coast, presents a more imposing and picturesque aspect than the little village of Elanchovi. Lying within an amphitheatre of cliffs, whose crests rise above the roofs of the houses, the port is protected from the surge of the sea by a handsome little jetty of chiselled stone; while the single street of which the village is composed, commencing at the inner end of the mole, sweeps boldly up against the face of the precipice. On both sides, the houses, disposed in a sort of *echelon*, rise, terrace-like, one above the other; so that viewed from a distance, the street presents the appearance of a gigantic stairway.

In these the common dwellings, there is not much variety of architecture; since the village is almost exclusively inhabited by poor fishermen. There is one building, however, that is conspicuous—so much so as to form the principal feature of the landscape. It is an old chateau—perhaps the only building of this character in Spain—whose slate roofs and gothic turrets and vanes, rising above the highest point of the cliffs, overlook the houses of the village.

This mansion belonged to the noble family of Mediana, and formed part of the grand estates of this ancient house. For a long period, the Counts of Mediana had not inhabited the chateau of Elanchovi, and it had fallen into a state of neglect and partial decay, presenting a somewhat wild and desolate aspect. However, at the beginning of the year 1808, during the troubles of the French invasion, the Count Don Juan, then head of the family, had chosen it as a safe residence for his young wife Doña Luisa, whom he passionately loved.

Here Don Juan passed the first months of his married life—a marriage celebrated under circumstances of sad augury. The younger brother of Don Juan, Don Antonio de Mediana, had also fervently loved the Doña Luisa; until finding her preference for his brother, he had given up his suit in anger, and quitted the country. He had gone, no one knew whither; and though after a time there came back a rumour of his death, it was neither confirmed nor contradicted.

The principal reason why the Count had chosen this wild spot as a residence for his lady was this:—He held a high command in the Spanish army, and he knew that duty would soon call him into the field. The *alcalde* of Elanchovi had been an old servant of the Mediana family, and had been raised to his present rank by their influence. Don Juan, therefore, believed he could rely upon the devotion of this functionary to the interests of his house, and that during his absence Doña Luisa would find security under the magisterial protection. Don Ramon Cohecho was the name of the chief magistrate of Elanchovi.

The Count was not permitted long to enjoy the happiness of his married life. Just as he had anticipated, he soon received orders to join his regiment; and parted from the chateau, leaving his young wife under the special care of an old and respectable domestic—the steward Juan de Dios Canelo. He parted from his home never more to return to it; for in the battle of Burgos, a French bullet suddenly terminated his existence.

It was sad tidings for the Doña Luisa; and thus to the joys of the first days of her married life succeeded the sorrows of a premature widowhood.

It was near the close of the year 1808, when the chateau was the sombre witness of Doña Luisa's grief, that our story commences, and though its scene lies in another land—thousands of leagues from, the Biscayan coast— its history is intimately woven with that of the chateau of Elanchovi.

Under ordinary circumstances, the village of Elanchovi presents a severe and dreary aspect. The silence and solitude that reigns along the summit of the cliffs, contrasted with the continuous roaring of the breakers against their base, inspires the beholder with a sentiment of melancholy. Moreover, the villagers, as already said, being almost exclusively fishermen, and absent during the whole of the day, the place at first sight would appear as if uninhabited. Occasionally when some cloud is to be observed in the sky, the wives of the fishermen may be seen at the door, in their skirts of bright colours, and their hair in long double plaits hanging below their waists. These, after remaining a while to cast anxious glances upon the far horizon, again recross the thresholds of their cottages, leaving the street deserted as before.

At the time of which we are writing—the month of November, 1808— Elanchovi presented a still more desolate aspect than was its wont. The proximity of the French army had produced a panic among its inhabitants and many of these poor people—forgetting in their terror that they had nothing to lose—had taken to their boats, and sought safety in places more distant from the invaders of whom they were in dread.

Isolated as this little village was on the Biscayan coasts, there was all the more reason why it should have its garrison of *coast-guards*; and such in reality it had. These at the time consisted of a company of soldiers—carabiniers, under the command of a captain Don Lucas Despierto—but the condition of these warriors was not one to be envied, for the Spanish government, although nominally keeping them in its pay, had for a long time neglected to pay them. The consequence was, that these poor fellows had absolutely nothing upon which to live. The seizure of smuggled goods—with which they might have contrived to indemnify themselves—was no longer possible. The contraband trade, under this system, was completely annihilated. The smugglers knew better than to come in contact with *coast-guards* whose performance of their duty was stimulated by such a keen necessity! From the captain himself down to the lowest official, an incessant vigilance was kept up—the result of which was that the fiscal department of the Spanish government was, perhaps, never so faithfully or economically served.

There was one of these coast-guards who affected a complete scepticism in regard to smuggling—he even went so far as to deny that it had ever existed! He was distinguished among his companions by a singular habit—that of always going to sleep upon his post; and this habit, whether feigned or real, had won for him the name of *the Sleeper*. On this account it may be supposed, that he was never placed upon guard where the post was one of importance.

José, or as he was more familiarly styled, *Pepé*, was a young fellow of some twenty-five years—tall, thin, and muscular. His black eyes, deeply set under bushy eyebrows, had all the appearance of eyes that *could* sparkle; besides, his whole countenance possessed the configuration of one who had been born for a life of activity. On the contrary, however—whether from a malady or some other cause—the man appeared as somnolent and immobile as if both his visage and body were carved out of marble. In a word, with all the exterior marks that denote the possession of an active and ardent soul, Pepé *the Sleeper* appeared the most inactive and apathetic of men.

His chagrin was great—or appeared to be so—when, upon the evening of the day in which this narrative commences the captain of the coast-guard sent a messenger to summon him to headquarters.

On receiving the unexpected order, Pepé rose from his habitual attitude of recumbence, stretched himself at his leisure, yawned several times, and then obeyed the summons, saying as he went out: "What the devil fancy has the captain got into his head to send for *me*?"

Once, however, on the way and alone, it might have been observed that the somnolent coast-guard walked with an energetic and active step, very unlike his usual gait!

On entering the apartment where the captain awaited him, his apathetic habit returned; and, while rolling a cigarette between his fingers, he appeared to be half asleep. The captain was buried in a profound meditation, and did not at first perceive him.

"*Bueno*! my captain," said the coast-guard, respectfully saluting his superior, and calling attention to his presence. "I am here."

"Ah! good! my fine fellow," began the captain, in a winning voice. "Well, Pepé!" added he more slowly and significantly, "the times are pretty hard with us—are they not?"

"Rather hard, captain."

"But you, *hombre*!" rejoined Don Lucas, with a laugh, "you don't appear to suffer much of the misery—you are always asleep I understand?"

"When I sleep, captain, I am not hungry," replied the coast-guard, endeavouring to stifle a yawn; "then I dream that the government has paid me."

"Well—at all events you are not its creditor for many hours of the day, since you sleep most of them. But, my fine fellow, it is not about this I desire to talk to you. I wish to give you a proof of my confidence."

"Ah!" muttered Pepé.

"And a proof of my regard for you," continued the officer. "The government has its eye open upon all of us; your reputation for apathy begins to be talked about, and you might be discharged one of these days as a useless official. It would be a sad affair if you were to lose your place?"

"Frightful! captain," replied Pepé, with perfect simplicity of manner; "for if I can scarce keep from dying of hunger in my place, what would be the result were I deprived of it? Frightful!"

"To prevent this misfortune, then," continued the captain, "I have resolved to furnish to those who calumniate you, a proof of the confidence which may be placed in you, by giving you the post of *Ensenada*—and this very night."

Pepé involuntarily opened his eyes to their fullest extent.

"That surprises you?" said Don Lucas.

"No," laconically replied the coast-guard.

The captain was unable to conceal from his inferior a slight confusion, and his voice trembled as he pronounced the interrogation:—

"What! It does not surprise you?"

"No," repeated Pepé, and then added in a tone of flattery: "The captain Despierto is so well-known for his vigilance and energy, that he may confide the most important post to the very poorest of his sentinels. That is why I am not astonished at the confidence he is good enough to place in me: and now I await the instructions your Honour may be pleased to give."

Don Lucas, without further parley, proceeded to instruct his sentinel in his duty for the night. The orders were somewhat diffuse—so much so that Pepé had a difficulty in comprehending them—but they were wound up by the captain saying to the coast-guard, as he dismissed him from his presence—

"And above all, my fine fellow, *don't go to sleep upon your post!*"

"I shall *try* not to do so, captain," replied Pepé, at the same time saluting his superior, and taking his leave.

"This fellow is worth his weight in gold," muttered Don Lucas, rubbing his hands together with an air of satisfaction; "he could not have suited my purpose better, if he had been expressly made for it!"

Chapter Two
The Sentinel of La Ensenada

The little bay of Ensenada, thus confided to the vigilance of Pepé the sleeper, was mysteriously shut in among the cliffs, as if nature had designed it expressly for smugglers—especially those Spanish *contrabandistas* who carry on the trade with a cutlass in one hand and a carbine in the other.

On account of its isolation, the post was not without danger, especially on a foggy November night, when the thick vapour suspended in the air not only rendered the sight useless, but hindered the voice that might call for assistance from being heard to any distance.

In the soldier who arrived upon this post, advancing with head erect and light elastic tread, no one could have recognised Pepé the sleeper—Pepé, habitually plunged in a profound state of somnolence—Pepé, of downcast mien and slow dragging gait—and yet it was he. His eyes, habitually half shut, were now sparkling in their sockets, as if even the slightest object could not escape him even in the darkness.

After having carefully examined the ground around his post, and convinced himself that he was entirely alone, he placed his lantern in such a position that its light was thrown along the road leading to the village. Then advancing some ten or twelve paces in the direction of the water, he spread his cloak upon the ground, and lay down upon it—in such an attitude that he could command a view both of the road and the bay.

"Ah, my captain!" soliloquised the coast-guard, as he arranged his cloak around him to the best advantage, "you are a very cunning man, but you have too much faith in people who are always asleep; and devil take me! if I don't believe that you are interested in my sleeping most soundly on this particular night. Well, *quien sabe?* we shall see."

For about the period of half an hour Pepé remained alone—delivering himself up to his reflections, and in turns interrogating with his glance the road and the bay. At the end of that time a footstep was heard in the loose sand; and looking along the pathway, the sentinel perceived a dark form approaching the spot. In another moment the form came under the light of the lantern, and was easily recognised as that of Don Lucas, the captain of the coast-guard.

The officer appeared to be searching for something, but presently perceiving the recumbent sentinel, he paused in his steps.

"Pepé!" cried he, in a low mincing voice.

No reply came from Pepé.

"Pepé!" repeated the captain, in a tone a little more elevated.

Still no reply from the sentinel, who remained obstinately silent.

The captain, appearing to be satisfied, ceased calling the name, and shortly after retraced his steps towards the village. In a few seconds his form was lost in the distance.

"Good!" said Pepé, as his superior officer passed out of sight; "just as I expected. A moment ago I was fool enough to doubt it. Now I am sure of it. Some smuggler is going to risk it to-night. Well, I shall manage badly if I don't come in for a windfall—though it be at the expense of my captain."

Saying this, the sentinel with one bound rose erect upon his feet.

"Here I am no more Pepé the Sleeper," continued he stretching himself to his full height.

From this time his eyes were bent continually upon the ocean; but another half hour passed without anything strange showing itself upon the bosom of the water—nothing to break the white line of the horizon where sea and sky appeared to be almost confounded together. Some dark clouds were floating in the heavens, now veiling and now suddenly uncovering the moon, that had just risen. The effect was fine; the horizon was one moment shining like silver, and the next dark as funeral crape; but through all these changes no object appeared upon the water, to denote the presence of a human being.

For a long while the coast-guard looked so intently through the darkness, that he began to see the sparks flying before his eyes. Fatigued with this sustained attention, he at length shut his eyes altogether, and concentrated all his powers upon the organs of hearing. Just then a sound came sweeping over the water—so slight that it scarce reached him—but the next moment the land-breeze carried it away, and it was heard no more.

Fancying it had only been an illusion, he once more opened his eyes, but in the obscurity he could see nothing. Again he shut them closely and listened as before. This time he listened with more success. A sound regularly cadenced was heard. It was such as would be made by a pair of oars cautiously dipped, and was accompanied by a dull knocking as of the oars working in their thole-pins.

"At last we shall see!" muttered Pepé, with a gasp of satisfaction.

A small black point, almost imperceptible, appeared upon the horizon. Rapidly it increased in size, until it assumed the form and dimensions of a boat with rowers in it, followed by a bright strip of foam.

Pepé threw himself suddenly *à plat ventre*, in fear that he might be seen by those on the water; but from the elevated position which he occupied, he was able to keep his eye upon the boat without losing sight of it for a single instant.

Just then the noises ceased, and the oars were held out of water, motionless, like some sea-bird, with wings extended, choosing a spot upon which to alight. In the next instant the rowing was resumed, and the boat headed directly for the shore of the bay.

"Don't be afraid!" muttered the coast-guard, affecting to apostrophise the rowers. "Don't be afraid, my good fellows—come along at your pleasure!"

The rowers, in truth did not appear to be at all apprehensive of danger; and the next moment the keel of the boat was heard grinding upon the sand of the beach.

"*Por Dios!*" muttered the sentinel in a low voice; "not a bale of goods! It is possible after all, they are not smugglers!"

Three men were in the boat, who did not appear to take those precautions which smugglers would have done. They made no particular noise, but, on the other hand, they did not observe any exact silence. Moreover their costume was not that ordinarily worn by the regular *contrabandista*.

"Who the devil can they be?" asked Pepé of himself.

The coast-guard lay concealed behind some tufts of withered grass that formed a border along the crest of the slope. Through these he could observe the movements of the three men in the boat.

At an order from the one who sat in the stern sheets, the other two leaped ashore, as if with the design of reconnoitring the ground. He who issued the order, and who appeared to be the chief of the party, remained seated in the boat.

Pepé was for a moment undecided whether he should permit the two to pass him on the road; but the view of the boat, left in charge of a single man, soon fixed his resolution.

He kept his place, therefore, motionless as ever, scarce allowing himself to breathe, until the two men arrived below him, and only a few feet from the spot where he was lying.

Each was armed with a long Catalonian knife, and Pepé could see that the costume which both wore was that of the Spanish privateers of the time—a sort of mixture of the uniform of the royal navy of Spain, and that of the merchant service; but he could not see their faces, hid as they were under the slouched Basque bonnet.

All at once the two men halted. A piece of rock, detached by the knees of the coast-guard, had glided down the slope and fallen near their feet.

"Did you hear anything?" hastily asked one.

"No; did you?"

"I thought I heard something falling from above there," replied the first speaker; pointing upward to the spot where Pepé was concealed.

"Bah! it was some mouse running into its hole."

"If this slope wasn't so infernally steep, I'd climb up and see," said the first.

"I tell you we have nothing to fear," rejoined the second; "the night is as black as a pot of pitch, and besides—the *other*, hasn't he assured us that he will answer for the man on guard, *who sleeps all day long?*"

"Just for that reason he may not sleep at night. Remain here, I'll go round and climb up. *Carramba!* if I find this sleepy-head," he added, holding out his long knife, the blade of which glittered through the darkness, "so much the worse—or, perhaps, so much the better for him—for I shall send him where he may sleep forever."

"*Mil diablos!*" thought Pepé, "this fellow is a philosopher! By the holy virgin I am long enough here."

And at this thought, he crept out of the folds of his cloak like a snake out of his skin, and leaving the garment where it lay, crawled rapidly away from the spot.

Until he had got to a considerable distance, he was so cautious not to make any noise, that, to use a Spanish expression, *the very ground itself did not know he was passing over it.*

In this way he advanced, carbine in hand, until he was opposite the point where the boat rested against the beach. There he stopped to recover his breath,—at the same time fixing his eye upon the individual that was alone.

The latter appeared to be buried in a sombre reverie, motionless as a statue, and wrapped in an ample cloak, which served both to conceal his person and protect him from the humidity of the atmosphere. His eyes were turned toward the sea; and for this reason he did not perceive the dark form of the carabinier approaching in the opposite direction.

The latter advanced with stealthy tread—measuring the distance with his eye—until at length he stood within a few paces of the boat.

Just then the stranger made a movement as if to turn his face towards the shore, when Pepé, like a tiger hounding upon its prey, launched himself forward to the side of the boat.

"It is I!" he exclaimed, bringing the muzzle of his carbine on a level with the man's breast. "Don't move or you are a dead man!"

"You, who?" asked the astonished stranger, his eyes sparkling with rage, and not even lowering their glance before the threatening attitude of his enemy.

"Why me! Pepé—you know well enough? Pepé, the Sleeper?"

"Curses upon him, if he has betrayed me?" muttered, the stranger, as if speaking to himself.

"If you are speaking of Don Lucas Despierto," interrupted the carabinier, "I can assure you he is incapable of such a thing; and if I *am here* it is because that he has been only too discreet, señor smuggler."

"Smuggler!" exclaimed the unknown, in a tone of proud disdain.

"When I say smuggler," replied Pepé, chuckling at his own perspicuity, "it is only meant as a compliment, for you haven't an ounce of merchandise in your boat, unless indeed," continued he, pointing with his foot to a rope ladder, rolled up, and lying in the bottom, "unless that may be a sample! *Santa Virgen!* a strange sample that!"

Face to face with the unknown, the coast-guard could now examine him at his leisure.

He was a young man of about Pepé's own age, twenty-five. His complexion had the hale tint of one who followed the sea for a profession. Thick dark eyebrows were strongly delineated against a forehead bony and broad, and from a pair of large black eyes shone a sombre fire that denoted a man of implacable passions. His arched mouth was expressive of high disdain; and the wrinkles upon his cheeks, strongly marked notwithstanding his youth, at the slightest movement, gave to his countenance an expression of arrogance and scorn. In his eyes—in his whole bearing—you could read that ambition or vengeance were the ruling passions of his soul. His fine black curling hair alone tempered the expression of severity that distinguished his physiognomy. With regard to his costume, it was simply that of an officer of the Spanish navy.

A look that would have frightened most men told the impatience with which he endured the examination of the coast-guard.

"An end to this pleasantry!" he cried out, at length. "What do you want, fellow? Speak!"

"Ah! talk of our affairs," answered Pepé, "that is just what I desire. Well, in the first place, when those two fellows of yours return with my cloak and lantern—which they are cunning enough to make a seizure of—you will give them your commands to keep at a distance. In this way we can talk without being interrupted. Otherwise, with a single shot of this carbine, which will stretch you out dead, I shall also give the alarm. What say you? Nothing? Be it so. That answer will do for want of a better. I go on. You have given to my captain forty *onzas*?" continued the carabinier, with a bold guess, making sure that he named enough.

"Twenty," replied the stranger, without reflecting.

"I would rather it had been forty," said Pepé. "Well, one does not pay so high for the mere pleasure of a sentimental promenade along the shore of the Ensenada. My intervention need be no obstruction to it—provided you pay for my neutrality."

"How?" asked the unknown, evidently desirous of putting an end to the scene.

"Oh, a mere bagatelle—you have given the captain forty *onzas*."

"Twenty, I tell you."

"I would rather it had been forty," coolly repeated the carabinier, "but say twenty, then. Now I don't wish to be indiscreet—he is a captain, I am nothing more than a poor private. I think it reasonable therefore, that I should have *double* what he has received."

At this extortionate demand the stranger allowed a bitter oath to escape him, but made no answer.

"I know well," continued Pepé, "that I am asking too little. If my captain has three times my pay, of course he has three times less need of money than I, and therefore I have the right to *triple* the sum he has received; but as the times are hard, I hold to my original demand—forty *onzas*."

A terrible struggle betwixt pride and apprehension appeared to be going on in the bosom of the stranger. Despite the coldness of the night the perspiration streamed over his brow and down his cheeks. Some imperious necessity it was that had led him into this place—some strange mystery there must be—since the necessity he was now under tamed down a spirit that appeared untamable. The tone of jeering intrepidity which Pepé held toward him caused him to feel the urgency of a compromise; and at length plunging his hand into his pocket he drew forth a purse, and presented it to the carabinier.

"Take it and go!" he cried, with impatience.

Pepé took the purse, and for a moment held it in his hand as if he would first count its contents.

"Bah!" he exclaimed, after a pause, "I'll risk it. I accept it for forty *onzas*. And now, señor stranger, I am deaf, dumb, and blind."

"I count upon it," coldly rejoined the unknown.

"By the life of my mother!" replied Pepé, "since it's not an affair of smuggling I don't mind to lend you a hand—for as a coast-guard, you see, I could not take part in anything contraband—no, never!"

"Very well, then," rejoined the stranger, with a bitter smile, "you may set your conscience at rest on that score. Guard this boat till my return. I go to join my men. Only whatever happens—whatever you may see—whatever you may hear—be, as you have promised, deaf, dumb, and blind."

As he uttered these words the stranger sprang out of the boat, and took the road leading to the village. A turning in the path soon bid him from the sight of the coast-guard.

Once left to himself, Pepé, under the light of the moon, counted out the glittering contents of the purse which he had extorted from the stranger.

"If this jewel is not false," muttered he to himself, "then I don't care if the government never pays me. Meanwhile, I must begin to-morrow to cry like a poor devil about the back pay. That will have a good effect."

Chapter Three
The Alcalde and his Clerk

It is not known how long Pepé remained at his post to await the return of the stranger: when the cock was heard to crow, and the aurora appeared in the eastern horizon, the little bay of Ensenada was completely deserted.

Then life began to appear in the village. The dark shadows of the fishermen were seen upon the stair-like street, descending to the mole; and the first beams of the morning lit up their departure. In a few minutes the little flotilla was out of sight; and at the doors of the cottages the women and children only could be seen, appearing and disappearing at intervals.

Among these wretched hovels of the village, there was one dwelling of greater pretensions than the rest. It was that of the alcalde, Don Ramon Cohecho of whom we have already spoken. It alone still kept its doors and windows closed against the morning light.

It was full day, when a young man, wearing a high-crowned beaver hat,—old, greasy and shining, like leather—walked up to the door of the alcalde's mansion. The limbs of this individual were scantily covered with a pair of pantaloons, so tightly fitting as to appear like a second skin to his legs, so short as scarce to touch his ankles, and of such thin stuff as to ill protect the wearer from the sharp air of a November morning. The upper half of this individual was not visible. A little cloak, of coarse shaggy cloth, known as an *esclavina*, covered him up to the very eyes. In the manner in which he so carefully guarded the upper part of his person with this pinched mantle, at the expense of his thighs and legs, an observer might have supposed that he was perfectly content with his pantaloons. Appearances, however, are often deceptive; for in truth the ambition of this youth; whose unsteady glance, miserable aspect, and a certain smell of old papers about him, proclaimed to be *un escribano*—his everyday dream was to have a pair of pantaloons entirely different from his own—in other words, a pair with long ample legs, of good wide waist, and made out of fine broadcloth. Such a pair would render him the most satisfied man in the world.

This young man was the *right hand* of the alcalde—his name Gregorio Cagatinta.

On reaching the door, he gave a modest knock with his horn ink-bottle, which he carried hanging to his button. The door was opened by an old housekeeper.

"Ah! it is you, *Don* Gregorio?" cried the housekeeper, with that superb courtesy so peculiar to the Spaniards—that even two shoeblacks on meeting lavish upon each other the epithet *Don*, as if each were a grand noble.

"Yes, it is I, Doña Nicolasa," replied Gregorio.

"*Santisima Virgen!*—since it is you, then I must be late, and my master will be waiting for his pantaloons that are not yet aired. Take a seat, Don Gregorio: he will soon be down."

The chamber into which the notary's clerk had been introduced would have been a large one, had it not been for the singular conglomeration of objects with which it was more than half filled. Nets of all sizes, masts, yards, and rudders of boats, oars, sails of every kind—both square and lateen—woollen shirts worn by sailors or fishermen, and a variety of other marine objects, were placed pellmell in every corner of the room. Notwithstanding, there was space enough left to hold three or four chairs around a large oaken table, upon which last stood a large cork ink-stand, with several goose-quill pens; with some sheets of half dirty paper placed ostentatiously around it to awe the visitors, who might have business with the alcalde.

The presence of this odd assortment of objects, it would have been difficult for a stranger to explain—though there was no mystery about it. The fact is, that besides his official character as first magistrate, the alcalde had another *rôle* which he played, of rather an unofficial character. He was the *pawnbroker* of the place—that is, he lent out money in small sums, charging a *real* for every dollar by the week—in other words, a simple interest of twenty per cent, by the month, or two hundred and fifty per cent, per annum! His clients being all fishermen, will account for the nautical character of the "pledges" that filled the chamber of audience.

Cagatinta scarce deigned to cast a look at this miscellaneous collection of objects. Had there been a pair of pantaloons among them, it might have been different; for to say the truth, the probity of Don Gregorio was scarce firm enough to have resisted so strong a temptation as this would have been. The notary's clerk was not exactly of that stuff of which honest men are composed. Nature, even in its crimes, does not leap to grand villainies at once; it proceeds from less to greater; and Cagatinta, though still but young, was yet capable of a little bit of "cribbing."

Don Ramon was not long in coming out of his sleeping-room. In a little while he showed his jovial face at the door of the audience chamber.

He was a person of portly and robust figure; and it was easily seen that one leg of his ample pantaloons would have been sufficient to have made a pair for the thin limbs and meagre body of the escribano.

"*Por Dios*! Señor alcalde," said the clerk, after having exchanged with his superior a profusion of matinal salutations, "what a splendid pair of pantaloons you have on!"

From the alcalde's answer, it was evident that this was not the first time that Cagatinta had made the remark.

"Ah! Gregorio, *amigo*!" replied he, in a tone of good-humour, "you are growing tiresome with your repetitions. Patience, patience, señor escribano! you know that for the services you are to render me—I say nothing of those already rendered—I have promised you my liver-coloured breeches, which have been only a very little used: you have only to gain them."

"But what services are to gain them, señor alcalde?" inquired the clerk, in a despairing tone.

"Eh—Dios!—who knows what—patience, *amigo*! Something may turn up all at once, that will give you that advantage over me. But come! let us to business—make out the deed of appropriation of the boat of that bad pay, Vicente Perez, who under pretence that he has six brats to feed, can't reimburse me the twenty dollars I have advanced him."

Cagatinta drew out from his little portfolio a sheet of stamped paper, and sitting down by the table proceeded to execute the order of the magistrate. He was interrupted by a hurried knocking at the outer door—which had been closed to prevent intrusion.

"Who dare knock in that fashion?" sharply inquired the alcalde.

"*Ave Maria purisima*!" cried a voice from without.

"*Sin pecado concebida*!" replied at the same time the two acolytes within.

And upon this formula, Gregorio hastened to the door, and opened it.

"What on earth can have brought you here at this hour, Don Juan de Dios Canelo?" inquired the alcalde in a tone of surprise, as the old steward of the Countess de Mediana appeared in the doorway, his bald forehead clouded with some profound chagrin.

"Ah, señor alcalde," replied the old man, "a terrible misfortune has happened last night—a great crime has been committed—the Countess has disappeared, and the young Count along with her!"

"Are you sure of this?" shouted the alcalde.

"Alas—you will only have to go up into the balcony that overlooks the sea, and there you will see in what state the assassins have left the Countess's chamber."

"Justice! justice! Señor alcalde! Send out your alguazils over the whole country; find the villains—hang them!"

This voice came from a woman still outside in the street. It was the *femme de chambre* of the Countess, who, to show a devotion which she very little felt, judged it apropos to make a great outcry as she precipitated herself into the chamber of audience.

"Ta-ta-ta, woman! how you go on!" interrupted the alcalde. "Do you think I have a crowd of alguazils? You know very well that in this virtuous village there are only two; and as these would starve if they didn't follow some trade beside their official one, they are both gone fishing hours ago."

"Ah, me!" cried the *femme de chambre*, with a hypocritical whine, "my poor mistress!—who then is to help her?"

"Patience, woman, patience!" said the alcalde. "Don't fear but that justice will be done."

The chamber-maid did not appear to draw much hope from the assurance, but only redoubled her cries, her excited behaviour strongly contrasting with the quiet manner in which the faithful old steward exhibited the sincerity of his grief.

Meanwhile a crowd of women, old men, and children, had gathered around the alcalde's door, and by little and little, were invading the sanctuary of the audience chamber itself.

Don Ramon advanced towards Cagatinta, who was rubbing his hands under his *esclavina*, charmed at the idea of the quantity of stamped paper he would now have an opportunity to blacken.

"Now, friend Gregorio," said the alcalde, in a low voice, "the time has come, when, if you are sharp, you may gain the liver-coloured breeches."

He said no more; but it was evident that the *escribano* understood him, at least, to a certain extent. The latter turned pale with joy, and kept his eye fixed upon every movement of his patron, determined to seize the first opportunity that presented itself of winning the breeches.

The alcalde reseated himself in his great leathern chair; and commanding silence with a wave of his hand, addressed his auditory in a long and pompous speech, with that profuse grandiloquence of which the Spanish language is so capable.

The substance of his speech was as follows:

"My children! We have just heard from this respectable individual, Don Juan de Dios Canelo, that a great crime has last night been committed; the full knowledge of this villainy cannot fail to arrive at the ears of justice, from which nothing can be kept hid. Not the less are we to thank Don Juan for his official communication; it only remains for him to complete the accusation by giving the names of the guilty persons."

"But, señor alcalde," interrupted the steward, "I do not know them, although, as you say, my communication may be official—I can only say that I will do all in my power to assist in finding them."

"You understand, my children," continued the alcalde, without taking notice of what the steward had said, "the worthy Canelo by his official communication asks for the punishment of the guilty persons. Justice will not be deaf to his appeal. I may now be permitted, however, to speak to you of my own little affairs, before abandoning myself to the great grief which the disappearance of the Countess and the young Count has caused me."

Here the alcalde made a sign to Cagatinta, whose whole faculties were keenly bent to discover what service was expected from him, by which he was to gain the object of his ambition—the liver-coloured breeches.

The alcalde continued:—

"You all know, my children, of my attachment to the family of Mediana. You can judge, then, of the grief which this news has given me—news the more incomprehensible, since one neither knows by whom, or for what reason such a crime should be committed. Alas, my children! I lose a powerful protector in the Countess de Mediana; and in me the heart of the old and faithful servant is pierced with anguish, while as a man of business I am equally a sufferer. Yes, my children! In the deceitful security, which I felt no later than yesterday, I was up to the chateau, and had an important interview with the Countess in regard to my rents."

"To ask time for their payment," Cagatinta would have added, for the clerk was perfectly acquainted with the alcalde's affairs. But Don Ramon did not allow him an opportunity of committing this enormous indiscretion, which would forever have deprived him of the promised breeches.

"Patience, worthy Cagatinta!" he exclaimed hastily, so as to prevent the other from speaking, "constrain this thirst for justice that consumes you!— Yes, my children!" he continued, turning to his auditory, "in consequence of this feeling of security, which I have now cause to regret, I placed in the hands of the unfortunate Countess,"—here the voice of Don Ramon quivered—"a sum equivalent to ten years of my rents *in advance*."

At this unexpected declaration, Cagatinta bounded from his chair as if stung by a wasp; and the blood ran cold in his veins when he perceived the grand blunder he had been so near committing.

"You will understand, then, my children, the terrible situation in which this disappearance of the Countess has placed me, when I tell you that I *took no receipt from the lady*, but this very morning was to have gone up for it."

This revelation produced a profound sensation among the auditory; and though perhaps not one of them really believed the story, no one dared to give utterance to his incredulity.

"Fortunately," continued the alcalde, "the word of persons worthy of credit may yet repair the mistake I have committed—fortunately there were witnesses of the payment."

Here Cagatinta—who like water that had been a long time dammed up and had now found vent—stretched out both his arms, and in a loud voice cried out:

"I can swear to it!"

"He can swear to it," said the alcalde.

"He can swear to it," mechanically repeated one or two of the bystanders.

"Yes, my friends!" solemnly added Cagatinta. "I swear to it now, and should have mentioned the matter sooner, but I was prevented by a little uncertainty. I had an idea that it was *fifteen* years of rent, instead of *ten*, that I saw the alcalde hand over to the unfortunate Doña Luisa."

"No, my worthy friend," interrupted the alcalde in a tone of moderation, likely to produce an effect upon his auditory. "It was only ten years of rent, which your valuable testimony will hinder me from losing."

"Yes, señor alcalde," replied the wily scribe, determined at all hazards to deserve the liver-coloured breeches, "I know it was ten years in advance, but there were also the two years of back rent which you paid—two years of arrears and ten in advance—twelve years in all. *Por Dios!* a large sum it would be to have lost!"

And with this reflection Cagatinta sat down again, fancying, no doubt, that he had fairly won the breeches.

We shall not detail what further passed during the scene in the alcalde's chamber of audience—where justice was practised as in the times of Gil Blas—long before and long after Gil Blas—for it is not very different in a Spanish law court at the hour in which we are writing.

Enough to say that the scene concluded, most of the dramatis personae, with the alcalde at their head, proceeded to the chateau, to inspect the chamber, and if possible find out some clue to the mysterious disappearance of the Countess.

Chapter Four
The Forsaken Chamber

On arriving at the chateau, the alcalde ordered the door of the Countess's chamber to be burst in—for it was still bolted inside. On entering the apartment a picture of confusion was presented. Drawers empty, others drawn out, but only half sacked of their contents.

All this did not indicate precisely that there had been any violence. A voluntary but hurried departure on the part of the Countess might have left just such traces as were discovered. The bed was still undisturbed, as if she had not lain down upon it. This fact appeared to indicate a foreknowledge, on the part of the lady, of what was to happen—as if she had had the intention of going off, but had made no preparation until the moment of departure. The furniture was all in its place—the window curtains and those of the alcove had not been disarranged, and no traces of a struggle were to be discerned within the chamber, which contained many light fragile objects of furniture that could not fail to have been destroyed by the slightest violence.

The fetid odour of an oil lamp filled the apartment despite the cold air that came in through the open window. It was evident, therefore, that this lamp had been left alight, and had continued to burn until the oil had become exhausted.

It could not be a robbery either. A thousand articles of value, likely enough to have tempted the cupidity of robbers, were left behind both on the tables and in the drawers.

The conclusion then was that neither assassination nor burglary had taken place.

Notwithstanding all these deceptive appearances, the old steward shook his head doubtfully. The signs were sufficient to baffle his reason, which was none of the strongest, but the faithful servant could not bring himself to believe that his noble mistress would take flight in a manner so extraordinary—his good sense revolted at the thought. In his belief some crime had been committed, but how was it to be explained—since the assassin had left no traces of his guilt? The devoted Don Juan looked with a sad eye upon that desolate chamber—upon the dresses of his beloved mistress scattered over the floor; upon the cradle of the young Count, where he had so lately slept, rosy and smiling, under the vigil of his mother.

Suddenly struck with an idea, the steward advanced towards the iron balcony that fronted upon the sea—that where the window had been found open. With inquiring eye he looked to the ground below, which was neither more nor less than the beach of the sea itself. It was at no great depth below; and he could easily have seen from the balcony any traces that might have been there. But there were none. The tide had been in and out again. No trace was left on the sand or pebbles that had the slightest signification in regard to the mysterious event. The wind sighed, the waves murmured as always; but amid the voices of nature none raised itself to proclaim the guilty.

On the fair horizon only were descried the white sails of a ship, gradually passing outwards and fading away into the azure of the sea.

While the old steward watched the disappearance of the ship with a sort of dreamy regard, he sent up a silent prayer that his mistress might still be safe. The others, with the exception of the alcalde and his clerk, stood listening to the mournful howling of the wind against the cliffs, which seemed alternately to weep and sigh as if lamenting the sad event that had just transpired.

As regards the alcalde and his assistant, they were under the same conviction as Don Juan—both believing that a crime had been committed—though they did not care to avow their belief, for reasons known to themselves. The absence of any striking evidence that might lead to the discovery of the delinquents, but more especially the difficulty of finding some interested individual able to pay the expenses of justice (the principal object of criminal prosecutions in Spain), damped the zeal of Don Ramon and the scribe. Both were satisfied to leave things as they stood—the one contented with having gained the recompense so much coveted—the other with the twelve years of rents which he felt sure of gaining.

"*Valga me Dios!* my children," said the alcalde, turning toward the witnesses, "I cannot explain what fancy the Countess may have had in going out by the window—for the door of the chamber, bolted inside, leaves no room to doubt that she went that way. Some woman's caprice, perhaps, which justice has no business to meddle with."

"Perhaps it was to escape from giving the alcalde his receipt," suggested one of the bystanders to another, in an undertone of voice.

"But how, Don Juan," continued the magistrate, addressing himself to the old steward, "how did you know of the Countess's disappearance, since you could not get into the room?"

"That is simple enough," replied the old man. "At the hour in which the chamber-maid is accustomed to present herself before the señora, she knocked as usual at the door. No answer was given. She knocked louder, and still received no answer. Growing anxious, she came to me to tell me. I went to the door myself, first knocked and then called; and receiving no reply, I ran round to the garden and got the ladder. This I placed against the balcony, and mounted up in order to see through the window. On reaching the window I found it open, and the chamber in the condition you now see it."

When the steward had finished this declaration, Cagatinta whispered some words in the ear of the alcalde; but the latter only replied by a shake of the shoulders, and an expression of disdainful incredulity.

"Who knows?" answered the scribe in reply to this dumb show.

"It might be," muttered Don Ramon, "we shall see presently."

"I persist, gentlemen," continued the alcalde, "in my belief that the Countess has gone out by the window; and however singular it may appear, I believe the lady is free to her fancy to go out as she pleases—even though it be by a window."

Cagatinta, and some others, complimented, with a laugh, this little bit of magisterial facetiousness.

"But, señor alcalde," spoke out Don Juan, disgusted with this ill-timed pleasantry, "a proof that there has been a forced entry into the chamber is this broken glass of the window, of which you see some pieces still lying on the balcony."

"This old fool," muttered the alcalde to himself, "is not going to let me have any breakfast. By this time everything will be cold, and Nicolasa— What do these bits of glass prove?" he continued, raising his voice; "don't you think that the breeze which was blowing roughly last night might have caused this? The window was hanging open, and the wind clashing it violently against the frame, would readily cause the breaking of a pane?"

"But why is it," answered Don Juan, "that the broken pane is precisely the one adjacent to the fastening? It must have been knocked out to get the window open."

"*Carramba*! Señor Don Juan de Dios!" cried the alcalde, in a peevish tone—at the same time biting his gold-headed cane, the emblem of his office—"Is it you or I who have here the right to ask questions? *Carrai*! it appears to me that you make me cut a strange figure!"

Here Cagatinta interposed with a modest air—

"I shall answer our friend Canelo, if you permit me. If the window was open with the design he has stated, it must of course have been done from the outside. The pieces of glass then would have fallen *into* the chamber; but such is not the case—there they lie on the balcony! It has been the wind therefore, as his honour the alcalde has reasonably stated, that has done this business. Unless, indeed," added he, with a feigned smile, "some trunk carried incautiously past the window might have struck one of the squares. This may have been—since it appears the Countess intends a prolonged absence, judging from the effects—taken with her, as testified by the empty drawers."

The old steward lowered his head at this proof which seemed completely to falsify his assertion. He did not hear the last observation of Cagatinta, who was cogitating whether he ought not to exact from the alcalde something more than the liver-coloured breeches, as a recompense of this new service he had done him.

While the faithful Don Juan was busy with painful reflections that threw their shadows upon his bald forehead, the alcalde approached and addressed him in a voice so low as not to be heard by the others.

"I have been a little sharp with you, Don Juan—I have not sufficiently taken into account the grief, which you as a loyal servant must feel under such an unexpected stroke. But tell me! independent of the chagrin which this affair has caused you, are you not also affected by some fears about your own future? You are old—weak in consequence—and without resources?"

"It is just because I am old, and know that I have not long to live, that I am so little affected. My grief, however," added he with an air of pride, "is pure and free from all selfishness. The generosity of Count de Mediana has left me enough to pass the remainder of my days in tranquillity. But I should pass them all the more happily if I could only see avenged the lady of my old master."

"I approve of your sentiments, Señor Don Juan! you are doubly estimable on account of your sorrow, and as to your *savings*—Notary! Señor Cagatinta!" cried the alcalde, suddenly raising his voice so as to be heard by all present, "Make out a *procès verbal*—that the Señor Don Juan Dios Canelo, here present, will become prosecutor in this case. It cannot be doubted that a crime has been committed; and it is a duty we owe to ourselves as well as to this respectable man, to seek out and punish the authors of it."

"But, señor alcalde!" interposed the steward, perfectly stupefied with this unexpected declaration, "I did not say—I have no intention to become *prosecutor*."

"Take care, old man!" cried Don Ramon, in a solemn tone; "if you deny what you have already confided to me, grievous charges may be brought against you. As friend Cagatinta has just this minute observed to me, the ladder by which you scaled the balcony might prove sinister designs. But I know you are incapable of such. Rest contented, then, at being the accuser in place of the accused. Come, gentlemen! our duty calls us outside. Perhaps underneath the balcony we may find some traces of this most mysterious matter."

So saying, the alcalde left the chamber, followed by the crowd.

Poor Don Juan found himself thus unexpectedly between two horns of a dilemma, the result in either case being the same—that is, the spoliation of the little *pecadillo* he had put away against old age. He shook his head, and with a sublime resignation accepted the voice of iniquity for that of God— consoling himself with the reflection, that this last sacrifice might be of some service to the family whose bread he had so long eaten.

No trace was found under the balcony. As already stated the waves must have obliterated any footmarks or other vestiges that may have been left.

It was believed for a while that an important capture had been made, in the person of a man found lying in a crevice among the rocks. This proved to be Pepé the Sleeper. Suddenly aroused, the coast-guard was asked if he had seen or heard anything? No, was the reply, nothing. But Pepé remembered his full pockets; and fearing that the alcalde might take a fancy to search him, saw that some *ruse* was necessary to put an end to the scene. This he succeeded in doing, by begging the alcalde for a *real* to buy bread with!

What was to be done with this droll fellow? The alcalde felt no inclination to question him farther, but left him to go to sleep again and sleep as long as he pleased.

Any further investigation appeared to Don Ramon to be useless—at least until some order might be received from higher quarters—besides it would be necessary to graduate the expenses of justice to the means of the prosecutor; and with this reflection, the alcalde went home to his breakfast.

In the evening of this eventful day for the village of Elanchovi—when the twilight had fallen upon the water—two persons might have been seen wandering along the beach, but evidently desirous of shunning one another. Both appeared in grief, though their sorrows sprang from a very different cause.

One was a poor old steward, who, while heaving a sigh at the thought that his worldly store was about to be absorbed in the inexorable gulf of justice, at the same time searched for some trace of his lost mistress, praying for her and her child, and calling upon God to take them under his protection.

The other pensive wanderer was Cagatinta, of whom the alcalde had again taken the advantage. Profiting by the confidence of the scribe, Don Ramon had induced the latter to commit his oath to stamped paper; and then instead of the liver-coloured breeches had offered him an old hat in remuneration. This Cagatinta had indignantly refused.

He was now lamenting his vanished dreams of ambition, his silly confidence, and the immorality of false oaths—*not paid for*. Nevertheless, he was meditating whether it would not be more prudent to accept the old hat in lieu of the liver-coloured breeches, alas! so well earned!

Chapter Five
Pepé's Revanche

When Pepé the Sleeper had made himself master of the secret of Captain Despierto—which he had found of such profitable service—he was not aware that the captain had held back another. Nevertheless, the coast-guard felt some kind of remorse of conscience—though he had as yet no idea of the terrible consequences that had resulted. His remorse was simply that he had betrayed his post of sentinel; and he determined that he would make up for it by a more zealous performance of duty whenever an opportunity should offer. To bring about this contingency, he went on the very next night, and requested to be once more placed on the post of Ensenada.

His wish was gratified; and while Don Lucas believed him asleep as usual, Pepé kept wide awake, as on the preceding night.

We shall leave him at his post, while we recount what was taking place off the coast not far from the Ensenada.

The night was as foggy as that which preceded it, when about the hour of ten o'clock a *coaster* was observed gliding in towards the cliffs, and entering among a labyrinth of rocks that lay near the mouth of the bay.

This vessel appeared well guided and well *sailed*. The shape of her hull, her rigging, her sails, denoted her to be a ship-of-war, or at the least a privateer.

The boldness with which she manoeuvred, in the middle of the darkness, told that her pilot must be some one well acquainted with this dangerous coast; and also that her commander had an understanding with some people on the shore.

The sea dashed with fury against both sides of the rocky strait, through which the coaster was making her way, but still she glided safely on. The strait once cleared, a large bay opened before her, in which the sea was more calm, and rippled gently up against a beach of sand and pebble.

The coaster at length succeeded in gaining this bay; and then by a manoeuvre directed by the officer of the watch she hove-to with a celerity that denoted a numerous crew.

Two boats were let down upon the water, and, being instantly filled with men, were rowed off in the direction of the upper end of the bay, where some houses, which could be distinguished by their whiteness, stood scattered along the beach.

To end the mystery, let us say that the little coaster was a French vessel—half-privateer half-smuggler—and had entered the bay with a double design—the disposing of merchandise and the procuring of provisions, of which the crew began to stand in need. Further we shall add, that the pilot was a skilful fisherman of Elanchovi, furnished by Don Lucas Despierto, captain of the coast-guard!

The officer of the watch silently walked the deck—now listening to the waves surging against the sides of the little vessel—now stooping a moment over the light of the binnacle—anon watching the sails that napped loosely upon the yards, now turned contrary to the direction of the wind.

An hour had been passed in this manner, when a brisk fusillade was heard from several points on the shore. Other reports of musketry appeared to respond and shortly after the two boats came hastening back to the coaster.

It was Pepé who had caused all this; Pepé, who, to the great chagrin of his captain, had given warning to the coast-guards. He had been too late, notwithstanding his zeal, for the boats came back laden with sheep and other provisions of every soft.

The last of the men who climbed over the gangway—just as the boats were being hoisted up—was a sailor of gigantic height, of colossal proportions, and Herculean vigour. He was a Canadian by birth. He carried in his arms a young child that was cold and motionless, as if dead. A slight trembling in its limbs, however, proclaimed that there was still life in it.

"What the deuce have you got there, Bois-Rose?" demanded the officer of the watch.

"With your leave, lieutenant, it's a young child that I found in a boat adrift, half dead with hunger and cold. A woman, quite dead, and bathed in her own blood, still held it in her arms. I had all the trouble in the world to get the boat away from the place where I found it, for those dogs of Spaniards espied it, and took it for one of ours. There was a terrible devil of a coast-guard kept all the while firing at me with as much obstinacy as awkwardness. I should have silenced him with a single shot, had I not been hindered in looking after this poor little creature. But if ever I return—ah!"

"And what do you intend to do with the child?"

"Take care of it, lieutenant, until peace be proclaimed, then return here and find out who it belongs to."

Unfortunately the only knowledge he was able to obtain about the infant was its name, Fabian, and that the woman who had been assassinated was its mother.

Two years passed during which the French privateer did not return to the coast of Spain. The tenderness of the sailor towards the child he had picked up—which was no other than the young Count Fabian de Mediana—did not cease for an instant, but seemed rather to increase with time. It was a singular and touching spectacle to witness the care, almost motherly, which this rude nurse lavished upon the child, and the constant *ruses* to which he had recourse to procure a supplement to his rations for its nourishment. The sailor had to fight for his own living; but he often indulged in dreams that some day a rich prize would be captured, his share of which would enable him to take better care of his adopted son. Unfortunately he did not take into his calculations the perilous hazards of the life he was leading.

One morning the privateer was compelled to run from an English brig of war of nearly twice her force; and although a swift sailer, the French vessel soon found that she could not escape from her pursuer. She disdained to refuse the combat, and the two vessels commenced cannonading each other.

For several hours a sanguinary conflict was kept up, when the Canadian sailor, dashed with blood, and blackened with powder, ran towards the child and lifting it in his arms, carried it to the gangway. There, in the midst of the tumult, with blood running over the decks, amidst the confusion of cries and the crash of falling masts, he wished to engrave on the child's memory the circumstance of a separation, of which he had a strong presentiment. In this moment, which should leave even upon the memory of an infant, a souvenir that would never be effaced, he called out to the child, while shielding it with his huge body, "Kneel, my son!"

The child knelt, trembling with affright.

"You see what is going on?"

"I am afraid," murmured Fabian, "the blood—the noise—" and saying this he hid himself in the arms of his protector.

"It is well," replied the Canadian, in a solemn tone. "Never forget, then, that in this moment, a sailor, a man who loved you as his own life, said to you—*kneel and pray for your mother!*"

He was not permitted to finish the speech. At that moment a bullet struck him and his blood spouting over the child, caused it to utter a lamentable cry. The Canadian had just strength left to press the boy to his breast, and to add some words; but in so low a tone that Fabian could only comprehend a single phrase. It was the continuation of what he had been saying—"*Your mother—whom I found—dead beside you.*"

With this speech ended the consciousness of the sailor. He was not dead, however; his wound did not prove fatal.

When he came to his senses again he found himself in the fetid hold of a ship. A terrible thirst devoured him. He called out in a feeble voice, but no one answered him. He perceived that he was a prisoner, and he wept for the loss of his liberty, but still more for that of the adopted son that Providence had given him.

What became of Fabian? That the history of the "Wood-Rangers" will tell us; but before crossing from the prologue of our drama—before crossing from Europe to America—a few events connected with the tragedy of Elanchovi remain to be told.

It was several days after the disappearance of the Countess, before anything was known of her fate. Then some fishermen found the abandoned boat driven up among the rocks and still containing the body of the unfortunate lady. This was some light thrown upon the horrid mystery; but the cause of the assassination long remained unknown, and the author of it long unpunished.

The old steward tied black crape upon the vanes of the chateau, and erected a wooden cross on the spot where the body of his beloved mistress had been found; but, as everything in this human world soon wears out, the sea-breeze had not browned the black crape, nor the waves turned green the wood of the cross, before the tragic event ceased to cause the slightest emotion in the village—ay, even ceased to be talked of.

Chapter Six
Sonora

Sonora, naturally one of the richest provinces of Mexico, is also one of the least known. Vast tracts in this State have never been explored; and others have been seen only by the passing traveller. Nevertheless, Nature has been especially bountiful to this remote territory. In some parts of it the soil, scarce scratched by the plough, will yield two crops in the year; while in other places gold is scattered over the surface, or mixed with the sands, in such quantity as to rival the *placers* of California.

It is true that these advantages are, to some extent neutralised by certain inconveniences. Vast deserts extend between the tracts of fertile soil, which render travelling from one to the other both difficult and dangerous; and, in many parts, of the province the savage aborigines of the country are still masters of the ground. This is especially the case in those districts where the gold is found in *placers*.

Those placers are not to be approached by white men, unless when in strong force. The Indians repel all such advances with warlike fury. Not that they care to protect the gold—of whose value they have been hitherto ignorant—but simply from their hereditary hatred of the white race. Nevertheless, attempts are frequently made to reach the desired gold fields. Some that result in complete failure, and some that are more or less successful.

The natural riches of Sonora have given rise to very considerable fortunes, and not a few very large ones, of which the origin was the finding a "nugget" of virgin gold; while others again had for their basis the cultivation of the rich crops which the fertile soil of Sonora can produce.

There is a class of persons in Sonora, who follow no other business than searching for gold *placers* or silver mines, and whose only knowledge consists of a little practical acquaintance with metallurgy. These men are called *gambusinos*. From time to time they make long excursions into the uninhabited portions of the State; where, under great privations, and exposed to a thousand dangers, they hastily and very superficially work some vein of silver, or wash the auriferous sands of some desert-stream, until, tracked and pursued by the Indians, they are compelled to return to their villages. Here they find an audience delighted to listen to their adventures, and to believe the exaggerated accounts which they are certain to give of marvellous treasures lying upon the surface of, the ground, but not to be approached on account of some great danger, Indian or otherwise, by which they are guarded.

These *gambusinos* are to mining industry, what the backwoodsmen are to agriculture and commerce. They are its pioneers. Avarice stimulated by their wonderful stories, and often too by the sight of real treasure brought in from the desert—for the expeditions of the *gambusinos* do not always prove failures—avarice thus tempted, is ready to listen to the voice of some adventurous leader, who preaches a crusade of conquest and exploration. In Sonora, as elsewhere, there are always an abundance of idle men to form the material of an expedition—the sons of ruined families—men who dislike hard work, or indeed any work—and others who have somehow got outside the pale of justice. These join the leader and an expedition is organised.

In general, however, enterprises of this kind are too lightly entered upon, as well as too loosely conducted; and the usual consequence is, that before accomplishing its object the band falls to pieces; many become victims to hunger, thirst, or Indian hostility; and of those who went forth only a few individuals return to tell the tale of suffering and disaster.

This example will, for a while, damp the ardour for such pursuits. But the disaster is soon forgotten; fresh stories of the *gambusinos* produce new dreams of wealth; and another band of adventurers is easily collected.

At the time of which I am writing—that is, in 1830—just twenty-two years after the tragedy of Elanchovi, one of these expeditions was being organised at Arispe—then the capital of the State of Sonora. The man who was to be the leader of the expedition was not a native of Mexico, but a stranger. He was a Spaniard who had arrived in Sonora but two months before, and who was known by the name, Don Estevan de Arechiza.

No one in Arispe remembered ever to have seen him; and yet he appeared to have been in the country before this time. His knowledge of its topography, as well as its affairs and political personages, was so positive and complete, as to make it evident that Sonora was no stranger to him; and the plan of his expedition appeared to have been conceived and arranged beforehand—even previous to his arrival from Europe.

Beyond doubt, Don Estevan was master of considerable resources. He had his train of paid followers, kept open house, made large bets at the *monté* tables, lent money to friends without appearing to care whether it should ever be returned, and played "grand Seigneur" to perfection.

No one knew from what source he drew the means to carry on such a "war."

Now and then he was known to absent himself from Arispe for a week or ten days at a time. He was absent on some journey; but no one could tell to what part of the country these journeys were made—for his well-trained servants never said a word about the movements of their master.

Whoever he might be, his courteous manner *à l'Espagnol*, his generosity, and his fine free table, soon gave him a powerful influence in the social world of Arispe; and by this influence he was now organising an expedition, to penetrate to a part of the country which it was supposed no white man had ever yet visited.

As Don Estevan almost always lost at play, and as he also neglected to reclaim the sums of money which he so liberally lent to his acquaintants, it began to be conjectured that he possessed not far from Arispe some rich *placer* of gold from which he drew his resources. The periodical journeys which he made gave colour to this conjecture.

It was also suspected that he knew of some *placer*—still more rich—in the country into which he was about to lead his expedition. What truth there was in the suspicion we shall presently see.

It will easily be understood that with such a reputation, Don Estevan would have very little difficulty in collecting his band of adventurers. Indeed it was said, that already more than fifty determined men from all parts of Sonora had assembled at the *Presidio of Tubac* on the Indian frontier—the place appointed for the rendezvous of the expedition. It was further affirmed that in a few days Don Estevan himself would leave Arispe to place himself at their head.

This rumour, hitherto only conjecture, proved to be correct; for at one of the dinners given by the hospitable Spaniard, he announced to his guests that in three days he intended to start for Tubac.

During the progress of this same dinner, a messenger was introduced into the dining-room, who handed to Don Estevan a letter, an answer to which he awaited.

The Spaniard, begging of his guests to excuse him for a moment, broke the seal and read the letter.

As there was a certain mystery about the habits of their convivial host, the guests were silent for a while—all watching his movements and the play of his features; but the impassible countenance of Don Estevan did not betray a single emotion that was passing his mind, even to the most acute observer around the table. In truth he was a man who well knew how to dissemble his thoughts, and perhaps on that very occasion, more than any other, he required all his self-command.

"It is well," he said, calmly addressing himself to the messenger. "Take my answer to him who sent you, that I will be punctual to the rendezvous in three days from the present."

With this answer the messenger took his departure. Don Estevan, turning to his guests, again apologised for his impoliteness; and the dinner for an instant suspended once more progressed with renewed activity.

Nevertheless the Spaniard appeared more thoughtful than before; and his guests did not doubt but that he had received some news of more than ordinary interest.

We shall leave them to their conjectures, and precede Don Estevan to the mysterious rendezvous which had been given him, and the scene of which was to be a small village lying upon the route to the Presidio of Tubac.

The whole country between Arispe and the Presidio in question may be said to be almost uninhabited. Along the route only mean hovels are encountered, with here and there a *hacienda* of greater pretensions. These houses are rarely solitary, but collected in groups at long distances apart. Usually a day's journey lies between them, and, consequently, they are the stopping-places for travellers, who may be on their way towards the frontier. But the travellers are few, and the inhabitants of these miserable hovels pass the greater part of their lives in the middle of a profound solitude. A little patch of Indian corn which they cultivate,—a few head of cattle, which, fed upon the perfumed pastures of the plains, produce beef of an exquisite flavour,—a sky always clear,—and, above all, a wonderful sobriety of living,—enable these dwellers of the desert steppes of Sonora to live, if not in a state of luxury, at least free from all fear of want. What desires need trouble a man who sees a blue sky always over his head, and who finds in the smoke of a cigarette of his own making, a resource against all the cravings of hunger?

At one part of the year, however, these villages of hovels are uninhabited—altogether abandoned by their occupants. This is the *dry season*, during the greater portion of which the cisterns that supply the villages with water become dried up. The cisterns are fed by the rains of heaven, and no other water than this can be found throughout most tracts of the country. When these give out, the settlements have to be abandoned, and remain until the return of the periodical rains.

In a morning of the year 1830, at the distance of about three days' journey from Arispe, a man was seated, or rather half reclining, upon his *serapé* in front of a rude hovel. A few other huts of a similar character were near, scattered here and there over the ground. It was evident, from the profound silence that reigned among these dwellings, and the absence of human forms, or implements of household use, that the *rancheria* was abandoned by its half nomad population. Such in reality was the fact, for it was now the very height of the dry season. Two or three roads branched out from this miserable group of huts, leading off into a thick forest which surrounded it on all sides. They were rather paths than roads, for the tracks which they followed were scarce cleared of the timber that once grew upon them. At the point of junction of these roads the individual alluded to had placed himself; and his attitude of perfect ease told that he was under no apprehension from the profound and awe-inspiring loneliness of the place. The croak of the ravens flitting from tree to tree hoarsely uttered in their flight; the cry of the *chaculucas* as they welcomed the rising sun, were the only sounds that broke the stillness of the scene.

Presently the white fog of the night began to rise upward and disappear under the strength of the sunbeams. Only a few flakes of it still hung over the tops of the mezquite and iron-wood trees that grew thickly around the huts.

Near where the man lay, there might be seen the remains of a large fire. It had been kindled no doubt to protect him from the chill dews of the night; and it now served him to prepare his breakfast. Some small cakes of wheaten meal, with few pieces of *tasajo*, were already placed upon the red embers of the fire; but notwithstanding that these would made but a meagre repast the man appeared eagerly to await the enjoyment of it.

Near at hand, with a frugality equal to that of his master, a horse was browsing upon the tufts of dry yellow grass, that grew thinly over the ground. This horse, with a saddle and bridle lying near, proved the solitary individual to be a traveller. Contrary to the usual custom of the country, the horse had no *lazo*, or fastening of any kind upon him; but was free to wander where he pleased.

The costume of the traveller consisted in a sort of jacket or vest of brick-coloured leather, without buttons or any opening in front, but drawn over the head after the manner of a shirt. Wide pantaloons of the same material, open from the knee downwards, and fastened at the waist by a scarf of red China crape. Under the pantaloons, and covering the calf of the leg nearly up to the knee, could be seen the *botas* of strong stamped leather, in one of which was stuck a long knife with a horn hilt—thus ready to the hand whether the owner was seated, standing, or on horseback. A large felt hat, banded with a *toquilla* of Venetian pearls, completed a costume sufficiently picturesque, the vivid colours of which were in harmony with that of the *serapé* on which the traveller was reclining. This costume denoted one of those men accustomed to gallop among the thorny jungles that cover the desert steppes of North Mexico; and who in their expeditions, whether against Indian enemies, or for whatever purpose, sleep with indifference under the shadow of a tree, or the open heaven itself,—in the forest, or upon the naked plain.

There was in the features of this traveller a singular mixture of brutal ferocity and careless good-humour. A crooked nose, with thick bushy eyebrows, and black eyes that sparkled from time to time with a malicious fire, gave to his countenance a sinister aspect, and belied the expression of his mouth and lips, that presented rather a pleasant and smiling contour. But the man's features, when viewed as a whole, could not fail to inspire a certain feeling of repulsiveness mingled with fear. A short carbine that lay by his side, together with the long knife, whose haft protruded above the top of his boots, did not in any way tame down the ferocious aspect of his face. On the contrary they proclaimed him one whom it would not be desirable to have for a companion in the desert.

Despite the *nonchalance* of his attitude, it was evident that he awaited some one; but as everything in these countries is on a large scale, so also is the virtue of patience. This outlaw—for everything about him signified that he was one of some sort—this outlaw, we say, having made three days' journey before arriving upon the ground where he now was, thought nothing of a few hours, less or more, spent in expectation. In the desert, he who has travelled a hundred leagues, will consider it a mere bagatelle to wait for a hundred hours: unlike to him who keeps an appointment in the midst of a great city, where a delay of a quarter of an hour will be endured with feverish impatience.

So it was with our solitary traveller; and when the hoof-strokes of a horse were heard at some distance off in the forest, he did nothing more than to make a slight change in the attitude in which he had been reclining; while his steed, also hearing the same sounds, tossed up his head and neighed joyously. The hoof-strokes each moment were heard more distinctly; and it was evident that a horseman was galloping rapidly in the direction of the huts. After a little the strokes became more gentle, and the gallop appeared to be changed to a walk. The rider was approaching with caution.

A few seconds intervened, and then upon one of the roads—that leading to Arispe—the horseman was perceived coming on at a slow and cautious pace.

On perceiving the traveller, still half reclining upon his *serapé*, the horseman drew his rein still tighter and halted, and the two men remained for some seconds regarding each other with a fixed and interrogative glance.

Chapter Seven
Two Honest Gentlemen

The new-comer was a tall man with a dark complexion, and thick black beard, costumed very similarly to the other—in vest and pantaloons of brick-red leather, felt sombrero, sash, and boots. He was mounted upon a strong active horse.

It may appear strange that during the period of mutual examination, each of these two men made a very similar reflection about the other; but it was scarcely strange either, considering that both presented an equally suspicious aspect.

"*Carramba!*" muttered the horseman as he eyed the man on the *serapé*, "if I wasn't sure that he is the gentleman I have been sent to meet, I should believe that I had chanced upon a very unlucky acquaintance."

At the same instant he upon the ground said to himself—

"*Por Dios*! if that infernal Seven of Spades had left any dollars in my purse, I should have considered them in danger of being taken out of it just now."

Despite the nature of his reflection, the horseman did not hesitate any longer, but spurring his horse forward to the edge of the fire, lifted his hat courteously from his head, and saluted him on the ground, at the same time saying interrogatively:—

"No doubt it is the Señor Don Pedro Cuchillo I have the honour to address?"

"The same, cavallero!" replied the other, rising to his feet, and returning the salute with no less politeness than it had been given.

"Cavallero! I have been sent forward to meet you, and announce to you the approach of the Señor Arechiza, who at this time cannot be many leagues distant. My name is Manuel Baraja, your very humble servant."

"Your honour will dismount?"

The horseman did not wait for the invitation to be repeated, but at once flung himself from the saddle. After unbuckling his enormous spurs, he speedily unsaddled his horse, fastened a long lazo around his neck, and then giving him a smart cut with the short whip which he carried, despatched the animal without further ceremony to share the meagre provender of his companion.

At this movement the *tasajo*, beginning to sputter over the coals, gave out an odour that resembled the smell of a dying lamp. Notwithstanding this, Baraja cast towards it a look of longing.

"It appears to me Señor Cuchillo," said he, "that you are well provided here. Carramba!—*tortillas*, of wheaten meal! *tasajo*!—it is a repast for a prince!"

"Oh, yes," replied Cuchillo, with a certain air of foppishness, "I treat myself well. It makes me happy to know that the dish is to your liking; I beg to assure you, it is quite at your service."

"You are very good, and I accept your offer without ceremony. The morning air has sharpened my appetite."

And saying this, Baraja proceeded to the mastication of the tassajo and tortillas. After being thus engaged for some time, he once more addressed himself to his host.

"Dare I tell you, Señor Cuchillo, the favourable impression I had of you at first sight?"

"Oh! you shock my modesty, señor. I would rather state the good opinion your first appearance gave me of *you*!"

The two new friends here exchanged a salute, full of affability, and then continued to eat, Baraja harpooning upon the point of his long knife another piece of meat out of the ashes.

"If it please you, Señor Baraja," said Cuchillo, "we may talk over our business while we are eating. You will find me a host *sans cérémonie*."

"Just what pleases me."

"Don Estevan, then, has received the message which I sent him?"

"He has, but what that message was is only known to you and him."

"No doubt of that," muttered Cuchillo to himself.

"The Señor Arechiza," continued the *envoy*, "started for Tubac shortly after receiving your letter. It was my duty to accompany him, but he ordered me to proceed in advance of him with these commands: 'In the little village of Huerfano you will find a man, by name Cuchillo; you shall say to him that the proposal he makes to me deserves serious attention; and that since the place he has designated as a rendezvous is on the way to Tubac, I will see him on my journey.' This instruction was given by Don Estevan an hour or so before his departure, but although I have ridden a little faster to execute his orders, he cannot be far behind me."

"Good! Señor Baraja, good!" exclaimed Cuchillo, evidently pleased with the communication just made, "and if the business which I have with Don Estevan be satisfactorily concluded—which I am in hopes it will be—you are likely to have me for a comrade in this distant expedition. But," continued he, suddenly changing the subject, "you will, no doubt, be astonished that I have given Don Estevan a rendezvous in such a singular place as this?"

"No," coolly replied Baraja, "you may have reasons for being partial to solitude. Who does not love it at times?"

A most gracious smile playing upon the countenance of Cuchillo, denoted that his new acquaintance had correctly divined the truth.

"Precisely," he replied, "the ill-behaviour of a friend towards me, and the malevolent hostility of the alcalde of Arispe have caused me to seek this tranquil retreat. That is just why I have established my headquarters in an abandoned village, where there is not a soul to keep company with."

"Señor Don Pedro," replied Baraja, "I have already formed too good an opinion of you not to believe that the fault is entirely upon the side of the alcalde, and especially on the part of your friend."

"I thank you, Señor Baraja, for you good opinion," returned Cuchillo, at the same time taking from the cinders a piece of the meat, half burnt, half raw, and munching it down with the most perfect indifference; "I thank you sincerely, and when I tell you the circumstances you may judge for yourself."

"I shall be glad to hear them," said the other, easing himself down into a horizontal position; "after a good repast, there is nothing I so much enjoy as a good story."

After saying this, and lighting his cigarette, Baraja turned upon the broad of his back, and with his eyes fixed upon the blue sky, appeared to enjoy a perfect beatitude.

"The story is neither long nor interesting," responded Cuchillo; "what happened to me might happen to all the world. I was engaged with this friend in a quiet game of cards, when he pretended that I had *tricked* him. The affair came to words—"

Here the narrator paused for an instant, to take a drink from his leathern bottle, and then continued—

"My friend had the indelicacy to permit himself to drop down dead in my presence."

"What at your words?"

"No, with the stab of a knife which I gave him," coolly replied the outlaw.

"Ah! no doubt your friend was in the wrong, and you received great provocation?"

"The alcalde did not think so. He pestered me in the most absurd manner. I could have forgiven the bitterness of his persecution of me, had it not been that I was myself bitterly roused at the ill-behaviour of my friend, whom up to that time I had highly esteemed."

"Ah! one has always to suffer from one's friends," rejoined Baraja, sending up a puff of smoke from his corn-husk cigarette.

"Well—one thing," said Cuchillo, "the result of it all is that I have made a vow never to play another card; for the cards, as you see, were the original cause of this ugly affair."

"A good resolution," said Baraja, "and just such as I have come to myself. I have promised never to touch another card; they have cost me a fortune—in fact, altogether ruined me."

"Ruined you? you have been rich then?"

"Alas! I had a splendid estate—a *hacienda de ganados* (cattle farm) with a numerous flock upon it. I had a lawyer for my *intendant*, who took care of the estate while I spent my time in town. But when I came to settle accounts with this fellow I found I had let them run too long. I discovered that half my estate belonged to him!"

"What did you do then?"

"The only thing I could do," answered Baraja, with the air of a cavalier, "was to stake my remaining half against his on a game, and let the winner take the whole."

"Did he accept this proposal?"

"After a fashion."

"What fashion?"

"Why, you see I am too timid when I play in presence of company, and certain to lose. I prefer, therefore, to play in the open air, and in some quiet corner of the woods. There I feel more at my ease; and if I should lose—considering that it was my whole fortune that was at stake—I should not expose my chagrin to the whole world. These were the considerations that prompted me to propose the conditions of our playing alone."

"And did the lawyer agree to your conditions?"

"Not a bit of it."

"What a droll fellow he must have been!"

"He would only play in the presence of witnesses."

"And you were forced to his terms?"

"To my great regret, I was."

"And of course you lost—being so nervous in presence of company?"

"I lost the second half of my fortune as I had done the first. The only thing I kept back was the horse you see, and even him my ex-intendant insisted upon having as part of the bet. To-day I have no other hope than to make my fortune in this Tubac expedition, and if I should do so I may get back, and settle accounts with the knave. After that game, however, I swore I should never play another card; and, carramba! I have kept my oath."

"How long since this happened?"

"Five days."

"The devil!—You deserve credit for keeping your word."

The two adventurers after having exchanged these confidences, began to talk over their hopes founded on the approaching expedition—of the marvellous sights that they would be likely to see—but more especially of the dangers that might have to be encountered.

"Bah!" said Baraja, speaking of these; "better to die than live wearing a coat out at elbows."

Cuchillo was of the same opinion.

Meanwhile the sun was growing hotter and hotter. A burning wind began to blow through the trees, and the horses of the two travellers, suffering from thirst, uttered their plaintive neighings. The men themselves sought out the thickest shade to protect them from the fervid rays of the sun, and for a while both observed a complete silence.

Baraja was the first to resume the conversation.

"You may laugh at me, Señor Cuchillo," said he, fanning himself with his felt hat, "but to say the truth the time appears very long to me when I am not playing."

"The same with myself," hastily responded Cuchillo.

"What do you say to our staking, on word of honour, a little of that gold we are going to find?"

"Just what I was thinking myself, but I daren't propose it to you;—I am quite agreeable."

Without further parley each of the two thrust a hand into his pocket, and drew forth a pack of cards—with which, notwithstanding the oath they had taken, both were provided.

The play was about to commence, when the sound of a bell, and the clattering of hoofs at a distance, announced the approach, most probably, of the important personage whom Cuchillo awaited.

Chapter Eight
The Senator Tragaduros

The two players suspended operations, and turned their faces in the direction whence came the sounds.

At some distance along the road, a cloud of dust suddenly rising, indicated the approach of a troop of horses.

They were without riders. One only was mounted; and that was ridden by the driver of the troop. In short, it was a *remuda*—such as rich travellers in the north of Mexico usually take along with them for a remount. These horses, on account of the half-wild life they lead upon the vast plains where they are pastured, after a gallop of twenty leagues without carrying a rider, are almost as fresh as if just taken out of the stable. On long routes, each is saddled and mounted at regular intervals; and in this way a journey is performed almost as rapidly as by a mail express, with relays already established.

According to usual custom, a *bell-mare* preceded this drove, which appeared to consist of about thirty horses. It was this bell that had first attracted the attention of the players.

When within a hundred yards or so of the huts, the driver of the *remuda* galloped to the front, and catching the bell-mare, brought her to a stop. The other horses halted on the instant.

Shortly after, five cavaliers appeared through the dust, riding in the direction of the huts. Two were in advance of the other three, who, following at a little distance, were acting as attendants or servants.

The most distinguished looking of the two who rode in advance, was a man of somewhat over medium height. He appeared to have passed the age of forty. A greyish-coloured *sombrero*, with broad brim, screened his face from the fervent sunbeams. He was habited in a pelisse, or *dolman*, of dark blue, richly laced with gold, and almost concealed under a large white kerchief, embroidered with sky-blue silk, and known in Mexico as *pano de sol*. Under the fiery atmosphere, the white colour of this species of scarf, like the *burnous* of the Arabs, serves to moderate the rays of the sun, and for this purpose was it worn by the cavalier in question. Upon his feet were boots of yellow Cordovan leather, and over these, large spurs, the straps of which were stitched with gold and silver wire. These spurs, with their huge five-pointed rowels, and little bells, gave out a silvery clinking that kept time to the march of the horse—sounds most agreeable to the ear of the Mexican *cavallero*.

A *mango*, richly slashed with gold lace, hung over the pommel of the saddle in front of the horseman, half covering with its folds a pair of wide pantaloons, garnished throughout their whole length with buttons of filigree gold. In fine, the saddle, embroidered like the straps of the spurs, completed a costume that, in the eyes of a European, would recall the souvenirs of the middle ages. For all that, the horseman in question did not require a rich dress to give him an air of distinction. There was that in his bearing and physiognomy that denoted a man accustomed to command and perfectly *au fait* to the world.

His companion, much younger, was dressed with far more pretension: but his insignificant figure, though not wanting in a certain degree of elegance, was far from having the aristocratic appearance of him with the embroidered kerchief.

The three servants that followed—with faces blackened by dust and sun, and half savage figures—carried long lances adorned with scarlet pennons, and *lazos* hung coiled from the pommels of their saddles. These strange attendants gave to the group that singular appearance peculiar to a cavalcade of Mexican travellers. Several mules, pack laden, and carrying enormous valises, followed in the rear. These valises contained provisions and the *ménage* necessary for a halt.

On seeing Cuchillo and Baraja, the foremost of the two cavaliers halted, and the troop followed his example.

"'Tis the Señor Don Estevan," said Baraja, in a subdued voice. "This is the man, señor," he continued, presenting Cuchillo to the cavalier with the *pano de sol*.

Don Estevan—for it was he—fixed upon Cuchillo a piercing glance, that appeared to penetrate to the bottom of his soul, at the same time the look denoted a slight expression of surprise.

"I have the honour to kiss the hands of your excellency," said Cuchillo. "As you see, it is I who—"

But in spite of his habitual assurance, the outlaw paused, trembling as vague souvenirs began to shape themselves in his memory; for these two men had met before, though not for a very long time.

"Eh! if I don't deceive myself," interrupted the Spaniard, in an ironical tone, "the Señor Cuchillo and I are old acquaintances—though formerly I knew him by a different name?"

"So too your excellency, who was then called—"

Arechiza frowned till the hairs of his black moustache seemed to stand on end. The outlaw did not finish his speech. He saw that it was not the time to tell what he knew; but this species of complicity appeared to restore him to his wonted assurance.

Cuchillo was, in truth, one of those gentlemen who have the ill luck to give to whatever name they bear a prompt celebrity; and for this reason he had changed his more than once.

"Señor Senator," said Arechiza, turning toward his *compagnon de voyage*, "this place does not appear very suitable for our noon siesta?"

"The Señor Tragaduros y Despilfarro, will find the shade of one of these cottages more agreeable," interposed Cuchillo, who knew the senator of Arispe. He knew, moreover, that the latter had attached himself to the fortunes of Don Estevan, in default of better cause: and in hopes of repairing his own fortune, long since dissipated.

Despite the low state of his finances, however, the Senator had not the less a real influence in the congress of Sonora; and it was this influence which Don Estevan intended using to his own advantage. Hence the companionship that now existed between them.

"I agree with all my heart to your proposal," answered Tragaduros, "the more so that we have now been nearly five hours in the saddle."

Two of the servants dismounting, took their masters' horses by the bridle, while the other two looked after the *cargas* of the mules. The camp-beds were taken from the pack saddles, and carried into two of the houses that appeared the most spacious and proper.

We shall leave the Senator reclining upon his mattress, to enjoy that profound slumber which is the portion of just men and travellers; while we accompany Don Estevan into the hut which he had chosen for himself, and which stood at some distance from that occupied by the legislator.

Chapter Nine
The Compact

After having followed Don Estevan, at the invitation of the latter, inside the hovel, Cuchillo closed behind him the wattle of bamboos that served as a door. He did this with great care—as if he feared that the least noise should be heard without—and then he stood waiting for the Spaniard to initiate the conversation.

The latter had seated himself on the side of his camp-bedstead, and Cuchillo also sat down, using for his seat the skull of a bullock,—which chanced to be in the house. It is the ordinary stool of this part of the country, where the luxury of chairs is still unknown—at least in the houses of the poor.

"I suppose," said Arechiza, breaking silence, "that you have a thousand reasons why I should know you by no other than your present name. I, with motives very different from yours, no doubt, desire to be here nothing more than *Don Estevan Arechiza.* Now! Señor Cuchillo," continued the speaker with a certain affectation of mockery; "let us have this grand secret that is to make your fortune and mine!"

"A word first, Señor Don Estevan de Arechiza," replied Cuchillo, in the same tone; "one word, and then you shall have it."

"I listen to you; but observe, sir, say nothing of the past—no more perfidy. We are here in a country where there are *trees,* and you know how I punish traitors."

At this allusion to some past event—no doubt some mysterious souvenir—the face of the outlaw became livid.

"Yes," replied he, "I remember that it is not your fault that I was not hung to a tree. It may be more prudent not to recall old wrongs—especially as you are no longer in a conquered country, but in one of forests—forests both sombre and dumb."

There was in this response of the outlaw such an evident air of menace, that, joined with his character and sinister antecedents, it required a firm heart on the part of Don Estevan not to regret having recalled the souvenir. With a cold smile he replied:

"Ha! another time I shall entrust the execution of a traitor in the hands of no human being. I shall perform that office myself," continued he, fixing upon Cuchillo a glance which caused the latter to lower his head. "As to your threats, reserve them for people of your own kind; and never forget, that between my breast and your dagger there is an insurmountable barrier."

"Who knows?" muttered Cuchillo, dissembling the anger which was devouring him. Then in a different tone, he continued: "But I am no traitor, Señor Don Estevan; and the proposal I am now about to make to you is frank and loyal."

"We shall see, then."

"Know, then, Señor Arechiza, that for several years past I have followed the profession of a *gambusino*, and have rambled over most of this country in the exercise of my calling. I have seen a deposit of gold such as mortal eye perhaps never looked upon!"

"You have seen it, and not possessed yourself of it?"

"Do not mock me, Don Estevan; I am in earnest. I have seen a *placer* so rich that the man who gets it might for a whole year play the game of hell with luck all the while against him, and not be impoverished! So rich as to satisfy the most insatiable avarice; so rich, in fact, as to buy a kingdom!"

At these words, which responded to some hopes and desires already conceived, Don Estevan could not hinder himself from the manifestation of a certain emotion.

"So rich," continued the outlaw, in an exalted tone, "that I would not hesitate for one instant to give my soul to the devil in exchange for it."

"The devil is not such a fool as to value so highly a soul which he knows he will get *gratis*. But how did *you* discover this *placer*?"

"Thus, señor. There was a *gambusino* called Marcos Arellanos, who was celebrated throughout the whole province. It was he who discovered this *bonanza* in company with another of the same calling as himself; but just as they were about to gather some of the gold, they were attacked by the Apache Indians. The associate of Marcos Arellanos was killed, and he himself had to run a thousand risks before he succeeded in making his escape.

"It was after he came home again that by chance I met him at Tubac. There he proposed to me to join him, and go back to the *placer*. I accepted his offer, and we started. We arrived safely at the *Golden Valley*, for by that name he called the place. Powers of Heaven!" exclaimed Cuchillo, "it only needed to see those blocks of gold shining in the sun to bring before one's eyes a thousand dazzling visions!

"Alas! we were only permitted to feast our eyes. The savages were upon us. We were compelled to fly in our turn, and I alone escaped. Poor Marcos! he fell under the horrible war clubs; and I—I have sorely grieved for him! Now, señor, this is the secret of the Golden Valley which I desire to sell to you."

"To sell to me:—and who is to answer for your fidelity?"

"My own interest. I sell you the secret, but I do not intend to alienate my rights to the *placer*. I have vainly endeavoured to get up an expedition such as yours, for without a strong force it would be of no use going there. It would be certain death to a party of only two or three. With your band, however, it will be easy, and success would be certain. I only ask the tenth part of all the gold that may be gathered, which I would deserve as guide of the expedition; and going as guide I will be at the same time a hostage for my good faith."

"Is that what I am to understand; you estimate the price of your secret and services a tenth part of the whole?"

"That and two hundred dollars paid down to enable me to equip myself for the expedition."

"You are more reasonable than I expected, Cuchillo. Very well, then let it be so; the two hundred dollars you shall have, and I promise you the tenth part."

"Agreed."

"Agreed, and you have my word upon it. Now, answer me some questions which I wish to put. Is this Golden Valley in that part of the country where I intended to have taken my expedition?"

"It is beyond the Presidio of Tubac; and since your men are to meet there you will not need to make any change in the dispositions you have already taken."

"Good. And you have seen this Golden Valley you say with your own eyes?"

"I have seen it without the power of touching it. I have seen it grinding my teeth as I looked upon it, like the damned in hell who get a glimpse of Paradise."

As Cuchillo spoke, his countenance betrayed beyond doubt the anguish he felt, at his cupidity having been balked.

Arechiza knew too well how to read the human physiognomy to doubt the truth of Cuchillo's report. Two hundred dollars were to him a mere bagatelle; and taking an ebony case from his bed, small but heavy, he drew from it a rouleau of gold pieces and handed them to the gambusino, who immediately put them in his pocket.

There was a little more in the rouleau than had been bargained for. The Spaniard took no notice of this, but forming a cross with his thumb and index finger of his right hand *à la mode Espagnole*, he held it before Cuchillo, directing him to make an oath upon it.

"I swear by the cross," said the latter, "to speak the truth, the whole truth, and nothing but the truth. At the end of ten days' journey beyond Tubac, going in a north-western direction, we shall arrive at the foot of a range of mountains. They are easy to recognise—for a thick vapour hangs over them both night and day. A little river traverses this range of hills. It is necessary to ascend it to a point where another stream runs into it. There in the angle where the two meet, is a steep hill, the summit of which is crowned by the tomb of an Indian chief. I was not near enough to distinguish the strange ornaments that surround this tomb; but at the foot of the hill there is a small lake by the side of a narrow valley in which the water from rain torrents has thrown to the surface immense treasures of gold, this is the *Golden Valley.*"

"The way will be easily found?" inquired Don Estevan.

"But difficult to travel," replied Cuchillo. "The arid deserts will be no obstacle compared with the danger from the hostility of Indians. This tomb of one of their most celebrated chiefs they hold in superstitious veneration. It is the constant object of their pilgrimages, and it was during one of these visits that we were surprised. Arellanos and myself."

"And this Arellanos—do you think, he has not revealed this secret to any one besides yourself?"

"You must know," replied Cuchillo, "that it is a custom of the gambusinos, before starting upon any expedition, to swear before the Holy Evangelists not to reveal the *bonanzas* they may find without the consent of their associates. This oath Arellanos took, and his death of course prevented him from betraying it."

"You have said that after his return from his first expedition, you met him in Tubac. Was there no woman whom he may perchance have had in his confidence?"

"His wife only—he may have told it to her. But yesterday a vaquero gave me the news that she has lately died. For all that, she may have revealed the secret to her son."

"Arellanos had a son then?"

"An adopted son—a young man whose father or mother no one knows anything about."

Don Estevan could not repress an involuntary movement.

"This young fellow is, no doubt, the son of some poor devil of this province?" said the Spaniard, in a careless way.

"No," replied Cuchillo, "he was born in Europe, and very likely in Spain."

Arechiza appeared to fall into a reverie, his head bending towards his breast. Some souvenirs were disturbing his spirit.

"This much at least is known," continued Cuchillo. "The commander of an English brig-of-war brought him to Guaymas. He stated that the child, who spoke both French and Spanish, had been captured in an affair between the brig and a French privateer. A sailor who was either killed in the fight or taken prisoner, was beyond doubt his father. The captain of the English brig, not knowing what to do with him, gave him to Arellanos— who chanced to be in Guaymas at the time—and Arellanos brought him up and has made a man of him—my faith! that he has. Young as the fellow is, there is not such a *rastreador* nor horse-tamer in the province."

The Spaniard, while apparently not listening to Cuchillo, did not lose a word of what he was saying; but whether he had heard enough, or that the subject was a painful one, he suddenly interrupted the gambusino:

"And don't you think, if this wonderful tracker and horse-breaker has been told the secret of his adopted father he might not be a dangerous rival to us?"

Cuchillo drew himself up proudly, and replied:—

"I know a man who will yield in nothing—neither at following a trail, nor taming a wild horse—to Tiburcio Arellanos; and yet this secret has been almost worthless in his keeping, since he has just sold it for the tenth part of its value!"

This last argument of Cuchillo's was sufficiently strong to convince Don Estevan that the Golden Valley was so guarded by these fierce Indians that nothing but a strong party could reach it—in short, that he himself was the only man who could set this force afoot. For a while he remained in his silent reverie. The revelations of Cuchillo in regard to the adopted son of Marcos Arellanos had opened his mind to a new set of ideas which absorbed all others. For certain motives, which we cannot here explain, he was seeking to divine whether this Tiburcio Arellanos was not the young Fabian de Mediana!

Cuchillo on his part was reflecting on certain antecedents relative to the gambusino Arellanos and his adopted son; but for powerful reasons he did not mention his reflections to Don Estevan. There are reasons, however, why the reader should now be informed of their nature.

The outlaw, as we have said, frequently changed his name. It was by one of these aliases used up so quickly, that he had been passing, when at the Presidio Tubac he made the acquaintance of the unfortunate Arellanos. When the latter was about starting out on his second and fatal journey—before parting with his wife and the young man whom he loved as well as if he had been his own son—he confided to his wife the object of his new expedition; and also the full particulars of the route he intended to take. Cuchillo was nevertheless ignorant of this revelation. But the knowledge which the outlaw carefully concealed, was that he himself after having reached the Golden Valley guided by Arellanos, murdered his companion, in hope of having all the treasure to himself. It was true enough that the Indians appeared afterwards, and it was with difficulty that the assassin could save his own scalp. We shall now leave him to tell his own story as to how he made the acquaintance of young Arellanos, and it will be seen that this story is a mere deception practised upon Don Estevan.

"Nevertheless," resumed Cuchillo in breaking the silence, "I was determined to free my mind from all doubt upon the subject. On my return to Arispe I repaired to the dwelling of the widow of Arellanos to inform her of the death of poor Marcos. But with the exception of the great grief which the news caused her, I observed nothing particular—nothing that could give me the least suspicion that I am not the sole possessor of the secret of the Golden Valley."

"One easily believes what he wishes to believe," remarked Arechiza.

"Hear me, Señor Don Estevan! There are two things on which I pride myself. One is, that I have a conscience easily alarmed; the other, that I am gifted with a perspicuity not easily deluded."

The Spaniard made no further objections. He was satisfied, not with the outlaw's conscience, but his perspicuity.

With regard to Tiburcio Arellanos, we need hardly state what the reader has no doubt already divined—that this young man was in reality no other than Fabian, the last descendant of the Counts of Mediana. Cuchillo has already related how the English brig brought him to Guaymas. Left without a guide to enable him to discover his family—disinherited of his rich patrimonial estates—an orphan knowing nothing of his parents, here he was in a strange land, the possessor of nothing more than a horse and a hut of bamboos.

Chapter Ten
The Afternoon Ride

When Cuchillo, after the interview just described, came forth from the hovel, the sun was no longer in the vertex of the heavens, but had commenced his downward course to the western horizon. The earth, burned up and dry as tinder, gave forth a thin vapoury mist, that here and there hung over the surface in condensed masses, giving that appearance known as the *mirage*. Limpid lakes presented themselves to the eye, where not a drop of water was known to exist—as if nature, to preserve a perfect harmony, offered these to the imagination in compensation for the absence of the precious fluid itself. Far off in the forest, could be heard at intervals the crackling of branches under the burning rays of the sun—just as if the woods were on fire. But the trees were beginning to open their leaves to the southern breeze that freshened as the hours passed on, and they appeared impatiently to await the twilight, when the night-dews would once more freshen their foliage.

Cuchillo gave a whistle, at which well-known signal his horse came galloping up to him. The poor beast appeared to suffer terribly from the thirst. His master, moved with pity, poured into a bowl a few drops of water from his skin bottle; and although it was scarce enough to moisten the animal's lips, it seemed to bring back the vigour of his spirit.

Cuchillo having saddled and bridled his horse, and buckled on a pair of huge spurs, called one of the attendants of Don Estevan. To this man he gave orders to have the pack of mules harnessed, as well as to collect the *remuda* to be sent on in advance—in order that the sleeping quarters for the night should be ready upon their arrival. The place where the travellers were to rest that night—as Cuchillo informed the domestic—was to be at the cistern known as *La Poza*.

"But *La Poza* is not on the route to Tubac!" objected the servant; "it lies out of the way and on the road leading to the *Hacienda del Venado*."

"*You* have nothing to do with the route," peremptorily answered Cuchillo, "your master intends spending some days at the Hacienda del Venado. Therefore do as I have ordered you."

The Hacienda del Venado was the most important estate between Arispe and the Indian frontier, and its proprietor had the reputation of being the most hospitable man in the whole province. It was, therefore, without repugnance that the attendants of Don Estevan heard this news from Cuchillo—since, although their route of march would be extended in making the détour by the Hacienda del Venado, they knew they would enjoy several days of pleasant repose at this hospitable mansion.

The man to whom Cuchillo had given his orders, immediately saddled his horse and set off to collect the *remuda*. He soon discovered the horses browsing in the woods near at hand, and collected, as usual, around the bell-mare.

As he approached, the troop bounded off in affright—just as wild horses would have done; but the active horseman was too quick for them, for already the running noose of his lazo was around the neck of one of them. The horse, perceiving that he was caught, and knowing well the lazo—whose power he had often felt—yielded without resistance, and permitted himself to be led quietly away. The *capitansa* (bell-mare) knew the signal and followed the horse of the servant, with all the others trooping at her heels.

Two of the freshest of the drove were left behind, for Don Estevan and the Senator. These would be enough to serve them as far as La Poza—the place of their intended night halt—which was only a few hours distant. The other horses, guided by the bell-mare, were taken on in advance, and the drove soon disappeared behind the cloud of dust thrown up by their hoofs.

Shortly after, the Senator made his appearance at the door of the hut where he had taken his siesta—a necessity almost imperious in these hot climates. At the same time, Don Estevan presented himself in the open air. The atmosphere, though a little fresher than when they had gone inside, was still sufficiently stifling to be disagreeable.

"Carramba!" cried the Senator, after inhaling a few mouthfuls of it, "it is fire, *not* air, one has to breathe here. If these hovels were not a complete nest of snakes and scorpions, I should prefer staying in them until night, rather than launch myself into this dreadful furnace."

After this doleful speech the Senator climbed reluctantly into his saddle, and he and Don Estevan took the route, riding side by side, as in the morning. Behind, at a few paces distance, followed Cuchillo and Baraja, and after these the little *recua* of mules with the other domestics.

For the first hour of their march the shade of the trees rendered the heat supportable, but soon the forest ended, and the road debouched upon the open plains that appeared interminable.

It is hardly possible to conceive a more dreary prospect than that presented by those arid plains of Northern Mexico—naked, white, and almost destitute of vegetation. Here and there at long distances on the route, may be seen a tall pole which denotes the presence of some artificial well-cistern; but as you draw near, the leathern buckets, by which the water is to be raised, show by their stiff contracted outlines that for a long time they have held no water, and that the well is dried up—a sad fortune for the traveller whose evil star has guided him into these deserts during the dry season, especially if at the end of his day's journey he reckons on a supply from these treacherous depositaries. If his canteen is not well filled, or if he is by any chance detained upon his route, his story is likely to be that of hundreds who have perished of thirst upon these plains, between a heaven and an earth that are equally unpitying.

"Is it true, then, Don Estevan," inquired the Senator, as he wiped the perspiration from his brow, "that you have been through this country before?"

"Certainly," replied Don Estevan; "and it is just because I have been here before that I am here now. But what brought me here formerly, and why I now return, is a secret I shall tell you presently. Let me say that it is a secret sufficient to turn a man's brain, provided he is not one with a bold, firm heart. Are you that man, señor Senator?" added the Spaniard, fixing his eyes upon his companion, with a calm regard.

The Senator made no reply, farther than by giving a slight shiver that was perceptible through his frame, and which denoted that he felt some apprehension as to the rôle he might be called upon to play.

The Spaniard did not fail to observe his uneasiness, as he resumed:

"Meanwhile, señor, let me ask you, are you decided to follow my advice, and restore your fortunes by some rich matrimonial alliance which I shall arrange for you?"

"Without doubt I am," replied the Senator, "though I can't see what interest that can be to you, Señor Don Estevan."

"That is my affair and my secret. I am not one of those who sell the skin of the bear before the animal is caught. It is enough for you to know, Don Vicente Tragaduros y Despilfarro, that I have a hundred thousand dollars at your disposal the moment you say the word—it only remains for you to hear my conditions, and subscribe to them."

"I don't say no," replied the Senator, "but I candidly avow that for the life of me I cannot think of any one possessing such an inheritance as you mention—not one in the whole province."

"Do you know the daughter of the rich landowner Augusta Peña—at whose hacienda, please God, we shall sleep to-morrow night?"

"Oh!" exclaimed the Senator, "the proprietor of the Hacienda del Venado? I have heard of her—*her* dowry should be a million if report speaks true; but what folly it would be for me to pretend—"

"Bah!" interrupted the Spaniard. "It is a fortress that well besieged may capitulate like any other."

"It is said that the daughter of Peña is pretty."

"Beautiful."

"You know her, then?" said the Senator, regarding his companion with an astonished look. "Perhaps," he added, "it is to the hacienda of Venado that you make those periodical and mysterious journeys, so much talked about at Arispe?"

"Precisely so."

"Ah! I understand you," said the Senator, turning a sly look upon his companion, "it was the beautiful eyes of the daughter that attracted you, the—?"

"You are mistaken. It was the father, who was simply the banker from whom, from time to time, I drew the funds necessary for my expenses at Arispe."

"Is that also the object of our present journey?"

"Partly," replied the Spaniard, "but not altogether—there is another object, which I will communicate to you hereafter."

"Well, señor," answered the Senator, "you are a mystery to me from head to foot; but I abandon myself blindly to your guidance."

"You do well," said Don Estevan, "and in all likelihood your sun, for a while eclipsed, will shine out again with more than its former splendour."

Chapter Eleven
An Unfortunate Traveller

It was now near sunset; the travellers were still about two leagues from La Poza, and the desert plains were nearly passed. Some *mezquite* trees appeared in front thinly covering the calcareous soil, but the twilight sun began to render less visible the objects here and there scattered over the plain.

All at once the horse of Don Estevan came to a stand, and showed signs of affright. The steed of the Senator acted in a similar fashion, though neither of the two horsemen could perceive the cause of this strange behaviour.

"It is the body of some dead mule?" suggested the Mexican.

Don Estevan spurred his horse forward, despite the repugnance of the animal to advance; and a few paces further on, behind a clump of wild aloe plants, he perceived the body of a horse stretched out upon the sand. Such a sight in these dry plains is by no means uncommon; and the travellers would not have given a moment's thought to it, but for the fact that the horse in question appeared to be saddled and bridled. This circumstance indicated some extraordinary occurrence.

Cuchillo had meanwhile ridden forward to the spot.

"Ah!" said he, after glancing a moment at the dead horse, "the poor devil who has ridden him has met with a double accident: he has not only lost his horse, but also his water-bottle. See!"

The guide pointed to an object lying upon the ground by the shoulder of the fallen horse, and still attached by a strap to the saddle. It was a leathern water-bottle apparently broken and empty. In fact, its position proved that the horse, enfeebled by the heat and thirst, had fallen suddenly to the earth, and the bottle, hardened by the sun, and coming in contact with the animal's shoulder, had got crushed either by the fall, or in the struggle that succeeded it. A large fracture was visible in the side of the vessel, through which the water had escaped to the very last drop.

"We are likely enough by and by to stumble upon his owner:" suggested Cuchillo, while he examined the trappings of the dead horse, to see if there might be anything worth picking up. "*Por Dios!*" he continued, "this reminds me that I have the very devil's thirst myself," and as he said this, he raised his own bottle to his head, and swallowed some gulps from it.

The tracks of a man upon the sandy surface, indicated that the traveller had continued his route on foot; but the footmarks showed also, that he must have tottered rather than walked. They were unequally distant from each other, and wanted that distinctness of shape, that would have been exhibited by the footsteps of a man standing properly on his legs.

These points did not escape the keen eyes of Cuchillo, who was one of those individuals who could read such dumb signs with an unfailing certainty.

"Beyond a doubt," said he, taking another gulp from his bottle, "the traveller cannot be far off."

His conjecture proved correct. A few moments after, the body of a man was seen by the side of the path, lying upon the ground, and perfectly motionless. As if this individual had intended that his countenance should be hidden from the eyes of any one passing, a broad palm-leaf hat covered the whole of his face.

The costume of this traveller in distress, betrayed a certain degree of poverty. Besides the hat already mentioned, which appeared old and battered, a rusty-coloured Indian shirt, somewhat torn, and a pair of pantaloons of nankeen, with common filigree buttons, appeared to be his only garments. At least they were all that could be noticed in the obscure twilight.

"Benito," said Don Estevan, calling to one of his servants, "knock off with the butt of your lance the hat that covers this man's face—perhaps he is only asleep?"

Benito obeyed the order, and tossed aside the hat without dismounting; but the man stretched on the ground did not appear to know what had been done—at least he made not the slightest movement.

When the hat was removed, however, the darkness, which had suddenly increased, rendered it impossible to distinguish his features.

"Although it is not exactly your speciality, Señor Cuchillo," said Don Estevan, addressing himself to the outlaw, "if you will do an act of humanity in trying to save the life of this poor devil, you shall have half an ounce of gold if you succeed."

"Cospita! Señor Don Estevan," cried Cuchillo, "you surely mistake my character. I am the most humane of mortals—that is," continued he in an undertone, "when it is my interest to be so. You may ride forward then; and it will not be my fault, if I don't bring this poor fellow safe to our halting-place at La Poza."

In saying these words Cuchillo dismounted, and laying his hands upon the neck of his horse, cried out:

"Now, good Tordilla, don't budge an inch from this spot till I call for you."

The animal, pawing the sand, and champing his bit, appeared to comprehend the words of his master, and remained in the place where he had been left.

"Shall we leave one of the servants to assist you?" inquired the Senator, as they were riding off.

"No, thank you, Señor Don Vicente," responded Cuchillo, fearing that if any one was left he might expect some share in the promised *demi-onza*; "it will not be necessary."

And the cavalcade riding off, left the outlaw alone with the recumbent body.

Chapter Twelve
Tiburcio Arellanos

Cuchillo approaching the body, bent down to examine the features, and see if there were any signs of life. At the first glance of that face the outlaw trembled.

"Tiburcio Arellanos, as I live!" he involuntarily muttered.

It was, in truth, the adopted son of his victim whom he saw before him.

"Yes—there is no mistake—it is he! *Santa Virgen*! if not dead he's not far off it," continued he, observing the mortal paleness of the young man's countenance.

A hellish thought at this moment arose in the mind of the outlaw. Perhaps the only man in all the world who shared with him that secret, which he himself had purchased by the crime of murder, was there before him—completely in his power. It only needed to finish him, if not already dead, and to report that he could not be saved. He was in the middle of the desert, under the shadow of night, where no eye could see, and no hand could hinder; why then should he not make his secret secure against every contingency of the future?

All the ferocious instincts of the villain were re-awakened; mechanically he drew the long knife from his boot, and held its point over the heart of the unconscious Tiburcio.

At that moment, a slight quivering of the limbs told that the latter still lived. The outlaw raised his arm, but still hesitated to strike the blow.

"It was just thus," reflected he, "that I stabbed the man he called his father—just in the same way, as he slept beside me, in full confidence of security. I see him now contesting with me for the life of this young fellow more than half gone. I feel at this moment the weight of his body upon my shoulders, just as I felt it when I carried him down to the river."

And the murderer, at these thoughts, in the middle of the darkness and solitude, cast around him a look that betrayed the terror with which the souvenir still inspired him.

That terror saved the life of Tiburcio; for the knife was thrust back into its singular scabbard, and the villain, seating himself beside the recumbent form, thrust his hand under the vest of the young man, and held it over his heart to try whether it was still beating.

In this attitude he remained for a short while—until satisfied that Tiburcio was yet alive. Then a bright thought seemed to startle him; for a voice had spoken to him from within, stronger than the voice of conscience. It was that of personal interest. Cuchillo knew the rare qualities of Tiburcio— his talents as a *rastreador*, or tracker—his daring prowess in Indian warfare; and after some consideration, he resolved to enrol him in the expedition of Don Estevan, to which he would no doubt prove of great value.

"That will be the best plan," said the outlaw, speaking in soliloquy. "What would his life be worth to me now?—Nothing; and if I wish to have it hereafter—why, then there will be no lack of opportunities. He cannot be otherwise than grateful for what I am going to do for him. But let me see how matters stand—of course it is thirst that is killing him—how lucky I have kept a little water in my canteen!"

He now opened the mouth of the dying man, and holding the neck of the leathern bottle to his lips, poured some drops down his throat. The water produced an almost instantaneous reanimation, and the young man opened his eyes, but soon closed them again.

"That shows he is coming round," muttered Cuchillo.

Twice or thrice he repeated the operation, each time doubling the dose of water. Finally, at the end of half an hour or so, Tiburcio was sufficiently recovered to be able to raise himself up, and to answer the questions put to him by the man who was, in reality, the preserver of his life.

Tiburcio Arellanos was still but a young man; but the sort of life he had led—solitary, and dependent on his own resources—had given to his judgment a precocious maturity. He therefore observed a degree of prudence in recounting to Cuchillo the death of his adopted mother, to which subject the outlaw had guided the conversation.

"During the twenty-four hours that I passed by the death-bed of my mother," said Tiburcio, "I quite forgot to attend to my horse; and after all was over I closed the door of the cottage, where I never wished to return, and I set out upon this journey. The poor animal, so long neglected, became feeble on the second day, and fell dead under me: and, to my misfortune, my water-bottle was broken in the fall, and the water spilled upon the sand. I remained on the spot till thirst brought on fever, and then I strayed away; and after wandering about, I know not how long, I fell, as my horse had done, expecting never more to rise."

"I comprehend all that," responded Cuchillo. "Well! it is astonishing how people will regret the death of parents, who do not leave them the slightest inheritance!"

Tiburcio could have told him, that on her death-bed his adopted mother had left him a royal, as well as a terrible legacy—the secret of the Golden Valley, and the vengeance of the murder of Marcos Arellanos. Both had been, confided to him—the golden secret upon the especial conditions that Tiburcio would, if necessary, spend the whole of his life in searching for the assassin.

Tiburcio appeared to take no notice of Cuchillo's last reflection, and perhaps his discretion proved the saving of his life: for had the outlaw been made sure that he was in possession of the secret of the Golden Valley, it is not likely he would have made any further efforts to save him, but the reverse.

"And is that a fact," continued Cuchillo, interrogatively, "that with the exception of a hut which you have abandoned, a horse which has dropped dead between your legs, and the garments you carry on your back, that Arellanos and his widow have left you nothing?"

"Nothing but the memory of their goodness to me, and a reverence for their name."

"Poor Arellanos! I was very sorry for him," said Cuchillo, whose hypocrisy had here committed him to an unguarded act of imprudence.

"You knew him then?" hastily inquired Tiburcio, with some show of surprise. "He never spoke to me of you!"

Cuchillo saw that he had made a mistake, and hastened to reply.

"No, I didn't know him personally. I have only heard him much spoken of as a most worthy man, and a famous gambusino. That is why I was sorry on hearing of his death. Was it not I who first apprised his widow of the unfortunate occurrence, having myself heard of it by chance?"

Notwithstanding the natural tone in which Cuchillo delivered this speech, he was one of those persons of such a sinister countenance, that Tiburcio could not help a certain feeling of suspicion while regarding it. But by little and little the feeling gave way, and the young man's thoughts taking another turn, he remained for some moments buried in a silent reverie. It was merely the result of his feebleness, though Cuchillo, ever ready to suspect evil, interpreted his silence as arising from a different cause.

Just then the horse of Cuchillo began to show evident signs of terror, and the instant after, with his hair standing on end, he came galloping up to his master as if to seek protection. It was the hour when the desert appears in all its nocturnal majesty. The howling of the jackals could be heard in the distance; but all at once a voice rising far above all the rest appeared to give them a signal to be silent. It was the voice of the American lion.

"Do you hear it?" inquired Cuchillo of his companion.

A howl equally loud, but of a different tone, was heard on the opposite side. "It is the puma and jaguar about to battle for the body of your horse, friend Tiburcio, and whichever one is conquered may take a fancy to revenge himself on us. Suppose you mount behind me, and let us be off?"

Tiburcio followed the advice; and notwithstanding the double load, the horse of Cuchillo galloped off like an arrow, impelled to such swift course by the growling of the fierce animals, that for a long time could be heard, as if they were following in the rear.

Chapter Thirteen
A Stumbling Horse

Far along the route these sounds accompanied the two riders—that is, the wailing of the jackals, mingled with the more fearful utterance of the great feline denizens of the desert. All at once, however, these noises became stilled, as a sound of a far different nature indicated the presence of some human being interfering in this scene of the desert. It was the crack of a gun, but with that quick sharp report that distinguishes the detonation of the rifle.

"A shot!" exclaimed Tiburcio. "But who can be amusing himself by hunting at this time of night, and in the middle of such a desert?"

"Very likely one of those American trappers we see now and then at Arispe, where they come to sell their beaver skins. These fellows think as little of a puma or a jaguar as they do of a jackal."

No other noise was afterwards heard to break the imposing silence of the night. The stars were shining brightly in the blue heaven, and the breeze, that had now become much cooler, scarce made the slightest rustling as it passed through the branches of the iron-wood trees.

"Where are you taking me?" asked Tiburcio, after an interval of silence.

"To La Poza, where I have some companions who are to pass the night there. To-morrow, if you like, on to the hacienda of Venado."

"To the hacienda of Venado! that is just where I was going."

Had it been daylight, Cuchillo might have seen a blush suddenly redden the cheeks of the young man as he pronounced these words; for it was an affair of the heart, that in spite of all the efforts he had made to resist it, was attracting him to the hacienda de Venado. The object of his interest was no other than the daughter of the *haciendado* himself—the young heiress already spoken of.

"For what purpose were you going there?" inquired Cuchillo, in a careless tone.

This simple question was nevertheless difficult to be answered. His companion was not the man to whom the young gambusino could give his confidence. He hesitated before making reply.

"I am without resources," said he at length, "and I go to ask Don Augustin Peña if he will accept me in the capacity of one of his *vaqueros*."

"'Tis a poor business you wish to undertake, *amigo*. To expose your life forever for such paltry pay as you will get—to keep watch at night and run about all the day; exposed to the burning heat of the sun, and by night to the cold—for this is the lot of a vaquero."

"What can I do?" replied Tiburcio. "Besides, it is just the sort of life I have been accustomed to; have I not always been exposed to privations and the solitude of the desert plains? These torn calzoneras and well-worn jacket are all that are left me—since I have now no longer my poor horse. Better turn vaquero than be a beggar!"

"He knows nothing of the secret then," reflected Cuchillo, "since he is meditating on an employment of this nature." Then raising his voice:—"You are in truth, then, a complete orphan, amigo; and have no one to mourn for you if you were to die—except myself. Have you by chance heard anything of this grand expedition that is being organised at Tubac?"

"No."

"Become one of it then. To an expedition of this kind a resolute young fellow like you would be a valuable acquisition; and upon your part, an expert gambusino, such as I fancy you must be—from the school in which you have been taught—might make his fortune at a single stroke."

If he parry this thrust, muttered the outlaw to himself, it will be proof positive that he knows nothing about it.

Cuchillo was thus pursuing his investigation with a twofold object, sounding Tiburcio about the secret, while at the same time trying to attach him to the expedition by the hope of gain. But cunning as was the outlaw, he had to do with a party that was no simpleton. Tiburcio prudently remained silent.

"Although between ourselves," continued Cuchillo, "I can tell you that I have never been beyond Tubac, yet I am to be one of the guides of this expedition. Now what say you?"

"I have my reasons," replied Tiburcio, "not to engage in it without reflection. I therefore demand of you twenty-four hours to think it over, and then you shall have my answer."

The expedition, of which this was the first news Tiburcio had heard, might, in fact, ruin or favour his own projects—hence the uncertainty he felt, and which he contrived so cleverly to conceal by his discreet reserve.

"Very well," rejoined Cuchillo, "the thing will keep that long."

And with this the conversation was discontinued.

Cuchillo, joyed at being disembarrassed of his apprehension about the secret, began carelessly whistling while he spurred forward his horse. The greatest harmony continued between these two men, who, though they knew it not, had each a motive of the deadliest hatred one against the other. Suddenly, as they were thus riding along, the horse that carried them stumbled upon the left fore-leg, and almost came to the ground. On the instant Tiburcio leaped down, and with eyes flashing fire, cried out in a threatening tone to his astonished companion.

"You say you have never been beyond Tubac? where did you get this horse, Cuchillo?"

"What business of yours, where I got him?" answered the outlaw, surprised by a question to which his conscience gave an alarming significance, "and what has my horse to do with the interrogatory you have so discourteously put to me?"

"By the soul of Arellanos! I will know; or, if not—"

Cuchillo gave the spur to his horse, causing him to bound to one side—while at the same time he attempted to unbuckle the straps that fastened his carbine to the saddle; but Tiburcio sprang after, seized his hand, and held it while he repeated the question:—

"How long have you owned this horse?"

"There, now! what curiosity!" answered Cuchillo, with a forced smile, "still, since you are so eager to know—it is—it is about six weeks since I became his master; you may have seen me with him, perhaps?"

In truth it was the first time Tiburcio had seen Cuchillo with this horse—that, notwithstanding his bad habits of stumbling, was otherwise an excellent animal, and was only used by his master on grand occasions. For this very reason Tiburcio had not seen him before.

The ready lie of the outlaw dissipated, no doubt, certain suspicions that had arisen in the mind of the young man, for the latter let go the horseman's wrist, which up to this time he had held in his firm grasp.

"Pardon me!" said he, "for this rudeness; but allow me to ask you another question?"

"Ask it!" said Cuchillo, "since we are friends; in fact, among friends, one question less or more can make no difference."

"Who sold you this horse six weeks ago?"

"Por Dios, his owner, of course—a stranger, whom I did not know, but who had just arrived from a long journey."

Cuchillo repeated these words in a slow and drawling manner, as if to gain time for some hidden purpose.

"A stranger?" repeated Tiburcio; "pardon me! one more question?"

"Has the horse been stolen from *you*?" asked the outlaw in an ironical tone.

"No—but let us think no more of my folly—pardon me, señor!"

"I pardon you," answered Cuchillo, in a tone of magnanimity, "the more so," added he mentally, "that you will not go much further, you son of a hound!"

Tiburcio, unsuspecting, was no longer on his guard, and the outlaw, profiting by the darkness, had already detached his carbine from the saddle. In another moment, beyond doubt, he would have carried into execution his demoniac purpose, had it not been for the appearance of a horseman, who was coming at full gallop along the road. Besides the horse which he rode, the horseman led behind him another, saddled and bridled. He was evidently a messenger from Don Estevan.

"Ah! is it you, Señor Cuchillo?" he cried out, as he rode up.

"The devil!" grumbled the outlaw, at this ill-timed interruption. "Ah! is it you, Señor Benito?" he inquired, suddenly changing his tone.

"Yes. Well, have you saved the man? Don Estevan has sent me back to you with a gourd of fresh water, and a horse to bring him on."

"He is there," replied Cuchillo, pointing to Tiburcio, who stood at a little distance, "thanks to me he is sound and safe—until I have a chance of being once more alone with him," he muttered, in a tone not intended to be heard.

"Well, gentlemen," remarked the servant, "we had better go on—the camping place is not far from here—we can soon reach it."

Tiburcio leaped into the empty saddle, and the three galloped silently toward the place where the travellers had halted—the servant thinking only of reaching it as soon as possible, and going to rest—Cuchillo mentally cursing the interruption that had forced him to adjourn his project of vengeance—and Tiburcio vainly endeavouring to drive out of his mind the suspicion which this curious incident had aroused.

In this occupation the three rode on for about a quarter of an hour, until the gleam of fires ahead discovered the halting-place of the travellers at La Poza. Soon afterwards their camp itself was reached.

Chapter Fourteen
La Poza

The place known by the name "La Poza" was the only one, within a circle of many leagues, where at this time of the year water could be found. There was here a natural cistern or well—partly nourished by a spring, and partly by rain from the skies. It was hollowed at the bottom of a little crater-shaped valley, only a few paces in circumference, the sloping side's of which served to conduct to the well the rain-water that fell around.

The ridges inclosing the little valley were crowned with trees of thick frondage, which, nourished by the evaporation of the water, appeared green and vigorous, and protected the cistern from the burning rays of the sun. The green grass that grew around, the cool shadow of the trees, and the freshness of the air, rendered the well of La Poza, in the middle of the desert, a delicious little oasis. Besides serving as excellent resting-place for travellers, it was a favourite resort of hunters, who used it as a stalking-ground for animals—elks and deer—as well as jaguars and other fierce beasts that in great numbers came to the well to drink.

At a short distance from the cistern of La Poza commenced a tract of thick forest through which ran the path leading to the Hacienda del Venado. Nearer to the edge of the little valley, upon the side of this path, the travellers had kindled an enormous fire, partly to defend themselves from the the cold night air, and partly to frighten off any jaguars or pumas that might be in the neighbourhood of the water.

Not far from this fire the servants had placed the camp-beds of the Senator and Don Estevan; and while a large saddle of mutton was being roasted for supper, a skin bottle of wine was cooling in the fresh water with which the trough had been filled.

After a painful day's march, it was an attractive spectacle which this scene presented to the eyes of the travellers.

"*Mine*! your halting-place, Tiburcio," said Cuchillo, as they rode into the camp, and speaking in a tone of pretended friendliness in order to conceal the real rancour which he felt. "Dismount here, while I go and report your arrival to our chief. It is Don Estevan de Arechiza himself under whose orders we are enrolled; so, too, may you be, if you desire it; and between ourselves, *amigo*, it is the best thing you can do."

Cuchillo fearing that his victim might escape him, now wished more than ever that he should join the expedition. He pointed out Don Estevan and the Senator seated on their camp-beds, and visible in the light of the great fire, while Tiburcio was not yet seen by them. Cuchillo himself advanced toward Don Estevan.

"I am desirous, Señor Don Estevan," said he, addressing himself to the Spaniard, "to say two words to your honour, with the permission of his excellency the Senator."

Don Estevan arose from his seat and made a sign to Cuchillo to accompany him into one of the dark alleys of the forest, the same by which the path entered that led to the hacienda.

"You could hardly guess, Señor Don Estevan, who is the man your generosity has saved—for I have brought him with me safe and sound, as you see?"

Without making answer, Don Estevan took from his purse the piece of gold he had promised, and handed it to Cuchillo.

"It is the young Tiburcio Arellanos to whom you have given life," continued the outlaw. "As for me I only followed the dictates of my heart; but it may be that we have both done a very foolish action."

"Why that?" asked the Spaniard. "This young man will be easily watched so long as he is near us; and I presume he is decided to be one of our expedition?"

"He has asked twenty-four hours to reflect upon it."

"Do you think he knows anything of—"

"I have my fears," replied Cuchillo, in a melancholy tone, little regarding the lie he was telling, and the purpose of which was to render the Spaniard suspicious of the man he had himself vowed to kill. "In any case," continued he, with a significant smile, "we have saved his life, and that will serve as *tit for tat*."

"What do you mean to say?"

"Only that my conscience assures me it will be perfectly tranquil if— if—Carramba!" added he, brusquely—"if I should send this young fellow to be broiled with his mother in the other world."

"God forbid that!" exclaimed the Spaniard, in a lively tone. "What need? Admit that he knows all: I shall be in command of a hundred men, and he altogether alone. What harm can the fellow do us. I have no uneasiness about him. I am satisfied, and so must you be."

"Oh! I am satisfied if you are," growled Cuchillo, like a dog whose master had hindered him from biting some one, "quite satisfied," he continued, "but perhaps hereafter—"

"I shall see this young man," said the Spaniard, interrupting him, and advancing in the direction where Tiburcio stood, while Cuchillo followed, talking to himself:

"What the devil possessed him to ask how long I had owned my horse? Let me see! the animal stumbled, I remember, and it was just then he dismounted and threatened me. I can't understand it, but I suspect what I do not understand."

When Arechiza and Cuchillo reached the camp, an excitement was observed among the horses, that gathered around the *capitansa*, at a short distance from the fire, and to all appearance in a state of extreme terror, were uttering a wild and continuous neighing. Some danger yet afar, but which the animals' instincts enabled them to perceive, was the cause of this sudden *stampede*.

"It is some jaguar they have scented," suggested one of the domestics.

"Bah!" replied another, "the jaguars attack only young foals—they wouldn't dare to assault a strong vigorous horse."

"Do you think so?" demanded the first speaker. "Ask Benito here, who, himself, lost a valuable animal taken by the jaguars."

Benito, hearing this reference to himself, advanced towards the two speakers.

"One day," he began, "or rather, one night just like this, I chanced to be at a distance from the Hacienda del Venado, where I was a *vaquero* at the time. I was in search of a strayed horse, and not finding him, had made up my mind to pass the night at the spring of *Ojo da Agua*. I tied my horse at a good distance off—where there was better grass—and I was sleeping, as a man sleeps after riding twenty leagues, when I was suddenly awakened by all the howlings and growlings of the devils. The moon shone so clear you might have fancied it daylight. All at once my horse came galloping toward me with the lazo hanging round his neck, which he had broken at the risk of hanging himself.

"'Here then,' said I, 'I shall now have two horses to go in search of instead of one.'

"I had scarce made this reflection, when I observed, under the light of the moon, a superb jaguar bounding after my horse. He scarce appeared to touch the ground, and each leap carried him forward twenty feet or more.

"I saw that my poor steed was lost. I listened with anxiety, but for a while heard nothing. At the end of a quarter of an hour, however, a terrible roar—"

The speaker paused, and stood trembling.

"*Virgen Santa!*" cried he, "that's it!" as the fearful cry of a jaguar at that moment echoed through the camp, succeeded by a deathlike stillness, as if both men and animals had been alike terrified into silence.

Chapter Fifteen
Nocturnal Visitors

The sudden shock occasioned by the perception of a peril so proximate and imminent paralysed every tongue. Even the ex-herdsman himself was silent, and appeared to reflect what had best be done to avoid the danger.

At this instant the voice of Don Estevan broke the temporary silence that reigned within the camp.

"Get your weapons ready!" shouted he.

"It is useless, master," rejoined the old vaquero, whose experience among jaguars gave a certain authority to his words, "the best thing to be done, is to keep the fire ablaze."

And saying this, he flung an armful of fagots upon it, which, being as dry as tinder, at once caught flame—so as to illumine a large circle around the camp.

"If they are not choking with thirst," said Benito, "these demons of darkness will not dare come within the circle of the fire. But, indeed, they are often choking with thirst, and then—"

"Then!" interrupted one of the domestics, in a tone of anxiety.

"Then," continued the herdsman, "then they don't regard either light or fire; and if we are not determined to defend the water against their approach, we had better get out of their way altogether. These animals are always more thirsty than hungry."

"How when they have drunk?" asked Baraja, whose countenance, under the light of the fire, betrayed considerable uneasiness.

"Why, then they seek to appease their hunger."

At this moment a second cry from the jaguar was heard, but farther off than the first. This was some relief to the auditory of Benito, who, relying upon his theory, was satisfied that the animal was not yet at the extreme point of suffering from thirst. All of them preserved silence—the only sounds heard being the crackling of the dry sticks with which Baraja kept the fire profusely supplied.

"Gently there, Baraja! gently!" called out the vaquero, "if you consume our stock of firewood in that fashion, you will soon make an end of it, and, *por Dios*! *amigo*, you will have to go to the woods for a fresh supply."

"There! hold your hand," continued he, after a pause, "and try to make the fagots last as long as possible, else we may get in darkness and at the mercy of the tiger. He is sure to come back again in an hour or two, and far thirstier than before."

If Benito had desired to frighten his companions, he could not have succeeded better. The eyes of one and all of them were anxiously bent upon the heap of dried sticks that still remained by the fire, and which appeared scarcely sufficient to last for another hour. But there was something so earnest in the tone of the ex-herdsman, despite the jesting way in which he spoke, that told he was serious in what he had said.

Of course, Don Estevan had postponed the interview with Tiburcio; and the young man, still ignorant that it was to Don Estevan he really owed his life, did not think of approaching to offer him thanks. Moreover, he saw that the moment would be ill-timed to exchange compliments of courtesy with the chief of the expedition, and for this reason he remained standing where Cuchillo had left him.

Nevertheless Don Estevan could not hinder himself from casting an occasional glance in the direction where the young man stood—though through the obscurity he could make no exact observation of his features.

The silence continued. Don Estevan and the Senator remained seated on their camp-beds, carbine in hand, while Benito, surrounded by the other domestics, formed a group by the side of the fire. The horses had all approached within a few feet of their masters, where they stood trembling and breathing loudly from their spread nostrils. Their behaviour indicated an instinct on their part that the danger was not yet over.

Several minutes passed, in which no human voice broke the silence. In the midst of greatest perils there is something consolatory in the sound of a man's voice—something which makes the danger appear less; and as if struck by this idea, some one asked Benito to continue the narrative of his adventures.

"I have told you then," resumed the ex-herdsman, "that I saw the tiger springing after my horse, and that in the chase both disappeared from my sight. The moment after, the horse came galloping back; but I knew that it was his last gallop, as soon as by the light of the moon I saw the terrible rider that he carried. The jaguar was upon his back, flattened over his shoulders, with the neck of the poor horse fast between his jaws.

"They had not gone a dozen paces before I heard a crackling sound—as if some bone had been crushed—and on the instant I saw the horse stumble and fall. Both tiger and horse rolled over and over in a short but terrible struggle, and then my poor steed lay motionless.

"For safety I stole away from the dangerous proximity; but returning after daylight, I found only the half-stripped skeleton of a horse that had carried me for many a long year.

"And now, amigo," continued the ex-herdsman, turning to the man who had first spoken, "do you still think that the jaguar attacks only foals?"

No one made reply, but Benito's audience turned their glances outward from the fire, fearing that in the circle around they might see shining the eyes of one of these formidable animals.

Another interval of silence succeeded to the narrative of the vaquero. This was broken by the young man Tiburcio, who, used to the wild life of the plains and forests, was very little frightened by the presence of the jaguars.

"If you have a horse," said he, "you need not much fear the jaguar; he is sure to take your horse first. Here, we have twenty horses and only one tiger."

"The young man reasons well," rejoined Baraja, reassured by the observation of Tiburcio.

"Twenty horses for one tiger—yes," replied Benito; "but suppose the horses don't choose to remain here. Supposing, what is likely enough to happen, we have an *estampeda*—the horses will be off. Now the jaguar knows very well he cannot overcome a horse unless he does so in the first bound or two. I will not follow the horses then, but will stay by the water, and of course by us as well. Besides, the jaguars that hunt by these springs are likely enough to have tasted human flesh before now; and if so, they will not, as the young man affirms, prefer the flesh of a horse."

"Very consoling, that," interrupted Cuchillo.

Benito appeared to be a man fond of the most frightful suggestions, for not contented with what he had already said, he continued—

"If there be but one jaguar, then he will be satisfied with one of us, but in case he should chance to be accompanied by his female, then—" "Then what, by all the devils?" demanded Cuchillo.

"Why, then—but I don't wish to frighten you."

"May thunder strike you! Speak out," cried Baraja, suffering at the suspense.

"Why, in that case," coolly added Benito, "the tiger would undoubtedly show his gallantry to his female by killing a pair of us."

"Carramba!" fervently exclaimed Baraja. "I pray the Lord that this tiger may be a bachelor," and as he said this he flung a fresh armful of fagots on the fire.

"Gently, amigo! gently," interrupted the ex-herdsman, lifting off some of the sticks again. "We have yet at least six hours of night, and these fagots will scarce serve to keep up the light for one. Gently, I say! We have still three chances of safety: the first that the jaguar may not be thirsty; the second, that he may content himself with one of our horses; and the third, that he may, as you have wished it, be a *bachelor* tiger."

There was no response, and another interval of silence succeeded. During this it was some consolation to the travellers to see the moon, which now, rising above the horizon, lit up the plains with her white beams, and flung her silvery effulgence over the trees. From the direction of the woods came the mournful notes of the great horned owl, and the sound of flapping wings, caused by the vampire bat, as it glided through the aisles of the forest. No other sounds appeared to indicate the presence of living thing except those made by the horses or the travellers themselves.

"Do you think," said Baraja, addressing himself to Benito, "that the jaguar is likely to return again? I have known these animals howl at night around my hut, and then go off altogether."

"Yes," replied Benito, "that may be when their drinking place is left free to them. Here we have intercepted their approach to the water. Besides, here are both men and horses—both food and drink in one place; it is not likely they have gone away from a spot that promises to furnish them with both. No, I warrant you, they are still in the neighbourhood."

At this moment the cry of the jaguar was heard once more, proving the correctness of Benito's judgment.

"There!" cried he, "just as I said; the beast is nearer too—no doubt his thirst is increasing—the more so that he is hindered from approaching the spring. Ha! do you hear that?"

This exclamation was caused by another roar of the jaguar, but evidently not the one that had been already frightening the travellers—for this cry came from the opposite side of the camp.

"Ave Maria!" screamed Baraja, in anguish, "the tiger has a wife!"

"You speak true," said Benito, "there are two of them, and they must be a male and female, since two male jaguars never hunt in company."

"*Carrai!*" exclaimed Cuchillo, "may the devil take me if ever I passed a night in the company of such a man as this old herdsman. He would frighten the hair off one's head if he could."

"After all," said Baraja, "I think there can't be much danger, so long as we have got the horses between us and these terrible brutes."

Unhappily, this chance of safety was not to exist much longer, for just then the jaguars recommenced their growling, both of them nearer than ever. The effect upon the horses was now exhibited in a complete *estampeda*,—for these animals, seeing they could no longer rely upon their masters for protection, preferred trusting to their heels, and one and all of them broke away in a wild gallop.

As this last chance of security was gone, the old vaquero, leaving the fire, approached the spot where Don Estevan and the Senator were seated, and thus addressed them:—

"Gentlemen," said he, "prudence requires that you will not remain so far from the rest of us. As you perceive there is danger on both sides, it will be best that we should all keep close together, and as near the fire as possible."

The affrighted look of the Senator offered a striking contrast to the countenance of Don Estevan, which still preserved its calm rigidity.

"It is good advice this faithful servant gives us," said Tragaduros, rising to do as Benito had suggested.

"Come, Benito," said Don Estevan, "these are nothing but hunter's stories you have been telling, and you wish to frighten these novices? Is it not so?"

"As I live, Señor Don Estevan, 'tis the truth!"

"There is a real danger, then?"

"Certain there is, my master!"

"Very well, in that case I shall remain where I am."

"Are you in earnest?" asked the frightened Tragaduros.

"Quite so—the duty of a leader is to protect his followers," said the Spaniard, proudly, "and that is what I mean to do. If the danger is only from the right and left as it appears to be—I shall guard the right here. There are two bullets in my gun, and with these and a sure eye, what care I for a jaguar? You, Señor Don Vicente, can take your stand on the left of the fire, and watch that side. If it appears prudent to you to keep near the men, do so."

This compromise appeared to the taste of Tragaduros, who had no idea of exposing the person of a man who was to be the future proprietor of a million of dollars dowry. He lost no time, therefore, in crossing over to the fire, and although he made a feint to keep watch on the opposite side from that guarded by Don Estevan, he took care to remain within a few feet of the group of attendants.

These dispositions had scarce been completed, when a formidable dialogue was struck up between the two fierce beasts that were approaching on opposite sides of the camp. Now they would utter a hoarse roaring, then a series of screams and yells, succeeded by a shrill mewing that resembled the caterwauling of cats—only louder and more terrific in its effect. Though Benito and Tiburcio knew that all these noises were caused by a single pair of tigers, the others imagined that not less than a dozen must be engaged in the frightful chorus.

The gun of the Senator shook in his hand—Baraja commended his soul to all the saints in the Spanish calendar—Cuchillo clutched his carbine, as if he would crush it between his fingers—while the chief himself coolly awaited the dénouement of the drama.

Chapter Sixteen
The Tiger Hunters

By the light of the fire Don Estevan could be seen walking in the direction whence proceeded the cries of the jaguar that was approaching on the right. He appeared calm as if going out in search of a deer. Tiburcio, at the aspect of the Spanish chief, felt within him that exultation of spirit which danger produces in certain energetic natures; but his dagger was the only weapon he possessed.

He cast a glance at the double-barrelled gun which the Senator held in his hand, and of which the latter was likely to make a use more fatal to his companions than to the jaguar.

On his part the Senator cast an envious look upon the safe position which Tiburcio occupied—in the centre of the group formed by Benito and his companions. Tiburcio read the meaning of this look.

"Señor Senator," said he, "it is not proper that you should expose your life thus—a life valuable to the state. You have relatives—a noble family; as for me, if I should be killed, there is no one to care for me."

"The fact is," said the Senator, "if others set upon my life one half the value I put upon it myself, my death would cause a great deal of unhappiness."

"Well, señor, suppose we change places? You give me your gun, and permit me to place my body in front of you as a rampart against the claws of the jaguars."

This proposal was made at the moment when the two cavernous voices of the ferocious beasts were heard loudly answering to one another. Under the impression produced by the terrible dialogue, Tiburcio's offer was hastily accepted. The Senator took his place; while the young man, with sparkling eyes and firm step, advanced several paces in the direction of the forest whence came theories of the jaguar. There he halted to receive the attack that appeared inevitable.

Don Estevan and he appeared motionless as a pair of statues. The unequal reflection of the fire gleamed upon these two men—whom chance had thus strangely united—neither of whom might yield to the other in pride or courage.

The moment was becoming critical. The two jaguars were about to find enemies worthy of them.

The fire, now burnt down, threw out only a pale light, scarce strong enough to illumine the group that stood near its edge.

At this moment an incident occurred which was likely to cause a change in the situation of affairs. In the midst of an interval of silence—in which the very stillness itself increased the apprehension of the travellers—was heard the long lugubrious whine of a prairie wolf. Melancholy as was this sound, it was sweet in comparison with the cries of the more formidable animals, the jaguars.

"The prairie wolf to howl in the presence of the tiger!" muttered the ex-herdsman. "Carramba! there's something strange about that."

"But I have heard it said," rejoined Tiburcio, "that it is the habit of the prairie wolf to follow the jaguar when the latter is in search of prey?"

"That is true enough," replied Benito, "but the wolf never howls so near the tiger, till after the tiger has taken his prey and is busy devouring it. Then his howl is a humble prayer for the other to leave him something.

"This is strange," continued the vaquero, as the prairie wolf was heard to utter another long whine. "Hark! another!—yes—another prairie wolf and on the opposite side too!"

In fact, another plaintive whine, exactly resembling the first, both in strength and cadence, was heard from a point directly opposite.

"I repeat it," said Benito, "prairie wolves would never dare to betray themselves thus. I am greatly mistaken if it be not creatures of a different species that make this howling, and who don't care a straw for the jaguars."

"What creatures?" demanded Tiburcio.

"Human creatures!" answered the ex-herdsman. "American hunters from the north."

"Trappers do you mean?"

"Precisely. There are no people in these parts likely to be so fearless of the jaguar, and I am pretty sure that what appears to be the call of the prairie wolf is nothing else than a signal uttered by a brace of trappers. They are in pursuit of the jaguars; they have separated, and by these signals they acquaint one another of their whereabouts."

Meanwhile the trappers, if such they were, appeared to advance with considerable precaution; for although the party by the fire listened attentively, not the slightest noise could be heard—neither the cracking of a branch, nor the rustling of a leaf.

"Hilloa! you by the fire there!" all at once broke out from the midst of the darkness a loud rough voice, "we are approaching you. Don't be afraid; and don't fire your guns!"

The voice had a foreign accent, which partly confirmed the truth of the vaquero's conjecture, and the appearance of the speaker himself proved it to a certainty.

We shall not stay to describe the singular aspect of the new arrival—further than to say that he was a man of herculean stature, and accoutred in the most *bizarre* fashion. He appeared a sort of giant armed with a rifle—proportioned to his size—that is, having a barrel of thick heavy metal nearly six feet in length.

As he approached the group his sharp eye soon took in the different individuals that composed it, and rested with a satisfied look on the form of Tiburcio.

"The devil take that fire of yours!" he said abruptly, but in a tone of good-humour. "It has frightened away from us two of the most beautiful jaguars that ever roamed about these deserts."

"Frightened them away!" exclaimed Baraja. "*Carramba*! I hope that may be true!"

"Will you allow me to put the fire out?" inquired the new-comer.

"Put out the fire—our only safeguard!" cried the astonished Senator.

"Your only safeguard!" repeated the trapper, equally astonished, as he pointed with his finger around him. "What! eight men wanting a fire for a safeguard against two poor tigers! You are surely making game of me!"

"Who are you, sir?" demanded Don Estevan, in a haughty tone.

"A hunter—as you see."

"Hunter, of what?"

"My comrade and I trap the beaver, hunt the wolf, the tiger—or an Indian, if need be."

"Heaven has sent you then to deliver us from these fierce animals," said Cuchillo, showing himself in front.

"Not very likely," replied the trapper, whose first impression of the outlaw was evidently an unfavourable one. "Heaven I fancy had nothing to do with it. My comrade and I at about two leagues from here chanced upon a panther and two jaguars, quarrelling over the body of a dead horse."

"I re was mine," interrupted Tiburcio.

"Yours, young man!" continued the trapper, in a tone of rude cordiality. "Well, I am glad to see you here, for we thought that the owner of the horse might be no longer among the living. The panther we killed, but the two jaguars made off, and we tracked them hither to the spring, which your fire now hinders them from approaching. Therefore, if you wish to be rid of these beasts, the sooner you put out the fire the better; and you will see how soon we shall disembarrass you of their presence."

"And your comrade?" asked Don Estevan, struck with the idea of making a brace of valuable recruits. "Where is he?"

"He'll be here presently; but to the work, else we must leave you to get out of your scrape as you best can."

There was a certain authority in the tone and words of the trapper—a cool assurance that produced conviction—and upon his drawing near to put out the fire, Don Estevan did not offer to hinder him, but tacitly permitted him to have his way.

In a few seconds the burnt fagots were scattered about over the grass, and the cinders quenched by a few buckets of water drawn from the trough. This done the trapper uttered an imitation of the voice of the coyote; and before its echoes had died away, his companion stepped forward upon the ground.

Although the second trapper was by no means a man of low stature, alongside his companion he appeared only a pigmy. He was not less strangely accoutred, but in the absence of the firelight his costume was not sufficiently visible for its style to be distinguished. Of him and his dress we shall hereafter speak more particularly.

"At last your devilish fire is out," said he, as he came up, "for the want of wood, no doubt, which none of you dared to go fetch."

"No, that is not the reason," hastily replied the first trapper; "I got leave from these gentlemen to put it out—so that we may have an opportunity to rid them of the presence of the tigers."

"Hum!" murmured the Senator; "I fear we have done wrong in letting the fire be put out. Suppose you miss them?"

"Miss them! *Por Dios!* how?" cried the second trapper. "*Caspita!* If I had not been afraid to frighten off one of the beasts, I could have killed the other long ago. Several times I had him at the muzzle of my carbine, when the signal of my comrade hindered me from firing. Miss them indeed!"

"Never mind!" interrupted the great trapper; "we shall end the matter, I have no doubt, by convincing this gentleman."

"You already knew, then, that we were here?" said Baraja.

"Of course. We have been two hours involuntarily playing the spy upon you. Ah! I know a part of the country where travellers that take no more precautions than you would soon find their heads stripped of the skin. But come, Dormilon! to our work!"

"What if the jaguars come our way?" suggested the Senator, apprehensively.

"No fear of that," replied the trapper. "Their first care will be to satisfy their thirst, which your fire has hindered them from doing. You will hear them howling with joy, as soon as they perceive that the fire is gone out. It was the light shining upon the water that frightened them more than the presence of men. All they want now is to get a drink."

"But how do you intend to act?" inquired Don Estevan.

"How do we intend to act?" repeated the second trapper. "That is simple enough. We shall place ourselves in the cistern—the jaguars will come forward to its brink; and then, if we are only favoured by a blink of the moon, I'll answer for it that in the twinkling of an eye the brutes will neither feel hunger nor thirst."

"Ah, this appears very simple!" cried Cuchillo, who was in reality astonished at the simplicity of the plan.

"Simple as bidding 'good-bye' to you," humorously responded one of the trappers. "Listen there!—what did I tell you?"

Two loud roars, as if from a brazen trumpet, were heard at the moment. They appeared to proceed from the same point, proving that the jaguars had joined company; and, moreover, proclaimed the joy which the fierce creatures felt at the darkness being restored. This was further evident from their repeated sniffing of the air, like horses who afar off scent with delight the fresh emanations of the water.

At this the two trappers, leaving the party by the fire, betook themselves to the cistern. The moon, for a moment shining out, glanced upon the barrels of their long rifles; but the next moment they had disappeared behind the ridge that surrounded the spring.

No doubt it is a grand pleasure to witness the spectacle of a bull-fight, as the huge bull dashes into the ring, and, pierced by the tormenting *bandrilleros*, with a crest erect, and eyes flashing fire, bounds over the arena. But, if the spectators were not separated from the actors by an impassable barrier, the sight would have in it less of enjoyment than of terror. The combats between men and tigers—which the Romans used to enjoy—must have been a still more exciting spectacle; but who can doubt that, if the iron railing which separated the audience from the combatants had been removed, scarce one of the former would have remained in the circus to witness the sanguinary struggle?

Only a short space—not wider than a jaguar could have passed over in a single leap—here separated the spectators from the actors in the drama about to be enacted. Supposing, then, that one of the actors should fail in performing his part, and the spectators have to take his place? Here was a situation, exceptional, and fertile in emotions, which most of the travellers felt keenly at the moment.

Meanwhile the trappers had descended into the little crater-like valley of the spring, and there placed themselves in readiness, rifle in hand, to await the approach of their terrible adversaries. They were both upon their knees, back to back, in order that they could keep at the same time under view the whole circumference of the circle. Both had placed their knives in readiness, in case that, by any chance, they should either miss their aim, or—what would be almost as unlucky—only wound the enemy; for they well knew that a wounded jaguar is a more dangerous adversary than one that escapes altogether from the touch of the bullet.

Fortunately the moon had again appeared; but being yet low down in the sky, her beams were not thrown into the bottom of the valley—and therefore the trappers themselves were still under the shadow. This circumstance was in their favour.

Notwithstanding the perilous position in which they had thus voluntarily placed themselves, neither made the slightest movement; and the long barrels of their rifles stood forth in front of them, as motionless as bronze cannon set in battery.

They well knew, in case either should miss with their firearms, that a hand-to-hand struggle with the ferocious tigers would be the result; a combat of knives and claws—a combat to the death. Yes; at the bottom of that little valley it would be necessary for them to conquer or die. They knew this without exhibiting the slightest show of fear.

Chapter Seventeen
Unexpected Recognitions

It was not long before the spectators, who awaited this terrible conflict, perceived the jaguars advancing toward the crest of the ridge. All at once, however, the two made an abrupt pause, uttering a loud roar that seemed to express disappointment. They had just scented the presence of the two men within the cistern—from which the animals were now only a few paces distant.

For a moment both male and female stood together, stretching their bodies out to their full length, and lashing their flanks with their long sinewy tails. Then, uttering another prolonged roar, they bounded simultaneously forward, passing, at a single leap, over a space of full twenty feet. A second spring brought them upon the crest of the ridge, upon which they had scarce rested an instant, before the quick sharp crack of a rifle, followed by a yell of agony, told that one of them had fallen to the hunter's bullet.

The second jaguar appeared for the moment to have escaped, but not to have retreated. He was seen to launch himself into the bottom of the little valley; and then was heard a confusion of noises—human voices mingling with the howls of the fierce brute, and the sound of a struggle, as if jaguar and hunters were rolling over one another. A second report now struck upon the ear, followed as before by the expiring yell of the tiger, and then succeeded a profound silence, which told that the wild scene was at an end.

The great trapper was now perceived scrambling up to the ridge—towards which the whole of the travellers had advanced to meet him.

"See!" he said, addressing himself to his admiring auditory, "see what a brace of Kentucky rifles and a good knife can do in the hands of those who know how to manage them!"

The darkness, however, hindered the spectators from making out the tableau which was exhibited at the bottom of the little valley.

A few minutes afterwards the moon lighted up the scene, and then could be observed the dead bodies of the two tigers, stretched along the ground by the water's edge, while the other trapper upon his knees was engaged in bathing with cold water a long scar, which he had received from the claws of the last killed jaguar, and which extended from behind his ear nearly down to his waist. Fortunately this ugly-looking wound was no more than skin-deep, and therefore not very dangerous.

"What signify the sharpest claws compared with the scratch of a knife!" cried he, pointing to the nearest of the jaguars, whose upturned belly exhibited a huge cut of more than a foot in length, and through which the entrails of the animal protruded.

"Can any of you tell us," continued he, without thinking further about his wound, "if there is a hacienda in this neighbourhood where one might sell these two beautiful jaguar skins, as well as the hide of a panther we've got?"

"Certainly," replied Benito, "there is the Hacienda del Venado, where we are going. There you may get not only five dollars apiece for the skins, but also the bounty of ten dollars more."

"What say you, Canadian?" inquired the trapper, addressing his great comrade. "Will that do?"

"Certainly," replied the Canadian, "forty-five dollars is not to be sneezed at; and when we have had a short nap we shall make tracks for the hacienda. We shall be likely to get there before these gentlemen, whose horses have taken a fancy to have a bit of a gallop, and I guess it will be some time before they lay hands on them again."

"Don't be uneasy about us!" rejoined the ex-herdsman. "It's not the first time I've seen a horse drove *stampedoed*, nor the first time I've collected them again. I've not quite forgotten my old business, and as soon as it is daylight, with the permission of the Señor Don Estevan, I shall go in search of them."

No one made any opposition to the rekindling of the fire, for the night had grown cooler, and it was not yet midnight. The domestics, no longer afraid of going out into the woods, collected fresh fagots—enough to last till morning—and the preparations for supper, which had been interrupted by the approach of the jaguars, were now continued with renewed zeal.

The blaze soon flared up bright and joyous as ever—the broiling mutton sent forth its delicious odour, sharpening to a keen edge the appetites of the travellers as they stood around the fire.

Don Estevan and the Senator now called before them the two intrepid hunters, who had rendered them a service that fully deserved their thanks.

"Come hither, brave hunters!" said the Senator, "you, whose daring behaviour has been of such service to us. A slice of roast mutton and a cup of Catalonian wine will not be out of place, after the rude struggle you have sustained."

"Ugh!" said the eldest of the trappers, in presenting his athletic form in front of the fire, "throwing a couple of poor tigers is no great feat. If it had been an affair of a dozen Comanches, or Pawnees, that would have been different. Howsomever, a chunk of roast mutton is welcome after a fight, as well as before one, and we're ready for it with your permission. Come along, comrade! Here's some chawing for you!"

"And you, young man," continued Don Estevan, addressing himself to Tiburcio, who stood at some distance apart, "you will also partake of our hospitality?"

Tiburcio by a sign accepted the invitation, and approached the fire. For the first time his countenance came fairly under the light; and as it did so, the eyes of the Spaniard seemed to devour him with their regard. In truth the physiognomy of Tiburcio Arellanos was of no ordinary character, and would have merited observation from one less interested in examining it than was Don Estevan Arechiza.

An aquiline nose, black eyes with thick dark eyebrows and long lashes, and olive complexion—that appeared almost white in contrast with the jetty blackness of his beard—but above all, the extreme contraction of a thin upper lip, indicated the countenance of a man of quick resolves and fiery passions. A shade of tranquil melancholy over these features to some extent tempered their half-fierce expression.

The hair was of a chestnut brown colour, and hung in luxuriant curls over a forehead large and of noble outline. Broad shoulders and well-developed limbs denoted a man of European vigour, whose personal strength would be equal, if occasion required it, to the execution of those passionate designs nourished under the tropical skies of Spanish America.

Tiburcio Arellanos was in truth the type of a noble and ancient race, transplanted into a country still less than half civilised.

"The very form and bearing of Don Juan de Mediana!" muttered Don Estevan to himself, more than half convinced that the young man before his eyes was the son of him whose name he had pronounced. No one could have read his suspicions, hidden under the mask of perfect calmness.

There was one other man in that group who was struck by the aspect of Tiburcio. This was the big trapper, who on first sight of the young man's face under the light of the fire started and closed his eyes, as if lightning had flashed before them. He was about to rush forward, when a second look seemed to convince him he had made a mistake; and smiling at his having done so, he kept his place. His eyes then wandered around the group of faces that encircled the fire, with that scrutinising glance, that showed a capacity for reading the characters of men in their looks.

Having finished this scrutiny, he called out to his companion, who had not yet got forward:—

"Come along, partner; or people will say you are ashamed to show yourself. Prove to these gentlemen that you know how to enjoy life like other folk."

"O certainly—I am coming—all right, comrade."

And the next moment the younger trapper made his appearance within the circle of light.

An odd-looking object he appeared, with his huge fur cap upon his head, drawn down in front, so as to cover his eyes, and an old striped cotton handkerchief fastened over his face and throat, in such a manner as to conceal the scar made by the claws of the tiger. With the cap and kerchief, the greater portion of his countenance was masked, leaving visible only his mouth, with a double row of grand teeth, that promised to perform their part upon the roast mutton.

Having reached the fire, he sat down with his back to it—so that his half-masked face was still further concealed in shadow—and being supplied, as well as his comrade, with a large cut from the joint, he at once set about satisfying the appetite of hunger.

"Are there many men of your size and strength where you come from?" inquired the Senator, addressing himself to the largest of the two hunters.

"In Canada," answered the latter, "I should not be remarked among others; ask my comrade there!"

"He speaks true," grumbled the other.

"But you are not both from the same country?" said Tragaduros.

"No—my comrade is a native of—"

"Of New York State," hastily interposed the younger of the two trappers—a reply which astonished the Canadian, but which he refrained from contradicting.

"And what is your calling?" continued the Senator, interrogatively.

"*Coureurs des bois*, wood-rangers," answered the Canadian. "That is to say, we pass our time in ranging the woods, with no other object than to avoid being shut up in towns. Alas! it is a profession likely soon to come to an end; and when we two are gone, the race of wood-rangers will run out in America, since neither of us has any sons to carry on the business of their father."

There was a tone of melancholy in the last words of the trapper's speech that contrasted strangely with his rude manner: something that seemed to evince a certain degree of regret. Don Estevan, noticing this, now entered into the conversation.

"I fear it is a poor business you follow, my brave fellows! But if you feel inclined to leave it off for a while, and take a part in an expedition that we are about to set on foot, I can promise to fill your caps with gold dust. What say you?"

"No!" brusquely responded the younger of the trappers.

"Each to his own business," added the Canadian. "We are not gold-seekers. We love to range freely where we please, without leader, and without being controlled by any one—in a word, free as the sun or the prairie breeze."

These answers were given in a tone so firm and peremptory that the Spaniard saw it would be of no use combating a resolution which was evidently not to be shaken, and therefore he declined to make any further offers.

Supper was soon over, and each of the travellers set about making himself as comfortable as possible for the remainder of the night.

In a short time all, with the exception of Tiburcio, were asleep. But Tiburcio was yet a mere youth, an orphan, who had lately lost a mother for whom he had a profound affection; and above all, Tiburcio was in love—three reasons why he could not sleep. A deep sadness had possession of his spirits. He felt himself in an exceptional situation—his past was equally mysterious with his future.

"Oh, my mother! my mother!" murmured he, despairingly, to himself, "why did you not tell me who I am!"

And as he said this he appeared to listen—as if the breeze, sighing through the leaves, would give a response to his interrogation. Little thought he at the moment that one of those men, lying near him under the light of the moon, could have given the desired answer—could have told him the name which he ought to hear.

Nevertheless, on her death-bed, the widow of Marcos Arellanos had revealed to him a secret—perhaps almost as interesting as that of his birth and parentage.

The secret of the Golden Valley, which had been made known to Tiburcio, had opened his eyes to a world of pleasant dreams. A prospect which hitherto had appeared to him only as a chimerical vision was now viewed by him in the light of a reality. A gulf that before seemed impassable was now bridged over as if by the hand of some powerful fairy.

Gold can work such miracles. Had he not in prospect the possession of a rich placer? Would not that enable him to overcome all obstacles both of the past and the future? Might he not, by the puissance of gold, discover who were his real parents? and by the same means, might he not realise that sweeter dream that had now for two years held possession of his heart?

As he lay upon the ground, kept awake by these hopeful reflections, a vision was passing before his mind's eye. It was a scene in which were many figures. A gentleman of rich apparel—a young girl his daughter—a train of servants all affrighted and in confusion. They have lost their way in the middle of the forest, and are unable to extricate themselves from the labyrinth of llianas and thickets that surround them. A guide appears in the presence of a young hunter, who engages to conduct them to the place whither they wish to go. That guide is Tiburcio himself, who in his reverie— as in the real scene that occurred just two years before—scarce observes either the gentleman in rich apparel nor the attendants that surround him, but only remembers the beautiful dark eyes and raven hair of the young girl. Tiburcio reassures them of safety, guides them, during a journey of two days—two days that appeared to him to pass only too rapidly.

In his waking dream one scene is forcibly recalled. He remembers a night halt in the woods. All were asleep around him—the attendants upon the grass—the rich gentleman upon his cloak, and the young girl upon the skin of a jaguar which the guide himself had supplied. He alone remained awake. The moon was shining upon all; and a delicious perfume from the blossoms of the sweet sassafras trees that grew near was wafted toward them upon the gentle breeze. The blue heaven above appeared in perfect harmony with the tranquil scene below. The guide, with admiring eyes, looked upon that lovely virgin form and listened to the soft breathing of that innocent bosom. To him it was a moment of delicious anguish...

Then the vision changed—the young girl at length reached her home, and entered the grand dwelling of her father. There the guide remained a whole week a welcome guest—drunk with love yet not daring to raise his eyes to the object of his passion.

Afterwards, too, at the festivals of the neighbouring villages, a hundred times had he gazed upon her; but what of that? he was only a poor *gambusino*, and she the daughter of the richest proprietor in the province!

But now—with the secret of the Golden Valley—Tiburcio suddenly saw himself powerful and rich; hope had sprung up within his bosom; and amidst the reverie occasioned by these delightful thoughts, he at last fell asleep.

It is scarce necessary to add that the young girl who recalled these sweet souvenirs, and who was now mingling in his dreams, was the daughter of Don Augustin Peña, the proprietor of the Hacienda del Venado.

At daybreak the sleepers were awakened by the ringing of a bell and the clatter of hoofs. It was the *cavallada* returning to camp, under the charge of Benito, who had thus kept his promise. The travellers were soon upon their feet, but it was soon perceived that the two trappers were not amongst them. These had gone away without any one having observed their departure!

The horses being saddled and bridled and the mules packed, the cavalcade continued its journey towards the hacienda—Don Estevan and the Senator, as before, riding in front.

It was after sunset before the walls of the hacienda were descried in the distance, already assuming a sombre hue under the fast increasing obscurity of the twilight. But through the wide forest tract which surrounded the hacienda a well-defined road led in the direction of the dwelling, which the travellers could follow even in the darkest night, and upon this road the cavalcade was now seen to enter.

A few minutes before they had passed into the forest from the open plain two men were seen standing near the edge of a thicket, by which they were hidden from the view of the travellers. These men might have been easily recognised by their long rifles as strangers to that part of the country; they were, in fact, the two trappers, the Canadian and his comrade, who had that morning so abruptly taken leave of the camp.

"You must have been deceived by some accidental resemblance," said the Canadian to his companion.

"No," replied the latter; "I am sure it is he. Twenty years have not made much change either in his face or figure. His voice is just the same as it was when I was the coast-guard, Pepé the Sleeper. My eyes and ears are as good as they were then, and I assure you, Bois-Rose, that he's the very man."

"Strange enough," answered Bois-Rose (for the great Canadian trapper was no other than Bois-Rose himself). "After all, one is more likely to meet an enemy he is in search of than a friend. It may be the same."

As he finished this speech, the Canadian, leaning upon his long rifle, stood looking after the cavalcade, which was just disappearing into the forest road that led to the hacienda.

After remaining a few minutes in this position, the two trappers turned back again into the forest, and soon disappeared under the shadows of the trees.

Chapter Eighteen
The Hacienda del Venado

The Hacienda del Venado—like all buildings of this kind situated upon the Indian frontier, and of course exposed to the attacks of the savages—was a species of citadel, as well as a country dwelling-house. Built with sun-dried bricks and hewn stone, crowned by a crenelled parapet, and defended by huge, massive doors, it could have sustained a siege from an enemy more expert in strategy than the tribe of Apaches who were its neighbours.

At one corner stood a tower of moderate height, which crowned the chapel belonging to the hacienda, serving for the great clock as well as for a belfry. In case the principal part of the building should be forced, this tower would answer for an asylum almost impregnable.

Finally, a strong stockade composed of trunks of the *palmetto*, completely encircled the building; within which enclosure were the quarters destined for the domestics of the hacienda—as also for the herdsmen, and such ordinary guests as from time to time came to seek a passing hospitality. Outside this privileged enclosure was a group of from twenty to thirty huts, composing a species of little village. These were inhabited by the day-labourers (peons) and their families attached to the hacienda—who, in case of danger, would escape within the enclosure for safety and protection.

Such was the Hacienda del Venado. The proprietor, Don Augustin Peña, was a man of great opulence. In addition to a rich gold mine which he worked, at no great distance off, he was the owner of countless herds of horses, mules, and cattle, that in a half-wild state roamed over the vast savannahs and forests that constituted the twenty leagues of land belonging to the hacienda. Such a vast tract of territory belonging to one man is by no means a rare thing in northern Mexico.

At this time Don Augustin was a widower, and his family consisted of only one daughter—the young girl already introduced to the reader. Considering the immense heritage that the Doña Rosario—or, as she was more gracefully called, Rosarita—was likely to bring to whoever should become her husband, it was natural that an alliance with Don Augustin should be the object of many an ambition; in fact her beauty without the grand fortune—which, at her father's death, she was to become mistress of—would of itself have been enough to have challenged a crowd of pretenders to her hand.

The Andalusian type has lost nothing in the northern provinces of Mexico. Its purity of outline is there associated with freshness of colour, and this happy mixture of graces was exhibited in the beautiful countenance of Rosarita. We have described her with black eyes and hair of raven hue; but hers was a beauty that words can but faintly portray, and about which all description would be superfluous.

And this lovely creature bloomed in the very midst of the desert, like the flower of the cactus which blossoms and fades under the eye of God alone.

The immense plain in the midst of which stood the Hacienda del Venado presented a double aspect. In front of the house only did the ground show any traces of cultivation. On that side fields of Indian corn and vast olive plantations denoted the presence and skilful labour of man.

Behind the hacienda—at some hundred paces distance from the stockade—the clearing ended, and thence extended the virgin forest in all its sombre and primitive majesty.

The cultivated ground was intersected by a considerable stream of water. During the dry season it ran gently and silently along, but in the season of rain it would suddenly change into an impetuous torrent that inundated the whole plain, bearing huge rocks along in its current, and every year widening its channel.

Perhaps the most powerful of Arab chiefs, the richest patriarch of ancient times, never counted such superb and numerous herds as roamed over the pasturage of the Hacienda del Venado.

About an hour before sunset—on that same day on which the travellers departed from La Poza—two men, one on horseback, the other mounted on a mule, were seen traversing the plain in the direction of the hacienda. Both horse and mule were each a splendid specimen of his kind—the horse with fiery eye, broad chest, and curving, swan-like neck, was scarce more to be admired than the mule, that with fine, delicate limbs, rounded flanks, and shining coat, walked side by side with him.

This horseman was the master of the hacienda, Don Augustin Peña. His costume consisted of a hat of Guayaquil grass, a shirt of the finest cambric, an embroidered vest, and silk velvet pantaloons fastened down the sides with large buttons of gold.

His companion, the rider of the mule, was the chaplain of the hacienda, a reverend Franciscan monk in a sort of half convent costume. This consisted of an ample blue frock confined around the waist with a thick cord of silk, the tassels of which hung down below his knees. Beneath this appeared a pair of large riding-boots heavily spurred. Upon his head a grey beaver, somewhat jauntily set, gave to the Franciscan an appearance rather soldier-like than monastic.

The haciendado appeared to be regarding with a look of pride his rich possessions—extending beyond view on every side of him—as if he was reflecting how much this kind of wealth was superior to golden ingots shut idly in a chest; while the monk seemed to be absorbed in some profound reverie.

"By Saint Julian! the patron saint of travellers!" said Don Augustin, breaking silence, "you have been more than twenty-four hours absent! I was afraid, reverend father, that some jaguar had swallowed both you and your mule."

"Man proposes, and God disposes," replied the monk. "When I took my departure from the hacienda, I did not except to be gone more than a few hours—giving Christian burial to poor Joaquin, that had been killed by one of the bulls—but just as I had blessed the earth where they had buried him, a young man came galloping up like a thunderbolt, both himself and horse all of a sweat, to beg that I would go along with him and confess his mother who was upon her death-bed. Only ten leagues he said it was, and I should have been glad for a pretext to get off from such a difficult turn of duty; but at the earnest entreaty of the young fellow, and knowing who he was, I could not refuse him. Who do you think he was?"

"How should I know?" replied the haciendado.

"Tiburcio, the adopted son of the famous gambusino, Marcos Arellanos."

"How! his mother dead! I am sorry. He is a brave youth, and I have not forgotten the service he once did me. But for him we should all have been dead of thirst, my daughter, my people, and myself. If he is left without resources, I hope you have said to him that he will find a welcome at the Hacienda del Venado."

"No—I have not," replied the monk.

"And why?"

"Because this young fellow is desperately in love with your daughter; it is my duty to tell you so."

"What signifies that, so long as my daughter does not love him?" replied Don Augustin. "And if she did, where would she find a man possessing higher physical or moral qualities than this same Tiburcio? I never dreamt of having for my son-in-law any other than an intelligent man, brave enough to defend the frontier against these hordes of savage Indians, and just such a man is young Arellanos. But in truth I forget myself; I have this day designed for Rosarita a husband of a more exalted station."

"And it may be that you have done wrong," rejoined the monk, in a serious tone; "from what I suspect—in fact, what I may say I know—this Tiburcio might make a more valuable son-in-law than you imagine."

"It's too late then," said Don Augustin. "I have given my word, and I cannot retract it."

"It is just about this matter I wish to speak to you, if you have time to hear me."

At this moment the two horsemen, having passed the stockade, had arrived at the foot of the stone stairway—which led up to the portico, and thence into the grand sala of the hacienda—and while dismounting, their dialogue was interrupted.

This sala was a large room, which, according to the practice in hot countries, was so arranged as to be continually kept cool by a current of air passing lengthwise through its whole extent. Fine Chinese mats covered the floor, while richly painted window-blinds prevented the rays of the sun from entering the apartment. The walls, whitened with stucco, were adorned with rare illuminated paintings set in gold frames, some leathern chairs called *butacas*, several side tables—upon one of which stood a silver brazero filled with red cinders of charcoal—these, with a *fauteuil* or two, and a mahogany couch of Anglo-American manufacture, completed the furniture of the apartment.

Upon a table of polished balsam-wood stood several porous jars containing water; beside them, on a large silver waiter, were confections of several kinds; while heaped upon other dishes, also of solid silver, were fruits both of the tropic and temperate climes—oranges, granadillas, limes, and pitayas, here brought together to tempt the appetite or assuage the thirst.

The appearance of these preparations denoted that Don Augustin expected company. As soon as they had entered within the sala, the monk, observing the well garnished tables, inquired if such was the case.

"Yes," answered the haciendado, "Don Estevan de Arechiza has sent me word that he will arrive this evening with a somewhat numerous train, and I have taken measures to entertain a guest of such importance. But you say you wish to speak to me about some business—what is it, Friar José Maria?"

The two now sat down, each choosing an easy-chair, and while Don Augustin was lighting a cigar the monk commenced speaking as follows:

"I found the old woman seated upon a bank outside the door of her hut, whither she had dragged herself to look out for my arrival. 'Bless you, good father!' said she, 'you have arrived in time to receive my last confession. But while you rest a little, I wish you to listen to what I am going to say to him whom I have always treated as my own child, and to whom I intend to leave a legacy of vengeance.'"

"What! holy father!" interrupted Don Augustin, "surely you did not permit this infraction of God's law, who says, *vengeance belongs only to Him?*"

"Why not?" replied the monk. "In these deserts, where neither laws nor tribunals exist, every man must be his own avenger."

With this strange apology for his conduct, the monk continued:

"I sat down and listened to what she had to say to this adopted son. It was this:—'Your father was *not* killed by the Indians, as we were led to believe. It was his companion who murdered him—for the purpose of being the sole possessor of a secret, which I shall presently disclose—but to you only, Marcos.'

"'God alone knows who this man was,' said Tiburcio, 'he alone knows him.'

"'He only!' cried the dying woman, with an air of disdain. 'Is this the language of a man? When the Indians come to steal his cattle from the vaquero, does he sit still and say: *God only can prevent them?* No!—with his eye bent, and his hand ready, he follows upon their traces, till he has recovered his herds, or perished in the attempt. Go you and do as the vaquero! Track out the assassin of your father. That is the last wish of her who nourished you, and has never failed in her affection.'

"'I shall obey you, my mother,' answered the young man, in a firm voice.

"'Listen, then, to what I have got to say!' continued the widow. 'The murder of Arellanos is no longer a supposition, but a reality. I have it from a herdsman who came from the country beyond Tubac. Some days before, he had met two travellers. One was your father Marcos; the other was a stranger to him. The herdsman was travelling on the same route, and followed them at some distance behind. At a place where certain signs showed that the two travellers had made their bivouac, the herdsman had found the traces of a terrible struggle. The grass was bent down, and saturated with blood. There were tracks of blood leading to a precipice that hung over a stream of water; and most likely over this the victim was precipitated. This victim must have been Marcos; for the herdsman was able to follow the trail of the murderer by the tracks of his horse; and a little further on he noticed where the horse had stumbled on the left fore-leg. The assassin himself must have been wounded in the struggle, for the herdsman could tell by his tracks leading to the precipice that he had limped on one leg.'"

Don Augustin listened with attention to this account—proving the wonderful sagacity of his countrymen, of which he had almost every day some new proof. The monk went on with his narration.

"'Swear then, Tiburcio, to avenge your father!' continued the dying woman. 'Swear it, and I promise to make you as rich as the proudest in the land; rich enough to bend to your wishes the most powerful—even the daughter of Augustin Peña, for whom your passion has not escaped me. This day you may aspire to her hand without being deemed foolish; for I tell you, you are as rich as her own father. Swear, then, to pursue to the death the murderer of Arellanos?'

"'I swear it,' rejoined Tiburcio, with a solemn gesture.

"Upon this, the dying woman placed in the hands of the young man a piece of paper, upon which Arellanos, before leaving his home for the last time, had traced the route of his intended journey.

"'With the treasure which that paper will enable you to find,' continued the dying woman, 'you will have gold enough to corrupt the daughter of a viceroy, if you wish it. Meanwhile, my child, leave me for a while to confess to this holy man: a son should not always hear the confession of his mother.'"

The monk, in a few more words, related the closing scene of the widow's death, and then finished by saying:—

"Now, Don Augustin, you perceive my reason for saying that this young fellow, whatever may be his family, is not the less likely to make a good match for the Doña Rosarita."

"I agree with you," responded the haciendado; "but, as I have said to you, my word is given to Don Estevan de Arechiza."

"What!" exclaimed the monk, "this Spaniard to be your son-in-law!"

Don Augustin smiled mysteriously as he replied:—

"He! no, good Fray José, not he, but another. Don Estevan does not wish this alliance."

"Caspita!" exclaimed the monk. "Does he think it beneath him?"

"It may be he has the right to think so," added Don Augustin, again smiling mysteriously.

"But who is this man?" inquired the monk, with an air of surprise.

Just as Don Augustin was about to reply, a servant entered the *sala*.

"Señor Don Augustin," said the servant, "there are two travellers at the gate, who beg of you to give them a night's lodging. One of them says that he is known to you."

"Bid them welcome!" replied the haciendado, "and let them enter. Whether they are known to me or not, two guests more or less will be nothing here."

A few seconds after, the two travellers had advanced to the foot of the stone stairway, where they stood awaiting the presence of the master of the house.

One of them was a man of about thirty years of age—whose open countenance and high forehead denoted courage, combined with intelligence. His figure presented an appearance of strength and vigorous activity, and he was somewhat elegantly dressed—though without any signs of foppery.

"Ah! is it you, Pedro Diaz?" cried Don Augustin, recognising him. "Are there any Indians to be exterminated, since I find you coming into these solitudes of ours?"

Pedro Diaz was, in truth, known as the most celebrated hater and hunter of Indians in the whole province—hence the strange salutation with which Don Augustin received him.

"Before answering you, Señor Don Augustin, permit me to introduce to you the king of *gambusinos* and prince of musicians, the Señor Don Diego Oroche, who scents a placer of gold as a hound would a deer, and who plays upon the mandolin as only he can play."

The individual presented under the name of Oroche, solemnly saluted the haciendado.

It must have been a long time since the prince of gambusinos had found an opportunity to exercise the subtle talent of which his companion spoke— or else the cards had been of late unlucky—for his outward man presented an appearance that was scarcely more than comfortable.

In reaching his hand to his hat, it was not necessary for him to disarrange the folds of his cloak. It only required that he should choose one of the numerous rents that appeared in this garment, to pass through it his long-clawed fingers—whose length and thinness denoted him a player on the mandolin. In reality, he carried one of these instruments slung over his shoulders.

Don Augustin invited both Diaz and his singular companion to enter. When they were seated in the saloon Diaz began the conversation.

"We have heard," said he, "of an expedition being got up at Arispe to proceed to *Apacheria*; and this gentleman and I are on our way to take part in it. Your hacienda, Señor Don Augustin, chanced to lie in our way, and we have entered to ask your permission to lodge here for the night. By daybreak we shall continue our route for Arispe."

"You will not have to go so far," replied Don Augustin, with a smile. "The expedition is already on foot, and I expect the leader of it here this very night. He will be glad of your services, I guarantee you, and it will save you several days' journey."

"A miracle in our favour!" exclaimed Diaz; "and I thank God for the lucky coincidence."

"The thirst of gold has caught you also, Pedro Diaz?" asked Don Augustin, smiling significantly.

"No, thank God!" replied Diaz, "nothing of the sort. Heave the searching for gold to experienced gambusinos, such as the Señor Oroche here. No— you know well that I have no other passion than hatred for the ferocious savages who have done so much ill towards me and mine. It is only because I hope through this expedition once more to carry steel and fire into their midst, that I take any part in it."

"It is right," said the haciendado, who like all dwellers upon the frontiers exposed to Indian incursions, nourished in his heart a hatred for the savages almost equal to that of Diaz himself. "I approve of your sentiments, Don Pedro Diaz; and if you will permit me to offer you a gage of mine, I beg you will accept from me the present of a horse I have—one that will carry you to your satisfaction. I promise you that the Indian you pursue, while on his back, will require to go as fast as the wind itself, if you do not overtake him."

"He shall be my war-horse," exclaimed Diaz, his eyes sparkling with pleasure at the gift. "I shall ornament his crest with Indian scalps, in honour of him who gave him to me."

"I cannot divine what has delayed Don Estevan," said the haciendado, changing the subject of conversation. "He should have been here three hours before this, that is, if he passed the night at La Poza."

Don Augustin had scarce finished his speech when a sudden and graceful apparition glided into the saloon. It was his daughter, the beautiful Rosarita.

As if the expected cavalcade only awaited her presence, the clattering of hoofs at the same instant was heard outside; and by the light of the torches which the domestics had carried out, Don Estevan and his suite could be seen riding up to the entrance of the hacienda.

Chapter Nineteen
Rosarita

On the route from La Poza it had fallen to the lot of Cuchillo and Tiburcio to ride side by side, but for all this few words had passed between them. Although Cuchillo had not the slightest idea of renouncing his dire design, he continued to hide his thoughts under an air of good-humour—which when need be he knew how to assume. He had made several attempts to read the thoughts of the young gambusino, but the latter was on his guard, seeking in his turn to identify Cuchillo with the assassin of his father. No opportunity offered, however; and in this game of mutual espionage, neither had the advantage. Nevertheless, an instinctive and mutual hatred became established between the two, and before the day's journey was over, each regarded the other as a mortal foe. Cuchillo was more than ever determined to execute his hellish purpose—since a crime less or more would be nothing to him—while Tiburcio, keenly remembering the oath which he had made to his adopted mother, was resolved on keeping it, and only awaited the time when he should be sure of the assassin. We need scarcely add that Tiburcio in the accomplishment of his vow, had no thought of playing the assassin. No. Whenever and wherever the murderer should be found, he was to die by Tiburcio's hand; but only in fair and open fight.

But there were other painful reflections that occupied Tiburcio's mind during the journey. The nearer he approached the object of his love the greater seemed to be the distance between them. Though a man may hope to obtain what he only wishes for in a moderate way, yet when anything is ardently yearned after, the obstacles appear insurmountable. Hence the secret of many a heroic resolution. When Tiburcio was reclining by the well of La Poza, his sweet dream hindered him from thinking of these obstacles; but now that the journey was nearly ended, and he drew near to the grand hacienda, his spirits fell, and a feeling of hopelessness took possession of his soul. Hence it was that he formed the resolution to put an end to the painful suspense which he had now a long time endured; and that very night, if possible, he intended to ascertain his position in the eyes of Doña Rosarita. Come what might, he resolved to ask that question, whose answer might render him at once the happiest or the most miserable of men.

When Tiburcio had first met Doña Rosarita, with her father and his servants, in the depth of the forest, he knew nothing of the rank of the party thus wandering astray. Even during the two happy days in which he acted as their guide, he was ignorant of the name of the beautiful young girl, to whom his eyes and his heart rendered a continual homage. He therefore permitted himself to indulge in those pleasant dreams which have their origin in a hopeful love. It was only after he had learned the quality of his fellow-travellers—that the young lady was the daughter of the opulent proprietor, Don Augustin Peña—it was only on ascertaining this that Tiburcio perceived the folly of his aspirations, and the distance that lay between him and the object of his love. If then the secret, so unexpectedly revealed to him, had given him a desire for the possession of riches, it was not for the sake of being rich. No; a nobler object inspired him—one more in keeping with his poetic character. He desired riches only that with them he might bridge over the chasm that separated him from Rosarita.

Unhappily he could not hide from himself the too evident fact that he was not the sole possessor of the secret.

All at once it occurred to him that the expedition to which he found himself thus accidentally attached could have no other object than this very placer of the Golden Valley. Most likely the very man who shared the secret with him—the murderer of Marcos Arellanos—was among the men enrolled under the orders of the chief Don Estevan. The ambiguous questioning of Cuchillo, his comprehension of events, the stumbling of his horse, with other slighter indications, appeared to throw some light upon the obscurity of Tiburcio's conjectures; but not enough. How was he (Tiburcio) to arrive at a complete understanding?

A still more painful uncertainty pressed upon his spirit, as they approached the dwelling of Don Augustin. What reception would he meet with from Doña Rosarita? he, a poor gambusino—without resources, without family—poorly dressed even—a mere follower, confounded with the common mob of adventurers who composed the expedition? Sad presentiments were passing in his mind, as the cavalcade of which he formed so humble an appendage arrived at the palisade enclosure of the hacienda.

The gates were soon open to receive them; and the moment after Don Augustin himself welcomed the travellers at the front entrance of the mansion. With that ease and elegance, almost peculiar to Spanish manners, he received Don Estevan and the Senator, while the cordiality with which he welcomed Tiburcio appeared to the young man a happy omen.

The travellers all dismounted. Cuchillo remained outside—partly out of respect to his chief and partly to look after his horse. As to Tiburcio, he had not the same motives for acting thus, and therefore entered along with Don Estevan and Tragaduros, his face pale and his heart beating audibly.

The room into which they had been shown was the grand sala already described, and in which certain preparations had been made for a magnificent banquet. But Tiburcio saw nothing of all this. His eyes beheld only one object—for there stood a beautiful girl whose lips rendered paler the carnation red of the granadillas, and the hue of whose cheeks eclipsed the rosy tint of the *sandias*, scattered profusely over the tables. It was Rosarita herself. A silken scarf covered her head, permitting the thick plaits of her dark hair to shine through its translucent texture, and just encircling the outline of her oval face. This scarf, hanging down below the waist, but half concealed her white rounded arms, and only partially hindered the view of a figure of the most elegantly voluptuous tournure. Around her waist another scarf of bright scarlet formed a sort of cincture or belt, leaving its long fringed ends to hang over the skirt of her silken robe, and blending its colours with those of the light veil that fell down from her shoulders. It was a costume that seemed well-suited to her striking beauty, and the effect of the *coup d'oeil* upon the heart of poor Tiburcio was at once pleasant and embarrassing.

Notwithstanding the gracious smile with which she acknowledged his presence, there was a certain hauteur about the proffered welcome—as if it was a mere expression of gratitude for the service he had formerly rendered.

Tiburcio observed this with a feeling of chagrin, and sighed as he contrasted her cold formality of speech with the abandon and freedom of their former relations. But he could not help noticing a still greater contrast when he looked at his own poor garments and compared them with the elegant costumes of his two travelling companions.

While Don Estevan was entertaining his host with some account of what had happened on their journey, the Senator appeared to have eyes only for the beautiful Rosarita—upon whom he was not slow in lavishing a string of empty compliments.

The young girl appeared to Tiburcio to receive these compliments with a smile very different from that she had accorded to himself; he also observed, with a feeling of bitterness, the superior easiness of manner in which those whom he regarded as his rivals addressed themselves to her. With anguish he noticed the colour become more vivid upon her cheeks; while the heaving of her bosom, as the scarf rose and fell in regular vibrations, did not escape the keen glance of jealousy. In fact the young girl appeared to receive pleasure from these gallantries, like a village belle who listens to the flatteries of some grand lord, at the same time that a voice from within whispers her that the sweet compliments she is receiving are also merited.

Don Estevan was not unobservant of this by-play that was passing around him. He easily read in the expressive looks of Tiburcio the secret of his heart, and involuntarily contrasted the manly beauty of the young man with the ordinary face and figure of the Senator. As if from this he apprehended some obstacles to his secret projects, more than once his dark eyebrows became contracted, and his eyes shone with a sombre fire.

By little and little he ceased to take part in the conversation, and at length appeared wrapped in a profound meditation. Insensibly also an air of melancholy stole over the features of Rosarita. As for Don Augustin and the Senator they appeared at once to be on good terms with each other, and carried on the conversation without permitting it to flag for a moment.

Just then Cuchillo, accompanied by Baraja, entered to pay their respects to the master of the hacienda. Their entrance within the sala of course created some slight disarrangement in the tableaux of the *dramatis personal* already there. This confusion gave Tiburcio an opportunity to carry out a desperate resolution he had formed, and profiting by it, he advanced nearer to Rosarita.

"I will give my life," said he to her, in a side whisper, "for one moment alone with you. I wish to speak of an affair of the highest importance."

The young girl regarded him for a moment with an air of astonishment, further expressed by a disdainful movement of the lip; although, considering their former relations, and also the free familiarity of Mexican manners, she might have been expected to have excused his freedom. Tiburcio stood waiting her reply in a supplicating attitude, and as everything seemed spontaneous with her, he had not long to wait. She answered in a few words:

"To-night then—at ten o'clock I shall be at my window."

Scarcely had the thrilling tones of her voice ceased to vibrate on the ear of Tiburcio, when supper was announced, and the guests were shown into another room. Here a table, splendidly set out, occupied the middle of the apartment, above which hung a great chandelier fitted with numerous waxen candles: these gave out a brilliant and cheerful light, that was reflected from hundreds of shining vessels of massive silver of antique forms, arranged upon the table below.

The upper end of the table was occupied by the host himself and his principal guests. His daughter sat on his left hand, while Don Estevan was placed upon the right. After them, the Senator and the chaplain, and Pedro Diaz. At the lower end were seated Tiburcio, Cuchillo, Baraja and Oroche.

The chaplain pronounced the *benedicite*. Although it was no longer the same jumbling formula, *sans façon*, which he had used at the death-bed of the widow of Arellanos, yet the air of mock solemnity and unction with which the grace was uttered, recalled to the heart of Tiburcio that sad souvenir, which recent events had for a time caused him to forget.

Cheerfulness soon reigned around the table. The expedition was talked of, and toasts drunk to its success. Vast silver goblets of antique shape were used for wine glasses, and these, passing rapidly from hand to mouth, soon produced an abundance of good-humour among the guests.

"Gentlemen!" said Don Augustin, when the festive scene was near its end, "before retiring I have the honour to invite you all to a hunt of the wild horse on my estate—which is to come off early in the morning."

Each of the guests accepted the invitation, with that *abandon* natural to people who have made a good supper.

With regard to Tiburcio, jealousy was devouring him. He scarce ate of the rich viands placed before him. He kept his eyes constantly fixed upon Don Estevan, who, during the supper appeared to pay marked attentions to Rosarita, and for every one of which Tiburcio thanked him with a look of hatred. As soon as the supper was ended, the young man silently left the room and repaired to the chamber that had been assigned to him for the night.

At an early hour—for such was the custom of the hacienda—all the guests had retired to their sleeping apartments—even the domestics were no longer to be seen in the great hall; and a profound silence reigned throughout the vast building, as if all the world had gone to rest. But all the world was not yet asleep.

Chapter Twenty
The Assignation

Alone in his chamber, Tiburcio awaited impatiently the hour named by Rosarita. From his window he cast a distracted glance over the plain that stretched away from the walls of the hacienda. The moon was up in the heavens, and the road leading to Tubac appeared under her light shining like a vast ribbon extended through the middle of the forest. The forest itself appeared asleep; not even a breath stirred the leaves of the trees, and the only sounds he heard were those caused by the half-wild herds that wandered through its glades. Now and then the bellowing of a bull denoted the uneasiness of the animal—perhaps from the presence of those terrible night robbers, the puma and jaguar. There was one other sound that reached the ear of Tiburcio, but this appeared to proceed from some part of the hacienda itself. It was the tinkling of a mandolin. The hour was appropriate to amorous reflections, as well as to thoughts of a graver character, and both presented themselves at that moment to the spirit of Tiburcio. Like all those whose life has been passed amid the depths of the desert, there was at the bottom of his heart a certain poetic temperament, at the same time that his soul exhibited that energetic vigour required by the dangers which surround such a life of solitude. His present position then was perfectly appropriate to this double character. His love was unreciprocated—the coolness of Rosarita, almost assured him of the painful fact—and some secret presentiment told him that he was encompassed by enemies.

While thus sadly reflecting on his situation, an object came under his eyes that attracted his attention. It was the gleam of a fire, which appeared to be kindled under cover of the forest at no great distance from the hacienda. The light was partly eclipsed by that of the moon, but still it could be traced by the greater redness of its rays, as they trembled mysteriously on the silver foliage of the trees. It denoted the halting-place of some traveller.

"So near the hacienda!" muttered Tiburcio, in entering upon a new series of reflections. "What can it mean? Why have these travellers not come here to demand hospitality? They have certainly some reason for keeping themselves at a distance? They may be unknown friends to me for heaven often sends such to those who stand in need of them. Cuchillo, Don Estevan, and this pompous Senator, all appear to be my enemies and all are secure under this roof! why might not these travellers, who appear to shun it for that very reason prove friends to me?"

The hour of rendezvous had at length arrived. Tiburcio took up his *serapé* and his knife—the last, the only weapon he had—and prepared to go out from his chamber without making any noise. A fearful conflict of emotions was passing in his bosom; for he knew that in a few minutes would be decided the question of his happiness or misery. Before leaving his chamber, he looked once more through the window in the direction of the forest fire. It was still gleaming in the same place.

While the lover, with cautious tread and wildly beating heart, was silently traversing the long gallery, and passing round to that side upon which opened the window of Rosarita, other scenes were passing elsewhere that must now be detailed.

Since his arrival at the hacienda, Don Estevan, in presence of the other guests, had scarce found an opportunity to speak with the *haciendado* on business that concerned both of them. Only for one moment had they been alone; and then the Spaniard had briefly related to Don Augustin the contract he had entered into with Cuchillo. When Don Estevan mentioned the secret of the Golden Valley, the haciendado appeared to make a slight gesture, as of disappointment, but their short dialogue ended abruptly by a promise to return to the subject at a later hour of the night.

Don Estevan awaited until all the other guests had retired to their chambers. Then drawing the Senator into the bay of one of the large windows of the sala, he requested him to look up at the stars that were shining in all their brilliance in the blue sky above.

"See!" said he, pointing to a particular constellation. "That is the *Chariot* that has risen above the eastern horizon. Do you perceive a single star farther down, which scarce shines through the vapour? That is the emblem of *your* star, which at present pale, to-morrow may be in the ascendant, and gleam more brightly than any of those that compose the brilliant cortege of the *Chariot*."

"What mean you, Señor Arechiza?"

"I shall tell you presently. Perhaps the hour is nearer than you think when you may be the future master of this hacienda, by a marriage with the charming daughter of its present owner, who is to be its heiress. Come presently to my apartment. The conversation which I am about to have with Don Augustin must be decisive, and I shall let you know the result."

With these words the Spaniard and the Senator parted—the heart of the latter beating at the same time with hope and fear.

Don Estevan now awaited the haciendado, who the moment after came up to him.

The proprietor of the Hacienda del Venado, as has already been seen, had given to the Spaniard more than an ordinary welcome. His politeness to him when in presence of witnesses, was even less respectful than when the two were alone. On his side Don Estevan appeared to accept the homage of the other as if it were due to him. There was in his polite condescension towards the rich proprietor, and in the deference of the latter towards him, something resembling the relation that might be supposed to exist between a powerful sovereign and one of his noble vassals.

It was not until after reiterated requests—orders they might almost be called—that Don Augustin consented to be seated in the presence of the other—whereas the Spaniard had flung himself into a *fauteuil* on the moment of entering the chamber, and with the most perfect abandon.

The haciendado waited silently for Don Estevan to speak.

"Well, what do you think of your future son-in-law?" inquired the Spaniard. "I presume you never saw him before?"

"Never," answered Don Augustin. "But if he was even less favoured by nature than he is, that would make no obstacle to our projects."

"I know him; he only needs to be known to prove that he has in him the stuff of a gentleman, besides being a senator of the illustrious congress of Arispe."

The Spaniard pronounced these words with a slight smile of contempt.

"But, señor," continued he, "that is not the difficulty, the important matter is whether *your daughter* will find him to her liking."

"My daughter will act according to my wish," said the haciendado.

"But supposing her heart is not free?"

"The heart of Rosarita is free, Señor Don Estevan; how could it be otherwise—she whose life has been spent in the midst of these deserts?"

"And what about this ragged young fellow, this Tiburcio Arellanos, whom you appear to know? he is in love with your daughter?"

"I have been made aware of it this very morning."

"If it is only a few hours, then, since you have been apprised of the secret of his passion, surely that of your daughter cannot have to this time escaped you?"

"The truth is," answered Don Augustin, smiling, "that I understand better how to follow the traces of an Indian, and read in the countenance of a savage his most secret thoughts, than to look into the heart of a young girl. But I repeat it, I have reason to believe that my daughter's heart is free of any such affection. I do not apprehend any difficulty in this regard. I dread an obstacle of a more important character—I mean an obstacle to the expedition you are about to conduct into the desert."

Here the haciendado communicated to Don Estevan the particulars which the monk had gathered at the death-bed of the widow of Arellanos, and which seemed to produce a strong impression on the Spaniard; but although the conversation continued for some time longer, I shall not here detail what was said, but return to the Senator, who with anxious heart was now awaiting Don Estevan in the apartment which had been assigned to the latter.

Chapter Twenty One
The Duke de Armada

The chamber set apart for the Señor Don Estevan de Arechiza was undoubtedly the best in the house; and, notwithstanding the little progress that luxury has made in the state of Sonora, was furnished with considerable elegance.

In this chamber Don Estevan found the Senator pacing to and fro, with an air that bespoke him a prey to the most vivid emotions.

"Well, Señor Don Vicente!" began Arechiza, who appeared to make light of the impatience of his *protégé*, "what do you think of the daughter of our host? have I exaggerated her beauty?"

"Oh, my friend!" exclaimed the Senator, with all that vivacity of pantomimic gesture so characteristic of the South, "the reality far exceeds the imagination. She is an angel! Even in our country, famous for its beautiful women, Doña Rosarita is certainly loveliest of all."

"And richest too," added the Spaniard, with a smile.

"Who would have expected to find, in the middle of the desert, such an accomplished beauty? such youthful freshness? Such charms were created to shine in afar higher sphere?"

"At the court of a king, for instance," carelessly rejoined Arechiza.

"Oh! Señor Don Estevan!" again exclaimed the Senator in an earnest voice, "do not keep me in suspense; the divine, the rich Doña Rosarita—is it possible I am to have her for my wife?"

"One word from me, one promise from you, and the thing is done. I have her father's word. Within fifteen days you may be the husband of his daughter."

"Agreeable as easy."

"A little later you will be rich."

"No harm in that."

"Later still you will be a grand proprietor."

more. I have therefore sought for glory and honour to satisfy my desires, and I have won them. I have conquered the right to stand uncovered in the presence of the king of Spain. Chevalier of the Order of Saint James of the Sword, I have taken part in the royal ceremonies of the *white cloak and red sword*; and I may say that for me fame has been no idle illusion. Chevalier also of Carlos the Third, I have shared with the royal princes the title of the Grand Cross. I have won successively the Order of Saint Ferdinand, of Saint Hermengildo, and the Golden Fleece of Calatrava. These honours, although coveted by all, were for me but sterile consolations."

This enumeration, made without the slightest show of ostentation, caused the Senator to regard the speaker with an air of respectful astonishment. Don Estevan continued:

"Wealth followed close upon these honours. Rich *appanages*, added to the fortune I derived from my ancestors, soon left far behind me, the time when, as a simple cadet of my family, I was worth nothing but my sword. Now I was rich, opulent, and—will I tell you?—I was still far from being content. My efforts continued; and I was made Comte de Villamares, and afterwards Duke de Armada—"

"Oh! Señor Duke," interrupted Despilfarro, in a humble voice, "permit me—but—I—"

"I have not yet finished," calmly continued the Spaniard; "when you have heard all, you will no longer doubt my words. Notwithstanding your mistrust, señor, I am still nothing more than the secret agent of a prince, and I desire to remain in your eyes, as ever, the simple gentleman Don Estevan de Arechiza—nothing more. It is necessary, however, that this distrust of me should not manifest itself again; for since you are presently to know the object which I am pursuing, you will be privy to my most secret thoughts."

The Senator continued to listen in the most respectful silence.

"As I have said, then, I followed ambition for twenty years for its own sake; or to speak more truly, I passed twenty years of my life to destroy a painful souvenir, at the same time that I was pursuing the path to fame. I fancied that in the middle of a turbulent life, this souvenir would in time be effaced from my memory. The favourite of a prince, the expectant heir to one of the first thrones in Christendom—elevated to the highest places of power—wealth prodigally lavished upon me—I hoped to be able to forget that terrible souvenir. Vain hope!" added the speaker in a solemn voice: "Alas! Nothing can banish remorse. The bloody sword of Saint James was no idle symbol in my hands; for remorse lends to ambition a fearful activity—like a voice continually crying, 'On—on forever!'"

"Oh! it is magnificent. Carramba! Señor de Arechiza, it is a perfect cataract of felicities to be lavished upon my head, it is a dream! it is a dream!" shouted the Senator, as he strode to and fro across the floor.

"Lose no time then in making it a reality," replied Don Estevan.

"But is the time so pressing?" inquired the Senator, suddenly pausing in his steps.

"Why this question? Is it possible to be too quick in obtaining happiness?"

The Senator appeared thoughtful, and for a moment presented an aspect of embarrassment, in strange contrast to his previous looks. He replied after a pause—

"The fact is, Don Estevan, I am willing to marry an heiress whose wealth, as is usually the case, would compensate for her ugliness. In this case it is the very beauty of the lady that confuses me."

"Perhaps she does not please you!"

"On the contrary, so much happiness awes me. It appears to me, for a reason which I cannot divine, that some sad disappointment lurks under the seductive prospect."

"Ah! just as I expected," answered Don Estevan; "it is the human heart. I knew you would make some objection of this kind, but I thought you were more a man of the world than to trouble yourself about the past with such a splendid fortune before you. Ah! my poor Despilfarro," added the Spaniard, with a laugh, "I thought you were more advanced."

"But why, Don Estevan?" inquired the Senator, intending to give a proof of his high diplomatic capacity,—"why is it, *entre nous*, that you desire to lavish this treasure of beauty—to say nothing of her grand wealth—upon another, while you yourself—"

"While I myself might marry her," interrupted the Spaniard. "Is that what you mean to say? Suppose I have no wish to get married. I had that desire long ago, like the rest of the world. My history has been like a great many others; that is, my sweetheart married another. It is true I adopted the means to re—to console myself, and quickly too," added Arechiza, with a dark scowl. "But who do you think I am, Don Vicente Tragaduros?"

"Who are you! why; Don Estevan de Arechiza, of course!"

"That does honour to your penetration," said the Spaniard, with a disdainful smile. "Well, then, since I have already demanded the hand of Doña Rosarita for the illustrious senator Tragaduros y Despilfarro, of course I cannot now take his place."

"But why, señor, did you not make the demand on your own account?"

"Why, because, my dear friend, were this young lady three times as beautiful, and three times as rich as she is, she would neither be beautiful enough nor rich enough for me!"

Despilfarro started with astonishment.

"Eh! and who are you then, señor, may I ask in my turn?"

"Only, as you have said, Don Estevan Arechiza," coolly replied the Spaniard.

The Senator made three or four turns across the room before he could collect his thoughts; but in obedience to the distrust that had suddenly sprung up within him, he resumed:

"There is something in all this I cannot explain, and when I can't explain a thing I can't understand it."

"Good logic," exclaimed Don Estevan, in a tone of raillery, "but am I really mistaken about you, my dear Senator? I did you the honour to believe you above certain prejudices; and even if there was anything in the past life of the beautiful Rosarita—for instance, any prejudice to be trampled under foot—is a million of dowry, besides three millions of expectation, nothing in your eyes?"

Don Estevan put this question for the purpose of sounding the morality of the man, or rather to try the strength of a tool, which he meant to make use of.

Despilfarro returned no reply.

"Now, then, I await your answer," said Don Estevan, after a pause, appearing to take pleasure in the Senator's embarrassment.

"Upon my word, Don Estevan," replied Despilfarro, "you are cruel to mystify one in this manner. I—I—Carramba! it is very embarrassing."

Don Estevan interrupted him. This hesitation on the part of Despilfarro told the Spaniard what he wished to know. An ironical smile played upon his lips, and laying aside his pleasantry, he resumed in a serious tone:

"Listen to me, Tragaduros! It would be unworthy of a gentleman to continue longer this badinage where a lady's reputation is concerned. I can assure you, then, that the past life of the Doña Rosarita is without a stain."

The Senator breathed freely.

"And now," continued Don Estevan, "it is necessary that you give me your full confidence, and I will set you an example by giving mine with a

perfect frankness: the success of the noble cause I have embraced depends upon it. First, then, hear who I am. Arechiza is only a borrowed appellation. As to my real name—which you shall soon know—I made oath in my youth, that no woman, however rich or beautiful, should share it with me; therefore, now that my hair is grey do you think that I should be likely to break the oath I have so long kept? Although a wife, such as I propose for you, may ofttimes be a stepping-stone to ambition, she is oftener an obstacle."

As he said this, Don Estevan rose, and in his turn paced the floor with an agitated air. Some traces of distrust were still perceptible upon the countenance of the Senator—they were noticed by him.

"You wish for a more precise explanation?" said he; "you shall have it."

The Spaniard approached the window and closed the shutters—as if fearful that their conversation might be heard outside. He then sat down again, and requested the Senator to be seated near him.

Tragaduros watched him with a lively curiosity, at the same time lowering his eyes whenever they met the fiery glances of the Spaniard.

The latter appeared suddenly to become transformed, as if looking grander and nobler.

"Now, Señor Senator!" began he, "I am going to make known to you some secrets sufficient to turn your head."

The Senator trembled.

"When the tempter carried the Son of Man to the top of a mountain, and promised him all the kingdoms of the earth if he would fall down and worship him, he scarce offered him more than I am offering to the Senator of Arispe. As the tempter, then, I lay at your feet honours, power, and riches, if you will subscribe to my conditions."

The solemnity of this exordium, and the imposing manner of Don Estevan, following so closely upon the jocular mien he had hitherto exhibited, made a painful impression upon the mind of the Senator. There was a short moment in which he regretted being so *advanced* in his opinions, and during this time the great dowry of Rosarita and her rosy lips had but slight prestige for him.

"It is now twenty years," continued the Spaniard, "since I took up my real vocation in the world. Previous to that time, I believed myself made for domestic life, and indulged in those absurd dreams of love natural to young hearts. An illusion soon destroyed—an evil hour—an accident showed me the deception; and I found out that I was made for ambition—nothing

Don Estevan paused, and for a time remained silent, during which the Senator regarded him with a timid look, at the same time admiring the imposing and solemn dignity of his countenance.

"But where to go on?" continued the speaker; "what object to follow next? Into what new course might I precipitate this torrent of ambition that was boiling within me? At length a new incident offered itself, and gave me a fresh opportunity for action—an opportunity to strive and combat—for in my case, to struggle and fight is to forget.

"In all likelihood you have scarce heard of our political troubles, Don Vicente? I am aware that all the kingdoms of Europe might be shaken to their bases, without your knowing anything of the matter, in this out of the way corner of the world. Well, then, I shall make known to you what occurred.

"It is now about two years since the king of Spain—by a total violation of the Salic law, hitherto observed by all his ancestors—violently cut off the succession to the throne in the person of his brother Don Carlos; and by this act kindled the fires of civil war throughout the kingdom. The Infanta Isabella was declared heiress to the crown, to the exclusion of her uncle, the legal heir. This prince it was of whom I spoke, and who is my august patron and protector. I did everything in my power to assuage the mortal grief that this unexpected event naturally caused to the man, whom I above all others have reason to esteem.

"Amidst the consolations which I offered him, and the plans which I proposed, one design of a gigantic nature offered itself to my imagination. True, it presented the prospect of countless dangers, and obstacles almost insurmountable; but for this very reason I adopted it.

"My dream, then, is to conquer for my master a kingdom as vast as the one of which he has been wrongfully deprived; to restore to him one of the brightest jewels of that Transatlantic crown, which his ancestors once so gloriously wore. I dream of conquering a kingdom—and that kingdom once conquered, I, a simple gentleman, intend to present it to the true heir of the Spanish monarchy—Don Carlos de Bourbon!

"Now, do you believe, Señor Senator, that Don Estevan de Arechiza has the power to bestow upon others, and without regretting it, the beauty and wealth of the daughter of a Mexican haciendado?"

The Spaniard pronounced these last words with an air of proud tranquillity, and then remained silent, awaiting their effect upon his listener.

Chapter Twenty Two
The New Kingdom

The Mexican senator, with his contracted, or rather egoistic views, was struck dumb by the gigantic and daring design of his companion. He could only exclaim, as he respectfully pressed the hand which the Spaniard held out to him:

"Oh, Don Estevan—if you permit me still to give you this modest title—I regret my suspicions; and for the happiness which you offer me, for the grand perspective which you open before me, I promise you my life, my heart, but—"

"But! another suspicion?" asked Don Estevan, with a smile.

"*No*, not a suspicion of you, but a fear of some one else. Have you noticed the young man whom chance brought into our company? I have a secret presentiment that there is something between him and Doña Rosarita. He is young—he is good-looking—and they appear to have known each other a long while."

"What!" exclaimed Don Estevan, "jealous of this ragged rustic?"

"I avow," replied the Senator, "that I cannot help it. I noticed two or three times their eyes fixed upon each other with a strange expression."

"Make yourself easy about that. I know, for certain—and from Don Augustin himself I have had my information—that the heart of his daughter is free. Besides, her vanity alone would hinder her from any fancy for this droll fellow, who appears to have all the pride of a Spanish beggar. He shall be watched; and, should he have the impudence to carry his pretensions so high, it will be an easy matter to send him about his business."

In pronouncing the last words the countenance of Don Estevan appeared for a moment to wear a troubled expression, and he could not hinder himself from adding:

"I have myself remarked what you say, but let us not dwell upon chimerical fears. Listen to me, Don Vicente, while I explain more categorically the object of which I have been speaking, in order that you may understand fully why I wish to reckon upon your assistance. I have not yet told you—either what resources I have, or the kingdom it is my design to conquer."

"True enough," assented Tragaduros, "you have not."

"The province then which I intend to transform into a kingdom is neither more nor less than this of Sonora."

"What! our republican state to be changed into a monarchy!" exclaimed the Senator. "Señor Don Estevan, to attempt this will be to play with your life."

"I know it."

"But what resources do you count upon?"

"Listen: Ten years ago I was in the Spanish army, and fought against the independence of your country in this very province. I then became acquainted with its resources—its incalculable richness—and when I quitted it to go home to Europe, I had a presentiment that some day I should again return to it—as I have done. Chance at that time made me acquainted with Don Augustin, then occupied in amassing the vast wealth which to-day he so freely spends. I had the fortune to render him a service—to save his life, in fact, and prevent his house from being pillaged by the insurgents, for he did not conceal his sympathy for the Spanish cause. I afterwards kept up with him a correspondence, and learned that Sonora became every day more discontented with the federal government. I then designed my great plan, which was approved of by the prince, and at his desire I came over here. Don Augustin was among the first to whom I opened my purpose. He was flattered by the promises I was able to make in the name of my royal master, and at once placed his fortune at my disposal.

"Notwithstanding the large pecuniary resources I have been able to dispose of, I am seeking to augment them still farther, and chance has favoured me. While here in my former campaign I made the acquaintance of an odd character—a young fellow who in turns betrayed both royalists and republicans. My relations with him recall a somewhat droll occurrence. I found that he was guiding the regiment I commanded into an ambuscade of the insurgents, and I ordered him to be hung to the first tree we should meet with. Fortunately for him my men translated the order in its most literal sense; and being at the time in the middle of vast savannahs entirely destitute of trees, the execution was held over, as it was an impossibility to perform it. The result was that in the middle of our marchings and counter-marchings the fellow escaped; and it appears did not, afterwards, hold any rancour towards me, since he has again offered his services to me. This fellow to-day goes by the name of Cuchillo. It was he whom I met at the village of

Huerfano, where you saw us renew our acquaintance; and at that interview he has made known to me the secret of an immense placer of gold—whither I intend to conduct my expedition. Besides ourselves, Cuchillo alone knows the object of this enterprise," (the Spaniard did not mention the name of Tiburcio), "which is generally supposed to be merely a new expedition—like many others that have been got up to go gold seeking by chance.

"And now, Señor Senator," continued Don Estevan, "you need not proceed farther with us. You may remain here, where you will have an easy part to play, in making yourself agreeable to the fair Rosarita, while I am braving the perils of this unknown frontier. As for Cuchillo, if he attempt to play the traitor with me a second time, I shall take care to be a little more prompt in punishing him.

"The product of this expedition," pursued the Spaniard,—"of which, as leader, I shall be entitled to a fifth part—will be added to the resources I have already. The men who compose it will be easily converted into devoted partisans of our design; and should it happen that the forces I expect from Europe should fail to come to hand in due time, these adventurers will serve a good purpose. But I have no fear for the want of followers. Europe is at the present moment overcrowded with people who lack employment: any enterprise will be welcome to them; and a leader in any part of the world needs only to speak the word for crowds to enrol themselves under his banner."

As he said this, Don Estevan paced the room, agitated by the grandeur of his thoughts. His dark eyes flashed with excitement, and his soul seemed inspired with a warlike ardour that caused him for a while to forget the presence of the Senator. It was only after some minutes spent in this wild enthusiasm that he remembered an important fact—that in all projects such as he was engaged in, *intrigue* should be the precursor of open action; and as this was to be the peculiar *rôle* which the Senator was expected to play, he again turned to address himself to this individual.

"Meanwhile," said he, "your tactics will be of a more pacific character. I take charge of the open fighting—while you manage the secret diplomacy of the affair. Your fortune, restored to you by this opulent alliance, will enable you to get back the influence you have lost. You will receive with the daughter of Don Augustin, at least two hundred thousand dollars of dowry. Half of this you are to employ in making partisans in the Senate, and in what you are pleased to call *your army*. This sum you will not lose: it will be repaid to you, and with usurious interest; or if it never should, you still make a good thing of it. The end you will keep in view, is to detach the Senate of Sonora from the Federal alliance. You will find no lack of reasons for this policy. For instance, your State has now scarcely the privileges of a simple territory; your interests differ entirely from those of the central States of the Republic. Every day your laws are becoming more centralised. The President, who deals with your finances, resides at a distance of seven hundred leagues from your capital—it is ridiculous! Besides, the funds of the treasury are misappropriated—the army badly paid, although you have to do your duty in raising the tax that is to pay it—a thousand grievances can be cited. Well, this will enable you to get up a *pronunciamento*, and before the news of your *grito* can reach the city of Mexico, and the Executive power there can send a force against you—ay, before the government troops could get half-way to Sonora, more than two-thirds of them would desert. The others would come upon the ground, only to find the insurrectionary party too strong for them, and they themselves would be certain to join us.

"Laws emanating from your own Senate—of which you yourself would have the control and guidance—laws suited to the manners and usages of your State, would soon become firmly established and respected, and Sonora would then be an independent government. This would be the first step and the most difficult. After that the rest would be easy enough; and the gold which I should furnish will bring it about. The Senate and the army would call for a European prince to place himself at their head—one who speaks the same language and professes the same religion as themselves. This prince I have already provided. Now hear me, Don Vicente! as to your own share in this business. The Senator Despilfarro is already a rich man, with a lady for his wife of whom a prince might be proud. He will be made noble—a count—a Grandee of Spain. A lucrative post will attach him to the person of the new king, and nothing is to hinder him from rising to the very summit of his ambition. All this I promise on the part of your future sovereign, *King Charles the First*."

With these words the Spaniard finished his harangue. The Mexican Senator, fascinated by the riches and honours thus promised him, grasped the hand of the bold conspirator, at the same time crying out with enthusiasm, "*Viva! Viva Carlos el Primero!*"

"Good!" rejoined Don Estevan, with a smile. "Don Carlos can count upon one powerful partisan already in Sonora, and there will soon be many. But it is getting late, Don Vicente, and I have yet much business to do before I can go to sleep. You will excuse me, then, if I bid good-night to you."

After exchanging the usual *buenas noches*, the Senator returned to his own chamber and couch, to dream of his future riches and grandeur.

Chapter Twenty Three
Quarrelsome Gamesters

In a remote chamber of the hacienda were lodged the four adventurers, Pedro Diaz, Oroche, Cuchillo, and Baraja. These gentlemen were not slow in becoming acquainted with one another, and this acquaintance was soon of the most familiar character. In the middle of the room in which all four were to pass the night, stood a strong oaken table, upon which, in an iron candlestick, was burning a long thin tallow candle, that gave forth a somewhat dim and doubtful light. By this light Cuchillo and Baraja— forgetful of all their promises and vows—were going on with the game, which had been so suddenly interrupted that morning at the village of Huerfano.

Pedro Diaz appeared to be merely an involuntary spectator; while Oroche, seated at one corner of the table, his right leg across his left, his elbow resting on his knee—the favourite attitude of mandolin players— accompanied his own voice as he sang the *boleros* and *fandangos* then most in vogue among the inhabitants of the coast region.

Wrapped as usual in his ragged cloak, Oroche appeared to have the true inspiration of an artist: since he could thus elevate himself upon the wings of music, above the vulgar consideration of the toilette, or the cleanliness and comfort of the person. A bottle of *mezcal*, already half empty, stood upon the table. From this the players occasionally helped themselves—as a finale to the elegant supper they had eaten and to which Cuchillo, Baraja, and Oroche had done ample honour. Notwithstanding the frequent bumpers which Cuchillo had quaffed, he appeared to be in the worst of humour, and a prey to the most violent passions. His shaggy eyebrows, contracted by the play of these passions, added to the evil aspect of his physiognomy, rendering it even more sinister than common. Just then he was observed to cut the cards with particular care. He was not playing with his friend Baraja for the mere sport of the thing; for a moiety of the half ounce he had received from Don Estevan had already gone into Baraja's pockets, and Cuchillo was in hopes that the attention which he had given to the cutting of the cards might change the luck that had hitherto been running against him. The careful cutting, however, went for nothing; and once more the sum he had staked was swept into the pocket of his adversary. All at once Cuchillo flew off into a passion, scattering his hand of cards over the table.

"Who the devil wants your music?" cried he to Oroche in a furious tone, "and I myself, fool that I am, to play in this fashion—only credit when I win, and cash whenever I lose."

"You offend me, Señor Cuchillo," said Baraja, "my word has always passed for its value in cash."

"Especially when you don't happen to lose," sneeringly added Cuchillo.

"That is not a very delicate insinuation," said Baraja gathering up the cards. "Fye, fye! Señor Cuchillo—to get angry about such a trifle! I myself have lost half a hacienda at play—after being robbed of the other half—and yet I never said a word about it."

"Didn't you indeed? what's that to me? I shall speak as I please, Señor Baraja, and as loudly as I please too," added he, placing his hand upon the hilt of his knife.

"Yes," coolly answered Baraja, "I know you use words *that cause your friends to drop dead*; but these words are harmless at a distance—besides I have got a tongue as sharp as yours, Señor Cuchillo."

As Baraja said this, he drew his knife from its sheath—in which action he was imitated by his antagonist—and both placed themselves simultaneously in an attitude for fight.

Oroche coolly took up his mandolin—which at the interference of Cuchillo he had laid aside—and, like a bard of ancient times was, preparing to accompany the combat with a chant, when Diaz suddenly interposed between the two champions.

"For shame, gentlemen!" cried he; "what! two men made to be mutual friends, thus to cut each other's throats for a few paltry dollars! on the eve too of becoming the owners of a hundred times as much! Have I not understood you to say, Señor Cuchillo, that you were to be the guide of our expedition? Your life is no more your own, then; it belongs to us all, and you have no right to risk it. And you, Señor Baraja! you have not the right to attempt the life of our guide. Come! put up your knives, and let there be no more of this matter."

This speech recalled the two combatants to their senses. Cuchillo remembering the grand interest he had in the success of the expedition, and perceiving that the risk of life was playing a little too high—for a combat of this sort usually ends in the death of one or the other—gave ready ear to the counsel of Diaz. Baraja, on his side, reflected that the dollars he had already pocketed might be better employed than in defraying the expenses of his own funeral; and on this reflection was equally ready to desist from his intention.

"Be it so, then!" cried Cuchillo, speaking first; "I sacrifice my feelings to the common good."

"And I," said Baraja, "I am willing to follow so noble an example. I disarm—but—I shall play no more."

The knives were again stuck into their scabbards, and the two adversaries mutually extended their hands to one another.

At this moment, Diaz, by way of preventing any allusion to the recent quarrel, suddenly turning to Cuchillo, demanded:

"Who, Señor Cuchillo, is this young man whom I saw riding by your side as you came up to the hacienda? Notwithstanding the friendship that appeared to exist between you and him, if I mistake not, I observed you regarding one another with an occasional glance of mistrust—not to say hostility. Was it not so?"

Cuchillo recounted how they had found Tiburcio half dead upon the road, and also the other circumstances, already known to the reader; but the question put by Diaz had brought the red colour into the face of the outlaw, for it recalled to him how his cunning had been outwitted by the young man, and also how he had been made to tremble a moment under Tiburcio's menace. Writhing under these remembrances, he was now determined to make his vengeance more secure, by enlisting his associates as accomplices of his design.

"It often happens," said he, in a significant tone, "that one man's interest must be sacrificed to the common welfare—just as I have now done—does it not?"

"Without doubt," replied several.

"Well then," continued Cuchillo, "when one has given himself, body and soul, to any cause, whatever it may be, it becomes his duty, as in my case, to put a full and complete constraint upon his affections, his passions, even his dearest interests—ay, even upon any scruples of conscience that might arise in an over-delicate mind."

"All the world knows that," said Baraja.

"Just so, gentlemen. Well, I feel myself in that difficulty; I have a too timid conscience, I fear, and I want your opinions to guide me."

His audience maintained an imperturbable silence.

"Suppose, then," continued the outlaw, "there was a man whom you all held in the highest esteem, but whose life compromised the success of our expedition, what should be done with him?"

"As God lives," cried Oroche, "I should be happy to find some occasion of sacrificing private interests to the common good."

"But is there such a man?" inquired Diaz, "and who may he be?"

"It's a long story," replied Cuchillo, "and its details concern only myself—but there *is* such a man."

"Carajo!" exclaimed Oroche, "that is enough; he should be *got rid of* as speedily as possible."

"Is that the advice of all of you?" asked Cuchillo.

"Of course," answered simultaneously Oroche and Baraja.

Diaz remained silent keeping himself out of this mysterious compromise. After a little, he rose from his seat, and under some pretext left the chamber.

"Well, then, gentlemen," said Cuchillo, addressing himself to his two more facile comrades, "you are fully of the opinion that the man should be got rid of? Let me tell you, then, that this man is no other than Tiburcio Arellanos."

"Tiburcio!" exclaimed the two acolytes.

"Himself—and although, since he is one of my dearest friends, it goes sadly against my heart, I declare to you that his life may render abortive all the plans of our expedition."

"But," interposed Baraja, "why may he not lose it?—to-morrow in this hunt of wild horses there will be a thousand opportunities of his losing it?"

"True enough," said Cuchillo, in a solemn voice. "It is of great importance he should not return from this hunt. Can I rely upon you, gentlemen?"

"Blindly!" replied the two adventurers.

The storm was gathering over the head of poor Tiburcio, but danger threatened him from still another quarter; and long before the expected hunt, that danger would be at its height.

The three adventurers continued their conversation, and were entering more particularly into the details of their design, when a knocking at the outer door interrupted their sinister councils.

Chapter Twenty Four
Tiburcio in Danger

Cuchillo opened the door, outside of which appeared one of the attendants of Don Estevan. Without entering the man communicated his message—which was to Cuchillo himself—to the effect that Don Estevan awaited him in the garden. The outlaw, without reply, followed the servant, who conducted him to an alley between two rows of granadines, where a man wrapped in his cloak was pacing to and fro, apparently buried in a deep meditation. It was Don Estevan himself.

The approach of Cuchillo interrupted his reverie, and a change passed over his countenance. Had Cuchillo not been preoccupied with his own thoughts and purposes of vengeance, he might have observed on the features of the Spaniard an expression of disdainful raillery, that evidently concerned himself.

"You have sent for me?" said he to Don Estevan.

"You cannot otherwise than approve of my discretion," began the Spaniard, without making answer. "I have allowed you time enough to sound this young fellow—you know whom I mean. Well! no doubt you have penetrated to the bottom and know all—you, whose perspicacity is only equalled by the tenderness of your conscience?"

There was an ascerbity in this speech which caused the outlaw to feel ill at ease, for it re-opened the wounds of his self-esteem.

"Well," continued Don Estevan, "what have you learnt?"

"Nothing," replied Cuchillo.

"Nothing!"

"No; the young man could tell me nothing, since he knew nothing himself. He has no secrets for me."

"What! does he not suspect the existence of the Golden Valley?"

"He knows no more of it than of the Garden of Eden," replied Cuchillo, with a confident swagger.

"What was bringing him to the hacienda, then—for that is upon the route? He must have some object in coming this way."

"O yes!—he came to ask Don Augustin to take him into his service as a vaquero."

"It is evident," said the Spaniard, in a tone of mockery, "that you have gained his full confidence and know all about him."

"I flatter myself, my perspicacity—"

"Is only equalled by the tenderness of your conscience," interrupted Don Estevan, still keeping up his tone of raillery. "Well, but has this young man not confided to you any other secret? You have had a long ride together, and an opportunity to talk of many things. For instance, has he said nothing to you about an affair of the heart?—has he not told you he was in love?"

"Por Dios! Who could Tiburcio be in love with in these deserts? The poor devil is likely to think more of a good horse than a pretty girl."

"Indeed!" exclaimed the Spaniard, with a mocking laugh that sent a shivering through the frame of Cuchillo. "Well, well! friend Cuchillo, your youth promised better than this. If your conscience is as callous as your perspicacity is obtuse—which God forbid—it is not likely to interfere with your sleep."

"What do you mean, señor?" demanded Cuchillo, evidently confounded by the reproach.

"I fear, my friend, that in the only good action you have ever done, you have made a bad hand of it."

"Good action!" repeated Cuchillo, embarrassed to know at what epoch of his life he had done such a thing.

"Yes—in saving this young man's life."

"But it was you who did that good action: as for me, it was only a lucrative one."

"Be it so. I will lend it to you, notwithstanding the proverb which says we should only lend to the rich. But now hear what I have ascertained—I, who do not boast either of my scruples of conscience or of my perspicacity. This young man has in his pocket, at this moment, a written direction of the route to the Golden Valley; moreover, he is passionately in love with Doña Rosarita, for whom he would give all the gold in this valley, or all the gold in the world, and all the horses in Sonora, if he had them. Moreover, his object in coming to the Hacienda del Venado, was to make himself its future proprietor."

"Blood and thunder!" cried Cuchillo, started as if bitten by a snake—"that cannot be—it is not possible I could be fooled in that manner by a child!"

"That child is a giant beside you, master Cuchillo," coldly replied Arechiza.

"It is impossible!" exclaimed the exasperated Cuchillo.

"Do you wish the proofs?—if you do you shall have them—but I may tell you they are of a nature to make you shudder from the crown of your head to the soles of your feet."

"No matter; I should like to hear them," said Cuchillo in a suppressed voice.

"I will not speak of your conscience—mark that well, Cuchillo! For I know that it never shudders—nor yet shall I speak of your timidity, which I observed last night while you were in the presence of the jaguars—"

Don Estevan paused, to let his words have their full effect. It was his design to crush by his superiority the man whose fidelity he had a thousand reasons to suspect.

"Tiburcio," continued he, "is of a race—or appears to be of a race—that unites intelligence with courage; and you are his mortal enemy. Do you begin to understand me?"

"No," said Cuchillo.

"Well, you will presently, after a few simple questions which I intend to ask you. The first is:—In your expedition with Arellanos, had you not a horse that stumbled in the left leg?"

"Eh!" ejaculated Cuchillo, turning pale.

"A second question:—Were they really *Indians* who murdered your companion?"

"Perhaps it was me?" replied the outlaw, with a hideous smile.

"Third question:—Did you not receive, in a deadly struggle, a wound in the leg? and fourth: Did you not carry upon your shoulder the dead body of Arellanos?"

"I did—to preserve it from being mutilated by the Indians."

"One more question:—Was it for this you flung the dead body into the neighbouring river—not quite dead, it may be?"

The beams of the moon, slanting through the leaves of the granadines, shone with a livid reflection on the face of the outlaw, who with haggard eyes listened, without comprehending whence they came, to the proofs of a murder which he believed forever buried in the desert.

Cuchillo, when imparting to Don Estevan the knowledge of his marvellous secret, had of course taken care not to give in detail the exact manner by which he had himself become master of it; he had merely stated such circumstances as were necessary to convince the Spaniard of the importance of the discovery. It would be impossible to paint the stupefied expression of his countenance, as he listened to these interrogatories. The very desert itself had spoken!

"Does Tiburcio know all this?" he asked, with an ill-dissembled anxiety.

"No; but he knows that the assassin of his father had a horse like yours; that he was wounded in the leg; that he flung the dead body in the water. Of one matter only is he still ignorant—the name of the murderer. But now let me say to you; if you give me the slightest cause to suspect your fidelity, I shall deliver the secret to this young man, who will crush you like a scorpion. Good blood never lies; so I repeat it, Cuchillo; no deception—no treason, or your life will answer for it!"

"Well, as regards Tiburcio," muttered Cuchillo to himself, "if you only keep the secret till this time to-morrow night, you may then shout it in his ears: I shall have no fear of his hearing you."

The outlaw was one of those characters who soon recover from a shock, similar to that he had just received. Almost on the instant he inquired, with impudent assurance:

"But your Excellency has not proved to me that this young fellow is in love with Doña Rosarita; and until I have proof of this I shall not doubt my penetration—"

"Hush!" interrupted the Spaniard; "I fancy I hear voices!"

Both remained silent. In advancing across the garden, the two men had approached nearer to the walls of the building, and on that side of it which fronted the window belonging to the chamber of Rosarita. They were still at a considerable distance from the window itself; but so tranquil was the night, that sounds could be heard along way off. As they stood to listen, a confused murmur of voices reached their ears—as of two persons engaged in conversation—but the words could not be distinguished.

"It is the voice of Tiburcio and Rosarita!" muttered the outlaw.

"Did I not tell you? You may take that, I think, as an instalment of the proof you are desirous of having."

A reflection, at this moment, came into the mind of the Spaniard, that struck upon his spirit like a thunderbolt. It was this:—"If the young girl, after all, is really in love with this fellow, what a dilemma! I may have to renounce all idea of the marriage, which I had designed as the corner-stone of my vast edifice!"

Don Estevan was the only one who at this time was aware of the real name and family of Tiburcio, and of course knew that he was not unworthy of the daughter of a Mexican haciendado. But it had never entered his mind that this young girl, who only regarded Tiburcio in the light of a poor gambusino, would think for a moment of reciprocating his passion. His ideas were suddenly altered, however, on hearing the voices of Tiburcio and Rosarita, alternating with each other, with no other witness to their conversation than the stars in the sky. It was evident, therefore, that Rosarita did not regard the young rustic with an unfavouring eye. An interview, such as this, could not be otherwise than a thing premeditated and prearranged.

The heart of the Spaniard swelled with rage at the thought. His ambition was suddenly alarmed: for this was an obstacle that had never occurred to him. His countenance exhibited a thoughtful and troubled expression. He found himself unexpectedly in the presence of one of those exigencies, which render diplomacy powerless, and absolve all reasons of state. He had behind him a man ready to destroy whatever victims he might point out; but he remembered that twenty years of expiation had failed to wash from his memory a murder of which he had been himself accused. Should he, then, after having passed the middle of his career, again embitter the remainder of his days by another deed of blood? On the other hand, so near the object of his ambition, was he to permit this barrier to stand in his way? or with a bold effort to rid himself of the obstacle?

Thus it is that the ambitious continually roll before them the rock of Sisyphus!

"Providence," said he to himself—and as he pronounced the word a bitter smile played upon his lips—"Providence offers me an opportunity to restore to this young man his name and his fortune, and the honours which he has lost. Such a good action in my ripe age would perhaps compensate for the crime of my youth. But, no—no—I spurn the occasion—it is but a slight sacrifice to the cause which I serve."

As he spoke, his face was turned towards Cuchillo, who was observing him attentively; but the shadow of the trees hindered the outlaw from noting the sombre expression of his countenance.

"The hour is come," said he, speaking to Cuchillo in a low voice, "when our doubts are to be solved. But remember! your projects of vengeance must remain subordinate to my wishes—now follow me!"

Saying this, he walked silently towards the hacienda, followed by the assassin.

The storm which threatened Tiburcio promised soon to break over his head. Two dangerous enemies were approaching him; Cuchillo with wounded self-esteem, and purposes of vengeance that caused, him to grind his teeth as he thought of them; and Don Estevan, smarting at the discovery of such an obstacle to his ambition.

Tiburcio in going forth from his chamber, and traversing the path that conducted him to the appointed rendezvous, was under the belief he had not been observed: neither was he; but unfortunately chance had now betrayed him.

The night was not so dark as Don Estevan and Cuchillo would have wished; nevertheless, by crouching low, and keeping well in to the wall that enclosed the garden, they succeeded in reaching a little grove of orange and citron trees, the foliage of which was thick enough to shelter them from view. From this grove, thanks to the calmness of the night, they could catch every word that was said—for under the shadow of the trees they were able to approach very near to the speakers.

"Whatever you may hear," whispered Don Estevan in the ear of the other, "remain motionless as I do."

"I will," simply answered Cuchillo.

The two now placed themselves in an attitude to see and hear. They were separated from the speakers by a slight barrier of leaves and branches, and by a distance not greater than an active man could pass over in two bounds. Little did the victims of their espionage suspect their proximity—little dreamt Tiburcio of the danger that was so near him.

Chapter Twenty Five
Love through the Window

For a time the listeners heard nothing beyond those commonplace speeches exchanged between lovers—when the young man, doubtful of his position, makes himself heard in reproaches, or arguments, which to him appear all-powerful, while the responses which he meets with show too plainly that he is either not loved at all, or that the advantages are on the side of the girl. But was this really the position of Tiburcio with Rosarita? It remains to be known.

According to the custom of country houses throughout Mexico, the window of Rosarita's chamber was unglazed. Strong iron bars, forming what is called the *reja*, hindered an entrance from without; and behind this reja, lit up by the lamp in the chamber, the young girl was standing in an attitude of graceful ease. In the calm and perfumed night she appeared even more charming than when seen in the brilliant saloon—for it is behind the railing of these balconies that the women of Spanish race appear to the greatest advantage.

A *reboso* of silk was thrown over her head, falling over her shoulders in graceful undulations. The window running quite down to the level of the floor concealed nothing of her person; she was visible from the crown of her head to the satin slipper that covered her pretty little foot; and the outline of her figure formed in a graceful silhouette against the light burning within.

Tiburcio, his forehead resting against the bars, appeared to struggle with a painful conviction that was fast forcing itself upon him.

"Ah!" said he, "I have not forgotten, as you, Rosarita, the day when I first saw you in the forest. The twilight was so sombre I could scarce make out your form, which appeared like the graceful shadow of some siren of the woods. Your voice I could hear, and there was something in it that charmed my soul—something that I had never heard till that moment."

"I have never forgotten the service you rendered us," said the young girl; "but why recall those times? they are long past."

"Long past! no, not to me, Rosarita—that scene appears to me as if it had happened yesterday. Yes," continued the young man, in a tone of melancholy, "when the light of the camp-fire by little and little enabled me to observe the radiant beauty of your face, I can scarce describe the emotion which it gave me."

Had Tiburcio, instead of looking to the ground, but raised his eyes at that moment, he might have noticed upon the countenance of Rosarita an expression of interest, while a slight blush reddened her cheeks. Perhaps her heart was scarce touched, but rarely does woman listen, without pleasure, to those impassioned tones that speak the praises of her beauty.

Tiburcio continued in a voice still softer and more marked by emotion:— "I have not forgotten the flowers of the llianas which I gathered for you, and that seemed to give forth a sweeter perfume when mingled with the tresses of your hair. Ah! it was a subtle poison that was entering into my heart, and which has resulted in filling it with an incurable passion. Ah! fool that I have been! Is it possible, Rosarita, that you have forgotten those sweet souvenirs upon which I have lived from that day up to the present hour?"

There are certain moments of indiscretion in the life of most women, of which they have a dislike to be reminded. Was it so with Rosarita? She was silent for a while, as if her rebellious memory could not recall the particulars mentioned by Tiburcio.

"No," at length answered she, in a tone so low as not to betray a slight trembling of her voice, "I do not forget, but we were then only children—to-day—"

"To-day," interrupted Tiburcio in a tone of bitter reproach, "to-day that is all forgotten, since a Senator from Arispe has condescended to comprise you in his projects of ambition."

The melodious voice of Rosarita was now heard in a tone of disdainful anger. Tiburcio had wounded her pride.

"Comprise me in his projects of ambition," said she, her beautiful nostrils curving scornfully as she spoke, "and who has told you, señor, that it is not I who condescend?"

"This stranger, too," continued Tiburcio, still preserving his reproachful manner, "this Don Estevan—whom I hate even worse than the Senator— has talked to you of the pleasures of Madrid—of the wonderful countries that lie beyond the sea—and you wish to see them with your own eyes!"

"Indeed I acknowledge," answered Rosarita, "that in these deserts life appears to me dull enough. Something tells me that I was not made to die without taking part in those splendours of the world of which I have heard so much. What can you offer to me—to my father?"

"I understand now," cried Tiburcio with despairing bitterness, "to be poor, an orphan, unhappy—these are not the titles to win the heart of a woman."

"You are unjust, Tiburcio. It is almost always the very reverse that happens—for it is the instinct of a woman to prefer those who are as you say. But it is different with fathers, who, alas! rarely share this preference with their daughters."

There was in these last words a sort of tacit avowal which Tiburcio evidently did not comprehend—for he continued his reproaches and bitter recriminations, causing the young girl many a sigh as she listened to them.

"Of course you love this Senator," said he. "Do not talk, then, of being compelled!"

"Who talks of being compelled?" said Rosarita, hastily interrupting the young man. "I said nothing of compulsion, I only spoke of the desire which my father has already manifested; and against his will, the hopes you may have conceived would be nothing more than chimeras or idle dreams."

"And this will of your father is to throw you into the arms of a ruined prodigal, who has no other aim than to build up the fortune he has squandered in dissipation, and satisfy his ambitious desires? Say, Rosarita, say! is this will in consonance with your own? Does your heart agree to it? If it is not, and there is the least compulsion upon you, how happy should I be to contest for you with this rival. Ah! you do not make answer—you love him, Rosarita? And I—Oh! why did they not leave me to die upon the road?"

At this moment a slight rustling was heard in the grove of oranges, where Don Estevan and Cuchillo were crouching in concealment.

"Hush!" said the young girl, "did you not hear a noise?"

Tiburcio turned himself quickly, his eye on fire, his heart beating joyfully with the hope of having some one upon which to vent the terrible anger that tortured it—but the rays of the moon shone only upon the silvery foliage—all was quiet around.

He then resumed his gloomy and pensive attitude. Sadness had again taken possession of his soul, through which the quick burst of anger had passed as lightning though a sombre sky.

"Very likely," said he, with a melancholy smile, "it is the spirit of some poor lover who has died from despair."

"Santisima Virgen!" exclaimed Rosarita, making the sign of the cross. "You make me afraid, Tiburcio. Do you believe that one could die of love?" she inquired in a tone of *naïveté*.

"It may be," replied Tiburcio, with a sad smile still playing upon his lips. Then changing his tone, he continued, "Hear me, Rosarita! you are ambitious, you have said so—hear me then! Supposing I could give you all that has been promised you? hitherto I have preferred to plead the cause of Tiburcio poor and an orphan; I shall now advocate that of Tiburcio Arellanos on the eve of becoming rich and powerful; noble too I shall become—for I shall make myself an illustrious name and offer it to you."

As he said these words the young man raised his eyes towards heaven: his countenance exhibited an altered expression, as if there was revived in his soul the pride of an ancient race.

For the first time since the commencement of the interview, Tiburcio was talking sensibly, and the daughter of Eve appeared to listen with more attention than what she had hitherto exhibited.

Meanwhile the two spies were also listening attentively from their hiding-place among the oranges. Not a word of what was said, not a gesture escaped them. The last speech of Tiburcio had caused them to exchange a rapid glance. The countenance of the outlaw betrayed an expression of rage mingled with shame. After the impudent manner in which he had boasted of his penetration, he felt confounded in the presence of Don Estevan, whose eyes were fixed upon him with a look of implacable raillery.

"We shall see now," whispered the Spaniard, "whether this young fellow knows no more of the situation of the Golden Valley than he does of the Garden of Eden."

Cuchillo quailed under this terrible irony, but made no reply.

As yet Don Estevan had learnt nothing new. The essential object with him was to discover whether Tiburcio's passion was reciprocated: the rest was of little importance. In the behaviour of Rosarita there was certainly something that betrayed a tender compassion for the adopted son of Arellanos; but was this a sign of love? That was the question to which Don Estevan desired to have the answer.

Meanwhile, having excited the evil passions of the outlaw to the highest pitch, he judged it prudent to moderate them again; an explosion at that moment would not have been politic on his part. A murder committed before his face, even though he had not ordered it either by word or gesture, would at least exhibit a certain complicity with the assassin, and deprive him of that authority which he now exercised over Cuchillo.

"Not for your life!" said he, firmly grasping the arm of the outlaw, whose hand rested upon his knife. "Not for your soul's safety! Remember! till I give the word, the life of this young man is sacred. Hush!" he continued, "listen!" and still holding the outlaw by the arm he turned his eyes upon Tiburcio, who had again commenced speaking.

"Why should I conceal it from you longer?" exclaimed the young man, in a tone to which the attentive attitude of Rosarita had lent animation. "Hear me, then! honours—riches—power I can lay at your feet, but you alone can enable me to effect this miracle."

Rosarita fixed her eyes upon the speaker with an interrogatory expression.

"Perhaps I should have told you sooner," continued Tiburcio, "that my adopted mother no longer lives—"

"I know it," interrupted the young girl, "you are alone in the world; I heard it this evening from my father."

The voice of Rosarita, in pronouncing these words, was soft as the breeze that sighed through the groves of oranges; and her hand, falling as if by chance into that of Tiburcio, did not appear to shun the pressure given to it.

At the sight of this, the hand of Don Estevan gradually relaxed its hold upon the arm of Cuchillo.

"Yes," continued Tiburcio, "my mother died in poverty, though she has left me a valuable inheritance, and at the same time a legacy of vengeance. True, it is a dangerous secret of which I am the heir, for it has already been death to those who possessed it; nevertheless it will furnish the means to raise myself to an opulence like your own. The vengeance which I have sworn to accomplish must be delayed, but it shall not be forgotten. I shall yet seek the murderer of Arellanos."

At these words Cuchillo turned pale, impatiently grinding his teeth. His arm was no longer restrained, Don Estevan grasped it no more, for he saw that the hand of Rosarita was still pressed by that of Tiburcio.

"Here me further!" continued the young man. "About sixty leagues from here, in the heart of the Indian country, there is a placer of gold of incalculable richness; it was discovered by my adopted father. My mother on her death-bed gave me full directions to find the place; and all this gold may be mine, Rosarita, if you will only love me. Without your love I care nothing for it. What should I do with such riches?"

Tiburcio awaited the answer of Rosarita. That answer fell upon his heart like the tolling of a funeral knell.

"I hope, Tiburcio," said she, with a significant smile, "that this is only a *ruse* on your part to put me to the proof—I hope so, because I do not wish to believe that you have acted so vile a part as to make yourself master of a secret that belongs to another."

"The secret of another!" cried the young man in a voice hoarse with astonishment.

"Yes, a secret which belongs only to Don Estevan. I know it—"

Tiburcio at once fell from the summit of his dreams. So his secret, too, was lost to him as well as her whom he loved, this secret upon which he had built his sweetest hopes; and to add to the bitterness of his disappointment, she too—for whose sake alone he had valued it—she to accuse him of treason!

"Ah!" cried he, "Don Estevan knows of the Golden Valley? perhaps then he can tell me who murdered my father! Oh! my God!" cried he, striking the ground with his heel, "perhaps it was himself!"

"Pray God rather to protect you,—you will need all his grace!" cried a rough voice, which caused Rosarita to utter a cry of terror as she saw a dark form—that of a man—rushing forward and flinging himself upon Tiburcio.

The young man, before he could place himself in an attitude of defence, received a severe wound, and losing his balance fell to the ground. The next moment his enemy was over him. For some minutes the two struggled together in silence—nothing was heard but their loud quick breathing. The knife of Cuchillo, already stained with blood, had escaped from his hand, and lay gleaming upon the ground without his being able to reach it.

"Now, villain, we are quits," cried Tiburcio, who with an effort of supreme strength had got uppermost, and was kneeling upon the breast of the outlaw. "Villain!" repeated he, as he endeavoured to get hold of his poignard: "you shall die the death of an assassin."

Places had suddenly changed—Tiburcio was now the aggressor, but at this moment a third personage appeared upon the scene. It was Don Estevan.

"Hold," screamed Rosarita, "hold, for the love of the Holy Virgin! This young man is my father's guest; his life is sacred under our roof."

Don Estevan grasped the arm that was raised to strike Cuchillo, and as Tiburcio turned to see what thus interfered between him and his vengeance, the outlaw glided from under him.

Tiburcio now sprang up, rolled his serapé around his left arm, and holding it as a shield, stood with his body inclined backward, his left leg advanced, and his right hand firmly grasping his weapon, in the attitude of an ancient gladiator. He appeared for a moment as if choosing upon which of his antagonists he would first launch himself.

"You call this being quits!" cried Cuchillo, his breast still heaving from the pressure to Tiburcio's knee. "Your life belongs to me—I only lent it to you, and I shall now take it back."

"Come on, dog!" shouted Tiburcio, in answer; "and you too, Don Estevan, you cowardly assassin! you who pay for the murder of defenceless people."

The countenance of the Spaniard turned livid pale at this unexpected accusation. He instantly drew his dagger, and crying out:—"Down with him, Cuchillo!" rushed furiously forward to the attack.

No doubt Tiburcio would soon have succumbed before two such formidable antagonists, but at this moment a red light flashed upon the combatants, as Doña Rosarita, with a flaming torch in her hand, rushed forward between them.

The aspect of Tiburcio, who, despite the odds against him, and the blood that was running from his arm, still fearlessly maintained his defensive attitude, caused the heart of Rosarita to beat with sympathetic admiration. This sanguinary *dénouement* to their interview, was pleading the cause of the lover far more eloquently than either his reproaches or promises!

The first impulse of Rosarita was to fling herself into the arms of the young man so daring and beautiful. She was restrained only from following this impulse, by a feeling of feminine delicacy; and for an instant Tiburcio seemed the one about whom she was least concerned.

"Oh! my God!" cried she, "are you wounded? Don Estevan? Señor Cuchillo? Señor Arechiza! retire; for the love of the Virgin, let not the world know that a crime has been committed in our house."

The excited bearing of the young girl, her bosom heaving under the light tissue of her dress, her reboso floating behind her, mingled with the long dark tresses of her dishevelled hair—all these, added to the proud savage beauty of her countenance—commanded respect; and as if by enchantment, the weapons of the combatants were restored to their sheaths.

Cuchillo growled like a dog newly muzzled, while Don Estevan preserved a sombre silence. Both walked away from the ground, and their forms were soon lost in the darkness.

Tiburcio, with face upturned, his eyes still flashing with rage, his features illuminated with the red light of the torch, remained for some moments without changing his attitude. His features exhibited that superb expression that danger only magnifies into grandeur. Gradually, however, their tone became softened, and an air of melancholy succeeded it, as his eyes rested upon Rosarita. The young girl had suddenly become pale, under the reaction of such vivid emotions, as well as under the influence of the powerful sentiment now rekindled within her heart. Acting under this influence as well, she hastily arranged her scarf in order to cover her nude shoulders, and the palpitating movements of her bosom. Even her motive for this was misunderstood by Tiburcio.

"Rosarita!" he said, speaking with perfect calmness, "I might have doubted your words, but your actions have spoken more plainly. It was to my enemies you first ran, though my blood was spilling; all your fears appeared to be for Don Estevan."

"God knows that I do not deserve this reproach," said the young girl, as with a look of terror she saw the blood streaming to the ground. At the same instant she advanced to examine the wound.

Tiburcio repulsed her by stepping backward.

"It is too late," said he with a bitter smile, "the evil is done. Adieu! I have been too long your guest. The hospitality of your house is fatal to me. Under your roof my life has been threatened, my dearest hopes have been crushed! Adieu, Rosarita! Adieu!"

As he pronounced the last words, he turned and walked hastily away. There was a broken place in the wall of the enclosure, and towards this he directed his steps. A hundred paces beyond, the forest commenced, and the dark sombre trees were visible through the opening. The mysterious light he had already noticed, was still glimmering feebly above their tops.

"Where are you going, Tiburcio?" cried the young girl, her hands joined and her eyes filling with tears, "my father's roof will protect you."

Tiburcio only answered by a negative shake of the head.

"But yonder," continued Rosarita, pointing to the woods, "yonder, alone and without defence—danger—death will await you."

"God will send me friends," answered Tiburcio, glancing towards the distant light. "The hospitality of the wandering traveller—a sleep by his camp-fire—will be safer for me than that of your father's roof." And Tiburcio continued to advance towards the breach with a gentle but resolute step.

"For the love of heaven do not expose yourself to dangers that may perhaps arise when I am no longer present to protect you! I tell you out yonder you will be risking your life;" then giving to her voice a tone of persuasive softness, she continued, "In what place, Tiburcio, will you be safer than with me?"

Tiburcio's resolution was for a moment shaken, and he paused to make answer.

"One word, Rosarita!" said he; "say that you hate my rival as I hate him—say this, and I remain."

A violent conflict appeared to arise in the breast of Rosarita. Her bosom swelled with conflicting emotions, as she fixed upon Tiburcio a glance of tender reproach, but she remained silent.

To a man of Tiburcio's age the heart of a woman is a sealed book. Not till we have lost the attractions of youth—so powerful, despite its inexperience—are we able to penetrate the mysteries of the female heart—a sad compensation which God accords to the maturity of age. At thirty years Tiburcio would have remained. But he was yet only twenty-four; he had spent his whole life in the desert, and this was his first love.

"You will not say it? Adieu, then," cried he, "I am no longer your guest," and saying this, he leaped over the broken wall, before the young girl could offer any opposition to his departure.

Stupefied by this unexpected movement, she mounted upon the fragments that lay at the bottom of the wall, and stretching her arms toward the forest, she cried out—

"Tiburcio! Tiburcio! do not leave us so; do you wish to bring upon our house the malediction of heaven?"

But her voice was either lost to his ears, or he disdained to reply.

She listened a moment, she could hear the sound of his footsteps fast dying in the distance—until they could be heard no more.

"Oh! my God," cried she, falling upon her knees in an attitude of prayer, "protect this young man from the dangers that threaten him. Oh God! watch over him, for alas! he carries with him my heart."

Then forgetting in her grief her projects of ambition, the will of her father, all that deceptive confidence, which had kept silent the voice of a love, of the existence of which she was hitherto almost ignorant—the young girl rose hastily from her knees, once more mounted upon the wall, and in a heart-rending voice called out, "*Come back! Tiburcio; come back! I love only you!*"

But no answer was returned, and wrapping her face in her reboso, she sat down and wept.

Before returning to her chamber she cast one more look in the direction of the forest, but the woods were still enveloped in the obscurity of night; all was sombre and silent, though in the distance the feeble light was still glimmering over the tree tops. All at once it appeared for an instant to flash more brightly, as if offering a welcome to him who had no longer a home!

Chapter Twenty Six
An Abrupt Departure

Don Estevan and Cuchillo, on leaving the ground of the combat, returned to the alley of granadines; but for some time not a word passed between them. Don Estevan was buried in a profound meditation. More skilled than his coarse companion in the mysteries of the female heart, he had divined, before the end of the dialogue between Rosarita and Tiburcio, that the young girl felt for the latter a tender sentiment. It was true it was just germinating in her soul; but the accents of her voice, her gestures, and other signs, discovered to the experienced intelligence of Don Estevan that she really loved Tiburcio, though herself not yet aware of the extent of that love.

For Tiburcio knowing the secret of the Golden Valley, Don Estevan cared little—that was a matter of secondary importance; but Tiburcio's love reciprocated by Doña Rosarita was a very different affair. This at once presented a series of obstacles to the ambitious projects of the Spaniard. Tiburcio then must be got out of the way at all hazards, and at any price. Such are the terrible exigencies of ambition.

It only remained to adopt some plan; but the Spaniard was not then in the spirit to think of one. He was writhing at the inadvertence that had just happened.

"The clumsy fool!" he muttered, but loud enough for his companion to hear him.

"Is it of me your excellency is speaking?" inquired Cuchillo, in a tone that savoured strongly of his usual impudence.

"Who else could I mean, you sot? You who neither know how to use strength or stratagem! A woman has accomplished what you could not do! I have told you that this child is a giant to you; and had it not been for me—"

"Had it not been for you," interrupted the outlaw, "this young fellow would not now have been living to trouble us."

"How sir?" demanded Don Estevan.

"Last night, as I was bringing him to your bivouac, the fellow did an outrage to my honour, and actually threatened me. I was about putting an end to our differences by a shot from my carbine, when your precious old fool of a servant, Benito, came galloping up, and of course I had to renounce my design. So you see, the only good action I have ever done, has brought me to grief. Such is the reward of our virtue!"

"Speak for yourself, my droll fellow!" said the Spaniard, whose pride revolted at being thus classed with such company as the outlaw. "But if that could be outraged which does not exist, may I ask what attempt this young man made upon your honour?"

"I do not know myself—it was something that happened with my horse, who has the fault—"

Cuchillo interrupted himself as one who has made an imprudent speech.

"The fault of stumbling in the left fore-leg?" added Don Estevan. "I see—this old history of the murder of Arellanos."

"I did not murder him," cried the outlaw, impudently. "I had reasons not to like him; but I pardoned him, for all that."

"Oh! you are so magnanimous! But come, an end to these pleasantries. It remains for you to get this young man out of the way. I have my reasons for wishing it so—among others, he knows our secret. I gave you a half *onza* to save his life. To-day I have different views regarding him; and I promise to give you twenty *onzas* when I am assured that he is no longer alive."

"Agreed, Don Estevan; and in to-morrow's hunt of these wild horses, it will be strange if Tiburcio Arellanos don't knock his brains out against either a rock or the trunk of a tree, or at least get himself into some corner, where he won't be able to find his way out again. The only regret I have is, that I shall have to share these twenty onzas with my friends, Baraja and Oroche."

"To-morrow!" exclaimed Don Estevan; "and who knows but that to-morrow may be too late? Is the night not better for your purpose? Are you not three to one? Who is to assure you that to-morrow I may not change my mind?"

This threat seriously alarmed Cuchillo.

"Carramba! your excellency is quick to decide; you are not one of those who leave for to-morrow what should be done to-day. *Pues*—then—I shall try my best. In fact, it is very quiet here—I wonder the cries of this young woman have not startled the whole house. There's not a creature about."

Such was in reality the case. Notwithstanding the noise of the struggle between Tiburcio and his assailants, and later still, the cries of Rosarita, no one had been awakened. The vast extent of the building prevented these sounds from being heard, particularly as all the domestics of the hacienda, as well as the proprietor himself, were buried in a profound slumber.

Cuchillo now directed himself toward the apartment where he had left his comrades; Don Estevan returning at the same time to his own chamber. The moon once more poured her soft, silvery light upon the grove of oranges, as if no crime had ever been attempted in that tranquil spot.

Don Estevan did not go to rest; but for a long time paced to and fro across his ample chamber, with the air of one accustomed to watch over ambitious projects while others were asleep.

After a lapse of time, Cuchillo was heard knocking softly at his door; and as soon as it was opened, the hired assassin stepped in. His confused looks caused Don Estevan to tremble. Was the deed already done? He wished it, yet feared to ask the question. Cuchillo relieved him from his embarrassment by speaking first.

"My twenty onzas are gone to the devil!" said he, in a lugubrious tone.

"How?" hastily inquired Don Estevan.

"The bird has flown: the young man is no longer about the place."

"Gone!" exclaimed Don Estevan. "And you have let him escape?"

"How could I hinder him? This brute, Baraja, as well as Oroche, were both drunk with mezcal; and Diaz refused to assist me, point-blank. While I was endeavouring to arouse the other two, the fellow had taken leg bail through an opening in the wall of the garden—at least that's all we can make out."

"And how have you arrived at this conjecture?" asked Don Estevan, angrily striking the floor with his foot.

"Why, when we arrived at the place, the Doña Rosarita was clinging over the wall, no doubt guided there by Tiburcio. He could not be far off at the time, for she was still calling upon him to return; and judging by the love-speeches she was making, she must have earnestly desired it."

"She loves him, then?"

"Passionately—or her words and her accents are all deceit. 'Come back!' she cried, 'Tiburcio, come back! I love only you!' These were the last words I heard; for shortly after she left the wall, and went back to her room."

"We must to horse and pursue him!" cried Don Estevan, hurrying to make ready; "yes, there is no help for it now. The success of our expedition depends upon the life of this ragged fellow. Go! arouse Benito and the others. Tell them to saddle the horses. Warn your friends in the chamber that we must be *en route* in an hour. Away! while I awake Don Augustin and the Senator."

"Just as I have known him for twenty years," muttered Cuchillo, as he hastened to his companions, "always awake, always ready for the greatest obstacles. Well, if with his character he has not made way in his own country, I fear that in Europe perseverance and energy are not worth much."

Don Estevan, as soon as Cuchillo had left him, spent a few minutes in putting himself once more in travelling costume, and then repaired to the chamber of the Senator. He found the door open—as is the custom in a country where people spend most of their lives outside their houses. The moon was beaming full through the large window, and her light illumined the chamber as well as the couch upon which the Senator was sleeping.

"What is it, Don Estevan?" cried the Senator, suddenly leaping up in his bed; "Señor Estevan, I should say." Tragaduros had been dreaming of the court of the King of Spain. "What is it, your grace?"

"I come to take leave of you, and to give you my final instructions."

"Eh! what?" said the Senator. "Is the hour late? or have I been three days asleep?"

"No," gravely replied the Spaniard, "but there is a serious danger that menaces our projects—both yours and mine. This young rustic, whom we found on the road, knows all about the Golden Valley; and what is still worse, he loves Doña Rosarita, and Doña Rosarita loves him."

Tragaduros, instead of starting up at this announcement, sank back upon his pillow, crying out.

"Adieu then to the million dollars of dowry! adieu to those beautiful plains covered with horses and cattle, which I already believed my own! adieu to the honours of the court of *Carlos el Primero!*"

"Come! all is not yet lost," said Don Estevan. "The evil may be remedied if taken in time. This young fellow has quitted the hacienda. It will be necessary to follow and find him before he gets out of the way. So much the worse for him, if his evil star is in opposition to yours."

The Spaniard said no more of his designs with regard to Tiburcio. As to the Senator, it was of little importance to him how he was to be disembarrassed of so dangerous a rival, so long as he himself should not be troubled with the matter.

"Whatever may be the end of it," added Don Estevan, "one thing is certain—the young fellow will never be allowed to come back to this house, for I shall arrange that with Don Augustin. You will therefore be master of the situation, and will have everything your own way. Make the young lady love you—it will be easy enough—your rival will be absent, he may be *dead*—for these deserts are dangerous, and you know the old proverb about absence?"

"I shall make myself irresistible!" said the Senator, "for since yesterday I feel as if I was on fire about this lovely creature, who appears to have come down direct from heaven—and with—such a dowry!"

"No man ever aimed at an object more desirable than this immense dowry and this fair flower of the desert. Spare no pains, therefore, to win both the lady and the fortune."

"If necessary I shall spin for her, as Hercules at the feet of Omphalé."

"Ha, ha ha!" laughed the Spaniard. "If Hercules had any merits in the eyes of Omphalé, it was not on account of his spinning, but because he was Hercules. No—do better than spin. To-morrow Don Augustin has a hunt among his wild steeds; there will be an opportunity for you to distinguish yourself by some daring exploit. Mount one of the wildest of the horses, for the honour of the beautiful eyes of Rosarita, and after having tamed him, ride him up panting into her presence. That will gain you more grace than handling the thread and distaff *à la Hercules*."

The Senator responded to these counsels with a sigh: and Don Estevan, having given him further instructions as to how he was to act during the absence of the expedition, took leave of him, and repaired to the chamber of Don Augustin.

The clank of his heavy spurs, as he entered the sleeping apartment of the haciendado, awoke the latter—who on opening his eyes and seeing his nocturnal visitor in full riding-costume, cried out:

"What! is it time to set forth upon the chase? I did not know the hour was so late!"

"No, Don Augustin," replied the Spaniard, "but for me the hour has come to set forth upon a more serious pursuit than that of wild horses. I hasten to pursue the enemy of your house—the man who has abused your hospitality, and who if not captured, may bring ruin upon all our projects."

"The enemy of my house! the man who has abused my hospitality!" cried the haciendado, starting up in astonishment, and seizing a long Toledo rapier that hung by the side of his bed, "Who is the man that has acted so, Don Estevan?"

"Be calm!" said Don Estevan, smiling inwardly at the contrast exhibited between the spirit of the haciendado and the pusillanimity of the Senator. "Be calm! the enemy I speak of is no longer under your roof—he has fled beyond the reach of your just vengeance."

"But who is he?" impatiently demanded Don Augustin.

"Tiburcio Arellanos."

"What! Tiburcio Arellanos my enemy! I do not believe it. Loyalty and courage are the characteristics of the young man. I shall never believe him a traitor."

"He knows the situation of the Golden Valley! Furthermore, he loves your daughter!"

"Is that all? Why, I was aware of these facts already!"

"Yes, but your daughter loves him—perhaps you were not aware of that fact?"

Don Estevan here detailed the events that had just transpired, and which proved that the passion of the young gambusino was reciprocated by Rosarita.

"Well!" calmly rejoined Don Augustin; "so much the worse for the Senator!"

This reply could not fail to astonish the Spaniard, and create a feeling of disappointment.

"Remember," said he, "remember, Don Augustin Peña; that you have engaged your word—not only to me, not only to Tragaduros, but to a prince of the blood royal of Spain, from whose brow this apparently simple incident—the caprice of a young girl—may snatch a crown. Think too of your country—its future glory and greatness—all dependent on the promise you have given—"

"Why," interrupted Don Augustin, "why set forth all these considerations? After my promise has been given, I never retract my word. But it is only to the Duke de Armada I have engaged myself, and he alone can free me from that engagement. Are you satisfied with this assurance?"

"How could I be otherwise?" cried the Spaniard, holding out his hand to the noble haciendado. "Enough! I have your word, it will be necessary forme to leave you without farther delay. This young fellow may find comrades to accompany him to the Golden Valley. There is not a moment, therefore, to be lost. I must at once proceed to Tubac. Adieu, my friend, adieu!"

Don Augustin would have risen to accompany his guest to the gates, but the Spaniard would not permit him, and they parted without farther ceremony.

When Don Estevan reached the court-yard, his attendants and domestics were found in readiness to depart. The mules had been packed, and the *remuda* collected in charge of the driver. The followers, Cuchillo, Baraja, Oroche, and Pedro Diaz were already in their saddles—the last mounted on a magnificent and fiery steed, which told that the generous haciendado had kept his promise.

Chapter Twenty Seven
The Lone Fire in the Forest

The motive for this hasty departure from the hacienda was unknown only to Benito and the other domestics. The cavalier adventurers were aware of its object though two of them, Baraja and Oroche, had no very clear understanding upon the matter. The fumes of the mezcal were still in their heads, and it was with difficulty they could balance themselves in the saddle. They were sensible of their situation, and did their best to conceal it from the eyes of the chief.

"Am I straight in my stirrups?" whispered Oroche addressing himself to Baraja.

"Straight as a bamboo!" replied the other. "Do I appear firm?" inquired he in turn.

"Firm as a rock," was the response.

Thanks to the efforts they were making to keep themselves upright, Don Estevan, as he glanced over the ranks of his followers, did not observe anything amiss. Cuchillo, however, knowing that they were not in a fit state for inspection regarded them with an anxious glance.

As Don Estevan was about to mount, the outlaw rode up to him, and pointing to the others with an expressive gesture, said, "If your honour desires me to act as guide, and give the order of march, I am ready to enter upon my duties."

"Very well," replied Don Estevan, springing into the saddle, "commence at any moment, but let us be gone as soon as possible."

"Benito!" shouted the newly appointed guide, "take the *remuda* and *recua* in advance; you will wait for us at the bridge of the *Salto de Agua*."

Benito, with the other attendants, obeyed the order in silence; and the moment after were moving with their respective charges along the road leading to Tubac. A little later the cavalcade rode out of the court-yard of the hacienda, and turning round the wall of the enclosure, guided by Cuchillo, proceeded toward the breach through which Tiburcio had passed. The guide was riding by the side of Don Estevan.

"We have found his traces," said he to the chief, as they moved forward; "he is down in the forest."

"Where?"

"Do you see a light yonder shining through the trees?"

The mysterious light was gleaming, just as Tiburcio had first seen it from his window. It was to this that Cuchillo directed the attention of the chief.

"Yes," replied the latter, "what of it?"

"It is the camp-fire of some travellers; and in all probability the fellow will be found there. So," continued he, with a hideous smile, "we are going to give chase to a wild colt—which will be better than hunting Don Augustin's wild horses—and here are the three hunters."

As the outlaw said this, he pointed with his whip, first to himself, and then to his two comrades, Oroche and Baraja.

"They have both espoused our quarrel," he added.

"From what motive?" inquired the Spaniard.

"That motive which the hound has in taking the part of the hunter against the stag," answered the outlaw, with a significant smile; "they only follow their instincts, and they are two animals with formidable teeth."

At this moment the moon shone out, and gleaming upon the carbines and knives of the two adventurers, seemed to confirm the assertion of Cuchillo. But the light proved disadvantageous to Baraja and Oroche, for it enabled Don Estevan to perceive that they were far from steady in their seats.

"Why, these fellows are drunk!" cried he, turning upon the guide a look of furious reproach. "Are these the assistants you count upon?"

"True, your honour," replied Cuchillo, "they are not exactly sober; but I hope soon to cure them. I know of a remedy that will set them all right in five minutes. It is the fruit of the *jocuistle*, which grows abundantly in these parts. I shall find it as soon as we have reached the woods."

Don Estevan was forced to swallow his chagrin in silence. It was not the time for vain recriminations; and above all, Tiburcio had first to be found, before the services of either of the inebriated gentlemen would be called into requisition.

In a few seconds' time the party had reached the breach in the wall. Cuchillo dismounted, and striking a light, pointed out to the others the traces left by Tiburcio. There could be seen some fragments freshly fallen from the wall, evidently detached by the feet of one passing over; but what was of more consequence, they were stained with drops of blood. This must have been Tiburcio's.

"You see," said the outlaw to Don Estevan, "that he must have passed this way. Ah! if I had only given him another inch or two. After all," added he, speaking to himself, "it is better I didn't. I shall be twenty onzas the richer that I didn't settle with him then. Now," continued he, once more raising his voice, "where can he have gone, unless to yonder fire in the woods?"

A little farther on in the direction of the forest, other spots of fresh blood were discovered upon the dry calcareous surface of the soil. This appeared to confirm the conjecture of the guide—that Tiburcio had proceeded towards the camp-fire.

"If your honour," resumed Cuchillo, addressing himself to his chief, "will go forward in company with the Señor Diaz, you will reach a stream running upon your left. By following down its bank for some distance, you will come to a bridge constructed with three or four trunks of trees. It is the bridge of the *Salto de Agua*. Just before reaching it, your honour will see a thick wood on the right. Under cover of that you can remain, until we three have finished our affair and rejoin you. Afterwards we can overtake the domestics. I have ordered them forward, for the reason that such people should not be privy either to our designs or actions."

In this arrangement Cuchillo exhibited the consummate skill of the practiced bandit. Don Estevan, without offering any opposition to his plan, rode off as directed, in company with Diaz; while the outlaw, with his two chosen acolytes turned their horses' heads in the direction of the fire.

"The fire betokens a halt of travellers, beyond doubt," remarked Diaz to Don Estevan; "but who these travellers can be is a thing that puzzles me."

"Travellers like any others, I suppose," rejoined the Spaniard, with an air of abstraction.

"No, that is not likely. Don Augustin Peña is known for his generous hospitality for twenty leagues around. It is not probable that these travellers should have halted so near his hacienda without knowing it. They must be strangers to the country I fancy, or if not, they have no good purpose in camping where they are."

Pedro Diaz was making almost the same observations that had occurred to Tiburcio at an earlier hour of the night.

Meanwhile, Cuchillo, with his two comrades, advanced towards the edge of the forest. As soon as they had reached it the guide dismounted from his horse.

"Stay here," said he, "while I go fetch something to cure you of your ill-timed drunkenness."

So saying he glided in among the trees, and in a few seconds came out again, carrying with him several oblong yellow-coloured fruits that resembled ripe bananas. They were the fruits of the *jocuistle*, a species of *asimina*, whose juice is an infallible remedy against the effects of intoxication. The two inebriates ate of the fruit according to Cuchillo's direction; and in a minute or two their heads were cleared of the fumes of the mezcal as if by enchantment.

"Now to business!" cried Cuchillo, without listening to the apologies his comrades were disposed to make—"to business! You will dismount and lead your horses forward by the bridle, until you can see the fire; and when you hear the report of my gun, be ready, for I shall then fall back upon you."

"All right," responded Oroche, "we are both ready—the Señor Baraja and myself—to sacrifice all private interests to the common good."

Cuchillo now parted with the two, leading his horse ahead of them. A little farther on he tied the animal to the branch of a tree, and then stooping downward he advanced on foot. Still farther on he dropped upon his hands and knees, and crept through the underwood like a jaguar stealing upon its prey.

Now and then he paused and listened. He could hear the distant lowing of the wild bulls, and the crowing of the cocks at the hacienda, mingled with the lugubrious notes of the great wood owl, perched near him upon a branch. He could hear the distant sound of water—the cataract of the *Salto de Agua*—and, in the same direction, the continuous howling of the jackals.

Again the assassin advanced—still creeping as before. Presently he saw before him the open glade, lit up by the flame of the camp-fire. On the edge nearest him, stood a huge button-wood tree, from whose base extended a number of flat ridge-like processes, resembling the bastions of a fortification. He perceived that, behind these he would be concealed from the light of the fire; while he himself could command a view of every object within the glade.

In another moment he was crouching under the trunk of the button-wood. His eyes gleamed with a fierce joy, as he gazed in the direction of the fire, around which he could distinguish the forms of three men—two of them seated, the other stretched along the ground, and apparently asleep.

Chapter Twenty Eight
The Wood-Rangers

Behind the Hacienda del Venado—that is, to the northward of it—the surface of the country was still in a state of nature; as we have already said, the edge of the forest lay almost within gun-shot of the walls; and this vast tract of woods extended for many leagues to the north, till it ended in the great deserts of Tubac.

The only road that trended in a northerly direction, was that leading to the Presidio of Tubac—though in reality it was not a road, but simply an Indian trail. At a short distance beyond the hacienda, it was crossed by a turbulent and rapid stream—the same that passed near the house— augmented by several tributaries that joined it in the woods. Where the road crossed it, and for a long distance above and below, this stream partook rather of the nature of a torrent, running in a deep bed, between rocky banks—a *cañon*. Over this cañon the crossing was effected by means of a rude bridge consisting simply of the trunks of two or three trees, laid side by side, and reaching from bank to bank. About half-way between the hacienda and this bridge, and but a short distance from the side of the road, was the fire which had already attracted so much attention.

This fire had been kindled near the centre of a little glade, but its flame cast a red glare upon the trees at a distance, until the grey bark of the button-wood, the pale foliage of the acacias, and the scarlet leaves of the sumac, all appeared of one colour: while the darker llianas, stretching from tree to tree, encircled the little glade with a series of festoons.

At the hour when Tiburcio was about leaving the hacienda, two persons were seated by this fire, in the attitude of men who were resting after a day of fatigue. These persons were the trappers, who had already made their appearance at La Poza.

There was nothing remarkable in two men having made their camp-fire in the woods; it was their proximity to a hacienda—and that, too, the Hacienda del Venado—that rendered the fact significant. The trappers knew well enough that the hacienda was close at hand; it followed, then, that they had some reasons of their own for not availing themselves of its hospitality. A large pile of fagots lay near the fire, evidently collected to feed it, and this proved that the men who had kindled it intended to pass the night on the spot.

The appearance of these two men would have been striking, even in the light of day; but under that of the fire it was picturesque—almost fantastic. The older of the two was habited in a costume half Indian, half Canadian; on his head was a sort of bonnet, shaped like a truncated cone, and made out of the skin of a fox; a blue striped cotton shirt covered his shoulders, and beside him upon the ground lay a sort of woollen surtout—the *capote* of the Canadians. His legs were encased in leathern leggins, reaching from the thigh downward to the ankle; but instead of moccasins he wore upon his feet a pair of strong iron-bound shoes, capable of lasting him for a couple of years at the least. A large buffalo-horn, suspended from the shoulder, contained his powder; and upon his right side hung a leathern pouch, well filled with bullets. In fine, a long rifle, with a barrel nearly six feet in length, rested near his hand; and this, with a large hunting-knife stuck in his belt, completed his equipment. His hair already showed symptoms of turning grey and a long scar which crossed his temples, and appeared to run all round his head, showed that if his scalp was still there he had some time or other run the risk of having it *raised*. His bronzed complexion denoted a long exposure to sun, wind, and rain; but for all this, his countenance shone with an expression of good-humour. This was in conformity with his herculean strength—for nature usually bestows upon these colossal men a large share of kind-heartedness.

The other trapper appeared to be some five or six years younger; and although by no means a man of small stature, he was but a pigmy alongside his gigantic companion. His countenance also lacked the serenity which distinguished that of the other—his black eyes gave out an expression of boldness approaching to effrontery; and the play of his features indicated a man whose passions, fiery by nature, once aroused, would lead him into acts of violence—even of cruelty. Everything about him bespoke the second trapper to be a man of different race from his companion—a man in whose veins ran the hot blood of the south. Although his style of dress did not differ very much from that of his comrade, there were some points in it that denoted him to be more of a horseman. Nevertheless, his well-worn shoes bore witness to his having made more than one long journey on foot.

The Canadian, half reclining upon the grass, was watching with especial interest a large piece of mutton, which, supported upon a spit of iron-wood, was frizzling and sputtering in the blaze of the fire. He appeared to enjoy the savoury odour that proceeded from the joint; and so much was his attention taken up by his gastronomic zeal, that he scarce listened to what his companion was saying.

"Well, I have often told you," said the latter, "that when one is on the trace of an enemy, whether it be an Indian or a white, one is pretty sure of coming on his tracks somewhere."

"Yes," rejoined the Canadian; "but you forgot that we shall just have time to reach Arispe, to receive the pay for our two years' campaign; besides, by our not going to the hacienda, we lose the bounty upon these three skins, and miss selling them besides."

"I never forget my interests," replied the other; "no more than I do the vows which I make: and the best proof of it is, that twenty years ago I made one which I believe I shall now be able to accomplish. We can always force them to pay us what is due at Arispe, and we shall find many an opportunity of getting rid of the skins: but the chance which has turned up in the middle of these deserts, of bringing me in contact with the man against whom I have sworn vengeance may not offer again during my whole lifetime."

"Bah!" exclaimed the Canadian, "vengeance is like many other kinds of fruit, sweet till you have tasted it, and afterwards bitter as gall."

"For all that, Señor Bois-Rose, you do not appear to practise your own doctrine with the Apaches, Sioux, Crows, and other Indians with whom you are at enmity! Your rifle has cracked many a skull—to say nothing of the warriors you have ripped open with your knife!"

"Oh! that is different, Pepé. Some of these would have robbed me of my peltries—others would have taken my scalp, and came very near doing so, as you see—besides, it is blessed bread to clear the prairies of these red vermin; but I have never sought to revenge myself against one of my own race and colour. I never hated one of my own kind sufficiently to kill him."

"Ah! Bois-Rose; it is just those of one's own race we hate most—that is when they have given us the reason for doing so—and this man has furnished me with such motives to hate him as can never be forgotten. Twenty years have not blunted my desire for vengeance; though, on account of the great distance that separated us, I supposed I should never find an opportunity of fulfilling my vow. Strange it is that two men, with relations like ours, should turn up together in the middle of these desert plains. Well! strange though it be, I do not intend to let the chance escape me."

Pepé appeared to have fixed his resolution upon this matter, and so firmly that his companion saw the folly of attempting to dissuade him by any further advice. The Canadian, moreover, was of an easy disposition, and readily yielded to the arguments of a friend.

"After all," said he, "perhaps, if I fully understood your motives, I might entirely approve of the resolution you have made."

"I can give them in two words," rejoined he whom the Canadian was addressing as Pepé. "It is just twenty years, as I have already told you, since I was a carabinier in the service of her Catholic majesty. I should have been content with my position and the amount of pay, had it only been *paid* which unfortunately it was not. We were obliged to do the duty of coast-guard as well, and this would have done well enough had there been any smuggling, with the capture of which we might have indemnified ourselves; but there was none. What a fool a smuggler would have been to have ventured on a coast, guarded by two hundred fellows at their wits' end with hunger! Well, then I reasoned that if any smuggler was to land it could only be with the concurrence of our captain, and I suspected that the captain would make no objection to such an arrangement—for he himself was, like the rest of us, a creditor of the government. In such case he would cast around among us for the man in whom he *could most* confide, and that would be he who was noted as being most careless upon his post. I resolved, therefore, to become the captain's confidential sentry.

"To arrive at this object I pretended to be all the day asleep; and, notwithstanding the reprimands I received, I managed also to be found asleep upon my post at all hours of the night. I succeeded in my design. The captain soon learnt all about my somnolent habits, and chose me for his favourite sentinel."

At this moment the Canadian detached the mutton from the spit, and having cut a large "hunk" from it with his knife passed the joint to his comrade.

This interrupted the narrative, for both narrator and listener were hungry. The two now sat face to face, their legs forming a sort of an ellipse, with the roast mutton in the centre, and for several minutes a formidable gritting of teeth, as huge pieces of the mutton passed through them, were the only sounds that broke the stillness of the night.

Chapter Twenty Nine
Old Souvenirs

"I have said then," resumed Pepé, after a time, "that I pretended to be always asleep. The *ruse* succeeded equal to my best expectations, and one night the captain sent for me. Good! said I to myself, there's an eel under the stone—the captain is going to confide a post to me. Just as I had anticipated he sent me to sleep—at least he thought so—on a most important post; but for all that I did not sleep a wink during the whole of that night."

Here Pepé paused for a moment, in order to swallow an enormous mouthful of the roast mutton, that hindered the free use of the tongue.

"To be brief, then," resumed he, "a boat arrived with men, and I permitted it to land. It was only afterwards that I learnt that it was no smuggling business these men were bent upon, but an affair of blood—of murder; and the thought that I was instrumental in aiding the assassins causes me to this hour a feeling of remorse. I did not conceal what I knew. Afterwards I denounced the murderer, by way of atoning for my fault. A trial took place, but as in Spain justice goes to the highest bidder, the assassin was set free, and I became a victim. I was drummed out of my regiment, and transported to the fisheries of Ceuta, on the unhealthy coast of Africa. There I was compelled to remain for many years, till at last having made my escape, after a thousand perilous adventures, I found myself on the prairies of America."

"It was a rich man then—some powerful person—whom you denounced?"

"Yes; a grand señor. It was the old story of the pot of clay broken against the pot of iron. But the desert here has no distinctions; and, by the Virgin of Atocha! I shall prove that before many suns have gone over my head. Ah! if I only had here a certain alcalde of the name of Don Ramon Cohecho, and his damned friend, one Señor Cagatinta, I fancy I should make them pass an uncomfortable quarter of an hour."

"Very well, then," said Bois-Rose, seeing the other had finished his narrative; "very well. I quite approve of your intentions—let the journey to Arispe stand over."

"It is an old story," said Pepé, in conclusion; "and if for ten years you have been teaching me to handle a rifle, after many more spent in the usage of a carbine in the service of her Catholic majesty, surely I should be able to manage it now. I think I would scarcely miss an object as large as him whom you have seen at the head of those horsemen journeying towards the hacienda."

"Yes—yes," replied the Canadian, with a laugh; "but I remember the time, Pepé, when you missed many a buffalo twice as big as he. Nevertheless, I fancy I have made a passable shot of you at last, although you still persist in mistaking the ear of an otter for his eye, which always depreciates the value of the skin. Well, you know that I myself was not brought up on the prairies. I was a sailor for many long years; and perhaps I should have continued one but for—a sad event—a melancholy affair—but what good is there in speaking of that which is no more. Let the past be past! I find the life of the desert something like that on the ocean—once a man has got used to it he cannot easily quit it."

"Yes," rejoined Pepé; "the life of the forest and prairie has its charms, and for my part—"

"Hush!" whispered the Canadian, interrupting the speech of his comrade and placing himself in an attitude to listen. "I heard a rustle among the branches. Other ears than mine may be listening to you."

Pepé cast a glance in the direction whence the sounds had been heard. The dark form of a man was perceived among the trees coming from the direction of the hacienda.

It was evident that the man was not trying to approach by stealth, for his form was erect and he made no attempt to conceal himself behind the branches.

This would have freed the mind of Pepé from all suspicion, but for the circumstance that the stranger appeared to be coming direct from the hacienda.

"Who goes there?" he hailed in a loud tone, as the dark shadow was seen entering the glade.

"One who seeks an asylum by your fire," was the ready reply, delivered in rather a feeble voice.

"Shall we allow him to come on? or beg him to continue his journey?" muttered Pepé to the Canadian.

"God forbid we should deny him! Perhaps they have refused him a lodging up at the house; and that voice, which I think I have heard before, plainly denotes that he is fatigued—perhaps ill."

"Come on, Señor!" called out Pepé, without hesitating farther; "you are welcome to our fire and our mess; come on!"

At this invitation the stranger advanced. It is needless to say that it was Tiburcio Arellanos, whose cheeks as he came within the light of the fire betrayed by their paleness the traces of some violent emotion, or else of some terrible malady. This pallor, however, was partly caused by the blood which he had lost in the conflict with Cuchillo.

As soon as the features of Tiburcio came fairly under the light, the trappers recognised him as the young man they had met at La Poza; but the ex-carabinier was struck with some idea which caused him to make an involuntary gesture. The Canadian, on the other hand, regarded the new-comer with that expression of condescending kindness which age often bestows upon youth.

"Have you parted with the gentlemen in whose company we saw you?" asked Pepé of Tiburcio.

"Yes."

"Perhaps you are not aware that there is a house close by. I do not know the owner, but I fancy he would not refuse you a night's lodging, and he could entertain you better than we. Perhaps," continued he, observing that Tiburcio made no reply, "you have been up to the house already?"

"I have," answered Tiburcio. "I have no reproach to make against its owner, Don Augustin Peña; he has not refused me hospitality; but there are other guests under his roof with whom my life is not safe."

"Oh, that!" exclaimed Pepé, appearing to become more interested; "has anything happened to you?"

Tiburcio lifted his serapé, exhibiting the wound in his right arm from which the blood was yet oozing.

Both Pepé and the Canadian rose hastily to their feet and stepped forward to examine the wound. Having done so, they immediately set about dressing it, which they effected with as much dexterity and despatch as might have been shown by practised surgeons; at the same time the rude physiognomy of each was marked by an expression of interest almost amounting to tenderness. While the Canadian kept bathing the wound with water from his canteen, Pepé proceeded into the woods in search of a peculiar plant noted for its healing properties. This plant was the *oregano*. Presently he returned, bringing with him several slices which he had cut from the succulent stem of the plant; the pulp of these, mashed between two stones, was placed over the wound, and then secured by Tiburcio's own scarf of China crape wound several times around the arm; nothing more could be done than await the effect of the application.

"Now," said the Canadian, "you will soon feel better. There is no danger of inflammation—nothing beats the oregano for preventing that, and you need not be afraid of fever. Meanwhile, if you feel inclined, there's a bit of roast mutton and a glass of *eau de vie* at your service; after which you had best lie down by the fire and take some sleep—for I can see that you're weary."

"In truth," replied Tiburcio, "I am fatigued. I thank you for your offer, but I do not feel inclined either to eat or drink; I have more need of sleep, and with your permission shall try and get some. One request I would make of you: that you will not permit me to sleep too long; there are reasons why I should soon be awake again."

"Very well," said Pepé; "we don't want your reasons. If you wish us to watch the hacienda, I beg you will only say so, and you shall have two pair of good eyes at your service; therefore make your mind easy, and sleep without fear of any enemy coming upon you unawares."

Tiburcio stretched himself upon the grass, and overcome by fatigue and the many violent emotions he had that day experienced, soon fell into a lethargic slumber.

For some time Bois-Rose sat regarding the sleeper in silence, but with an air of strange interest.

"What age do you think he is?" he at length inquired of his comrade.

"Twenty-four, I should fancy," replied the ex-coast-guard.

"Just what I was thinking," said the Canadian, speaking in a tone of half soliloquy, while a melancholy expression appeared to tone down his rude physiognomy. "Yes, just the age he ought to be if still alive."

"He! who are you talking of?" brusquely interrupted his companion, in whose heart the words of the Canadian seemed to find an echo.

"No matter," said Bois-Rose, still speaking in a tone of melancholy; "the past is past; and when it has not been as one would have wished it, it is better forgotten. But come! let us have done with idle regrets and finish our supper—such souvenirs always spoil my appetite."

"The same with me," agreed Pepé, as he seized hold of a large mutton-bone, and commenced an attack upon it in a fashion that proved that his appetite was not yet quite gone.

After a while Pepé again broke the silence.

"If I had the pleasure," said he, "of a personal acquaintance with this Don Augustin Peña, who appears to be the proprietor here, I would compliment him upon the fine quality of his mutton; and if I thought his horses were of as good a sort, I think I should be tempted to borrow one—one horse would never be missed out of the great herds we have seen galloping about, no more than a sheep out of his vast flocks; and to me a good horse would be a treasure."

"Very well," said the Canadian. "If you feel inclined for a horse, you had better have one; it will be no great loss to the owner, and may be useful to us. If you go in search of one, I can keep watch over this young fellow, who sleeps as if he hadn't had a wink for the last month."

"Most probably no one will come after him; nevertheless, Bois-Rose, keep your eye open till I return. If anything happens, three howls of the coyote will put me on my guard."

As he said this, Pepé took up a lazo that lay near, and turning his face in the direction in which he was most likely to find a drove of horses, he walked off into the woods.

Bois-Rose was left alone. Having thrown some dry branches upon the fire, in order to produce a more vivid light, he commenced regarding anew the young man who was asleep; but after a while spent in this way he stretched himself alongside the prostrate body, and appeared also to slumber.

The night-breeze caused the foliage to rustle over the heads of these two men, as they lay side by side. Neither had the least suspicion that they were here re-united by strange and providential circumstances—that twenty years before, they had lain side by side—then lulled to sleep by the sound of the ocean, just as now by the whispering murmurs of the forest.

Chapter Thirty
Bois-Rose and Fabian

For twenty years the murderer of the Countess de Mediana had gone unpunished. For twenty years the justice of heaven had remained suspended; but the time of its accomplishment was not far off. Soon was it to open its solemn assizes; soon would it call together accuser and criminal, witness and judge—not from one part of a country to another, but from opposite sides of the globe; and, as if led by some invisible hand, all would have to obey the terrible summons.

Fabian de Mediana and the Canadian sailor lay side by side—just as they had done twenty years ago, at three thousand leagues distance from Sonora. And yet they had no suspicion of ever having met before, though a single chance word might at that moment have brought either to the memory of the other.

It was just about this time that Don Estevan and his party rode off from the hacienda.

The Canadian, according to the counsel of his comrade Pepé, slept with one eye open. At short intervals he contrived to awake himself, and raising his head slightly, cast around him a scrutinising glance. But on each of these occasions, the light of the fire showed him Tiburcio still tranquilly asleep; and this appearing to satisfy him, he would again compose himself as before.

About an hour had passed, when the sound of heavy footsteps awakened him once more, and listening a moment, he distinguished them as the hoof-strokes of a horse.

A few moments after, Pepé made his appearance within the circle of the blaze, leading a horse at the end of his lazo—a magnificent animal, that snorted and started back at sight of the fire. Pepé, however, had already given him more than one lesson, and his obedience was nearly complete; so that, after a short conflict, the trapper succeeded in bringing him nearer and attaching him to the trunk of a tree.

"Well," said Pepé, wiping the perspiration from his forehead with an old ragged handkerchief, "I've had a tough struggle with him; but he's worth it, I fancy. What think you, Bois-Rose? Isn't he the most splendid quadruped that ever galloped through these woods?"

In truth it was a beautiful creature, rendered more beautiful by the terror which he was exhibiting at the moment, as he stood with his fine limbs stretched, his head thrown high in the air, his mane tossed over his wild savage eyes, and his nostrils spread and frothy. Strange enough that fear, which renders vile and degraded the lord of the creation, should have an opposite effect on most of the lower animals—especially on the horse. This beautiful creature under its impulse only appears more beautiful!

Little as Bois-Rose delighted in horse-flesh, he could not withhold his approval of the capture which his comrade had made.

"He looks well enough," was his sober reply; "but he'll be a rough mount, I reckon."

"No doubt of that," assented Pepé. "I know he'll be rough at first; but the main thing was to get hold of him. I had a lucky hand to hook him as I did."

"I hope your neck will prove as lucky as your hand. For my part, I'd rather walk ten leagues than be on his back for ten minutes. But see, comrade!" continued the big trapper, pointing to the stars, "they're gone down yonder! you'll need some sleep before morning. Lie down while I take my turn of the watch."

"I'll take your advice," replied Pepé, at the same time stretching himself out upon his back, with his feet to the fire—in which attitude he was soon asleep.

The Canadian rose to his feet, took several turns round the fire—as if to drive away any remains of sleep that might be lurking in his eyes—then sat down again, with his back resting against the stump of a tree.

He had not been long seated before he got up once more, and, approaching with caution, stood over Tiburcio. For several minutes he remained in this attitude, attentively examining the features of the young man: he then returned to his seat by the stump.

"Just about *his* age, if he is still living," muttered he to himself. "But what chance have I to recognise in a grown man the features of an infant scarce four years old?"

A smile of disdain played for an instant on his lips, as if he were chiding himself for the silliness of his conjectures.

"And yet," he continued, his countenance changing its expression, "I have seen and taken part in too many strange events—I have been too long face to face with Nature—to doubt the power of Providence. Why should I consider this a miracle? It was not one when I chanced upon the boat adrift that carried that poor infant and its murdered mother! No, it was the hand of God. Why might not the same hand restore him to me in the midst of the desert? The ways of Providence are inscrutable."

As if this reflection had given birth to new hopes, the Canadian again rose to his feet, and approaching, stooped once more over the prostrate form of Tiburcio.

"How often," said he, "have I thus gazed on my little Fabian as he slept! Well, whoever you are, young man," continued he, "you have not come to my fire without finding a friend. May God do for my poor Fabian what I am disposed to do for you!"

Saying this, he once again returned to his seat, and remained for a long time reflecting upon incidents that had transpired twenty years before in the Bay of Biscay.

It should here be stated that up to this hour Bois-Rose and Pepé had not the slightest suspicion that they had ever met, before their chance encounter upon the prairies of America. In reality they had never met—farther than that they had been within musket-range of each other. But up to this hour Pepé knew not that his trapping comrade was the gigantic smuggler he had fired at from the beach of Ensenada; and Bois-Rose was equally ignorant that Pepé was the coast-guard whose "obstinacy and clumsiness" he had spoken of to his lieutenant.

The cause of this mutual ignorance of each other's past was that neither of them had ever mentioned the word Elanchovi in the hearing of the other. The Canadian had never thought of communicating the incidents of that night to his prairie comrade; and Pepé, on his side, would have given much to have blotted them altogether from the pages of his memory.

The night became more chilly as the hours passed on, and a damp dew now fell upon the grass and the foliage of the trees. It did not wake the sleepers, however, both of whom required a long rest.

All at once the silence was broken by the horse of Pepé, that neighed loudly and galloped in a circle at the end of his lazo: evidently something had affrighted him. Bois-Rose suddenly started from his reverie, and crept silently forward, both ear and eye set keenly to reconnoitre. But nothing could be heard or seen that was unusual; and after a while he glided back to his seat.

The noise had awakened Tiburcio, who, raising himself into a sitting posture, inquired its cause.

"Nothing," answered the trapper, whose denial, however, was scarce sincere. "Something indeed," continued he, "has frightened the horse. A jaguar, I fancy, that scents the skins of his companions, or, more likely, the remains of our roast mutton. By the way, you can eat a bit now; I have kept a couple of pieces for you."

And as he said this he handed two goodly-sized pieces of mutton to Tiburcio.

This time the young man accepted the invitation to eat. Rest had given him an appetite; and after swallowing a few mouthfuls of the cold mutton, warmed up by a glass of the brandy already mentioned, he felt both his strength and spirits restored at the same time. His features, too, seemed to have suddenly changed their hue, and now appeared more bright and smiling.

The presence of the hunter also added to the pleasure thus newly arisen within his breast. He remembered the solicitude which the Canadian had exhibited in dressing his wound—which he now extended even to giving him nourishment—and the thought occurred to him that in this man he might find a friend as redoubtable for his herculean strength as for his dexterity and courage. He no longer felt so lone in the world—so abandoned.

On the other hand, Bois-Rose sat looking at his *protégé* and apparently delighted to see him enjoy his repast. The heart of the trapper was fast warming into a strong friendship for this young man.

"Stranger!" said he, after a considerable interval of silence, "it is the custom of the Indians never to inquire the name or quality of a guest until after he has eaten of their bread. I have followed their example in regard to you; and now may I ask you who you are, and what happened at the hacienda to drive you forth from it?"

"I shall willingly tell you," answered Tiburcio. "For reasons that would have no interest for you, I left my hut and started on a journey to the Hacienda del Venado. My horse, overcome by thirst and fatigue, broke down on the way. It was his dead body, as you already know, that attracted the jaguars, so adroitly destroyed by you and your brave comrade."

"Hum!" interrupted the Canadian, with a smile; "a poor feat that—but go on. I long to hear what motive any one could have for hostility to a mere youth scarce twenty years old, I should fancy."

"Twenty-four," answered Tiburcio, and then proceeded with his narrative. "I came very near sharing the fate of my poor horse; and when, about two hours after, you saw me at La Poza, I had just arrived there— having been saved by the party in whose company you found me. But what motive those gentlemen could have, first to rescue me from death, and then afterwards attempt to take my life, is what I am unable to comprehend."

"Perhaps some rivalry in love?" suggested the Canadian, with a smile; "it is usually the history of young men."

"I acknowledge," rejoined Tiburcio, with an air of embarrassment, "there is something of that; but there is also another motive, I believe. Possibly it is to secure to themselves the sole possession of an important secret which I share with them. Certain it is, that there are three men whom my life appears to discommode; there is one of them against whom I have myself sworn vengeance, and although I am but one against three I must accomplish the vow which I made at the death-bed of a person who was very dear to me."

The three men whom Tiburcio meant—and whose names he repeated to Bois-Rose—were Cuchillo, who had attempted to assassinate him; the Senator, his rival: and Don Estevan, whom Tiburcio now believed to be the murderer of Marcos Arellanos.

Bois-Rose tacitly applauded this exhibition of youthful ardour and reckless courage.

"But you have not yet told me your name?" said he, interrogatively, after a moment's hesitation.

"Tiburcio Arellanos," was the reply.

At the mention of the name the Canadian could not restrain a gesture that expressed disappointment. There was nothing in the name to recall the slightest souvenir. He had never heard it before.

The young man, however, observed the gesture.

"You have heard the name before?" he asked abruptly. "Perhaps you knew my father, Marcos Arellanos? He has often been through the wildest parts of the country where you may have met him. He was the most celebrated gambusino in the province."

Instead of calling Marcos Arellanos his father, had Tiburcio said his *adopted father*, his explanation might have elicited a different response from the Canadian. As it was, he only said in reply:

"It is the first time I have heard the name. It was your face that recalled to me some memories of events that happened—long, long ago—"

Without finishing what he meant to have said, the Canadian relapsed into silence.

Tiburcio, too, ceased speaking for a while; he was reflecting on some hopes that had suddenly sprung up within him. His meeting with the two trappers appeared to him not so much a mere chance as a providential circumstance. The secret which he possessed, almost useless to him alone, might be rendered available with the assistance of two auxiliaries such as they—it might become the key to the favour of Don Augustin. It was not without repugnance that he reflected on this means of winning the heart of Rosarita—or rather of purchasing it at the price of gold—for Tiburcio believed that it was closed against any more tender appeal. He had mentally resolved never to return to the hacienda; but notwithstanding this vow he still indulged in a slight remnant of hope—perhaps the echo of his own profound passion. This hope overcame his repugnance; and he resolved to make known his design to the trappers, and endeavour to obtain assistance in carrying it out.

With this view he again opened the conversation.

"You are a hunter by profession—I think I have heard you say?"

"Yes; that is the vocation both of my comrade and myself."

"It is not a very profitable one, and yet attended with many dangers."

"Ah! it is a noble calling, my boy! My fathers followed it before my time, and I, after a few years of interruption, have resumed the profession of my fathers. Unfortunately I have no son to succeed me; and I can say, without boasting, that when I am gone a brave and strong race perishes with me."

"I, too," said Tiburcio, "follow the profession of my father—who, as I have told you, was a gambusino."

"Ah! you are one of a race whom God has also created—in order that the gold which He has given to the world should not be lost to the use of man."

"My father," continued Tiburcio, "has left me a grand legacy—the knowledge of a deposit of gold, not far from the frontier; and if two men, such as you and your comrade, would join me in obtaining it, I could promise to make you richer than ever you dreamt of becoming."

Tiburcio awaited the reply of the trapper, feeling almost certain of his adhesion, notwithstanding the refusal the latter had made in his presence to the proposal of Don Estevan. His astonishment, therefore, was great when the Canadian, with a negative shake of the head, replied as follows:

"Your proposal, young man, might be seductive to many—there was a time when it would have been so to myself—but now it is no longer so. What would gold be to me? I have no one to whom either to give it or leave it. I have no longer a country. The woods and prairies are my home, and gold would be of no service to me there. I thank you, young friend, for your offer, but I must decline to accept it."

And as he said this, the Canadian covered his face with his huge hand, as if to shut out from his eyes the seductive prospect which had been offered to his view.

"Surely this is not your final answer?" said Tiburcio, as soon as he had recovered from his surprise. "A man does not so readily refuse a treasure that he has only to pick up from the ground?"

"Nevertheless," responded the trapper, "it is my resolution, fixed and firm. I have other objects to follow. I have given myself, body and soul, to aid my comrade there in an enterprise—my comrade of ten years' standing."

During this conversation the words *gold* and *treasure*, frequently pronounced, appeared to produce their magic influence on Pepé. Every now and then he turned himself, as if about to protest against the refusal of Bois-Rose, so definitively given. It was evident he was not sleeping very soundly while the talk was going on.

"This Don Estevan de Arechiza, of whom you speak," resumed the Canadian; "he is the same we saw at La Poza is he not—the chief of the expedition?"

"The same."

"Ha! is that the name he goes by here?" cried Pepé, suddenly rousing himself from his apparent sleep.

"You know him, then?" said Tiburcio, interrogatively.

"Yes—yes," replied Pepé; "he is an old acquaintance, with whom I have some back debts to settle—and that is why you see me in this part of the country. But if you desire to have the whole story—and from what has happened I fancy you will—I promise to tell it to you by-and-bye. I begin to fancy that our cause is a common one; and if so, I shall be able to lend you a hand. But there's a time for everything; and now, the most important thing for me is to get some sleep, so as to be ready for whatever turns up."

As Pepé said this, he made a movement to return to the horizontal position from which he had temporarily raised himself.

"Stay! Pepé!" interrupted the Canadian, with an air of good-humour; "one instant before you fall asleep, or I shall say that you deserved the name of Pepé the Sleeper. Hear me! This young man has made us an offer. He wishes us to accompany him to a *placer* he knows of, where you have only to stoop down and gather the gold in handfuls."

"Carramba!" exclaimed Pepé; "you have accepted the offer, of course?"

"On the contrary, I have refused it."

"Then you've done wrong, Bois-Rose! That's a thing that deserves consideration; but we can talk it over by-and-bye—I must have some sleep first." And as he uttered the last words he lay down again; and the instant after a loud snore announced that he was soundly asleep!

Chapter Thirty One
The Recognition

The conversation, for a moment interrupted, was resumed by Bois-Rose.

"So you shall find," said he, "in my comrade Pepé, a man ready to join you against this Don Estevan; and, as Pepé's enemies are mine, I shall be equally your partisan. We shall be able to offer you a brace of good rifles that never miss their aim. There is one, at all events, I think I can answer for."

As the trapper said this, he pointed to the long piece that rested by his side.

Tiburcio cast his eyes upon the gun, and for a moment regarded it with some surprise. He appeared to look more particularly at the wood-work of the stock, which was notched and carved in a somewhat fantastic manner. Here there was a row of simple notches, and there another row of marks resembling crosses. Then there were rows of double crosses; and also one of triple crosses; and finally a series of stars. All these hieroglyphics appeared to have been cut with the blade of a knife; but their purpose was a puzzle to Tiburcio.

Bois-Rose, noticing an interrogative expression upon the face of the young man, at once entered upon an explanation.

"These marks," said he, "are the scores I keep of the savages that have fallen by my rifle. They themselves keep count by the number of scalps; but this, you see, is more Christian and decent. That row of crosses stands for Apache—there is a dozen in all. The double crosses are for Sioux—seven of them. Those with the triple branch are Pawnees—eight of them I have sent to the land of spirits. The stars are Crows—and number only four, that my rifle has caused to utter their death-yell. You see nine parallel notches?— well, these are nine Flatheads that, thanks to me, will rob no longer in this world; and finally, those marks of a roundish shape, which I needn't count, are so many Blackfeet, who have gone to their happy hunting-grounds. Now," added the trapper, "I think I can promise you a rifle that is not likely to miss fire, and the hand of a friend that will not fail you."

And as he said this, he stretched forth his huge hand, and grasping that of Tiburcio, pressed it frankly and firmly.

The young man accepted the offer with a profusion of thanks.

"I had a presentiment," said he, "when I saw the light of your fire, that I should find friends around it."

"You are not deceived," warmly responded Bois-Rose; "you have found friends;—but, pardon me when I ask you, have you no relatives or connections with whom you could find a home?"

For a moment the colour mounted to the cheeks of Tiburcio; but after a slight hesitation, he replied:

"Why should I not be frank with you?—I shall! Know then, brave trappers, that surrounded as I am by enemies who seek my life; disdained by the woman I have loved, and still love—I am alone in the world: I have neither father, nor mother, nor any relative that I know of?"

"Your father and mother—are they dead?" inquired Bois-Rose, with an air of interest.

"I never knew either of them," answered the young man in a sad voice.

"You have never known them!" cried the Canadian, rising suddenly, and laying hold of a blazing fagot, which he held up to the face of Tiburcio.

This fagot, light as it was, appeared as if a hundredweight in the hand of the giant, that trembled like an aspen, under the convulsive emotions that were agitating his bosom. He held the flame closed to the countenance of the young man, and scanned his features with eager anxiety.

"But surely," said he, "you at least know in what country you were born?"

"I do not," answered Tiburcio. "But why do you ask me? What interest—"

"Fabian! Fabian!" interrupted Bois-Rose, in a soft, appealing tone, as if he was speaking to an infant—"what has become of you?"

"Fabian!" repeated the young man; "I do not know the name."

"Oh, my God!" exclaimed the Canadian, as if speaking to himself, "since this name recalls nothing to him, it is not he! Why did I indulge in such a foolish hope? And yet his features are just as Fabian's should be at his age. Pardon me," he continued, addressing himself to Tiburcio—"pardon me, young friend. I am a fool! I have lost my senses!"

And throwing the fagot back upon the fire, he returned to his seat, placing himself with his back to the light, so that his countenance was concealed from the eyes of his companion.

Both were for some minutes silent. Tiburcio was endeavouring to penetrate the past, and recall some vague reminiscences of infancy, that still lingered in his memory. The widow of Arellanos had told him all she knew of his early history—of the gigantic sailor who had nursed him; but it never occurred to Tiburcio that the great trapper by his side, a *coureur de bois* of the American wilderness—could ever have been a seaman—much less that one of whom he had heard and read, and who was believed to have been his father. The strange interest which the trapper had exhibited and the questions he had asked were attributed by him to mere benevolence. He had no idea that the latter referred to any one whom he had formerly known, and who was now lost to him; for Bois-Rose had as yet told him nothing of his own history.

As Tiburcio continued to direct his thoughts upon the past, certain vague souvenirs began to shape themselves in his memory. They were only dim shadows, resembling the retrospect of a dream, and yet he was impressed with the belief that they had once been realities. He was the more confirmed in this idea, because such visions had occurred to him before—especially upon the night when he sat by the death-bed of his adopted mother—the widow of Arellanos. The revelations which she made to him before dying had revived in some mysterious way these shadowy souvenirs.

After a while the young man made known his thoughts to his companion by the camp-fire, whose interest appeared to be forcibly re-awakened, and who listened with eager attention to every word.

"I fancy I can remember," said Tiburcio—"that is, if it be not a dream I have sometimes dreamt—a terrible scene. I was in the arms of a woman who held me closely to her breast—that I was rudely snatched from her embrace by a wicked man—that she screamed and cried, but then all at once became silent; but after that I remember no more."

These words appeared to produce an effect upon the Canadian; and his interest visibly increased as he listened.

"You can remember no more?" he inquired, in an eager tone. "Can you not remember what sort of place it was in? Was it in a house? or do you not remember whether the sea was around you? That is a thing one is not likely to forget."

"No," answered Tiburcio, "I saw the great ocean for the first time at Guaymas—that was four years ago—and yet from what has been told me I should have also seen it when I was a child."

"But, when you saw it four years ago, did it not recall anything to your memory?"

"No, nothing."

"Nothing?" repeated the Canadian, interrogatively, and in a despairing tone.

"Nothing more than this same dream, which I have mistaken no doubt for reality."

Bois-Rose again resumed his attitude of melancholy, and remained silent.

After a pause Tiburcio continued:

"One figure appears to me in these visions that is different from the rest."

"What sort of figure?" inquired the Canadian, with renewed interest.

"That of a man of a hale rude countenance, but notwithstanding one of kindly expression. This man loved me, for I now have his face before me more clearly than I ever had; and I can trace that expression upon it."

"And did you love him? can you remember that?" inquired the Canadian, while his heart beat with anxiety, as he awaited the answer.

"I am sure I did, he was so kind to me. I can remember he was kind to me."

A tear stole over the bronzed cheek of the trapper as he listened to these words; and then turning his face once more so that it was hidden from the view of Tiburcio, he murmured to himself—

"Alas, poor Fabian! he too loved me—I know he did."

Then once more facing round to the fire, he hazarded a last question:

"Do you not remember one circumstance above all? Do you not remember that this man was suddenly separated from you in the midst of a terrible affray—?"

The emotion under which Bois-Rose was suffering hindered him from finishing his interrogatory. His head fell between his knees, and he awaited in trembling the response which Tiburcio might make.

The latter was silent for some seconds, as if endeavouring to arrange the confused thoughts that had suddenly sprung up in his mind.

"Hear me!" said he at length, "you who appear to be a beacon guiding my memories of the past—hear what I can remember at this moment. There was one day of terror and confusion; I saw much blood around me. The ground appeared to tremble—there was thunder or the noise of cannon. I was in great fear within a dark chamber where I had been shut up—a man came to me; it was the big man who loved me—"

Tiburcio paused for an instant, as if to grapple freshly with the vague reminiscences that were endeavouring to escape from him, while the Canadian appeared like one suffering the agony of suspense.

"Yes," resumed Tiburcio, "this man came to me—he lifted me up in his arms and carried me into the light—there he caused me to kneel down—oh! I now remember what he said—'*kneel!*' said he, '*kneel, my child! and pray for your mother!*' That is all I can remember."

The Canadian, who was still seated, appeared to tremble convulsively, as he listened to these last words; but when Tiburcio had finished speaking, he rose suddenly to his feet; and rushing forward threw his arms wildly around the young man, while at the same time he cried out in a broken voice:

"*Your mother whom I found dead beside you.* Oh! my God! Once more in need of a father, hast thou sent him to me. Oh! Fabian! Fabian! Come to my heart! It was I who caused you to kneel—I am that man! who in the bay of Elanchovi—"

At this moment the report of a carbine echoed in the woods; and a bullet whistling through the air, passed close to the head of Tiburcio, striking a tree that stood behind him.

This unexpected intruder at once put an end to the dialogue; suddenly changing the tableaux of figures around the fire. Pepé, who had heard the shot, sprang instantaneously to his feet, and all three stood grasping their weapons, ready to receive the enemy who had committed the dastardly attempt.

Chapter Thirty Two
Souvenirs of Elanchovi

While these incidents were passing by the trappers camp-fire, Don Estevan was actively pursuing the execution of his plans.

From what little he had heard and seen of Diaz he had conceived a high opinion of this person. He had observed in him a man of very different character from the crowd of adventurers who usually make up expeditions of the kind he was about to lead. Don Augustin had pronounced upon his courage; and the chief himself had noticed the reserve with which Diaz treated his new associates Cuchillo and Baraja. Moreover, some words with Diaz himself had confirmed Don Estevan's favourable impression, and convinced him that the Indian fighter was a man of brave and loyal heart. He regarded Diaz, therefore, as a valuable member of the expedition, and resolved to attach him as much as possible to his service—not merely with a view to his assistance in the search and conquest of the Valley of Gold, but for that higher aim which he had proposed to himself—the establishment of a kingdom.

While proceeding to the rendezvous designated by Cuchillo, Don Estevan took the opportunity of sounding Diaz on this important question. His bravery and address as a soldier were already known; but these two qualities were not sufficient for the purposes of the Spaniard. Something more would be required of the man of whom it was his design to make both his lieutenant and confidant.

The reply of Diaz to his very first question, convinced Don Estevan that Diaz was the very man he stood in need of; but the time had not yet arrived for the leader to open himself fully. He contented himself by simply observing, that in the event of the expedition being crowned with success, it might lead to an important affair—the separation of Sonora from the Federal Republic.

At this moment the conversation between the chief and Pedro Diaz was interrupted by the report of a carbine. It was the shot fired by Cuchillo, which had caused the sudden alarm at the camp-fire of the trappers, but which as already known had failed in its aim.

If the outlaw had not yielded to his own cupidity, it is possible that Tiburcio would have fallen at that moment. The assassin would have taken with him his two associates Baraja and Oroche; and as three bullets instead of one would thus have been aimed at the intended victim, the chances are that some of them would have reached his life. But Cuchillo did not desire to have a partner in the deed who could claim a share in the promised reward, he was determined to have the twenty onzas to himself; and this it was that induced him to leave Baraja and Oroche behind him. His design was well conceived, and might have been executed to his satisfaction. No doubt his aim had been true enough; but it chanced to be taken at an inopportune moment—just as Tiburcio sprang forward under the impulse of the revelation which Bois-Rose had made to him.

Having delivered his fire the outlaw did not even stop to ascertain its effect; but turning suddenly away, he ran to recover his horse. The dread of being pursued and overtaken by the two trappers caused him to fly at full speed. He dreaded the vengeance of two men of whose singular courage and dexterity he had already been a witness. Fear, however, so confused his senses, that on facing round, he was unable to remember in what direction he had come, or where the horse had been left; and for some seconds he stood hesitating and doubtful.

Short as was the time, it might have proved fatal to him, but that his unexpected attack had somewhat disconcerted the camp. Both Bois-Rose and Tiburcio, interrupted while suffering the most vivid emotions, stood for some moments in a state of stupor, while Pepé was stretched out at full length, and supposed to be asleep.

This was only apparent, however, for at the report he sprang to his feet as if he had heard the "hish" of the bullet as it passed close to his ears.

"*Carramba!*" cried he, "I am curious to know which of us that bit of lead was intended for, you or myself, young man; for I have heard your conversation, and I am no stranger to this affair of Elanchovi."

"Elanchovi!" exclaimed the Canadian. "What! do you know anything of Elanchovi?"

"Ah, well do I," answered Pepé. "I have good reasons to know Elanchovi—but there's no time to talk of it now; I will settle that business by-and-by, for it's a secret you can't comprehend without my help. So indeed it is the young count, and you have found him again! Well that's enough at present. Now, Bois-Rose, forward! You take to the right of where the shot came from, while this young man and I go to the left. The cowardly rascal who fired will no doubt be trying to turn our camp, and by going both ways, one or other of us will be likely to chance upon him. Away, Bois-Rose, away!"

Hurriedly pronouncing these words, Pepé grasped his rifle and struck off to the left, followed by Tiburcio, who had no other weapon than his knife. The Canadian, suddenly stooping, till his huge body was almost horizontal, glided off to the right under the branches of the trees, and then moved on with a silence and rapidity that showed how accustomed he was to this mode of progression.

The camp-fire was abandoned to the guard of the half-wild horse, that, freshly affrighted by the report of the carbine, once more plunged and reared, until he had almost strangled himself in the noose of his lazo.

Meanwhile the day was beginning to break, and the red light of the fire was every moment growing paler under the first rays of the morning.

"Let us stop here," said Pepé to Tiburcio, as soon as they had reached a thicket where they could have the advantage of seeing without being seen, and from which they commanded a view of the road leading to the Salto de Agua. "Stand closely behind this sumac bush," continued he; "I have an idea that this *picaron*, who has such a crooked sight, will pass this way. If he do, I shall prove to him that the lessons Bois-Rose has given me have not been altogether lost upon me. I manage my piece somewhat better now than when I was in the service of her Catholic majesty. There now, stand close, and not a word above a whisper."

Tiburcio—or, as we may now call him, Fabian de Mediana—obeyed with pleasure the injunctions of his companion. His spirit, troubled with a few strange words he had heard from Bois-Rose and Pepé, was full of hope that the latter would be able to complete the revelation just begun; and he waited with anxious silence to hear what the ex-carabinier might say.

But the latter was silent. The sight of the young man—whom he had himself assisted in making an orphan, and despoiling not only of his title and wealth, but even of his name—renewed within him the remorse which twenty years had not sufficed to blot out from his memory. Under the dawning light he looked sadly but silently on the face of that child whom he had often seen playing upon the beach of Elanchovi. In the proud glance of the youth, Pepé saw once more the eyes of his high-born mother; and in the elegant and manly form he recognised that of Don Juan de Mediana, his father; but twenty years of a rude and laborious life—twenty years of a struggle with the toils and dangers of the desert—had imparted to Fabian a physical strength far superior to that of him who had given him being.

Pepé at length resolved to break the silence. He could no longer restrain himself, suffering as he was from such bitter memories.

"Keep your eye fixed upon the road," said he, "at yonder point, where it is lost among the trees. Watch that point whilst I talk to you. It is the way in which Bois-Rose and I do when there is any danger threatening us. At the same time listen attentively to what I say."

"I listen," answered Fabian, directing his glance as his companion, had instructed him.

"Do you remember nothing of your young days, more than you have just related to the Canadian?"

"Nothing—ever since I learnt that Arellanos was not my father, I have tried to remember something, but to no purpose. I do not even know who took care of me in my infancy."

"No more know they of you, my poor young man. I am the only one who can tell you these things of which you are ignorant."

"For heaven's sake speak!" impatiently cried Fabian.

"Hush! not so loud!" cautioned the trapper. "These woods, remote and solitary as they seem, nevertheless contain your deadliest enemy—unless, indeed, it was at me that the bullet was aimed. That may make a difference in your favour. In fact, since I have not been able to recognise you, I do not see how *he* can?"

"Who—of whom do you speak?" brusquely demanded Fabian.

"Of your mother's murderer—of the man who has robbed you of your titles, your honours, your wealth, and your name."

"I should be noble and rich then?" cried Fabian, interrogatively. "Oh that I had but known it sooner—only yesterday!"

Fabian's thoughts were upon Rosarita. If he could have told this to her, in that sad parting interview, perhaps the result might have been different!

"Noble! yes!" replied Pepé, "you should be and shall yet, if I mistake not—but rich—alas! you are no more rich."

"What matters it?" responded Fabian, "to-day it would be too late."

"Yes, but it does matter—ah! I knew two men—one at least—who shall restore to you what you have lost, or die in the attempt."

"Of whom do you speak?"

"Of one who, without knowing it, aided to some extent in the assassination of your mother—of one whom that sad souvenir has a thousand times troubled the conscience—who, in the silence of the night in the midst of the woods, has often fancied he could hear that cry of anguish, which at the time he mistook for the wailing of the breeze against the cliffs of Elanchovi. It was the death scream of your poor mother. Ah! Don Fabian de Mediana," continued the speaker, in reply to the gesture of horror made by the young man, "Ah! that man's conscience has reproached him in stronger terms than you could use; and at this hour he is ready to spill the last drop of his blood for you."

The impetuous passions of Fabian, for a moment softened by thoughts of Rosarita, were again inflamed to their utmost. He had already sworn to avenge the death of Arellanos, and here was anew object of vengeance, the murderer of his own mother! The bland image of Rosarita at once disappeared, paling away as the firelight eclipsed by the brighter gleams of the rising sun.

"My mother's assassin!" cried he, his eyes flashing with furious indignation. "And you know him?"

"You also—you have eaten with him at the same table—under the same roof—that which you have just now quitted!"

Pepé without further interrogation went on to recount what he knew of the events of Elanchovi. He told Fabian who he was—that Don Estevan was no other than his uncle, Antonio de Mediana—of the marriage of his mother with Don Juan his father—of the consequent chagrin of the younger brother—of his infamous design, and the manner it had been carried into execution. How Don Antonio, returning from the wars in Mexico, with his band of piratical adventurers, had landed in a boat upon the beach at Ensenada—how he had entered the chateau, and with the help of his two subordinate villains had abstracted the Countess and her infant—himself Fabian—how the assassination of the mother had been committed in the boat, and the child only spared in the belief that the murderer's steel was not necessary—in the belief that the waves and the cold atmosphere of a November night would complete the deed of death.

Nor did Pepé conceal his own conduct connected with this affair. He disclosed all to his half-frantic listener—the after actions of Don Antonio with regard to himself—his imprisonment and subsequent banishment to the fisheries of Ceuta—his escape at a later period to the prairies of America, and his meeting with Bois-Rose—with whom, however, no recognition had ever been established about the events of Elanchovi—since neither had ever mentioned that name in hearing of the other.

All these things Pepé narrated in turn, but briefly as the circumstances required. The rest of his history Fabian already knew—at least, the greater part of it; Bois-Rose had partially made the revelation.

Chapter Thirty Three
The Man in the Yellow Jacket

Bois-Rose, as already stated, had gone alone in a direction opposite to that taken by his comrades. His mind full of the danger with which Fabian was surrounded—Fabian restored to him as if by a miracle—the Canadian continued to advance with rapid strides. He examined every opening and aisle of the forest with an eye keenly bent, and an ear straining to catch the slightest sound.

After making a distance of a hundred yards or so, he stopped in his tracks, and laying himself flat along the grass, placed his ear to the ground and listened attentively. In a few seconds' time a dull sound reached him—the hoof-strokes of a horse that seemed to approach the spot where he lay.

"Pepé is right," muttered he to himself, as he started to his feet; "the skunk is coming this way. Good! he has the advantage of me in being mounted; but I have a rifle that I dare say will make up for the difference—*enfant de grâce!* he is here!"

As this exclamation escaped him, the trapper was seen suddenly to raise his long rifle to his shoulder. At the same instant a leathern jacket of yellowish colour appeared at some distance off among the leaves, and at about the height of a man on horseback.

The sharp crack of a rifle was instantly followed by the disappearance of the leathern jacket: and, since for marksmen like Bois-Rose to take aim is to hit, the latter had no doubt that his enemy had fallen to the ground either dead or wounded. For a moment he thought of reloading; but the ardour of his vengeance urged him to rush forward and make sure of his victim. In the event that the assassin should have companions, the trapper trusted to his great strength to equalise the chances of a hand-to-hand conflict. Neglecting all further precautions, therefore, like the hunter rushing upon the wounded stag, he dashed forward through the trees toward the spot where his enemy had fallen.

As he drew near, he could perceive a horse rearing furiously in front of him, crushing the underwood as he plunged violently from side to side. The horse was saddled and bridled, but there was no one in the saddle. This led Bois-Rose to the belief that his bullet had dismounted the rider.

All at once a shrill whistle rang through the trees; and the horse uttered a loud neigh—as if in reply—galloping off in the direction from which the signal had come. After making several lengths through the bushes, the horse came to a stop. Bois-Rose ran after, and in a few bounds was beside the animal. It was still dark under the shadow of the trees, but the Canadian could make out the form of a man upon the ground, at that moment struggling in the act of raising himself. Just then the horse dropped upon his knees, the man grasping the pommel of the saddle succeeded in crawling into it; a signal started the animal to his feet again; and before the trapper could come up to the spot, both horse and man were fast disappearing behind the foliage of the trees.

Bois-Rose launched after them a furious malediction; and reloading his rifle as rapidly as he could, sent a bullet in the same direction; but the continued strokes of the horse's feet falling upon his ear told him that his random shot had been delivered to no purpose.

Without following further, he turned in the opposite direction, and after imitating three times in succession, the howling of the prairie wolf—a signal for Pepé—he strode off to the spot where the yellow jacket had fallen from the saddle.

There he perceived the grass pressed down as if where a man's body had fallen upon it; and at about the height of a man on horseback, the branches of the sumac tree were broken, as though the horseman had caught at them in falling. There were no traces of blood, however—not a drop could be seen; but a carbine lying upon the ground showed that the horseman, in his hurry to escape, had left his weapon behind him.

"My poor Fabian!" muttered he, "this will serve for him. In these woods a knife is not much worth; this will be a better weapon for him."

Somewhat consoled by this reflection, the trapper now turned to go back in the direction of the camp-fire. He had not made a dozen steps, when the sharp report of a rifle fell upon his ear.

"It is Pepé's!" he cried. "I know it. God grant he may have made a better shot than I have done!"

Just then a second report echoed through the woods. It sounded sadly on the ear of the Canadian—who did not recognise it—and being now the victim of a terrible uncertainty, he ran with all speed in the direction whence the sound had come.

Another report that now reached him added to the anguish of his suspense; for this time, like the last, it was not the well-known crack of his comrade's rifle.

Almost at the same instant, however, he heard Pepé's voice calling out:

"Come back, Fabian! come back! What is the use of—"

A third detonation seemed to cut short the speech of the ex-coast-guard—as if he had fallen by the bullet—while no voice of Fabian was heard to make reply. A profound and frightful silence followed the last shot, which was broken only by the voice of the mock-bird, who appeared imperfectly to imitate the words that had been spoken, and then commenced chanting a plaintive song—as if mourning the death of those who had fallen by the shots.

The Canadian ran on for some moments, until—unable longer to restrain himself—he paused, and cried out, at the risk of exposing himself to some ambushed enemy:

"Hola! Pepé!—where are you?"

"Here!" answered the voice of the ex-carabinier. "We are here, straight before you—Don Fabian and myself. Come on!"

A cry of joy was all the response the Canadian could give; and the next moment another joyous shout, as he came upon the ground and perceived that both his companions were still in safety.

"The skunk ought to be wounded," said he; "my shot caused him to tumble out of his saddle. You were perhaps more fortunate than I? I heard your piece speak—have you throwed him, Pepé?"

Pepé shook his head in the negative.

"If you mean the fellow in the yellow jacket," said he, "I fancy the devil has *him* under his protection; for I had a fair sight on him—and yet he's off! He's not alone, however; there are four other horsemen along with him; and in one of these gentleman I have recognised him whom they here call Don Estevan de Arechiza, but who is no other than—"

"I have seen only the fellow in the leather jacket," interrupted the Canadian; "and here is his gun, Fabian, for you. But are you quite safe?" continued he, in an anxious tone. "You are sure you are not wounded?"

"No, no—my friend—my father!" cried Fabian, flinging himself into the trapper's arms, as if they had just met after a long separation.

"Oh, Pepé!" cried the Canadian, his eyes filling with tears, as he pressed Fabian convulsively against his great bosom, and then held him at a distance as if to get a better view of him. "Is he not grand? Is he not beautiful? He—once my little Fabian—oh!"

"Pepé has told me all," said Fabian. "Among these men is the murderer of my mother."

"Yes," exclaimed Pepé; "and by the Virgin of Atocha let us not delay here. There is no time for sentiment—the villain must not escape us. Justice, so long evaded, must now have its due."

"As God wills!" rejoined Fabian.

The three friends now held a rapid council as to what course was best to be taken. It was concluded by their resolving to follow the horsemen as rapidly as possible along the road which these had taken—the road to Tubac.

Chapter Thirty Four
The Blood of the Medianas

After having uselessly discharged their carbines several times, from too great a distance for the balls to be dangerous, Oroche and Baraja had rejoined Cuchillo.

The outlaw was as pale as death; the ball fired at him by the Canadian had creased his head, and it was this had caused him to fall from his horse. Doubtless Bois-Rose would then have crushed him, like a venomous reptile, but for the horse. The noble animal, seeing that his master could not raise himself unaided, bent down that he might seize his mane, and so reach the saddle, and when he felt his master once more firmly seated on his back, he had set off at full gallop, and carried him away beyond the reach of Bois-Rose.

This was not the only danger run by the outlaw. When his accomplices had rejoined him and all three had come up with Don Estevan and Diaz, another danger was in store for him. The Spaniard had no need to interrogate Cuchillo in order to learn that Fabian had once more escaped. From the disappointed air of the two followers, and the paleness of the outlaw, who was still tottering in his saddle, Don Estevan guessed all.

Deceived in his expectation, the rage of the Spaniard burst out. He rode up to Cuchillo, crying, in a voice of thunder, "Cowardly and clumsy knave!" and in his blind fury, without reflecting that Cuchillo alone knew the secret of the Golden Valley, he drew his pistol. Luckily for the outlaw, Pedro Diaz threw himself quickly between him and Don Estevan, whose fury gradually subsided.

"And those men who are with him—who are they?" cried he.

"The two tiger-killers," replied Baraja.

A short deliberation took place in a low voice between Don Estevan and Pedro Diaz, which ended by these words, pronounced aloud:

"We must destroy the bridge of the Salto de Agua, and the devil is in it if they overtake us before we reach Tubac;" and at this they all set off at full gallop.

Fabian had heard Don Estevan say to Cuchillo, the night before, that he should only pass two hours at the hacienda before his departure; and as the last events which had taken place at Don Augustin's must have tended to shorten his stay, there was no time to hesitate. The horse of Pepé became a precious auxiliary in following the fugitives, and, if necessary, for cutting off their retreat. It remained to be decided who should mount him, and undertake an enterprise so perilous as opposing singly the flight of five armed horsemen.

"I shall follow them," said Fabian.

So saying, he rushed towards the animal, who recoiled in terror; but seizing the cord by which he was tethered, the young man threw a handkerchief over his eyes. Trembling in every limb, the horse remained quiet, while Fabian brought Pepé's saddle, which he placed on his back, and then arranged the lazo so as to form at once a bridle and a snaffle. He was about to mount without removing the handkerchief, when Pepé, at a sign from Bois-Rose, interposed.

"Gently," said he, "if any one here has a right to mount this animal, it is I—I who captured him, and to whom he belongs."

"Do you not see," cried Fabian, impatiently, "that he is not *branded*, which shows that he has never yet been mounted? if you care for the safety of your limbs, I advise you not to try him."

"That is my business," said Pepé, advancing; but scarcely had the animal felt his hand on the pommel, and his foot on the stirrup, than with a furious bound he threw him ten feet off. Pepé uttered an angry oath, but Fabian vaulted into the saddle without touching the stirrups.

"Stop! Fabian, stop!" cried Bois-Rose, in a tone of anguish, "you must not go alone and risk falling into their hands."

But already Fabian had removed the handkerchief; and the noble animal, his eyes restored to the light, made furious efforts to free himself from a weight which he felt for the first time, but at last stood motionless and trembling. Bois-Rose profited by this moment to seize the bridle, but was shaken off by another furious bound, and the terrified animal rushed away with such impetuosity that it was no longer in human power to restrain him. For a few moments the Canadian watched the intrepid rider struggling with the fury of the horse, and then both disappeared from his sight.

"They will kill him," cried he; "they are five to one. Let us follow as closely as we can, Pepé, to protect once more my lately recovered child."

Bois-Rose threw his rifle over his shoulder, and was already taking gigantic strides after Fabian.

"The horse is difficult to manage," cried he; "I am certain that he will not go straight! we shall perhaps arrive as soon as he. Ah! Don Estevan, your evil star has guided you to these outlaws."

Fabian, like those legendary cavaliers whom nothing appals, passed with fearful rapidity over hillocks, ravines, and fallen trunks of trees. Pepé was not wrong; in spite of the start that the pursued had of him, Fabian would soon have overtaken them, could he have guided his horse; but luckily, or unluckily for him, the intractable animal deviated constantly from the track; and it was only after prodigious efforts that he could bring him back to the road, which wound through the wood, and on which the traces of the five fugitives were visible, and thus the pursuer constantly lost ground.

However, after an hour of this struggle, the horse began to find that he had met with his master, and that his strength was becoming exhausted; the curb, held by a vigorous hand, compressed his jaws, his speed gradually relaxed, his bounds became less violent, and he ended by obeying the hand which guided him. As if by common consent, man and horse stopped to take breath. Fabian profited by this rest to look around him; his heart began to beat less rapidly and he could both hear and see. Trampled leaves, newly broken branches and the prints of horses' feet, were clear indications of the passage of those who fled before him.

Suddenly the sound of falling water struck upon his ear. In another moment the fugitives would have gained the rustic bridge which crossed the wide and deep bed of the torrent; their united efforts might destroy it, and then all pursuit would be useless. While he was seeking for a ford Don Estevan would escape through the vast plains which extended to Tubac. This thought aroused anew the young man's passion; and, pressing his horse's side he galloped along the path, the windings of which still hid his enemies from view. This time his horse had grown docile and flew along the road.

The noise of the torrent soon drowned that of the horse's feet, but before long human voices mingled with it. This sound produced upon Fabian as powerful an effect as his repeated blows did upon his horse; a few minutes more and he would confront the enemies whom he was burning to reach. The impetuous pace of a horse excites a man to the greatest degree; horse and rider react upon each other, and Fabian in his excitement forgot the inequality of numbers, therefore the spectacle which met his eyes was one that caused him a bitter disappointment.

As already stated, a bridge composed of trunks of trees roughly cut, joined the two steep banks, between which roared the Salto de Agua. This bridge, broad enough for a horse to pass over, rested at each end on the bare rock without anything to secure it, and the strength of a few men might overturn the trees and render the crossing impossible.

Just as Fabian reached the bridge, four horses, urged on by their riders, were pulling vigorously, with ropes attached to the trees, which at that moment yielding, fell with a crash into the torrent.

Fabian uttered a cry of rage. A man turned round—it was Don Estevan, but Don Estevan separated from him by an impassable barrier, and looking triumphantly at him.

Fabian, his clothes torn to pieces by the brambles, and his face so transformed by fury as to be scarcely recognisable, rushed forward in his blind rage to cross the river. But his horse reared violently and refused to proceed.

"Fire on him!" cried Don Estevan, "or the madman will derange all our plans. Fire, I tell you!"

Three carbines were already pointed at Fabian, when at some distance behind him loud voices were heard, and Pepé and the Canadian appeared. At the sight of these formidable rifles, the outlaws hesitated; Fabian made a new effort, but the frightened horse plunged and reared as before.

"Fire!" again cried Don Estevan.

"Woe to him who does!" shouted the Canadian, "and you, Fabian, in heaven's name, retire!"

"Yes, it is I, Fabian!" cried the Count, in a voice which drowned the thunder of the torrent and the cries of the hunters, "Fabian, who comes to avenge his mother's blood upon the infamous Don Antonio de Mediana!"

Then, while his voice still sounded in the ears of Don Estevan, who for the first time in his life stood motionless with terror, the impetuous young man drew his knife and pricked his horse with it.

This time the animal gave a furious leap across the gulf and reached the opposite bank; but one of his feet slipped, and after a short struggle he fell backwards, both horse and rider disappearing in the flood. A cry of anguish burst from the Canadian and one of triumph from the opposite bank; but both were quickly drowned by the roar of the torrent as it closed over its double prey.

Chapter Thirty Five
A Bird's Eye View of the Desert

About a fortnight after the events just related, other scenes were taking place in a part of the desert which extends from Tubac to the American frontier. But before referring to the actors let us describe the theatre on which they once more met.

The vast plains which separated Mexico from the United States are known only by the vague reports of hunters or gold-seekers—at least that part watered by the river Gila and its tributaries. This river, which takes its rise in the distant mountains of the Mimbres, passes under various names through an immense extent of sandy barren country, the arid monotony of which is interrupted only by the ravines hollowed by the waters, which in their erratic course, ravage without fertilising.

The reader must imagine himself at a spot distant about sixty leagues from Tubac. The sun, inclining towards the west, was already darting oblique rays; it was the hour when the wind, although still hot, no longer seems to come out of the mouth of a furnace. It was about four o'clock in the afternoon, and light white clouds tinted with rose colour, indicated that the sun had run two-thirds of his course; above, in the deep blue sky, an eagle hung motionless over the desert, the only visible inhabitant of the air. From the height where the king of birds balanced himself majestically, his eye could perceive on the immense plain, many human beings, some of whom were in groups, and others at so great a distance apart as to be visible to him alone, and not to each other.

Just beneath the soaring bird was a kind of irregular natural circle formed by a hedge of cacti, with their fleshy leaves and thorny points, with which were mingled the pale foliage of the *bois de fer*. At one end of this hedge was an elevated piece of ground two or three feet high, with a flat top, which overlooked it on all sides. All around this entrenchment, untouched by the hand of man, stretched arid plains or a succession of little hillocks which appeared like motionless waves in a sea of sand.

A troop of about sixty men on horseback had alighted in this place. The steaming horses showed that they had travelled fast. There was a confused noise of human voices, the neighing of horses, and the rattling of every kind of weapon—for it did not appear to be a regular cavalry corps. Lances with red pennons, muskets, carbines and double-barrelled guns were hanging from the saddle-bows.

Some of the men were cleaning their horses, while others were lying on the sand under the shelter of the cacti; a little further back were a number of mules advancing towards the halting-place, and behind them again, some twenty carts, heavily laden.

Visible to the eyes of the eagle, in the road along which these travellers must have passed, were corpses of men and animals strewn on the arid plain, marking the bloody track of this band of adventurers. Doubtless our readers have already recognised the Gold-seekers under the command of Don Estevan de Arechiza.

When the mules and the carts joined the horsemen, the mules were unharnessed and the horses unsaddled; the carts were unloaded and then linked together with iron chains, while the saddles of the animals were piled upon one another, and served with the cacti to fill up the spaces between the wheels and form a formidable barricade. The animals were tied to the carts, and the cooking utensils placed by the side, of the brushwood brought from a distance; a portable forge was established; and this colony, which seemed as though it had risen from the ground as by a miracle, was soon busily employed, while the anvil resounded with the blows which were fashioning horses' shoes and repairing wheels.

A man richly dressed, but whose clothes were faded with sun and dust, alone remained on horseback in the middle of the camp, looking earnestly around him. This man was the chief of the troop. Three other men were occupied meanwhile in fixing the poles of a tent, and then placing on its summit a red banner on which was painted a scutcheon with six golden stars on an azure ground, with the motto, "I will watch." The chief then alighted, and after having given an order to one of his men, who mounted and left the camp he entered the tent. All these preparations had occupied barely half-an-hour, so much were they simplified by habit.

To the right of the camp, but far distant, arose from the sand a mass of gum-trees and *ironwoods*, the only trees produced by these arid plains. Here a second troop had halted. They had neither carts nor baggage mules, but were about double the number of the other party. By the bronzed complexions of the riders, some almost naked, others covered with skins and with waving plumes of eagle's feathers, and by the brilliant red and yellow with which they were painted, it was easy to recognise a party of Indians.

Ten of them—doubtless the chiefs—gravely seated round a fire which produced more smoke than flame, were passing from hand to hand the calumet or pipe of council. Their arms, consisting of leathern bucklers—surrounded by a thick fringe of feathers—axes, and knives, were laid by their side. At some little distance and out of hearing, five warriors held a number of horses, strangely accoutred with wooden saddles covered with skins. These horses belonged to the chiefs, and seemed difficult to restrain.

As one of the chiefs passed the calumet to the others, he pointed to a spot in the horizon. The eyes of a European would only have seen a slight grey cloud against the blue sky, but the Indian recognised a column of smoke—that rising from the camp of the whites.

At that moment an Indian messenger arrived with some news, and all the party crowded round him.

Now between the two camps the eye of the eagle could discover another rider, but alone and out of sight of both parties. It was doubtless he who was being sought for by the messenger despatched from the camp of the gold-seekers. This man rode a grey horse, and seemed to be seeking a track; he was dressed as a European; and his complexion, though much bronzed, denoted that he belonged to that race.

It was Cuchillo, who, resuming his course, caused his horse to mount one of the hillocks, where he could perceive the columns of smoke arising from the two camps. The Indians perceived him at the same time; for a long howl, like that of a hundred panthers, arose, and the king of birds, terrified by the tumult, soon became only a black speck in the clouds. The outlaw fled rapidly in the opposite direction and the Indians rushed after him.

Still further in the horizon, placed so as to form a triangle with the other camps, was a third group of men scarcely visible to the eagle himself. They were encamped upon a small islet in the midst of a river fringed with trees, and over which rested a light fog. The desert of Tubac ended at this river, which, flowing from east to west, divided, a league below the island, into two branches, and formed a vast delta—bounded by a chain of hills which were now shrouded by the fog.

In this delta, more than a league square, lay the Golden Valley.

All these different groups of people will soon meet, like the waves which, raised by opposing winds, break against each other in the immensity of the ocean.

Thanks to a skillful manoeuvre of Pedro Diaz, the expedition, on arriving near the Golden Valley, had concealed for two days from the Indians the route they had taken. But to associate himself with sixty companions did not please Cuchillo, who, under the pretence of reconnoitring the country, had separated himself from his companions. It was to indicate the position of their bivouac that they had lighted a fire in the camp, and to find him that Don Estevan had sent out a messenger. Cuchillo, indeed, was the only one who could guide them to the Golden Valley.

A bold thought was in Cuchillo's mind, but the executions of this project was yet to lead him to a fearful punishment, which he well deserved. We cannot, however, speak of this at present.

A man, as we have said, had arrived at the Indian camp with news. This man, in seeking the enemies whom they were pursuing, had reached the bank of the river, and concealed by the willows, had perceived three white men. These three men could only be Bois-Rose, Pepé the Spaniard, and Fabian de Mediana. It was indeed this trio of friends.

We left Bois-Rose and Pepé on the banks of the torrent in which the young Spaniard, excited by the tale he had heard of his mother's assassination, and full of fury, had nearly found a tomb. Fortunately the fall had been fatal only to the horse, and the rider had escaped by a miracle. The three friends had resumed their pursuit; but, forced to proceed on foot while their enemies were on horseback, they had only arrived at Tubac on the day the expedition left it, after having travelled sixty leagues in five days.

Then it became more easy to follow the adventurers—who were retarded by their baggage—and ten days' march had brought the intrepid companions to the same point as their enemies; for although forced for safety to take a different route, they had rarely lost sight of the fires of their bivouacs. Surrounded as he was, however, Don Estevan could not be easily captured.

When the Indian messenger had finished his report, the warriors deliberated afresh. The youngest of the ten called upon to speak first, said:

"The whites have sometimes the legs of a deer, sometimes the courage of the puma, and the cunning of the jackal. They have concealed their route for two days from eyes which can trace that of the eagle in the air; it is another ruse on their part to scatter their warriors, and we must seek them near the island in river Gila."

After a minute's silence, another spoke:

"The whites have doubtless a thousand stratagems at their service, but can they increase their stature? No; and if on the contrary they could make themselves so small that the Indian eye could not perceive them, they would do it. Our enemies are from the south—these men just discovered come from the north—it is not therefore towards the island that we must go."

In the midst of these contradictory opinions, the shouts of the Indians, at the sight of Cuchillo, burst forth, compelling the chiefs to suspend their deliberations until the warriors who pursued him had returned. When they reappeared, they reported that they had discovered the trail of the whites. Then the second chief who had spoken—a man of tall stature and darker in colour than most of his tribe—whence his name of the *Blackbird*—again spoke:

"I have said that the men who come from the north could not form part of those who come from the south. I have always seen that the south and the north are enemies of one another like the winds which flow from opposite quarters. Let us send a message to the three warriors on the island and ask them to join us against the other whites, and the Indian will be gladdened at the death of his enemies by the hands of each other."

But this advice, dictated by prudence and knowledge of mankind, found no support in the council. The Blackbird was forced to yield, and it was agreed that the mass of the troop should march against the camp, while only a small detachment should be sent to the island.

A quarter of an hour after, one hundred men set off for the camp; while twenty others went towards the island, thirsting for the blood of the three men who had taken shelter there.

It is towards the end of the month of March that we find the gold-seekers and their chief in the camp described, after they had lost by the Indians and by the numberless dangers of the desert, forty of their men. But although weakened by this loss, still the chances between them and the Indians, ever ready to defend their territory, were nearly equal. On each side was cunning, and the habit of following an almost invisible track, while the cupidity of the one was equalled by the ferocity of the other.

Nevertheless the enthusiasm was no longer so great as on the day when, after having celebrated a mass for the success of their expedition, the adventurers had set off from Tubac, uttering cries of triumph, which were accompanied by the sound of cannon and the acclamations of the inhabitants. No precaution had been omitted by Don Estevan, who seemed to foresee everything. Until then, in these kind of expeditions, each man had acted for himself, and trusted to himself and his own horse for his safety; but the Spaniard had disciplined this band, and forced them to obey him, while the carts that he had brought served both for transport and for defence. Thus moved the ancient people of the north in their invading journeys towards the south of Europe. No former expedition had penetrated so far into the desert as had this one, under the guidance of its skillful chief.

The responsibility which weighed upon Don Estevan would of itself have been enough to account for the clouds upon his brow; but perhaps he thought more of the past than of the present or the future. He had been able to compare the energy of Fabian with the pusillanimity of the Senator Tragaduros. Carried away by the course of events, he had thought only of removing his nephew from his path; but when the young man disappeared in the gulf shouting a fierce menace to his father's brother, he had suddenly felt an immense void, and a scarcely-closed wound had re-opened in his heart. He missed one thing amidst all his prosperity, and in spite of himself, the pride of race revived in his breast, and an ardent sympathy had seized upon him for the ardent young man, loved by Doña Rosarita, who might perhaps have replaced the Senator in the execution of his bold plan.

He regretted having allowed himself to be led away by circumstances, and at the moment when the last of the Medianas—except himself—disappeared from his eyes, he regretted an heir so worthy to bear the name. Now, when on the eve of mounting another step by the conquest of the Golden Valley, this regret became more vivid.

This was not the only care, however, which then preoccupied Antonio de Mediana; the absence of Cuchillo made him uneasy, and he began to have a suspicion of this man's perfidy.

Cuchillo had gained considerably upon the Indians who pursued him; but no sooner did he perceive through the hedge the entrenchment raised by his companions than he slackened his pace. The distance at which he still was from the camp was too great to enable him to be perceived by the sentinels; and when he saw the Indians who pursued him halt at sight of the column of smoke, he stopped altogether. His plan was to go into the camp as late as possible, so as only to give the alarm at the last moment. He knew enough of the Indians to play this dangerous game with the most perfect *sang froid*; he knew that they never attacked but with superior numbers, also that some hours would elapse before they decided on attacking the camp at all; that, satisfied with having recovered the track of their enemies, his pursuers would return and carry the report to their companions.

He was right; and enchanted at the effect of his ruse, the outlaw lay down behind a mound of earth, ready to resume his course when his senses should warn him of the approach of danger. By regaining the camp only a few minutes before the attack, he hoped also to escape the questions of Don Estevan.

"We should have sixty to divide the treasure," thought he, "had I not taken care to diminish that number. Then, while the whites and reds are fighting together, I—"

A distant explosion, like that of a rifle, interrupted his meditations. This sound appeared to come from the north, and indeed proceeded from the river, where were Bois-Rose and his companions.

"It is strange that such a sound should proceed from that quarter," said Cuchillo, "for the white camp is eastward and the red westward."

A second shot was heard; then a third, followed by a short silence, to which succeeded a continual firing. Cuchillo trembled. He fancied that a second white party, distinct from his, were about to seize the coveted treasures. Then he feared that Don Estevan had despatched a detachment to take possession of the Golden Valley. But reason soon showed him the little probability of either of these surmises. A party of men must have left traces which he should have discovered during the two days he had been scouring the country; and then it was not probable that Don Estevan would have dared to weaken his force by dividing it. He therefore lay still, and concluded that the sounds proceeded from some party of American hunters surprised by the natives.

We must return to the camp of Don Antonio, where the firing had also been heard, and where it had given rise to a host of conjectures.

Evening had come on, and red clouds marked the fiery trace of the setting sun; the earth began to freshen up at the approach of night, and the crescent of the moon to grow more and more brilliant, under the light of which the camp appeared picturesque.

On the rising ground which overlooked the whole entrenchment, arose, as we have said, the chief's tent with its floating banner. A feeble light from within indicated that he was still watching, and several fires, made in holes dug in the sand or surrounded by stones—lest their light should betray their position—threw a subdued red glare around; while, in case of attack, fagots were prepared to illumine the camp. Groups of men lying down, and others preparing the evening meal, were mingled with the horses and mules, who were eating their rations of maize.

The careless and satisfied look upon every face, showed that these men confided the care of their defence wholly to their chief. At the entrance to the tent lay a man, like a dog watching over his master; and from his long hair and the guitar by the side of his rifle, it was easy to recognise Oroche. His time seemed to be divided between the contemplation of a heaven glittering with stars, and the care of keeping up a fire of green wood, the smoke of which rose in a vertical column silvered by the moon. Beyond the entrenchments the moonlight whitened the plain, and even the fog which covered the summits of a chain of mountains which were visible in the horizon.

Behind the carts paced the sentinels, carbine in hand. Among the various groups of men scattered about were Benito, the servant of Don Estevan, and Baraja. They were engaged in conversation.

"Señor Benito," said Baraja, speaking to the old herdsman, "you who are so well acquainted with all the affairs of these deserts, can you explain to me what is the cause of these shots, which we have been hearing ever since noon, and which can only be fired by our enemies, the Indians?"

"It is difficult to say," answered Benito; "but certainly they must have some good reason for wasting so much powder—a scarce article among them. It appears probable enough that poor Cuchillo is captured; or may be the Señor Gayferos, who was sent after him."

"But why should they keep firing from time to time?—one shot would be enough to put an end to either Cuchillo or Gayferos; whereas we have heard volleys."

"Ah! it may be that the savages are practising one of their horrible modes of punishment—perhaps they are firing at their victims merely for the sport. There is one terrible torture they inflict—I remember to have been—"

"Hold there, friend Benito!" cried Baraja, interrupting him, "no more of your horrible stories; I have not forgotten that frightful night by the well of La Poza."

"Well," rejoined the herdsman, "unless they are firing at either Cuchillo or Gayferos—or perhaps at both—I cannot divine the cause of their continued fusillade. These Indians are as curious as the very devil; and they can extract a secret almost as effectually as the Holy Inquisition itself. Perhaps they are frightening either the guide or Gayferos to betray the situation of our camp."

"God forbid they should succeed!" exclaimed Baraja.

"I join you in the prayer," said the ex-herdsman: "but I cannot help remarking, how imprudent in our chief to permit the fire. The smoke has been rising all day like a column. In an atmosphere like this it may be seen for leagues off!"

"I agree with you," replied Baraja; "but then you know it was kindled at the express wish of the guide—so that he might find the way to where we should be encamped. Both humanity towards Cuchillo, as well as our own interest in his safety, required us to light the fire."

"Ah! that is not so certain. Between ourselves, I haven't much confidence in this Cuchillo. He appears to be one of those guides whose paths always end in quagmires."

"But have you not heard the rumour of the camp?"

"What rumour? That Don Estevan is not going by mere hazard to search for a mine of gold; but that he already knows of the existence of a rich placer? Is it that you mean?"

"Yes—or rather that Don Estevan knows of the existence of the placer; but not *where* it is, or the road that leads to it. This is only known to Cuchillo, whose death would therefore be an irreparable loss to all of us."

"Bah!" replied the ex-herdsman, with a shake of the head; "Cuchillo's face is one that could never deceive an experienced eye. For my part I hope I am deceived in him, though I doubt it."

"Oh, Señor Benito, you always look upon the dark side of things."

"Well, perhaps so—and on this very night I may especially appear a bird of ill omen, for I cannot help feeling the presentiment that there is danger near us. See! look yonder! The animals have left off eating—both mules and horses. Observe how they stand listening, as if they heard something. Well, what is to come will come; and I have not much to lose—even my life is not worth much."

And with this consolatory speech the old shepherd wrapped himself up in his cloak and lay down to sleep.

Not so Baraja. The words of his comrade had produced their effect, and he was unable to compose himself to rest. His imagination depicted to him a thousand phantoms, and every moment he fancied he could hear the yells of the savages, as they rushed forward to attack the camp. Not that the ex-haciendado was altogether a coward; but there was reason for his fears; and the darkness of the night, as well as the strange behaviour of the animals, was sufficient cause to render even a brave man apprehensive of danger.

After the long day's march, all the adventurers were asleep—stretched here and there upon the ground. The sentinels alone were awake, and watching—now and then raising along the lines their monotonous cry of "*Sentinela alerte!*" It was the only sound that for a long time interrupted the silence of the night.

After remaining awake for a considerable time, Baraja began to feel confidence, and perhaps would have gone to sleep, like the others, when all at once he heard several shots, similar to those that had been heard during the day, and which appeared to proceed from the same direction.

"They are still firing over there," said he, nudging the old herdsman so as to awake him.

"No matter," grumbled Benito; "let them fire away. If it be not Cuchillo or Gayferos, we needn't care. So, friend Baraja, I wish you good-night—go to sleep yourself. In the desert, time for sleep is precious, although at any minute you may be sent to sleep in eternity—Good-night!"

After this terrifying speech, the ex-herdsman drew his cloak over his eyes to keep out the rays of the moon, when a noise made by the mules caused him to raise his head again, "Ah!" said he, "the red devils are not far off."

The neigh of a horse was now heard from a distance, accompanied by a cry of alarm, and the next moment a man was seen riding up at full gallop.

"It is Cuchillo," cried the servant; then, in a low voice, to Baraja, "Let the travellers take care when the will-o'-the-wisp dances on the plain!"

Chapter Thirty Six
The Alarm

That evening, as usual, Don Estevan watched in his tent, while his people reposed. By the light of a smoky candle, the Spaniard, in spite of the modest appearance of his lodgings and of his dust-covered clothes, seemed to have lost nothing of the dignity of his appearance or of his grand air. His complexion, more sunburnt than usual, gave his countenance a still more energetic character. He appeared pensive, but his thoughts were no longer so uneasy as they had been; on the eve, after so many dangers, of realising his vast designs, Don Estevan had, for the time at least, shaken off gloomy thoughts, and fixed his mind on the hope of a success which he believed infallible.

He had raised the canvas, which served as a door, in order to glance upon the men who reposed around, and seemed to wish to compare his means of action with the aim he was pursuing.

"Nearly twenty years ago," thought he, "I commanded a party of sailors, nearly equal in number, and as determined as these. I was then only an obscure younger son, and they aided me to recover my inheritance—yes, it was mine. But I was then in the flower of my age, and had an aim in the future to pursue. I have attained this aim—I have even surpassed it; and now that I have nothing more to desire, I find myself, in my mature age, scouring the desert as I formerly scoured the sea. Why?"

The conscience of Mediana cried to him, that it was in order to forget one day of his life, but at that moment he wished to remain deaf to its voice. The moon shone upon the firearms piled in the centre of the camp, and cast its light upon sixty men inured to peril and fatigue, and who laughed at heat and thirst. In the distance a luminous vapour rested upon the mountains beyond which lay the Golden Valley.

"Why?" repeated Don Estevan; "because there remains to me still an immense treasure and a vast kingdom to conquer."

The eyes of Mediana sparkled with pride; then this expression passed away, and he fixed on the horizon a melancholy look.

"And yet," continued he, "what of this treasure shall I keep for myself? Nothing. The crown will be placed on the head of another, and I shall not even have a son or any descendant bearing the name of Mediana, who one day might bow before my portrait and say, 'This man could be tempted neither by gold nor by a throne.' But they will say it of me now, and is not that enough?"

At this moment Pedro Diaz raised the door of the tent, and said, "You sent for me, Señor Don Estevan?"

"I wish to speak to you of important things, which I could not do yesterday, and ought to do to-day; I have some questions to ask; and although this is the hour for repose, they must not be adjourned. If I do not deceive myself, Diaz, you are one of those men who repose only when they have nothing better to do. The ambitious are such," added Don Estevan, with a smile.

"I am not ambitious, Señor," replied the adventurer quietly.

"You are so without knowing it, Diaz; and I will prove it to you, presently. But first tell me what you think of this distant firing?"

"Men meet on the sea whose surface is incomparably more extensive than that of this desert; it is not astonishing that they should meet here. Travellers and Indians have encountered one another, and are fighting."

"That is what I think. One more question and then we will return to the first subject which I have at heart. Has Cuchillo returned?"

"No, Señor, and I much fear that we have lost the guide who has conducted us till now."

"And to what do you attribute this strange absence?" asked Don Estevan, with an anxious look.

"Probably he has gone too far upon the track of the Apaches, and has been surprised by them. In that ease his absence may prove eternal, in spite of the fires which we have lighted for two days to show him our encampment."

"Is that really your idea?" said the chief, looking fixedly at Diaz.

"It is; although, to say the truth, Cuchillo is one of those people whom one is rarely wrong in accusing of perfidy; but I do not see what object he could have in betraying us."

Don Estevan pointed to the fog which hid the tops of the mountains in the horizon. "The neighbourhood of those mountains," said he, "might explain the absence of Cuchillo." Then, with a changed tone, "Are our men still of the same mind."

"Yes, Señor, and have more confidence than ever, in the chief who watches while they sleep, and fights like the humblest of them."

"I have battled in many parts of the world," said Don Estevan, sensible to praise, the sincerity of which he believed in, "and I have rarely commanded men more determined than these. Would they were five hundred instead of sixty, for then on the return of this expedition my projects would be easy of accomplishment."

"I am ignorant what these projects are, of which you now speak to me for the first time," said Diaz in a reserved tone. "But perhaps Don Estevan thinks me ambitious, only because he does me the honour to judge me by himself."

"It is possible, friend Diaz," replied Don Estevan, smiling; "the first time that I saw you I thought that your mind was of the same stamp as my own. We are made to understand each other, I am sure."

The Mexican had all the vivacious intelligence of his country; he had judged Don Estevan, but he waited for him to take the initiative. He therefore bowed and kept silence.

The Spaniard pushed open the curtains of the tent, and, pointing one more to the horizon, "Another day's march," said he; "and we shall encamp at the foot of those mountains."

"Yes, we are scarcely six leagues distant."

"And do you know what is below that mass of fog which crowns their top?"

"No," replied the Mexican.

Don Estevan cast upon Diaz a look which seemed as if meant to penetrate his soul, at the moment of revealing a secret until then so carefully kept. The Spaniard wished to assure himself that the confidant he was about to choose was worthy of his confidence. The honest look of Diaz—on whose countenance could be traced none of that cupidity which spurred on his companions—reassured him, and he went on:

"Well, it is towards those mountains that we have been marching. I shall now tell you why I have directed the expedition to this place, as the pilot conducts the ship to some point in the ocean known only to himself; this evening you shall read my mind clearly. That mass of fog, which the sun itself will not wholly disperse, serves as a veil to treasures which have been amassing perhaps from the beginning of the world. For centuries the rains have been washing them into the plains: the whites only suspected, and the Indians spared them; to-morrow they shall be ours! This has been my aim. Well, Diaz! do you not fall on your knees to thank God for being one of those called to share in these treasures?"

"No," replied Diaz, simply; "cupidity would not have made me brave the dangers that a wish for revenge has done. I would have sought from the work of my arms what others seek by easier, if by less sure, methods. But the Indians have ravaged my fields, pillaged my flocks, and murdered my father and brothers. Of my people I alone escaped. Since that time I have made fierce war upon the savages, have slain many, have sold their sons by dozens, and it is still the hope of vengeance which brings me here—neither ambition nor cupidity. But I love my country and all that I should care for riches would be to enable me to make a last effort against that distant congress which tyrannises over but cannot protect us."

"Good! friend Diaz!" cried the Spaniard, holding out his hand to the adventurer, and then added with vehemence:

"Strong by the aid of this gold, I will confide my plans to those sixty men now buried in sleep. On our return our numbers will swell like the stream which widens as it flows, and we shall shake off the yoke of a capital—which is capable only of constantly changing its men and its principles."

Don Estevan had already noticed, in former conversations with Diaz, his great hatred of the federal system, but wishing to be sure whether or not it was founded on personal motives, he continued—

"The congress is far from you, and the government of Mexico has neither troops nor money to protect provinces so distant as yours. Is that the only reproach you have to make of it!"

"The only reproach! No. Independence is for us but an empty name, and we have to bear only the burden of a distant government."

Don Estevan now unveiled to Diaz the project which he had discussed with the Senator. Then passing from principles to persons, he named the King, Don Carlos, as him whom they were to introduce.

"A king! King Charles! so be it," replied Diaz, "but we shall have many obstacles to overcome."

"Less than you imagine, Diaz. Gold will level all obstacles, and to-morrow we shall gather it by handfuls. We will pave the way to the new kingdom with gold, and pay largely the founders and guardians of a throne which will want only its king."

Thus, as he had promised his master, the bold partisan laid, even in the desert, the foundation of a future dynasty. What the influence of the Senator was to effect in the congress, that of a man renowned by his exploits was to obtain from his equals.

After this conversation Diaz retired to seek repose from his fatigues, and Don Estevan accompanied him out of the tent. The latter threw around him a glance of tranquil pride; all obstacles were surmounted, the incessant vigilance of the Indians had been eluded, thanks to Diaz, and an immense treasure, untouched since the commencement of the world, awaited only the hands which were about to be extended to seize it.

"See!" said he, "from those will rise the elements of a new kingdom, and our names will belong to history. Now I have but one fear—that is, treachery on the part of Cuchillo—and you will share this fear with me when you hear that it is he who sold me the secret of this golden deposit."

Diaz was looking earnestly at the plain.

"There!" cried he, "I see a man approaching at full gallop: it is Gayferos or Cuchillo?"

"Pray God it be the latter," said Don Estevan. "I prefer having him near rather than far from my sight."

"I think I recognise his grey horse."

In a minute, indeed, they recognised Cuchillo himself.

"To arms! to arms!" cried the guide, "here are the Indians," and he rushed precipitately through the opening made for him by the sentinels.

"Cuchillo! the Indians! both names of bad augury," said Don Estevan, as he turned towards his companion.

Chapter Thirty Seven
The Attack

At the cry of Cuchillo, which resounded throughout the camp, the Spaniard and Diaz exchanged looks of intelligence.

"It is strange that the Indians should have found our trail again?" said Don Estevan, interrogatively.

"Very strange," replied Diaz, and without saying another word, both descended from the eminence, on which they stood.

The camp was already in motion, and confusion reigned everywhere; there was a general movement among these intrepid men, who were accustomed to such surprises, and who had already more than once measured their strength with their implacable enemies. Each armed hastily, but soon the tumult subsided, and all stationed themselves at the posts assigned to them in case of attack. The first who interrogated Cuchillo were the shepherd and Baraja.

"Unless you drew the Indians on to our track, how could they have discovered us?" said the former, with a suspicious look.

"Certainly it was I," replied Cuchillo, impudently. "I should have liked to have seen you pursued by a hundred, of these demons, and whether you would not, like me, have galloped to the camp to seek an asylum!"

"In such a case," replied Benito, severely, "a man to save his companions, does not fly, but gives up his life sooner than betray them. I should have done so."

"Every one in his own way," replied Cuchillo, "but I have an account to render only to the chief, and not to his servants."

"Yes," murmured the other, "a coward and a traitor can but commit baseness and perfidies."

"Are the Indians numerous?" asked Baraja.

"I had not time to count them; all that I know is that they must be near."

And crossing the camp he proceeded to where Don Estevan—after having attended to the most important precautions—stood at the door of his tent waiting for him. As Cuchillo went on without replying to any of the questions with which he was assailed, a man advanced with a lighted torch in his hand to set fire to the fagots piled in various places, but Don Estevan cried—

"Not yet; it is, perhaps, a false alarm, and until we have the certainty of attack we must not light up the camp to betray ourselves."

At the words "false alarm," a smile played over Cuchillo's features.

"However," added Don Estevan, "let every one saddle his horse and be prepared." Then he returned to his tent, making a sign to Diaz to accompany him.

"That means, friend Baraja," said Benito, "that if the orders are given to light the fires, we are sure to be attacked—at night too; it is terrible."

"Who knows that better than I?" said Baraja, "have you ever been present at such a thing?"

"Never; that is why I dread it so much."

"Well, if you had, you would dread it more."

Cuchillo, as he drew near the tent, arranged his countenance and threw back his long hair—as though the wind had blown it about in his rapid flight—and then entered the tent like a man out of breath and pretending to wipe the perspiration from his forehead. Oroche had glided in with Diaz.

Cuchillo's story was brief: in reconnoitring the places towards which the expedition should advance, he had gone further than was prudent.

Diaz interrupted him.

"I had taken such precautions to deceive the Indians by false tracks," said he, "I had so misled them, that you must have quitted the line of march and gone from right to left."

"Yes," replied the outlaw, "I lost my way, deceived by the monotony of these endless plains where each hillock resembles the other."

"What!" cried Diaz, ironically. "Had a dweller in cities been so deceived it might be believed; but you—fear must have thrown a mist before your eyes!"

"Fear!" replied Cuchillo; "I know it no more than you do."

"Then you must be growing shortsighted, Señor Cuchillo."

"However it happened, I lost myself; and, but for the column of smoke, I should not have regained my way so quickly. I was, however, forced to make a circuit on perceiving a party of Indians, and only owe the start I have got upon them to the speed of my good horse."

As he spoke, Don Estevan frowned more than once. Oroche left the tent, but immediately re-entering, said—

"The Indians are there! Look at those black shadows on the plain over which the moon throws a distant light; those are men sent to reconnoitre our encampment."

Over the sand of the desert they could indeed see men on horseback advancing, and then disappearing in the shadows of the sand heaps.

Pedro Diaz consulted an instant with Don Estevan, and then cried loudly—

"Light the fires everywhere! we must count our enemies."

A few minutes after, a red light, almost as bright as the sun, lit up the whole camp, and showed the adventurers at their post, rifles in hand; while the horses stood saddled and bridled, only waiting for their riders in case of a sortie being necessary. At the same time Don Estevan's tent was struck, and a calm succeeded to the tumult.

The desert was silent also; the moon no longer shone on the Indians, who had all disappeared like a bad dream chased away by the return of morning. It was a dead silence—the precursor of the storm—and there seemed in this silence something fearful. It did not announce one of those surprises in which an enemy inferior in number disguises his weakness under the impetuosity of his attack, and ready to run if he is resisted: it was the respite before the combat, granted by pitiless enemies, preparing for a deadly struggle.

"Yes, trust to me," said old Benito to Baraja, "in a quarter of an hour you will hear the howlings of these red devils sound in your ears like the trumpets of the last judgment!"

"Carramba! you are the most skilled man about tigers and Indians that I ever met with, but you might be more consoling. I wish to God I could doubt the truth of your words!"

"There are some things always easy to foresee," continued the old man. "One may predict to the traveller who goes to sleep in a bed of a torrent that he will be carried away by the waters; and that Indians who have discovered their enemies will draw off a little, and count their men before making an attack. One may also predict that several of them will utter their death-cry, as many among us will have to say their last prayer; but who those will be no one can say. Do you know any prayers for the dying, Señor Baraja?"

"No," replied the latter, dolefully.

"I am sorry for that; those are little services that friends may render each other, and if I had the grief, as is very possible, of seeing you first scalped then murdered—"

Further conversation was interrupted by outcries which seemed drawing near to the camp. In spite of the terrifying words of the old shepherd, his *sang froid* in the greatest perils and his resolution full of consoling fatalism, sustained the more wavering courage of Baraja.

As he shuddered at the horrible sounds—which must be heard to be appreciated—he cast upon Benito a glance in order to catch from him a little of his philosophy. For the first time a cloud of sadness appeared on the ex-herdsman's brow, and his eyes looked as though tears stood in them. Baraja was struck by the change, and laid his head upon the old man's arm. Benito raised his head.

"I understand you," said he, "but man has his moments of weakness. I am like him who is called from his hearth by the sound of the trumpet at a time he least thought to quit it. Amidst those howls I hear from above the sound of the last trumpet calling me, and although I am old, it grieves me to go. I leave neither wife nor children to regret, nor those who would weep for me; but there is an old companion of my solitary life from whom I cannot separate without grief. It is at least a consolation for the Indian warrior to know that his war-horse will share his tomb, and to believe that he shall find him again in the land of spirits. How many times have we scoured the woods and the plains together. How often have we borne together heat, hunger, and thirst! This old and faithful friend is my horse, as you may have guessed. I give him to you, friend Baraja. Treat him kindly—love him as I love him, and he will love you as he loves me. His companion was killed by a tiger, and he will now be left alone."

So saying, the old man pointed to a noble courser, champing his bit proudly, among the other horses. He then went towards him, caressed him, and, this moment of weakness over, his countenance recovered its habitual serenity. As he recovered his calmness, he renewed his predictions, careless of the terror he excited in others.

"Listen!" said he to Baraja; "to recompense you for the care you will take of my old friend, I shall teach you, while there is still time, a verse of the psalm for the dying, that may serve you as—"

"Well!" said Baraja, as he did not go on, "what more terrifying things have you to say?"

Benito did not reply, but his companion felt him press his arm convulsively, and then the sight which struck Baraja was more terrible than any answer. The old man's eyes were rolling wildly, and he was vainly trying to stanch the blood which flowed from a wound made by an arrow that had just pierced his throat.

He fell, crying: "What is ordained must happen. No," added he, repulsing the assistance that Baraja was endeavouring to render him, "my hour is come—remember—my old friend—" and the flowing blood cut short his speech.

At that moment the best mounted among the Indians showed themselves in the moonlight. Travellers who have met only with civilised Indians can with difficulty form any idea of the savage tribes. Nothing less resembled those degenerate Indians than these unconquered sons of the desert; who—like the birds of prey, wheeling in the air before pouncing on their victims—rode howling around the camp. Their figures hideously marked with paint, were visible from time to time; their long hair streaming in the wind, their cloaks of skins floating in their rapid course, and their piercing cries of defiance and bravado, giving them the appearance of demons, to whom they have justly been compared.

There were few among the Mexicans who had not some revenge to take on these indefatigable spoilers, but none of them were animated by such deadly hatred as Pedro Diaz. The sight of his enemies produced on him the effect that scarlet does on a bull, and he could scarcely refrain from indulging in one of those exploits which had rendered his name formidable to their tribes. But it was necessary to set an example of discipline, and he curbed his impatience. Besides, the moment of attack could not be far off, and the superior position of the gold-seekers compensated for the inequality of their numbers.

After having assigned to each his post behind the intrenchments, Don Estevan placed on the rising ground, where his tent had stood, those of his men whose rifles carried farthest, or whose sight was the best, and the fires gave light enough for their aim. As for himself, his post was everywhere.

The piercing eyes of the Indians, and the reports of those who had preceded them had doubtless instructed them as to the position of the whites. For a moment an indecision seemed to reign among them, but the truce did not last long. After a short interval of silence, a hundred voices at once shrieked out the war-cry; the earth trembled under an avalanche of galloping horses; and amidst a shower of balls, stones, and arrows, the camp was surrounded on three sides by a disorderly multitude. But a well-sustained fire proceeded from the top of the hill.

Under this murderous discharge riderless horses were seen galloping over the plain, and riders disengaging themselves from their wounded steeds. Before long, however, the combat became one of hand to hand; the Mexicans behind their carts, the Indians trying to scale them.

Oroche, Baraja, and Pedro Diaz pressed one against the other, sometimes retiring to avoid the long lances of their enemies—sometimes advancing and striking in their turn—encouraging each other, and never pausing but to glance at their chief. As already stated, the report had vaguely spread that he knew the secret of the immense riches, and cupidity supplied to Oroche and Baraja the place of enthusiasm.

"Carramba!" cried Baraja, "a man possessing such a secret should be invulnerable."

"Immortal!" said Oroche, "or only die after—"

A blow from a hatchet on his head cut short his words. He fell to the ground, and but for the solidity of his hat, and the thickness of his hair, all had been over with him. His adversary, carried away by the violence of his own blow, placed his hand for support on the shafts of the cart which separated them. Diaz immediately seized the Indian's arm, and leaning on the nave of the wheel, dragged him towards him with such force that he fell off his horse into camp; and, almost before he touched the ground, the Mexican's sword severed his head from his body.

Useless now on their elevated position—for the *mêlée* was so thick that their shots might have been as fatal to friends as foes—the sharpshooters had come down and mingled with the other combatants.

In the corner of the intrenchments where they stood, Don Estevan and Cuchillo had to sustain an attack not less furious. The first, while he defended himself, yet cast an eye over the whole of the intrenchments; but it was with the greatest difficulty that amidst the tumult he could make heard his orders and advice. More than once his double-barrelled rifle of English make—and which he loaded and discharged with wonderful rapidity—stayed the knife or axe which was menacing one of his men—a feat which was greeted each time with loud hurrahs. He was, in a word, what the adventurers had seen him from the beginning of this dangerous campaign, the chief who thought of all, and the chief who feared nothing.

Accompanied by his horse, which followed his movements with the intelligence of a spaniel, Cuchillo stood behind the chief—as much out of the way as possible—with more prudence than bravery. He seemed to be following with an anxious eye the chances of attack and defence: when all at once he tottered as though struck by a mortal wound, and fell heavily behind the carts. This incident passed almost unperceived amidst the confusion—every one being in so much danger as to be able to think only of himself.

"There is a coward the less," said Don Estevan, coldly, while Cuchillo's horse drew near him with a terrified air.

For some minutes Cuchillo remained motionless; then, little by little, he raised his head and cast around him a glance which seemed undimmed by the approach of death. A few minutes after, he rose on his feet, like a man to whom death lends some strength at the last, and apparently, mortally hurt, his hand on his breast, as though endeavouring to retain the spark of life ready to escape, tottered backwards, and then fell again some way off. His horse followed him once more; and then, if every one had not been too much occupied, they might have seen the outlaw rolling over and over towards an open place in the intrenchments. He then stopped again; and finally glided under the cart wheels out of the camp.

There he rose upon his legs as firm as ever, while a smile of joy played over his lips. The darkness and the tumult favoured his manoeuvre. He silently unfastened the iron chains of two carts, and opened a passage. He whistled and his horse glided after him; in a second he was in the saddle, almost without touching the stirrup; when after a moment's thought, he spurred on the animal, who set off like the wind, and horse and rider soon disappeared in the darkness!

On both sides of the intrenchment corpses covered the ground; half burnt-out piles of wood cast their red light upon the bloody scenes of this struggle; the shouts of enemies, the repeated discharge of firearms, and the whistling of bullets followed each other uninterruptedly. The hideous figures of the Indians looked more hideous still in the strange light.

One point in the intrenchment had given way before the incessant attacks; and here, dead or wounded, its defenders had yielded to enemies who seemed to swarm from the ground. At this point there was an instant of horrible confusion. A *pêle mêle* of bodies interlaced, over which appeared the plumes of the Indian warriors. Soon, however, the line of the adventurers, broken for an instant, reformed before a group of Indians who were rushing like wild beasts into the middle of the camp.

Oroche and Baraja left the point which they were still defending, and found themselves face to face with their enemies, this time with nothing to separate them. Amidst the group of Indians, whose lances and hatchets fell indiscriminately upon horses, mules and men, the chief was recognisable by his vast height, the painting of his face and his great strength.

It was the second time that he had faced the whites since the commencement of the campaign, and his name was known to them.

"Here, Diaz," cried Baraja, "here is the *Spotted Cat!*"

At the name of Diaz, which had already reached him, the Indian chief looked round for him who bore it, with eyes which seemed to dart flames, and raised his lance to strike Diaz, when a blow from Oroche's knife wounded his horse. The Indian thrown to the ground, let fall his lance. Diaz seized it, and while the chief raised himself on one knee and endeavoured to draw his sword, the lance which he had dropped, pierced his naked breast, and came out between his shoulders. Although mortally wounded, the Indian uttered no cry, his eyes never lost their haughty menace, and his face expressed only rage.

"The Spotted Cat dies not so easily," said he, and with a vigorous hand he seized the wood of the lance still held by Diaz. A fierce struggle ensued, but at every effort of the Indian to draw Diaz towards him, and envelop him in a last deadly clasp, the murdering, lance pierced farther and farther. Soon his strength failed, and violently torn from his body the bloody weapon remained in the hands of Diaz. The Indian fell back, gave one glance of defiance, and then lay motionless upon the earth.

Their chief fallen, the others soon shared the same fate, while their companions vainly tried to force the line a second time. Victims of their temerity, the Indians, without asking for a mercy which they never showed, fell like their chief facing the enemy, and surrounded by the corpses of those who had preceded them in their journey to the land of spirits.

Of all the savages in the camp but one remained. He looked round him for a minute with eyes fierce as those of the hunted tiger; then, instead of seeking to hide his presence, he uttered anew his war-cry, but it was confounded with those from without—and profiting by a moment of confusion, during which the adventurers, attacked from without, left the breach almost clear—he caused his horse to leap over, and found himself once more among his own people.

Pedro Diaz alone saw him, and regretted his prey, but the implacable enemy of the Indians never indulged in sterile regrets. He was mounted on the war-horse presented to him by Don Augustin Peña. From his left hand hung by the sword-knot a long Toledo rapier, with the Spanish device:

Do not draw me without cause,
Or sheathe me without honour.

The blade was red with blood. Diaz shaded his eyes with his right hand, and tried to pierce the distant obscurity. All at once he perceived at the end of the luminous zone projected by the fires, the man he was seeking. He was making furious evolutions on his horse, and uttering shouts of defiance. Diaz remembered the speech of the haciendado about the horse he had given him—"The Indian whom you pursue must be mounted on the wings of the wind if you do not catch him," and he resolved to make the attempt. The noble animal, excited by the spur, leaped over the intrenchments overthrown by the Indians, and the two were soon side by side. The Indian brandished his hatchet, Diaz his sword, and for some seconds there was a trial of agility, courage, and address. Each sustained his country's reputation, but the Indian's hatchet broke to pieces the sword of the Mexican. The two combatants then seized one another round the body and tried to drag each other from their horses, but like centaurs, each seemed to form a part of the animal he bestrode.

At last Diaz disengaged himself from his adversary's clasp, and backed his horse, still facing the Indian. Then, when he was a little way off, he caused his horse to rear so furiously that the animal seemed for a moment to be raised over the Indian. At the same moment Diaz lifted his right leg, and with a blow from the large heavy iron-bound stirrup, broke his adversary's skull, whom his horse carried away dead from the spot.

This last magnificent exploit seemed to end the battle; some arrows flew harmlessly around Diaz, who was welcomed back with shouts of triumph by his companions.

"Poor Benito!" cried Baraja; "may God rest his soul, I regret even his terrific histories."

"What is still more to be regretted," interrupted Oroche, "is the death of the illustrious Cuchillo, the guide of the expedition."

"Your ideas are still confused from the blow you received on your head," said Diaz, as he tried the flexibility of a new sword. "But for the illustrious Cuchillo, as you call him, we should not have lost to-night at least twenty brave comrades. Cuchillo unluckily died a day too late, and I cannot say 'God rest *his* soul.'"

Meanwhile the Indians were deliberating. The last exploit of Diaz, the death that so many of their party had met with in the camp, and those killed by the filing, had thinned their ranks.

The Indian never persists in a hopeless struggle: a singular mixture of prudence and contempt of life characterises this singular race, and prudence counselled them to retreat; they did so precipitately as they had attacked.

But the tactics of the white men were different; they were anxious to profit by a victory the fame of which would penetrate to the furthest end of the desert, and render their future more secure. Therefore an order to pursue the fugitives given by Don Estevan was received with acclamations. Twenty cavaliers instantly rushed forward, Pedro Diaz among the foremost. Sword in one hand, and lasso and bridle in the other, he was soon out of sight.

Those who remained behind, though nearly all more or less wounded, occupied themselves first with reconstructing the intrenchment in case of any new attack; then, overwhelmed with fatigue, hunger, and thirst, after clearing the camp of the dead bodies which encumbered it, they lay down on the earth, still wet with blood, to seek for repose.

Chapter Thirty Eight
After the Fight

In the calm which succeeded to the noise of the combat, a single man rose slowly up, and by the light of a torch which he held, examined all the corpses lying at his feet, as if seeking to identify the livid or bloody faces of the dead. Sometimes the light fell on the strange paint of an Indian face, and the pale one of a white man, lying side by side in an eternal sleep; occasionally a deep groan proceeded from some one who was wounded, but the seeker did not appear to find what he sought.

All at once, amidst the silence, a weak voice attracted his attention, and he tried in the half-light to discover whence the sound proceeded. The feeble movement of a hand guided him, and he approached the dying man—in whom he immediately recognised Benito.

"Ah! it is you, my poor Benito?" said he, with a look of profound pity.

"Yes," replied the old shepherd, "it is old Benito, dying in the desert where he has nearly always lived. As for me—I know not who you are; my eyes are dim. Is Baraja living?"

"I trust so; he is now pursuing the Indians, and will return in time, I hope, to bid you a last adieu."

"I doubt it," replied Benito; "I wished to teach him a verse of the hymn for the dying. I can no longer remember it now. Do you not know something?"

"Not a word."

"Ah! I must do without it," said Benito, whose accustomed stoicism did not forsake him even at that moment. Then, in a still more feeble voice, he added, "I have bequeathed to Baraja an old companion—an old friend; whoever you may be, recommend him to observe my last request, to love him as I did."

"A brother doubtless."

"Better than that; my horse."

"I shall remind him—do not fear."

"Thank you," said the old man. "As for myself, I have finished my travels. The Indians did not kill me when they took me prisoner in my youth—now they have killed me in my old age without taking me prisoner. That—" he stopped, and then added some words in so low a tone that they did not reach the ear of the listener. He spoke no more; those were his last words, for death had abruptly ended his speech.

"He was a brave man—peace be with him!" said the speaker, who then continued his search, until at last, fatigued by its uselessness, he returned with an anxious look to his place, and after he had gone the silence of death seemed to pervade the camp.

Before long, however, a confused noise of voices and horses' feet indicated the return of the adventurers who had started in pursuit of the Indians, and by the doubtful light of the half extinct fires, they entered the camp.

The same man who had been recently inspecting the dead, went out to meet them. While some of them were dismounting to open a passage through the barricades, Pedro Diaz advanced towards him, a stream of blood flowing from a wound in his forehead.

"Señor Don Estevan," said he, "we have not been lucky in our pursuit. We have but wounded one or two of the Indians, and have lost one of our own men. However I bring you a prisoner; do you wish to interrogate him?"

So saying, Diaz detached his lasso from the saddle-bow, and pointed to a mass held in its noose. It was an Indian, who, pitilessly dragged along over the sand and stones, had left behind at every step pieces of flesh, and now scarcely retained any vestige of humanity.

"He was alive when I took him, however," cried Diaz, "but it is just like these dogs of Indians, he must have died in order not to tell anything."

Without replying to this ferocious jest, Don Estevan signed to Diaz to accompany him to a place where they might converse without being overheard. When the new-comers had lain down and silence reigned anew, Don Estevan began:

"Diaz," said he, "we are close on the end of our expedition: to-morrow, as I told you, we shall encamp at the foot of those mountains; but in order that success may crown our efforts, treason must not throw obstacles in our way. It is on this subject that I wish to consult you to-night. You have known Cuchillo long, but not so long as I have; and certainly, not as thoroughly. From his earliest youth he has always betrayed those to whom he appeared most devoted. I know not which of all the vices with which he is endowed has the ascendant; but in a word, the sinister look of his face is but a feeble reflection of the blackness of his soul. It was he who sold to me the secret of the rich and mysterious placer to which I am leading you—and of this secret he had made himself the sole master by murdering the friend who had freely confided it to him, and who thought to find him a faithful companion in his dangers.

"I have ever, therefore, kept a watchful eye over him. His disappearance for the last two days alarmed me, but it might have been the result of an accident common in these deserts. The attack, however, from which we have so narrowly escaped has confirmed my suspicions. He has advanced under our protection, until we have reached the place where he would, be able to seize a part of these immense treasures. He had need of auxiliaries in order to murder our sixty men, and the Indians who have attacked us were but his instruments."

"Indeed," replied Diaz, "his report seemed to me suspicious. But the simplest method will be to hold a court-martial, interrogate him, and if he be convicted of treason, let us shoot him at once."

"At the commencement of the attack, I assigned him a post near me, in order to watch him more easily. I saw him totter and then fall apparently mortally wounded, and I was glad to be rid of a traitor and a coward. But I have just turned over and examined all the dead, and Cuchillo is not amongst them. It is therefore urgent that without loss of time we should follow him; he cannot be far off. You are accustomed to this sort of expedition; we must, without delay, set off in pursuit of him, and execute prompt justice on a villain whose life must pay for his treachery."

Diaz appeared to reflect for a moment, and then said, "To trace him can neither be tedious nor difficult. Cuchillo must have gone towards the Golden Valley—therefore in that direction we must seek him."

"Go rest for an hour, for you must be worn out," said the chief. "Ah! Diaz, if all these men were like you, how easy our path would be—gold in one hand, and the sword in the other."

"I have only done my duty," said Diaz, simply.

"Say to our men that it is necessary for us to reconnoitre the environs of the camp, and tell the sentinels to keep strict watch until our return, and then we shall proceed towards the valley."

"Cuchillo must certainly be there, and we shall catch him either going or returning."

"We shall find him in the valley," said Don Estevan. "When you have seen it, you will find it a place that a man like Cuchillo could not make up his mind to leave."

Diaz departed to execute his orders, and Don Estevan caused his tent to be pitched again, that even in his absence his starry banner might float over the camp as a sign of his protective authority. This done, he threw himself on his couch, and slept the sleep of a soldier after a day of fighting and fatigue.

Little more than an hour after, Diaz stood before him, "Señor Don Estevan," said he, "all is prepared for starting."

The chief rose and found his horse awaiting him ready saddled.

"Diaz," said he, "ask the sentinels if Gayferos has returned."

Diaz questioned one of the men, who replied, "The poor fellow will probably never return. The Indians must have surprised and killed him before attacking us, and that probably was the cause of the firing that we heard in the afternoon."

"I fear it is but too certain that he has been murdered," replied Diaz; "but as for the firing that we heard, I believe that had a different origin."

Don Estevan now mounted his horse, and the two set off in, the direction of the mountains.

Chapter Thirty Nine
The Islet

While the Indians, united in council, were deliberating on the means of attacking the camp of the gold-seekers, let us see how the three men on the island were occupied.

It was about four o'clock, and the fog was beginning to rise slowly from the water. Willows and aspens grew on the shores of the river Gila, within rifle-range of the little island, and so near the water that their roots were in the river. The spaces between the trees were filled up by vigorous osier and other shoots; but just in front of the island was a large open space. This had been made by the troops of wild horses and buffaloes, that came down to drink at the river; and through this opening any one on the island could see clearly over the plain.

The little island had been formed originally by trees that had taken root in the bed of the river; other trees, some green and others without branches or foliage, had rested against these, and their roots had become interlaced. Since then, many summers and winters must have passed; and grasses and sedges, detached from the banks by the water, had filled up the interstices. Then the dust, brought there by the wind, had covered these with a crust of earth, and formed a kind of solid ground for the floating island. Plants had grown along the banks; the trunks of the willows had sent forth vigorous shoots, and, with the reeds, had surrounded the island with a fringe of verdure. The island was only a few feet in diameter; but a man lying, or even kneeling upon it, was completely hidden by the willow-shoots.

The sun was going down, and a little shade was thrown by the leaves and trees; in this shade was stretched the form of Fabian asleep. Bois-Rose seemed to be watching over his sleep, hastily taken after the fatigues of a long march, while Pepé refreshed himself by plunging in the water. While Fabian slumbers, we shall raise the veil by which the young Count hid from the eyes of his two friends his most secret and dearest thoughts.

After his fall into the torrent, Pepé had forgotten that the enemy on whom he had sworn vengeance was escaping, and both he and Bois-Rose had thought only of rendering prompt assistance to Fabian. On returning to consciousness, Fabian's first thought was to resume his interrupted pursuit. The acquisition of the Golden Valley, and even the remembrance of Doña Rosarita, were forgotten by the ardent wish of revenging his mother.

Pepé, on his side, was not the man to draw back from his vow; and as for Bois-Rose, his whole affections were centred in his two companions, and he would have followed them to the end of the world. Their first failure, far from discouraging them, did but excite their ardour; in hatred as in love, obstacles are always a powerful stimulant to vigorous minds. The pursuit had gradually presented a double object to Fabian; it brought him near to the Golden Valley in the desert; and he nourished a vague hope that the place pointed out to him was not the same as that which the expedition led by Antonio de Mediana proposed to conquer.

Fabian said to himself, that the daughter of Don Augustin doubtless only yielded obedience to the ambitious views of her father, and that it might yet be easy for him, noble and rich, to win the day against such a rival as Tragaduros.

Still, discouragement often seized upon Fabian; he loved the daughter of the haciendado with his whole soul; and the thought of owing her love only to the treasures that he might possess, distressed him. Moreover, he felt that the ardent and jealous affection of the Canadian, had founded on him the sole aim of his life, and that, like the eagle who carries away his young one and places it in an eyrie, inaccessible to the hand of man, Bois-Rose, who had forever quitted civilised life, wished to make of him his inseparable companion in the desert; and that, to disappoint the old man would be to throw a shadow over his whole future life. As yet, no confidence as to their future had been exchanged between them; but in face of a love that he believed hopeless, and of the ardent, though secret wishes of the man who now acted as a father to him, and who would half break his heart at a separation, Fabian had generously and silently sacrificed his tastes and hopes that would not die. He who had but to hold out his hand to seize the things that the whole world desires—riches, titles, and honours—was like one whose life tortured by an unhappy love, disclaiming the future, seeks within the cloister forgetfulness of the past. For Fabian de Mediana, the desert was the cloister; and his mother once revenged, it only remained to him to bury himself in it forever. Sad and inefficacious, as a remedy, would be solitude, with its mysterious voice, and the ardent contemplations that it awakens, for a passion so fondly awakened in the young heart of Fabian.

One single hope remained to him—that amidst the ever-renewed dangers of an adventurous life, the day was not far distant when his life would be cut short in some contest with the Indians, or in one of those desperate attempts that he meditated against the murderer of his mother. He had carefully hidden from the Canadian the love that he buried in the depths of his heart; and it was in the silence of the night that he dared to look into his own bosom. Then, like the light which shines in the horizon above great cities, and which the traveller contemplates with joy, a radiant and cherished image rose before his eyes in the desert, standing on that breach in the wall of the hacienda, where his last souvenirs carried him. But during the day, the heroic young man tried to hide under an apparent calm, the melancholy that devoured him. He smiled, with sad resignation, at those plans for the future which the Canadian sometimes enlarged on before him—he so happy in having found him, and who trembled to lose again his beloved Fabian, whose hand he hoped would one day close his eyes. The blind tenderness of Bois-Rose did not divine the abyss under the calm surface of the lake, but Pepé was rather more clear-sighted.

"Well," said Pepé, after a long silence, "the inhabitants of Madrid would pay dearly for such a stream of water in the Manzanares; but we have not the less lost a day which might have brought us nearer to the Golden Valley, and from which we cannot now be far distant."

"I allow that," replied Bois-Rose, "but the child," for so he called the vigorous young man before them, "is not so accustomed as we are to long marches, and though sixty leagues in twelve days is not very much for us, it begins to tell on him. But before he has been a year with us, he will be able to walk as far as ourselves."

Pepé could not help smiling at this answer, but the Canadian did not perceive it.

"See," said the Spaniard, pointing to Fabian, "how the poor lad has changed in a few days. For my part, at his age, I should have preferred the glance of a damsel and the Puerta del Sol at Madrid to all the magnificence of the desert. Fatigue alone has not produced this change in him. There is some secret which he does not tell us, but I will penetrate it one of these days," added Pepé mentally.

At these words the Canadian turned his head quickly towards his beloved child, but a smile of joy from Fabian chased away the sudden cloud from the brow of his adoptive father. Fabian indeed smiled; he was dreaming that he was on his knees before Rosarita, listening to the sweet voice of the young girl, who was recounting her anguish during his long absence, and that Bois-Rose stood behind them leaning on his rifle and blessing them both. Ah! it was only a dream.

The two hunters looked for a moment silently at the sleeper.

"There lies the last descendant of the Medianas," said Pepé, with a sigh.

"What care I for the Medianas and their powerful race?" replied the Canadian. "I know but Fabian. When I saved him, and attached myself to him as though he had been my own, did I ask about his ancestors?"

"You will wake him if you talk so loud," said Pepé; "your voice roars like a cataract."

"Why are you always recalling to me things that I do not wish to know, or rather wish to forget. I know that some years in the desert will accustom him—"

"You deceive yourself strangely, Bois-Rose, if you imagine that with the prospects that await him in Spain, and the rights that he can claim, this young man will consent to pass his whole life in the desert. It is good for us, but not for him."

"What! is not the desert preferable to cities?" cried the old sailor, who vainly tried to conceal from himself that Pepé was right. "I undertake to make him prefer a wandering life to a settled one. Is it not for movement, for fighting, and for the powerful emotions of the desert that man is born?"

"Certainly," said Pepé, gravely, "and that is just why the towns are deserted and the deserts peopled!"

"Do not jest, Pepé; I am speaking of serious things. While I leave Fabian free to follow his own inclinations, I shall make him love this captivating life. Is not this short sleep, snatched hastily between two dangers, preferable to what one tastes after a day of idle security in the towns. You yourself, Pepé—would *you* wish to return to your own country, since you have known the charms of a wandering life?"

"There is between the heir of the Medianas," replied Pepé, "and the old coast-guard man a great difference. To him will come a fine property, a great name, and a beautiful Gothic castle with towers like the cathedral at Burgos; while I should be sent to fish for mackerel at Ceuta—which is the most execrable life I know of and which I should have but one chance of escaping from—that of waking some fine morning, at Tunis or Tetuan, as a slave to our neighbours the Moors. I have here, it is true, the daily chance of being scalped or burnt alive by the Indians. Still the town is worse for me—but for Don Fabian—"

"Fabian has always lived in solitude, and will, I trust, prefer the calm of the desert to the tumult of cities. How solemn and silent is all around us! See here!" and he pointed to Fabian, "how the child sleeps, softly lulled by the murmur of the waters, and by the breeze in the willows. Look there, in the horizon at those fogs just coloured by the sun, and that boundless space where man wanders in his primitive liberty, like the birds in the air!"

The Spaniard shook his head doubtfully, although he partook the ideas of the Canadian, and like him felt the charm of this wandering life.

"Look," continued the old hunter, "at that troop of wild horses coming down to drink before going for the night to their distant pasturage. See how they approach in all the proud beauty that God gives to free animals — ardent eyes, open nostrils, and floating manes! Ah! I should almost like to awake Fabian in order that he might see and admire them."

"Let him sleep, Bois-Rose; perhaps his dreams show him more graceful forms than those horses of the desert — forms such as abound in our Spanish towns, in balconies or behind barred windows."

Bois-Rose sighed, as he added —

"Yet this is fine sight — how these noble beasts bound with joy at their liberty!"

"Yes, until they are chased by the Indians, and then they bound with terror!"

"There! now they are gone like the cloud driven by the wind!" continued the Canadian. "Now the scene changes. Look at that stag, who shows from time to time his shining eyes and black nose through the trees; he snuffs the wind, he listens. Ah! now he also approaches to drink. He has heard a noise, he raises his head; do not the drops that fall from his mouth look like liquid gold? I will wake the lad!"

"Let him sleep, I tell you; perhaps his dream now shows him black eyes and rosy lips, or some nymph sleeping on the banks of a clear stream."

The old Canadian sighed again.

"Is not the stag the emblem of independence?" said he.

"Yes, until the time when the wolves assemble to pursue and tear him to pieces. Perhaps he would have more chance of life in our royal parks. Everything to its time, Bois-Rose; old age loves silence, youth noise."

Bois-Rose still fought against the truth. It was the drop of gall that is found at the bottom of every cup of happiness; it is not permitted that there should be perfect felicity, for it would then be too painful to die; neither is unmixed misery allowed to mortals, or it would be painful to live. The Canadian hung his head and looked sad as he glanced at the sleeping youth, while Pepé put on his buffalo-skin buskins.

"Well! what did I tell you?" said he, presently; "do you not hear from afar those howlings—I mean those barkings, for the wolves have voices like dogs when they hunt the stags. Poor stag! he is, as you said, the emblem of life in the desert."

"Shall I wake Fabian now?" said Bois-Rose.

"Yes, certainly; for after a love dream a stag hunt is the thing most worthy of a nobleman like him, and he will rarely see such a one as this."

"He will see nothing like it in the towns," cried the Canadian, enchanted; "such scenes must make him love the desert."

And he shook the young man gently.

With head thrown back, to inhale more freely the air necessary to his lungs, the stag flew like an arrow along the plain. Behind him a hungry pack of wolves, a few white, but the greater number black, pursued him at full speed. The stag had an immense start, but on the sand heaps, almost lost in the horizon, the piercing eye of the hunter might distinguish other wolves watching. The noble animal either did not see, or else disdained them, for he flew straight towards them. As he neared them he halted a moment. Indeed, he found himself shut in by a circle of enemies, who constantly advanced upon him as he stopped to take breath. All at once he turned round, faced the other wolves, and tried one last effort to escape. But he could not now clear the solid masses that had formed around him, and he fell in the midst of them. Some rolled under his feet, and two or three were tossed in the air. Then, with a wolf hanging to his flanks, bleeding and with tongue protruding, the poor animal advanced to the edge of the water, in front of the three spectators of the strange chase.

"It is magnificent!" cried Fabian clapping his hands, and carried away by the hunter's enthusiasm, which for the time silences humanity in the heart of men.

"Is it not fine?" cried Bois-Rose, doubly pleased, happy at Fabian's pleasure, and at his own. "And we shall witness many such fine sights, my Fabian! here you see only the worst side of these American solitudes, but when you go with Pepé and me to the great rivers, and the great lakes of the north—"

"The animal has got rid of his enemy," interrupted Fabian, "he is about to spring into the river!"

The water bubbled after the leap of the stag, then a dozen times more as the wolves followed; then amidst the foam were visible the head of the stag, and those of the wolves who were pursuing him, howling with hunger, while the more timid ones ran along the banks uttering their lamentable howls. The stag had neared the island, when the wolves on the bank suddenly ceased their cries and fled precipitately away.

"What is that?" cried Pepé; "what causes this sudden panic?" but no sooner had he spoken than he cried again, "Hide yourselves, in God's name! the Indians are in chase also."

Other and more formidable hunters now appeared in their turn upon the arena. A dozen of the wild horses, which they had seen before, were now seen galloping wildly over the plain, while some Indians, mounted bareback on their horses (having taken their saddles off for greater speed), with their knees almost up to their chins, were pursuing the terrified animals. At first there were but three Indians visible; but one by one about twenty appeared, some armed with lances, and others brandishing their lassoes of plaited leather—all uttering those cries by which they express their joy or anger.

Pepé glanced at the Canadian as though to ask whether he had calculated these terrible chances when he wished to make Fabian share their adventurous career. For the first time, at such a crisis, the intrepid hunter looked deadly pale. An eloquent but sad glance was his reply to the Spaniard's mute interrogation.

"A too great affection in the heart of the bravest man," thought Pepé, "makes him tremble for him who he loves more than life; and adventurers like us should have no ties. There is Bois-Rose trembling like a woman!"

However, they felt almost certain that even the practiced eyes of the Indians could not discover them in their retreat; and the three men, after their first alarm had passed over, watched coolly the manoeuvres of the Indians. These continued to pursue the flying horses; the numberless obstacles so thickly strewn over the plain—the ravines, the hillocks, and the sharp-pointed cacti—could not stop them. Without slackening the impetuosity of their pace or turning aside from any obstacle, these horsemen cleared them with wonderful address. Bold rider as he was himself, Fabian looked with enthusiasm on the astonishing agility of these wild hunters, but the precautions which they were forced to take, in order to conceal themselves, made the three friends lose a part of this imposing spectacle.

The vast savannahs, late so deserted, were suddenly changed into a scene of tumult and confusion. The stag, returning to the bank, continued to fly, with the wolves still after him. The wild horses galloped before the Indians—whose howlings equalled that of the wolves—and described great circles to avoid the lance or the lasso, while numerous echoes repeated these various sounds.

The sight of Fabian, who followed with an ardent eye all these tumultuous evolutions, not appearing to disquiet himself about a danger which he now braved for the first time, deprived Bois-Rose of that confidence in himself which had brought him safe and sound out of perils apparently greater than this.

"Ah!" muttered he, "these are scenes which the inhabitants of cities can never see, it is only in the desert one can meet with them."

But his voice trembled in spite of himself; and he stopped, for he felt that he would have given a year of his life that Fabian had not been present. At this moment a new subject of apprehension added to his anguish.

The scene became more solemn; for a new actor, whose *rôle* was to be short though terrible, now appeared upon it. It was a man, whom by his dress the three recognised with terror as a white man like themselves. The unlucky man suddenly discovered in one of the evolutions of the chase, had become in his turn the exclusive object of pursuit. Wild horses, wolves, the stag, had all disappeared in the distant fog. There remained only the twenty Indians scattered over a circle, of which the white man occupied the centre. For an instant the friends could see him cast around him a glance of despair and anguish. But, excepting on the river-side, the Indians were everywhere. It was, therefore, in this direction that he must fly; and he turned his horse towards the opening opposite to the island. But his single moment of indecision had sufficed for the Indians to get near him.

"The unhappy man is lost, and no help for it," said Bois-Rose; "he is too late now to cross the river."

"But," said Fabian, "if we can save a Christian, shall we let him be murdered before our eyes?"

Pepé looked at Bois-Rose.

"I answer for your life before God," said the Canadian, solemnly, "if we are discovered we are but three against twenty. The life of three men— yours especially, Fabian—is more precious than that of one; we must let this unhappy man meet his fate."

"But intrenched as we are?" persisted Fabian.

"Intrenched! Do you call this frail rampart of osiers and reeds an intrenchment? Do you think these leaves are ball proof? And these Indians are but twenty now; but let one of our shots be fired at them, and you will soon see one hundred instead of twenty. May God pardon me if I am unfeeling, but it is necessary."

Fabian said no more; this last reason seemed conclusive, for, like his companions, he was ignorant that the rest of the Indians were at the camp of Don Estevan.

Meanwhile the white fled like a man the speed of whose horse is his last resource. Already they could see the terror depicted on his face, but just as he was about twenty feet from the river, the lasso of an Indian caught him, and the unlucky wretch, thrown violently from his saddle fell upon the sand.

Chapter Forty
An Indian Diplomat

After the cries of triumph which announced the capture of the unlucky white man, there was a moment of profound silence. The men on the island exchanged looks of consternation and pity. "Thank God! they have not killed him!" said Fabian.

The prisoner indeed arose, although bruised with his fall, and one of the Indians disengaged him from the lasso. Bois-Rose and Pepé shook their heads.

"So much the worse for him, for his sufferings would now be over," said Pepé; "the silence of the Indians shows that each is considering what punishment to inflict. The capture of one white is more precious in their eyes than that of a whole troop of horses."

The Indians, still on horseback, surrounded the prisoner, who, casting around him a despairing glance, saw on every side only bronzed and hardened faces. Then the Indians began to deliberate.

Meanwhile, one who appeared to be the chief, and who was distinguished by his black plumes, jumped off his horse, and, throwing the bridle to one of the men, advanced towards the island. Having reached the bank, he seemed to seek for footsteps on the sand. Bois-Rose's heart beat violently, for this movement appeared to show some suspicion as to their presence.

"Can this wretch," whispered he to Pepé, "smell flesh like the ogres in the fairy tales?"

"*Quien sabe*—who knows?" replied the Spaniard, in the phrase which is the common answer of his native country.

But the sand trampled over by the wild horses who had come to drink, showed no traces of a human foot, and the Indian walked up the stream, still apparently seeking.

"The demon has some suspicion," said Bois-Rose; "and he will discover the traces that we left half-a-mile off when we entered the bed of the river to get at this island. I told you," added he, "that we should have entered two miles higher up; but neither you nor Fabian wished it, and like a fool, I yielded to you."

The deliberation as to the fate of the prisoner was now doubtless over; for cries of joy welcomed some proposition made by one of the Indians. But it was necessary to await the return and approbation of the chief, who was the man already known to us as the "Blackbird." He had continued his researches, and having reached the place where they had left the sand to enter the river, no longer doubted that the report brought to them had been correct; and having his own private objects, he determined to follow it. Once assured of the presence of the three whites, he returned to his men, listened gravely to the result of their deliberations, answered in a few words, and then advanced slowly towards the river—after having given an order to five of his men who set off at full gallop to execute it.

The aquatic plants were open in the sunshine; the breeze agitated the leaves of the osiers on the banks of the island, which was to all appearance as uninhabited as when the stream flowed only for the birds of heaven, and the buffaloes and wild horses of the plains. But an Indian could not be deceived by this apparent calm. The "Blackbird" made a speaking-trumpet of his hand, and cried in a language half Indian, half-Spanish—

"The white warriors of the north may show themselves; the 'Blackbird' is their friend. So, too, are the warriors he commands."

At these words, borne to them distinctly by the wind, the Canadian pressed the arm of Pepé; both understood the mixed dialect of the Indian.

"What shall we reply?" said he.

"Nothing," answered Pepé.

The breeze which murmured through the reeds was the only answer the Indian could hear.

He went on—

"The eagle may hide his track in the air from the eye of an Apache; the salmon in the stream leaves no trace behind him; but a white man who crosses the desert is neither a salmon nor an eagle."

"Nor a gosling," murmured Pepé; "and a gosling only betrays himself by trying to sing."

The Indian listened again, but hearing no sound, continued, without showing any signs of being discouraged, "The white warriors of the north are but three against twenty, and the red warriors engage their word to be friends and allies to them."

"Wagh!" said Bois-Rose, "for what perfidy has he need of us?"

"Let him go on, and we shall hear; he has not yet finished, or I am much mistaken!"

"When the white warriors know the intentions of the Blackbird, they will leave their hiding-place," continued he, "but they shall hear them. The white men of the north are the enemies of those of the south—their language, their religion is different. The Apaches hold in their toils a whole camp of southern warriors."

"So much the worse for the gold-seekers," said Bois-Rose.

"If the warriors of the north will join the Indians with their long rifles, they shall share the horses and the treasures of the men of the south; the Indians and the whites will dance together round the corpses of their enemies, and the ashes of their camp."

Bois-Rose and Pepé looked at each other in astonishment, and explained to Fabian the proposal made to them, but the fire of their eyes and their disdainful looks, showed that the noble trio had but one opinion on the subject—that of perishing rather than aiding the Indians to triumph even over their mortal enemies.

"Do you hear the miscreant," cried Bois-Rose, using in indignation an image fit for the Indians, "he takes jaguars far jackals. Ah! if Fabian were not here, a bullet would be my answer."

Meanwhile, the Indian feeling certain of the presence of the hunters in the island, began to lose patience—for the orders of the chiefs had been peremptory to attack the whites—but he, having his own opinions, wished to prove them right. He knew that the American or Canadian rifle never misses its aim, and three such allies seemed to him not to be despised. He therefore continued to speak:

"The buffalo of the prairies is not more easy to follow than the white man; the track of the buffalo tells the Indian his age, his size, and the time of his passing. There are behind the reeds of the floating island a man as strong as a bison, and taller than the tallest rifle, a warrior of mingled north and south blood, and a young warrior of the pure south, but the alliance of these two with the first, indicates that they are enemies of the southern whites—for the weakest ever seek the friendship of the strongest and espouse their cause."

"The sagacity of these dogs is admirable," said Bois-Rose.

"Because they flatter you," said Pepé, who seemed somewhat annoyed at what the Indian had said.

"I await for the answer of the whites," continued the Blackbird. "I hear only the sound of the river, and the wind which says to me, 'the whites imagine a thousand errors; they believe that the Indian has eyes behind his back, that the track of the bison is invisible, and that reeds are ball proof.' The Blackbird laughs at the words of the wind."

"Ah!" said Bois-Rose, "if we had entered but two miles higher up the river!"

"A friend disdained becomes a terrible enemy," continued the chief.

"We say something similar among us," muttered Pepé.

The Blackbird now signed to the captive to approach. The latter advanced, and the chief pointed out to him the little island, and said, "Can the rifle of the pale-face send a ball into the space between those bushes?"

But the prisoner had understood only the little Spanish mixed with the Indian dialect, and he remained mute and trembling. Then the Blackbird spoke to one of his warriors, who placed in the hands of the prisoner the rifle that he had taken from him, and by gestures made him understand what was wanted of him. The unlucky man tried to take aim, but terror caused him to shake in such a fashion that his rifle was unsteady in his hands.

"If the Indian has no better way than that to make us speak," said Pepé, "I will not say a word until to-morrow!"

The white man fired indeed, but the ball, directed by his trembling hands, fell into the water some distance from the island. The Blackbird glanced contemptuously at him, and then looked around him.

"Yes," said Pepé; "seek for balls and powder among the lances and lassoes of your warriors."

But as he finished this consoling reflection, the five men who had gone away, returned armed for combat, with rifles and quivers full of arrows. They had been to fetch the arms which they had laid down, in order to follow the wild horses more freely. Five others now went off.

"This looks bad," said Bois-Rose.

"Shall we attack them while they are but fifteen," said Pepé.

"No, let us remain silent; he still doubts whether we are here."

"As you like."

The Indian chief now took a rifle and advanced again to the bank.

"The hands of the Blackbird do not tremble like a leaf shaken by the wind," said he, pointing his rifle steadily towards the island. "But before firing, he will wait while he counts one hundred, for the answer of the whites who are hidden in the island."

"Get behind me, Fabian," said Bois-Rose.

"No, I stay here," said Fabian, decidedly. "I am younger, and it is my place to expose myself for you."

"Child! do you not see that my body exceeds yours six inches on every side, and your remaining in front is but presenting a double mark."

And without shaking a single one of the reeds around the island, he advanced and knelt before Fabian.

"Let him do it, Fabian," said Pepé. "Never had man a more noble buckler, than the heart of the giant which beats in fear for you."

The Indian chief, rifle in hand, listened as he counted, but excepting the murmur of the water, a profound silence reigned everywhere.

He fired at length, and the leaves of the trees flew into the air; but as the three hunters knelt in a row they did not present a large aim, and the ball passed at some little distance from them.

The Blackbird waited a minute and cried again: "The Indian was wrong, he acknowledges his error, he will seek for the white warriors elsewhere."

"Who believes that?" said Pepé; "he is more sure than ever. He is about to leave us alone for a few minutes, until he has finished with that poor devil yonder, which will not belong—since the death of a white is a spectacle which an Indian is always in a hurry to enjoy."

"But had we better not make some effort in favour of the unlucky man?" said Fabian.

"Some unexpected circumstances may come to our assistance," replied Bois-Rose. "Whatever Pepé says, the Indians may still doubt, but if we show ourselves, all is over. To accept an alliance with these Indians, even against Don Estevan de Arechiza, would be an unworthy cowardice. What can we do?" added he, sadly.

One fear tormented him; he had seen Fabian in danger when his blood was boiling with passion, but had he the calm courage which meets death coolly? Had he the stoical resignation of which he himself had given so many proofs? The Canadian took a sudden resolution.

"Listen, Fabian," said he; "can I speak to you the language of a man? Will the words which your ears will transmit to your heart not freeze it with terror?"

"Why doubt my courage?" replied Fabian in a tone of gentle reproach. "Whatever you say, I will hear without growing pale; whatever you do, I will do also, without trembling."

"Don Fabian speaks truly, Pepé; look at his eye," said the Canadian, pressing Fabian in his arms; then he continued solemnly: "Never were three men in greater peril than we are now; our enemies are seven times our number; when each of us has killed six of them, there would still remain a number equal to our own."

"We have done it before," said Pepé.

"And we shall do it again," cried Fabian.

"Good, my child," said Bois-Rose, "but whatever happens, these demons must not take us alive. See, Fabian!" added the old man, in a voice that he tried to keep firm while unsheathing a long knife, "if we were left without powder or ammunition at the mercy of these dogs, about to fall into their hands, and this poignard in my hand was our only chance, what would you say?"

"I would say, strike, father, and let us die together!"

"Yes, yes," cried the Canadian, looking with indescribable tenderness at him who called him father, "it will be one means of never being separated." And he held out to Fabian his hand trembling with emotion, which the latter kissed respectfully.

"Now," said Bois-Rose, "whatever happens we shall not be separated. God will do the rest, and we shall try to save this unlucky man."

"To work then!" said Fabian.

"Not yet, my child; let us see what these red demons are about to do."

Meanwhile the Indians had ranged themselves in two lines, and the white man was placed a little in advance of them.

"I see what they are going to do," said Bois-Rose, "they are going to try if the poor wretch's legs are better than his arms. They are about to chase him."

"How so?" said Fabian.

"They will place their captive a little in advance, then at a given signal he will run. Then all the Indians will run after him, lance and hatchet in hand. If the white is quick enough to reach the river before them, we will call to him to swim to us. Some shots will protect him, and he may reach here safe and sound. But if terror paralyses his limbs, as it did his hands just now, the foremost Indian will break his head with a blow from a hatchet. In any case we shall do our best."

At this moment the five other Indians returned armed from head to foot, and now joined the rest. Fabian looked with profound compassion at the unlucky white man, who with haggard eye, and features distorted by terror, waited in horrible anguish until the signal was given. But the Blackbird pointed to the bare feet of his warriors, and then to the leather buskins which protected the feet of the white man. They then saw the latter sit down and take them off slowly, as if to gain a few seconds.

"The demons!" cried Fabian.

"Hush!" said Bois-Rose, "do not by discovering yourself destroy the last chance of life for the poor wretch!"

Fabian shut his eyes so as not to witness the horrible scene about to take place. At length the white man rose to his feet, and the Indians stood devouring him with their looks, until the Blackbird clapped his hands together, and then the howlings which followed could only be compared to those of a troop of jaguars in pursuit of a deer. The unlucky captive ran with great swiftness, but his pursuers bounded after him like tigers. Thanks to the start which he had had, he cleared safely a part of the distance which separated him from the river, but the stones which cut his feet and the sharp thorns of the nopals soon caused him to slacken his pace, and one of the Indians rushed up and made a furious thrust at him with his lance. It passed between his arm and his body, and the Indian losing his equilibrium, fell on the sand.

Gayferos, for it was he, appeared to hesitate a moment whether he should pick up the lance which the Indian had let fall, but then rapidly continued his course. That instant's hesitation was fatal to him. All at once, amidst the cloud of dust raised by his feet, a hatchet shone over the head of the unfortunate Mexican, who was seen falling to the earth.

Bois-Rose was about to fire, but the fear of killing him whom he wished to defend, stopped his hand. For a single moment the wind cleared away the dust, and he fired, but it was too late, the Indian who fell under his ball was brandishing in his hand the scalp of the unhappy man. To this unexpected shot, the savages replied with howls, and then rushed away from what they believed to be only a corpse. Soon, however, they saw the man rise, with his head laid bare, who after straggling a few paces, fell again, while the blood flowed in torrents from his wounds.

"Ah!" cried Bois-Rose, "if there remains in him a spark of life—and people do not die only from scalping—we shall save him yet; I swear we shall!"

Chapter Forty One
Indian Cunning

As the Canadian uttered the generous oath, wrung from him by indignation, it seemed to him that a supplicating voice reached him. "Is not the poor wretch calling for aid?" And he raised his head from behind its shelter.

At sight of the fox-skin cap which covered the head of the giant, and of the long and heavy rifle which he raised like a willow wand, the Indians recognised one of their formidable northern enemies, and recoiled in astonishment—for the Blackbird alone had been instructed as to whom they were seeking. Bois-Rose, looking towards the shore now perceived the unlucky Gayferos stretching out his arms towards him, and feebly calling for help. The dying Indian still held the scalp in his clenched hand.

At this terrible spectacle the Canadian drew himself up to his full height. "Fire on these dogs!" cried he, "and remember—never let them take you alive."

So saying, he resolutely entered the water, and any other man would have had it up to his head, but the Canadian had all his shoulders above the surface.

"Do not fire till after me," said Pepé to Fabian; "my hand is surer than yours, and my Kentucky rifle carries twice as far as your Liege gun." And he held his rifle ready to fire at the slightest sign of hostility from the Indians.

Meanwhile, Bois-Rose still advanced, the water growing gradually shallower, when an Indian raised his rifle ready to fire on the intrepid hunter; but a bullet from Pepé stopped him, and he fell forward on his face.

"Now you, Don Fabian!" said Pepé, throwing himself on the ground to reload, after the American custom in such cases.

Fabian fired, but his rifle having a shorter range, the shot only drew from the Indian at whom he aimed a cry of rage. But Pepé had reloaded, and stood ready to fire again.

There was a moment's hesitation among the Indians, by which Bois-Rose profited to draw towards him the body of the unlucky Gayferos. He, clinging to his shoulders, had the presence of mind to leave his preserver's arms free; who, with his burden, again entered the water, going backwards. Then his rifle was heard, and an Indian's death-cry immediately followed. This valiant retreat, protected by Pepé and Fabian, awed the Indians, and some minutes after, Bois-Rose triumphantly placed the fainting Gayferos on the island.

"There are three of them settled for," said he, "and now we shall have a few minutes' truce. Well, Fabian, do you see the advantage of firing in file? You did not do badly for a beginner, and I can assure you that when you have a Kentucky rifle like us, you will be a good marksman." Then to Gayferos, "We came too late to save the skin of your head, my poor fellow, but console yourself, it is no such dreadful thing. I have many friends in the same condition, who are none the worse for it. Your life is saved—that is the great thing—and we shall endeavour to bind up your wounds."

Some strips torn from the shirt of Gayferos served to bind around his head a large mass of willow leaves crushed together and steeped in water, and concealed the hideous wound. The blood was then washed from his face.

"You see," said Bois-Rose, still clinging to the idea of keeping Fabian near him, "you must learn to know the habits of the desert, and of the Indians. The villains, who see, by the loss of three of their men, what stuff we are made of, have retired to concoct some stratagem. You hear how silent all is after so much noise?"

The desert, indeed, had recovered its silence, the leaves only trembled in the evening breeze, and the water began to display brilliant colours in the setting sun.

"Well, Pepé, they are but seventeen now!" continued Bois-Rose, in a tone of triumph.

"Oh! we may succeed, if they do not get reinforcements."

"That is a chance and a terrible one; but our lives are in God's hands," replied Bois-Rose. "Tell me, friend!" said he to Gayferos, "you probably belong to the camp of Don Estevan?"

"Do you know him then?" said the wounded man, in a feeble voice.

"Yes; and by what chance are you so far from the camp?"

The wounded man recounted how, by Don Estevan's orders, he had set off to seek for their lost guide, and that his evil star had brought him in contact with the Indians as they were hunting the wild horses.

"What is the name of your guide?"

"Cuchillo."

Fabian and Bois-Rose glanced at each other.

"Yes," said the latter, "there is some probability that your suspicions about that white demon were correct, and that he is conducting the expedition to the Golden Valley; but, my child, if we escape these Indians, we are close to it; and once we are installed there, were they a hundred, we should succeed in defending ourselves."

This was whispered in Fabian's ear.

"One word more," said Bois-Rose to the wounded man, "and then we shall leave you to repose. How many men has Don Estevan with him?"

"Sixty."

Bois-Rose now again bathed the head of the wounded Gayferos with cold water: and the unhappy man, refreshed for the moment, and weakened by loss of blood, fell into a lethargic sleep.

"Now," continued Bois-Rose, "let us endeavour to build up a rampart which shall be a little more ball and arrow-proof than this fringe of moving leaves and reeds. Did you count how many rifles the Indians had?"

"Seven, I believe," said Pepé.

"Then ten of them are less to be feared. They cannot attack us either on the right or the left—but perhaps they have made a détour to cross the river, and are about to place us between two fires."

The side of the islet opposite the shore on which the Indians had shown themselves was sufficiently defended by enormous roots, bristling like chevaux-de-frise; but the side where the attack was probably about to recommence was defended only by a thick row of reeds and osier-shoots.

Thanks to his great strength, Bois-Rose, aided by Pepé, succeeded in dragging from the end of the islet which faced the course of the stream, some large dry branches and fallen trunks of trees. A few minutes sufficed for the two skilful hunters to protect the feeble side with a rough but solid entrenchment, which would form a very good defence to the little garrison of the island.

"Do you see, Fabian," said Bois-Rose, "you'll be as safe behind these trunks of trees as in a stone fortress. You'll be exposed only to the balls that may be fired from the tops of the trees, but I shall take care that none of these redskins climb so high."

And quite happy at having raised a barrier between Fabian and death, he assigned him his post in the place most sheltered from the enemy.

"Did you remark," said he to Pepé, "how at every effort that we made to break a branch or disengage a block of wood, the island trembled to its foundation?"

"Yes," said Pepé, "one might think that it was about to be torn from its base and follow the course of the stream."

The Canadian then cautioned his two companions to be careful of their ammunition, gave Fabian some instructions as to taking aim, pressed him to his heart, squeezed the hand of his old comrade, and then the three stationed themselves at their several posts. The surface of the river, the tops of the aspens growing on the banks, the banks themselves and the reeds, were all objects of examination for the hunters, as the night was fast coming on.

"This is the hour when the demons of darkness lay their snares," said Bois-Rose, "when these human jaguars seek for their prey. It was of them that the Scriptures spoke."

No one replied to this speech, which was uttered rather as a soliloquy.

Meanwhile, the darkness was creeping on little by little, and the bushes which grew on the bank began to assume the fantastic forms given to objects by the uncertain twilight.

The green of the trees began to look black; but habit had given to Bois-Rose and to Pepé eyes as piercing as those of the Indians themselves, and nothing, with the vigilance they were exerting, could have deceived them.

"Pepé," whispered Bois-Rose, pointing to a tuft of osiers, "does it not seem to you that that bush has changed its form and grown larger?"

"Yes; it has changed its form!"

"See, Fabian! you have the piercing sight that I had at your age; does it not appear to you that at the left-hand side of that tuft of osiers the leaves no longer look natural?"

The young man pushed the reeds on one side, and gazed for a while attentively.

"I could swear it," said he, "but—" He stopped, and looked in another direction.

"Well! do you see anything?"

"I see, between that willow and the aspen, about ten feet from the tuft of osiers, a bush which certainly was not there just now."

"Ah! see what it is to live far from towns;—the least points of the landscape fix themselves in the memory, and become precious indications. You are born to live the life of a hunter, Fabian!"

Pepé levelled his rifle at the bush indicated by Fabian.

"Pepé understands it at once," said Bois-Rose; "he knows, like me, that the Indians have employed their time in cutting down branches to form a temporary shelter; but I think two of us at least may teach them a few stratagems that they do not yet know. Leave that bush to Fabian, it will be an easy mark for him; fire at the branches whose leaves are beginning to wither—there is an Indian behind them. Fire in the centre, Fabian!"

The two rifles were heard simultaneously, and the false bush fell, displaying a red body behind the leaves, while the branches which had been added were convulsively agitated. All three then threw themselves on the ground, and a discharge of balls immediately flew over their heads, covering them with leaves and broken branches, while the war-cry of the Indians sounded in their ears.

"If I do not deceive myself, they are now but fifteen," said Bois-Rose, as he quitted his horizontal posture, and knelt on the ground.

"Be still!" added he. "I see the leaves of an aspen trembling more than the wind alone could cause them to do. It is doubtless one of those fellows who has climbed up into the tree."

As he spoke, a bullet struck one of the trunks of which the islet was composed, and proved that he had guessed rightly.

"Wagh!" said the Canadian, "I must resort to a trick that will force him to show himself."

So saying, he took off his cap and coat, and placed them between the branches, where they could be seen. "Now," said he, "if I were fighting a white soldier, I would place myself by the side of my coat, for he would fire at the coat; with an Indian I shall stand behind it, for he will not be deceived in the same manner, and will aim to one side of it. Lie down, Fabian and Pepé, and in a minute you shall hear a bullet whistle either to the right or the left of the mark I have set up."

As Bois-Rose said this, he knelt down behind his coat, ready to fire at the aspen.

He was not wrong in his conjectures; in a moment, the balls of the Indians cut the leaves on each side of the coat, but without touching either of the three companions, who had placed themselves in a line.

"Ah," cried the Canadian, "there are whites who can fight the Indians with their own weapons; we shall presently have an enemy the less."

And saying this he fired into the aspen, out of which the body of an Indian was seen to fall, rolling from branch to branch like a fruit knocked from its stem.

At this feat of the Canadian, the savage howlings resounded with so much fury, that it required nerves of iron not to shudder at them. Gayferos himself, whom the firing had not roused, shook off his lethargy and murmured, in a trembling voice, "Virgen de los Dolores! Would not one say it was a band of tigers howling in the darkness?—Holy Virgin! have pity on me!"

"Thank her rather," interrupted the Canadian; "the knaves might deceive a novice like you, but not an old hunter like me. You have heard the jackals of an evening in the forest howl and answer each other as though there were hundreds of them, when there were but three or four. The Indians imitate the jackals, and I will answer for it there are not more that a dozen now behind those trees. Ah! if I could but get them to cross the water, not one of them should return to carry the news of their disaster."

Then, as if a sudden thought had flashed across his mind, he directed his companions to lie down on their backs—in which position they were protected by the trunks of the trees. "We are in safety as long as we lie thus," said he, "only keep your eye on the tops of the trees; it is from these only they can reach us. Fire only if you see them climb up, but otherwise remain motionless. The knaves will not willingly depart without our scalps, and must make up their minds at last to attack us."

This resolution of the hunter seemed to have been inspired by heaven, for scarcely had they laid down before a shower of balls and arrows tore to pieces the border of reeds, and broke the branches behind which they had been kneeling a minute before. Bois-Rose pulled down his coat and hat, as though he himself had fallen, and then the most profound silence reigned in the island, after this apparently murderous fire. Cries of triumph followed this silence, and then a second discharge of bullets and arrows.

"Is not that an Indian mounting the willow?" whispered Pepé.

"Yes, but let us risk his fire without stirring; lie all of us as if we were dead. Then he will go and tell his companions that he has counted the corpses of the palefaces."

In spite of the danger incurred by this stratagem, the proposition of Bois-Rose was accepted, and each remained motionless, watching, not without anxiety, the manoeuvres of the Indian. With extreme precaution the red warrior climbed from branch to branch, until he had reached a point from which he could overlook the whole islet.

There remained just sufficient daylight to observe his movements when the foliage itself did not hide them. When he had reached the desired height, the Indian, resting on a thick branch, advanced his head with precaution. The sight of the bodies extended on the ground appeared not to surprise him, and he now openly pointed his rifle towards them. This he did several times, apparently taking aim, but not one of the hunters stirred. Then the Indian uttered a cry of triumph. "The shark takes the bait," muttered Bois-Rose.

"I shall recognise this son of a dog," rejoined Pepé, "and if I do not repay him for the anxiety he has caused me, it is because the bullet he is about to send will prevent me."

"It is the Blackbird," said Bois-Rose, "he is both brave and dexterous— lie close!"

The Indian once more took aim, and then fired; a branch knocked from a tree just above Pepé, fell upon him and hurt his forehead. He stirred no more than the dead wood against which he leaned, but said, "Rascal of a redskin, I'll pay you for this before long."

Some drops of blood fell upon the face of the Canadian.

"Is any one wounded?" said he, with a shudder.

"A scratch, nothing more," said Pepé, "God be praised!"

Just then the Indian uttered a cry of joy, as he descended from the tree on which he had mounted, and the three friends again breathed freely.

And yet some doubt seemed to remain in the minds of the Indians, for a long and solemn silence followed the manoeuvre of their chief.

The sun had now set, the short twilight had passed away, night had come on, and the moon shone on the river, yet still the Indians did not stir.

"Our scalps tempt them, but they still hesitate to come and take them," said Pepé, who was becoming very tired of doing nothing.

"Patience!" whispered Bois-Rose, "the Indians are like the vultures, who dare not attack a body until it begins to decay. We may look out for them by-and-bye. Let us resume our position behind the reeds."

The hunters again quickly knelt down and continued to watch their enemies.

Before long an Indian showed himself very cautiously, another then joined him, and both approached with increasing confidence, followed by others, until Bois-Rose counted ten in the moonlight.

"They will cross the river in file, I expect," said he. "Fabian, you fire at the first, Pepé will aim at the centre, and I at the last but one. In that way they cannot all attack together. It will be a hand-to-hand struggle, but you, Fabian, while Pepé and I wait for them knife in hand, shall load our rifles and pass them to us. By the memory of your mother, I forbid you to fight with these wretches."

As the Canadian uttered these words, a tall Indian entered the river, followed by nine others. All advanced with the utmost caution; they might have been taken for the shades of warriors returned from the land of spirits.

Chapter Forty Two
The Blackbird

Death seemed to the eyes of the Indians to reign over the island—for the hunters held even their breath—and yet they advanced with the utmost care.

The foremost man, who was the "Blackbird" himself, had reached a place where the water began to be deep, as the last man was just leaving the bank. But just as Fabian was about to take aim against the chief, to the great regret of Pepé, the "Blackbird," either fearful of danger, or because a ray of moonlight gleaming on the rifles told him his enemy still lived dived suddenly under the water.

"Fire!" cried Bois-Rose, and immediately the last Indian of the file fell to rise no more, and two others appeared struggling in the water, and were quickly borne off by the stream. Pepé and Bois-Rose then threw their rifles behind them as agreed upon, for Fabian to reload, while they themselves stood upon the bank, knives in hand.

"The Apaches are still seven," shouted Bois-Rose, in a voice of thunder, anxious to finish the struggle, and feeling all his hatred of the Indians awakened within him, "will they dare to come and take the scalps of the whites?"

But the disappearance of their chief and the death of their comrades had disconcerted the Indians; they did not fly, but they remained undecided and motionless, as black rocks bathed by the shining waters of the river.

"Can the red warriors only scalp dead bodies?" added Pepé with a contemptuous laugh. "Are the Apaches like vultures who only attack the dead? Advance then, dogs, vultures, women without courage!" shouted he, at the sight of their enemies, who were now rapidly regaining the bank. Suddenly, however, he noticed a body floating on its back, whose bright eyes showed that it was not a corpse, as the extended arms and motionless body seemed to indicate.

"Don Fabian, my rifle! there is the 'Blackbird' pretending to be dead and floating down the stream."

Pepé took the rifle from Fabian, and aimed at the floating body, but not a muscle stirred. The hunter lowered his rifle. "I was wrong," said he, aloud, "the white men do not, like the Indians, waste their powder on dead bodies."

The body still floated, with outspread legs and extended arms. Pepé again raised his rifle and again lowered it. Then, when he thought that he had paid off anguish for anguish to the Indian chief, he fired, and the body floated no longer.

"Have you killed him?" asked Bois-Rose.

"No, I only wished to break his shoulder bone, that he may always have cause to remember the shudder he gave, and the treason he proposed to me. If he were dead, he would still float."

"You might have done better to have killed him. But what is to be done now? I hoped to finish with these demons, and now our work is still to be done. We cannot cross the river to attack them."

"It is the best thing we can do."

"With Fabian, I cannot decide to do it, or I should be now on the bank opposite, where you know as well as I do they still are breathing their infernal vengeance."

The Spaniard shrugged his shoulders with stoical resignation.

"Doubtless," said he, "but we must decide either to fly or to stay."

"Carramba!" continued he, "if we two were alone we would gain the opposite bank in a minute; the seven who are left would catch us no doubt, but we should come out of it, as we have out of more difficult situations."

"It would be better than to stay here like foxes in their hole."

"I agree: but Fabian! and the unlucky scalped man, whom we cannot abandon thus to the mercy of the wretches who have already treated him so cruelly. Let us wait at least until the moon has set, and darkness comes on."

And the old man hung his head with an air of discouragement—which made a painful impression on the Spaniard—raising it only to glance anxiously at the sky; where the moon held on her ordinary course over the starry blue.

"So be it," said Pepé; "but, stay! we killed first five Indians, then three, that makes eight; there should have been twelve left; why did we only count ten in the water? Depend upon it, the Blackbird has sent the two others to seek for reinforcements."

"It is possible: to remain here or to fly are both terrible."

For some time the hunters thus continued to deliberate; meanwhile the moonbeams began to fall more obliquely, and already a part of the tops of the trees were in shadow. More than an hour had elapsed since the attempt of the Indians, and Pepé, less absorbed than Bois-Rose, was watching anxiously.

"That cursed moon will never go down," said he, "and it seems to me that I hear something like the noise of feet in the water; the buffaloes do not come down to drink at this time of night."

So saying, he rose and leaning right and left, looked up and down the stream, but on each side extended an impenetrable veil of fog. The coolness of the American nights which succeeds the burning heat of the day, condenses thus in thick clouds the exhalations of the ground, and of the waters heated by the sun.

"I can see nothing but fog," said he.

Little by little the vague sounds died away, and the air recovered its habitual cairn and silence. The moon was fast going down, and all nature seemed sleeping, when the occupants of the island started up in terror.

From both sides of the river rose shouts so piercing that the banks echoed them long after the mouths that uttered them were closed. Henceforth flight was impossible; the Indians had encompassed the island.

"The moon may go down now," cried Pepé with rage. "Ah! with reason I feared the two absent men, and the noises that I heard; it was the Indians who were gaining the opposite bank. Who knows how many enemies we have around us now?"

"What matter," replied Bois-Rose gloomily, "whether there are one hundred vultures to tear our bodies, or a hundred Indians to howl round us when we are dead?"

"It is true that the number matters little in such circumstances, but it will be a day of triumph for them."

"Are you going to sing your death-song like them, who, when tied to the stake, recall the number of scalps they have taken?"

"And why not? it is a very good custom, it helps one to die like a hero, and to remember that you have lived like a man."

"Let us rather try to die like Christians," replied Bois-Rose.

Then drawing Fabian towards him, he said:

"I scarcely know, my beloved child, what I had dreamed of for you; I am half savage and half civilised, and my dreams partook of both. Sometimes I wished to restore you to the honours of this world—to your honours, your titles—and to add to them all the treasures of the Golden Valley. Then I dreamed only of the splendour of the desert, and its majestic harmonies, which lull a man to his rest, and entrance him at his waking. But I can truly say that the dominant idea in my mind was that of never quitting you. Must that be accomplished in death? So young, so brave, so handsome, must you meet the same fate as a man who would soon be useless in the world?"

"Who would love me when you were gone?" replied Fabian, in a voice which their terrible situation deprived neither of its sweetness nor firmness. "Before I met you, the grave had closed upon all I loved, and the sole living being who could replace them was—you. What have I to regret in this world?"

"The future, my child; the future into which youth longs to plunge, like the thirsty stag into the lake."

Distant firing now interrupted the melancholy reflections of the old hunter; the Indians were attacking the camp of Don Estevan. The reader knows the result.

Suddenly they heard a voice from the bank, saying, "Let the white men open their ears!"

"It is the 'Blackbird' again," cried Pepé. It was indeed he, supported by two Indians.

"Why should they open their ears?" answered Pepé.

"The whites laugh at the menaces of the 'Blackbird,' and despise his promises."

"Good!" said the Indian; "the whites are brave, and they will need all their bravery. The white men of the south are being attacked now; why are the men of the north not against them?"

"Because you are a bird of doleful plumage! because lions do not hunt with jackals, for jackals can only howl while the lion devours. Apply the compliment; it is a fine flower of Indian rhetoric," cried Pepé, exasperated.

"Good! the whites are like the conquered Indians, insulting his conqueror. But the eagle laughs at the words of the mocking-bird, and it is not to him that the eagle deigns to address himself."

"To whom then?" cried Pepé.

"To the giant, his brother, the eagle of the snowy mountains, who disdains to imitate the language of other birds."

"What do you want of him?" said Bois-Rose.

"The Indian would hear the northern warrior ask for life," replied the Blackbird.

"I have a different demand to make," said the Canadian.

"I listen," replied the Indian.

"If you will swear on the honour of a warrior, and on your father's bones, that you will spare my companions' lives, I shall cross the river alone without arms, and bring you my scalp on my head. That will tempt him," added Bois-Rose.

"Are you mad, Bois-Rose?" cried Pepé.

Fabian flew towards the Canadian: "At the first step you make towards the Indian, I shall kill you," cried he.

The old hunter felt his heart melt at the sound of the two voices that he loved so much. A short silence followed, then came the answer from the bank.

"The Blackbird wishes the white man to ask for life, and he asks for death. My wish is this, let the white man of the north quit his companions, and I swear on my father's bones, that his life shall be saved, but his alone; the other three must die."

Bois-Rose disdained to reply to this offer, and the Indian chief waited vainly for a refusal or an acceptance. Then he continued: "Until the hour of their death, the whites hear the voice of the Indian chief for the last time. My warriors surround the island and the river. Indian blood has been spilled and must be revenged; white blood must flow. But the Indian does not wish for this blood warmed by the ardour of the combat, he wishes for it frozen by terror, impoverished by hunger. He will take the whites living; then, when he holds them in his clutches, when they are like hungry dogs howling after a bone, he will see what men are like after fear and privation; he will make of their skin a saddle for his war-horse, and each of their scalps shall be suspended to his saddle, as a trophy of vengeance. My warriors shall surround the island for fifteen days and nights if necessary, in order to make capture of the white men."

After these terrible menaces the Indian disappeared behind the trees. But Pepé not willing that he should believe he had intimidated them, cried as coldly as anger would permit, "Dog, who can do nothing but bark, the whites despise your vain bravados. Jackal, unclean polecat, I despise you—I—I"—but rage prevented him from saying more, and he finished off by a gesture of contempt; then with a loud laugh he sat down, satisfied at having had the last word. As for Bois-Rose he saw in it all only the refusal of his heroic sacrifice.

"Ah!" sighed the generous old man, "I could have arranged it all; now it is too late."

The moon had gone down; the sound of distant firing had ceased, and the darkness made the three friends feel still more forcibly how easy it would have been to gain the opposite bank, carrying in their arms the wounded man. He, insensible to all that was passing, still slept heavily.

"Thus," said Pepé, first breaking silence, "we have fifteen days to live; it is true we have not much provision, but carramba! we shall fish for food and for amusement."

"Let us think," said Bois-Rose, "of employing usefully the hours before daylight."

"In what?"

"Parbleu! in escaping!"

"But how?"

"That is the question. You can swim, Fabian?"

"How else should. I have escaped from the Salto de Agua?"

"True! I believe that fear confuses my brain. Well! it would not be impossible, perhaps, to dig a hole in the middle of this island, and to slip through this opening into the water. The night is so dark, that if the Indians do not see us throw ourselves into the water, we might gain a place some way off with safety. Stay, I shall try an experiment." So saying, he detached, with some trouble, one of the trunks from the little island; and its knotty end looked not unlike a human head. This he placed carefully on the water, and soon it floated gently down the stream. The three friends followed its course anxiously; then, when it had disappeared, Bois-Rose said:

"You see, a prudent swimmer might pass in the same manner; not an Indian has noticed it."

"That is true; but who knows that their eyes cannot distinguish a man from a piece of wood?" said Pepé. "Besides, we have with with us a man who cannot swim."

"Whom?"

The Spaniard pointed to the wounded man; who groaned in his sleep, as though his guardian angel warned him that there was a question of abandoning him to his enemies.

"What matter?" said Bois-Rose; "is his life worth that of the last of the Medianas?"

"No," replied the Spaniard; "and I, who half wanted a short time ago to abandon the poor wretch, think now I would be cowardly."

"Perhaps," added Fabian, "he has children, who would weep for their father."

"It would be a bad action, and would bring us ill luck," added Pepé.

All the superstitious tenderness of the Canadian awoke at these words, and he said—

"Well, then, Fabian, you are a good swimmer, follow this plan: Pepé and I will stay here and guard this man, and if we die here, it will be in the discharge of our duty, and with the joy of knowing you to be safe."

But Fabian shook his head.

"I care not for life without you; I shall stay," said he.

"What can be done then?"

"Let us think," said Pepé.

But it was unluckily one of those cases in which all human resources are vain, for it was one of those desperate situations from which a higher power alone could extricate them. In vain the fog thickened and the night grew darker; the resolution not to abandon the wounded man opposed an insurmountable obstacle to their escape, and before long the fires lighted by the Indians along each bank, threw a red light over the stream, and rendered this plan impracticable. Except for these fires, the most complete calm reigned, for no enemy was visible, no human voice troubled the silence of the night. However, the fog grew more and more dense, the stream disappeared from view, and even the fires looked only like pale and indistinct lights under the shadowy outline of the trees.

Chapter Forty Three
A Feat of Herculean Strength

Let us now glance at the spot occupied by the Blackbird. The fires lighted on the banks threw at first so strong a light that nothing could escape the eyes of the Indians, and a sentinel placed near each fire was charged to observe carefully all that passed on the island. Seated and leaning against the trunk of a tree, his broken shoulder bound up with strips of leather, the Blackbird only showed on his face an expression of satisfied ferocity; as for the suffering he was undergoing, he would have thought it unworthy of him to betray the least indication of it. His ardent eye was fixed continually on the spot where were the three men, whom he pictured to himself as full of anguish.

But as the fog grew thicker, first the opposite bank and then the island itself, became totally invisible. The Indian chief felt that it was necessary to redouble his surveillance. He ordered one man to cross the river, and another to walk along the bank, and exhorted every one to watchfulness.

"Go," said he, "and tell those of my warriors who are ordered to watch these Christians—whose skins and scalps shall serve as ornaments to our horses—that they must each have four ears, to replace the eyes that the fog has rendered useless. Tell them that their vigilance will merit their chief's gratitude; but that if they allow sleep to deaden their senses, the hatchet of the Blackbird will send them to sleep in the land of spirits."

The two messengers set off, and soon returned to tell the chief that he might rest satisfied that attention would be paid to his orders. Indeed, stimulated at once by their own hatred of the whites, and by the hope of a recompense—fearing if sleep surprised them, not so much the threatened punishment as the idea of awaking in the hunting-grounds of the land of spirits, bearing on their foreheads the mark of shame which accompanies the sentinel who gives way to sleep—the sentinels had redoubled their vigilance. There are few sounds that can escape the marvellous ears of an Indian, but on this occasion the fog made it difficult to hear as well as to see, and the strictest attention was necessary. With closed eyes and open ears, and standing up to chase away the heaviness that the silence of nature caused them to feel, the Indian warriors stood motionless near their fires, throwing on on from time to time some fagots to keep them ablaze.

Some time passed thus, during which the only sound heard was that of a distant fall in the river.

The Blackbird remained on the left bank, and the night air, as it inflamed his wounds, only excited his hatred the more. His face covered with hideous paint, and contracted by the pain—of which he disdained to make complaint—and his brilliant eyes, made him resemble one of the sanguinary idols of barbarous times. Little by little, however, in spite of himself, his eyes were weighed down by sleep, and an invincible drowsiness took possession of his spirit. Before long his sleep became so profound, that he did not hear the dry branches crackle under a moccasin, as an Indian of his tribe advanced towards him.

Straight and motionless as a bamboo stem, an Indian runner covered with blood and panting for breath, waited for some time until the chief, before whom he stood, should open his eyes and interrogate him. As the latter showed no signs of awaking, the runner resolved to announce his presence, and in a hollow, guttural voice, said—

"When the Blackbird shall open his eyes, he will hear from my mouth words which will chase sleep far from him."

The chief opened his eyes at the voice, and shook off his drowsiness with a violent effort. Ashamed at having been surprised asleep, he muttered:

"The Blackbird has lost much blood; he has lost so much that the next sun will not dry it on the ground, and his body is more feeble than his will."

"Man is made thus," rejoined the messenger, sententiously.

The Blackbird continued without noticing the reflection:

"It is some very important message doubtless, since the Spotted Cat has chosen the fleetest of his runners to carry it?"

"The Spotted Cat will send no more messengers," replied the Indian. "The lance of a white man has pierced his breast, and the chief now hunts with his fathers in the land of spirits."

"What matter! he died a conqueror? he saw, before he died, the white dogs dispersed over the plain?"

"He died conquered; and the Apaches had to fly after losing their chief and fifty of their renowned warriors."

In spite of his wound, and of the empire that an Indian should exercise over himself, the Blackbird started up at these words. However, he restrained himself, and replied gravely, though with trembling lips—

"Who, then, sends you to me, messenger of ill?"

"The warriors, who want a chief to repair their defeat. The Blackbird was but the chief of a tribe, he is now the chief of a whole people."

Satisfied pride shone in the eye of the Indian, at his augmented authority.

"If the rifles of the north had been joined to ours, the whites of the south would have been conquered." But as he recalled to mind the insulting manner in which the two hunters had rejected his proposal, his eyes darted forth flames of hatred, and pointing to his wound, he said, "What can a wounded chief do? His limbs refuse to carry him, and he can scarcely sit on his horse."

"We can tie him on; a chief is at once a head and an arm—if the arm be powerless the head will act, and the sight of their chief's blood will animate our warriors. The council fire was lighted anew after the defeat, and the warriors wait for the Blackbird to make his voice heard; his battle-horse is ready—let us go!"

"No," replied the Blackbird, "my warriors encompass, on each bank, the white hunters whom I wished to have for allies; now they are enemies; the ball of one of them has rendered useless for six moons, the arm that was so strong in combat; and were I offered the command of ten nations, I would refuse it, to await here the hour when the blood that I thirst for shall flow before my eyes."

The chief then recounted briefly the captivity of Gayferos, his deliverance by the Canadian, the rejection of his proposals and the vow of vengeance he had made.

The messenger listened gravely; he felt all the importance of making a new attack on the gold-seekers, at the moment when, delighted at their victory, they believed themselves safe, and he proposed to the Blackbird to leave some one behind in his place to watch the island; but the Blackbird was immovable.

"Well!" said the runner, "before long the sun will begin to rise; I shall wait until daylight to report to the Apaches that the Blackbird prefers his personal vengeance to the honour of the entire nation. By deferring my departure, I shall have retarded the moment when our warriors will have to regret the loss of the bravest among them."

"So be it," said the chief, in a grave tone, although much pleased by this adroit flattery, "but a messenger has need of repose after a battle followed by a long journey. Meanwhile, I would listen to the account of the combat in which the Spotted Cat lost his life."

The messenger sat down near the fire, with crossed legs, and with one elbow on his knee and his head leaning on his hand, after a few minutes' rest, gave a circumstantial account of the attack on the white camp—omitting no fact which might awaken the hatred of the Blackbird against the Mexican invaders.

This over, he laid down and slept, or seemed to sleep. But the tumultuous and contrary passions which struggled in the heart of the Blackbird—ambition on the one hand, and thirst for vengeance on the other—kept him awake without effort. In about an hour the runner half rose, and pushing back the cloak of skin which he had drawn over his head he perceived the Blackbird still sitting in the same attitude.

"The silence of the night has spoken to me," said he, "and I thought that a renowned chief like the Blackbird might, before the rising sun, have his enemies in his power and hear their death-song."

"My warriors cannot walk on the water as on the warpath," replied he; "the men of the north do not resemble those of the south, whose rifles are like reeds in their hands."

"The blood that the Blackbird has lost deceives his intellect and obscures his vision; if he shall permit it, I shall act for him, and to-morrow his vengeance will be complete."

"Do as you like; from whatever side vengeance comes, it will be agreeable to me."

"Enough. I shall soon bring here the three hunters, and him whose scalp they could not save."

So saying the messenger rose and was soon hidden by the fog from the eyes of the Blackbird.

On the island more generous emotions were felt. From the eyes of its occupants sleep had also fled—for if there be a moment in life, when the hearts of the bravest may fail them, it is when danger is terrible and inevitable, and when not even the last consolation of selling life dearly is possible to them. Watched by enemies whom they could not see, the hunters could not satisfy their rage by making their foes fall beneath their bullets as they had done the evening before. Besides, both Bois-Rose and Pepé knew too well the implacable obstinacy of the Indians to suppose that the Blackbird would permit his warriors to reply to their attacks; a soldier's death would have seemed too easy to him.

Oppressed by these sad thoughts, the three hunters spoke no more, but resigned themselves to their fate, rather than abandon the unlucky stranger by attempting to escape.

Fabian was as determined to die as the others. The habitual sadness of his spirit robbed death of its terrors, but still the ardour of his mind would have caused him to prefer a quicker death, weapon in hand, to the slow and ignominious one reserved for them. He was the first to break silence. The profound tranquillity that reigned on the banks was to the experienced eyes of the Canadian and Pepé only a certain indication of the invincible resolution of their enemies; but to Fabian it appeared reassuring—a blessing by which they ought to profit.

"All sleeps now around us," said he, "not only the Indians on the banks, but all that has life in the woods and in the desert—the river itself seems to be running slower! See! the reflections of the fires die away! would it not be the time to attempt a descent on the bank?"

"The Indians sleep!" interrupted Pepé, bitterly, "yes, like the water which seems stagnant, but none the less pursues its course. You could not take three steps in the river before the Indians would rush after you as you have often seen wolves rush after a stag. Have *you* nothing better to propose, Bois-Rose?"

"No," replied he as his hand sought that of Fabian, while with the other he pointed to the sick man, tossing restlessly on his couch of pain.

"But, in default of all other chance," said Fabian, "we should at least have that of dying with honour, side by side as we would wish. If we are victorious, we can then return to the aid of this unfortunate man. If we fall, God himself, when we appear before him, cannot reproach us with the sacrifice of his life, since we risked our own for the common good."

"No," replied Bois-Rose; "but let us still hope in that God, who re-united us by a miracle; what does not happen to-day, may to-morrow; we have time before us before our provisions fail. To attempt to take the bank now, would be to march to certain death. To die would be nothing, and we always hold that last resource in our own hands; but we might perhaps be made prisoners, and then I shudder to think of what would be our fate. Oh! my beloved Fabian, these Indians in their determination to take us alive give me at least the happiness of being yet a few days beside you."

Silence again resumed its reign; but as Bois-Rose thought of the terrible dénouement he clutched convulsively at some of the trunks of the dead trees, and under his powerful grasp the islet trembled as though about to be torn from its base.

"Ah! the wretches! the demons!" cried Pepé, with a sudden explosion of rage. "Look yonder!"

A red light was piercing gradually through the veil of vapour which hung over the river, and seemed to advance and grow larger; but, strange to say, the fire floated on the water, and, intense as was the fog, the mass of flames dissipated it as the sun disperses the clouds. The three hunters had barely time to be astonished at this apparition, before they guessed its cause. A long course of life in the desert and its dangers had imparted to the Canadian a firmness which Pepé had not attained; therefore, instead of giving way to surprise, he remained perfectly calm. He knew that this was the only way to surmount any difficulty.

"Yes," said he, "I understand what it is as well as if the Indians had told me. You spoke once of foxes smoked out of their holes; now they want to burn us in ours."

The globe of fire which floated on the river advanced with alarming rapidity, and confirmed the words of Bois-Rose. Already amidst the water, reddened by the flame, the twigs of the willows were becoming distinct.

"It is a fire-ship," cried Pepé, "with which they want to set fire to our island."

"So much the better," cried Fabian; "better to fight against the fire than wait quietly for death."

"Yes," said Bois-Rose; "but fire is a terrible adversary and it fights for these demons."

The besieged could oppose nothing to the advancing flames; and they would soon devour the little island, leaving to its inmates no other chance of escape but by throwing themselves into the water—where the Indians could either kill them by rifle-shots, or take them alive, as they pleased.

Such had been the idea of the Indian messenger. By his order, the Apaches had cut down a tree with its leaves on, and a thick mass of wet grass interlaced in its branches formed a sort of foundation, on which they placed the branches of a pine tree; and after setting fire to this construction, they had sent it floating down the stream. As it approached, the crackling of the wood could be heard; and out of the black smoke which mixed with the fog arose a bright, clear flame.

Not far from the bank they could distinguish the form of an Indian. Pepé could not resist a sudden temptation. "Yon demon," cried he, "shall at least not live to exult over our death."

So saying, he fired and the plume of the Indian was seen to go down.

"Sad and tardy vengeance," remarked Bois-Rose; and as if, indeed, the Apaches disdained the efforts of a vanquished foe, the shore preserved its gloomy solitude, and not a single howl accompanied the last groans of the warrior.

"Never mind," cried Pepé, stamping his foot in his impotent fury; "I shall die more calmly, the greater number of those demons I have sent before me." And he looked round for some other victim.

Meanwhile Bois-Rose was calmly reconnoitring the burning mass, which, if it touched the island, would set fire to the dried trees which composed it.

"Well," cried Pepé, whose rage blinded his judgment, "it is useless to look at the fire; have you any method of making it deviate from its course?"

"Perhaps," replied the Canadian. Pepé began to whistle with an affected indifference.

"I see something that proves to me that the reasonings of the Indians are not always infallible; and if it were not that we shall receive a shower of balls, to force us to stay hidden while the islet takes fire, I should care as little for that burning raft as for a fire-fly in the air."

In constructing the floating fire, the Indians had calculated its thickness, so that the wet grass might be dried by the fire and become kindled about the time when it should touch the island. But the grass had been soaked in the water, and this had retarded its combustion; besides the large branches had not had time to inflame; it was only the smaller boughs and the leaves that were burning. This had not escaped the quick eye of the Canadian, who, advancing with a long stick in his hand, resolved to push it underwater; but just as he was about to risk this attempt, what he had predicted took place. A shower of balls and arrows flew towards them; though these shots seemed rather intended to terrify than to kill them.

"They are determined," said Bois-Rose, "only to take us alive!"

The fire almost touched the island, a few minutes and it would be alight, when with the rapidity of lightning, Bois-Rose glided into the water and disappeared. Shouts rose from each side of the river, when the Indians, as well as Fabian and Pepé, saw the floating mass tremble under his powerful grasp. The fire blazed up brightly for a moment, then the water hissed and the mass of flame was extinguished in foam, until darkness and fog once more spread their sombre covering over the river. The blackened tree, turned from its course, passed by the island, while, amidst the howls of the Indians Bois-Rose rejoined his friends. The whole island shook under his efforts to get back upon it.

"Howl at your ease," cried he, "you have not captured as yet; but," he added, in a more serious tone, "shall we be always as lucky?"

Indeed, although this danger was surmounted, how many remained to be conquered! Who could foresee what new stratagems the Indians might employ against them? These reflections damped their first feeling of triumph. All at once Pepé started up, crying out as he did so:

"Bois-Rose, Fabian, we are saved!"

"Saved!" said Bois-Rose, "what do you mean?"

"Did you not remark how a few hours ago the whole islet trembled under our hands when we tore away some branches to fortify ourselves with, and how you yourself made it shake just now? well, I thought once of making a raft, but now I believe we three can uproot the whole island and set it floating. The fog is thick, the night dark and to-morrow—"

"We shall be far from here!" cried Bois-Rose. "To work! to work! we have no time to spare, for the rising wind indicates the approach of morning, and the river does not run more than three knots an hour."

"So much the better, the movement will be less visible."

The brave Canadian grasped the hands of his comrades as he rose to his feet.

"What are you going to do?" said Fabian, "cannot we three uproot the island, as Pepé said?"

"Doubtless, Fabian, but we risk breaking, it in pieces, and our safety depends upon keeping it together. It is, perhaps, some large branch or root which holds it in its place. Many years must have elapsed since these trees were first driven here, and the water has probably rendered this branch or root very rotten—that is what I wish to find out."

At that moment the doleful screech of an owl interrupted them, and those plaintive cries troubling the silence of night, just as they were about to entertain some hope, sounded ominous in the ears of Pepé.

"Ah!" said he, sadly, all his superstition reviving, "the voice of the owl at this moment seems to me to announce no good fortune to us."

"The imitation is perfect, I allow," said Bois-Rose, "but you must not be thus deceived. It is an Indian sentinel who calls to his companions either to warn them to be watchful, or what is more like their diabolical spirit, to remind us that they are watching us. It is a kind of death-song with which they wish to regale us."

As he spoke, the same sound was repeated from the opposite bank with different modulations, confirming his words, but it sounded none the less terrible as it revealed all the perils and ambushes hidden by the darkness of the night.

"I have a great mind to call to them to roar more like tigers that they are."

"Do not; it would only enable them to know our exact position."

So saying, the Canadian entered the water with extreme care, while his comrades followed his movements with anxious eyes.

"Well," said Pepé, when Bois-Rose came to the surface to take breath, "are we firmly fixed?"

"All is well, I think," replied Bois-Rose, "I see at present but one thing that keeps the islet at anchor. Have patience a while."

"Take care not to get too far under," said Fabian, "or you may be caught in the roots and branches."

"Have no fear, child; a whale may sooner remain fixed to a fishing-boat which it can toss twenty feet into the air, than I under an islet that I could break to pieces with a blow."

The river closed again over his head, and a tolerably long space of time elapsed during which the presence of Bois-Rose was indicated only by the eddies formed round the islet, which now tottered on its foundation. His comrades felt that the giant was making a powerful effort, and Fabian's heart sank as he thought that he might be struggling with death; when a crash was heard under their feet, like that of a ship's timbers striking against a rock, and Bois-Rose reappeared above the surface, his hair streaming with water. With one bound he regained the island, which began to move slowly down the river. An enormous root, some depth in the water, had given way to the vigorous strength of the colossus, and the islet was set free.

"God be praised!" cried he, "the last obstacle is vanquished and we are afloat." As he spoke the island could be perceived advancing down stream, slowly it is true, but surely.

"Now," continued he, "our life rests in the hands of God. If the island floats down the middle of the stream we shall soon, thanks to the fog, be out of sight or reach of the Indians. Oh! my God," added he, fervently, "a few hours more of darkness and your creatures will be saved."

Chapter Forty Four
The Floating Islet

The three men kept silence as they followed with anxious eyes the movement of the floating island. Day would soon break, but the freshness of the night, which always increases an hour or two before sunrise, had condensed more and more the vapours which rose from the water. The fires on the bank appeared only like stars, which grow pale in the heavens at the approach of dawn. From this source, therefore, they had little to fear; but another danger menaced the three hunters. The island followed the stream, but turned round as it went, and they feared that in this continual rotation it might deviate from the centre of the liver and strike on one of the banks on which the Indians were encamped.

Like the sailor who, with a heart full of anguish, follows the movements of his ship, almost disabled by the storm, and contemplates with terror the breakers into which he is perhaps destined to be driven, thus the three hunters—a prey to the most cruel anxiety—regarded in silence the uncertain progress of their island. When sometimes the border of osiers and reeds which surrounded the island trembled in the breeze which proceeded from one of the banks, it seemed then to be driven towards the opposite side. Sometimes it went straight along with the current, but in any event, the efforts of those who were on it could do nothing to direct it. Luckily the fog was so thick that the very trees which bordered the river were invisible.

"Courage," muttered Pepé; "as long as we cannot see the trees it is a sign that we are going on rightly. Ah! if God but favour us, many a howl will resound along these banks, now so peaceful, when at daybreak the Indians find neither the island nor those it sheltered."

"Yes," replied Bois-Rose, "it was a grand idea, Pepé; in the trouble of my mind I should not have thought of it, and yet it was such a simple thing."

"Simple ideas are always the last to present themselves," rejoined Pepé. "But do you know, Bois-Rose," added he, in a low voice, "it proves that in the desert it is imprudent to venture with one whom you love more than life, since fear for him takes away a man's senses. I tell you frankly, Bois-Rose, you have not been like yourself."

"It is true; I scarcely recognise myself," replied the Canadian, simply; "and yet—"

He did not finish, but fell into a profound reverie, during which, like a man whose body only is present, and his soul absent, he appeared no longer to watch the movements of the island. For the hunter who, during twenty years has lived the free life of the desert, to renounce this life seemed like death; but to renounce the society of Fabian, and the consolation of having his eyes closed by his adopted son, was still worse than death. Fabian and the desert were the two dominant affections of his life, and to abandon either seemed impossible.

His reverie, however, was soon interrupted by Pepé, who had for some minutes been casting uneasy glances towards one of the banks. Through the fog he fancied he could perceive the fantastic forms which trees appear to take in a mist. They looked like indistinct phantoms, covered with long draperies, hanging over the river.

"We are going wrong, Bois-Rose," said he, "are not those the tops of the willows on the bank?"

"It is true," cried Bois-Rose, rousing himself; "and by the fires being still visible it is evident how little progress we have made in the last half hour."

At that moment the island began to move more rapidly, and the trees became more distinct. The hunters looked anxiously at each other. One of the fires was more clearly seen, and they could even distinguish an Indian sentinel in his frightful battle-costume. The long mane of a bison covered his head, and above that waved a plume of feathers. Bois-Rose pointed him out to Pepé, but luckily the fog was so thick that the Indian, rendered himself visible by the fire, near which he stood, could not yet see the island. However, as if an instinct had warned him to be watchful, he raised his head and shook back the flowing hair which ornamented it.

"Can he have any suspicion?" said Bois-Rose.

"Ah! if a rifle made no more noise than an arrow, with what pleasure I should send that human buffalo to mount guard in another world," replied Pepé.

Just then they saw the Indian stick his lance in the ground, and leaning forward, shade his eyes with his hands so as to concentrate their power. A keen anxiety was in their hearts as they watched him. The ferocious warrior bending down like a wild beast ready to spring, his face half covered with the straggling hair, was hideous and terrible to look upon; but the fugitives would only have laughed at the spectacle had they not had so much to dread. All at once, the Apache after remaining a few minutes in this attentive attitude, walked towards the bank and disappeared from sight—for nothing was visible except in the circle of light thrown by the fire. It was a moment of intense anxiety for the fugitives, as the island continued to glide silently on.

"Has he seen us?" murmured Pepé.

"I fear so."

A doleful cry now caused them to start. It was repeated from the opposite side; it was the signal of the sentinels one to the other, but all became again silent. Bois-Rose uttered a murmur of relief, as he saw the man return to his former place and attitude. It was a false alarm.

Still the island continued to approach the bank.

"At this rate," said Bois-Rose, "in ten minutes we shall fall into the hands of the Indians. If we could but paddle a little with that great branch, we should soon be in the right direction again, but the noise, I fear, would betray us."

"Nevertheless," replied Pepé, "it is what we must do, it is better to run the chance of betraying ourselves, than be drifted into the hands of our enemies. But first, let us see if the current in which we now are, runs towards the bank. If it does, we must hesitate no longer, and although the branch of a tree is more noisy in the water than an oar, we must do our best to paddle in silence."

Pepé then gently broke off a piece of wood and placed it on the water, and leaning over the edge, he and Bois-Rose watched it anxiously. There was in that place a violent eddy, caused by some deep hole in the bed of the river. For a moment the wood turned round as though going to sink, then it took a direction opposite to the bank, towards which they were driving. Both uttered a stifled exclamation of joy, as their island also, after a moment's stoppage, began to float away from the shore, and the increasing thickness of the fog assured them that they were taking the right course.

About an hour passed thus, amidst poignant alternatives of fear and hope; then the bivouac fires were lost in the distance, and the fugitives perceived that they were nearly out of danger. Reassured by this belief Bois-Rose placed himself at one end of the islet, and paddled vigorously, until the raft, ceasing to gyrate, advanced more swiftly down the current, like a horse long abandoned to his own caprices, who feels at last the hand and spur of an able rider. Keeping where the water was deepest, they now proceeded at a considerable rate of speed, and began to think themselves entirely out of danger.

"Daylight will not be long in appearing," said Bois-Rose, "and we must now land and endeavour to get on faster; we shall go twice as fast on foot as on this island, which sails slower than a Dutch lugger."

"Well! land where you like, Bois-Rose, and we will follow. Let us wade down the stream a bit, so as to hide our traces from the Indians; and even if we have to carry the wounded man, we can manage two leagues an hour. Do you think, Don Fabian, that the Golden Valley is far off?"

"You saw the sun go down behind the foggy mountains which shut in this valley," replied Fabian. "It lies at their foot—we cannot be many hours' march from it."

Bois-Rose now gave to the island an oblique direction, and in about a quarter of an hour, it struck violently against the bank. While Pepé and Fabian jumped ashore, the Canadian took the wounded man in his arms, and laid him gently down. This awoke him, and opening his eyes and throwing round him an astonished glance, he murmured, "Virgen Santa! shall I again hear those frightful howls which troubled my sleep?"

"No, my lad, the Indians are far off now, and we are in safety. Thank God, who has permitted me to save all that are dear to me—my child Fabian and my old friend."

They then prepared to continue their course.

"If you are not able to walk," said Pepé to Gayferos, "we shall construct a kind of litter to carry you on. We have no time to lose if we wish to escape these wretches, who, as soon as daylight appears, will begin to chase us as eagerly as ever they chased a white enemy."

So great was the desire of Gayferos to escape, that he almost forgot the pain he was enduring, and declaring that he would follow his liberators as quickly as they could go themselves, he begged them to set off at once.

"We have some precautions to take first," said Bois-Rose; "rest a few minutes while we break to pieces and commit to the current this raft, which has been so useful to us. It is important the Indians should not trace us."

All three set to work, and already disjointed by the breaking of the root which held it, and by the shock it had received on touching the shore, the floating island opposed no great resistance to their efforts. The trunks of the trees which composed it, were torn asunder and pushed into the current—which carried them quickly away—and there soon remained no vestige of what it had taken years to construct. When the last branch had disappeared from their eyes, Bois-Rose and Pepé busied themselves in raising up the stalks of the plants, to efface the marks of their feet, and then all prepared to start. They first entered the water and walked along the edge, so as to leave no footmarks, and to lead the Indians to suppose that they had remained on the island. It was too fatiguing for them to walk very quickly; but, in about an hour, just as their wounded feet were about to force them to make halt, they arrived at the fork of two rivers which formed a delta. In this delta lay the Golden Valley. Daylight was just beginning to appear in the horizon, and a grey tint upon the sky was taking the place of darkness. Luckily the arm of the river that they had to cross was not deep, the mass of the water flowing in the opposite direction. This was fortunate, for the wounded man could not swim. Bois-Rose lifted him on his shoulders, and all three waded through the water, which scarcely reached to their knees. The chain of mountains was only about a league off, and after a short rest, all resumed their way with renewed ardour.

Soon the country changed its aspect. To the fine sand—for the triangle formed by the junction of the two rivers was inundated during part of the year—succeeded deep ruts, and then dry beds of streams, hollowed out by the torrents in the rainy season. Instead of the narrow border of willows and cotton-trees which shaded the deserted banks, green oaks rose up, and the landscape terminated in the line of the foggy mountains. All looked strange and imposing, and rarely had the foot of a white man pressed this desert clothed in its virgin wildness. Perhaps Marcos Arellanos and Cuchillo were the only white men who had ever wandered to this remote place. A vague sentiment of awe caused the hunters involuntarily to lower their voices before the supernatural charm of this austere landscape. Those hills, enveloped in mist—even when the plains shone with the blazing rays of the sun—seemed to hide some impenetrable mystery. It might be fancied that the invisible guardians of the treasures, the lords of the mountains according to Indian superstition, were hidden under this veil of eternal vapour.

Chapter Forty Five
The Finger of God

After a short journey, fatigue and suffering overcame the wounded man; and as it was imperative that he should not become acquainted with the situation of the Golden Valley, or even be made aware of its existence, Bois-Rose and Pepé resolved, now that he was in safety, to leave him for some hours and employ the time in reconnoitring the places described to Fabian by his adopted mother.

"Listen, my lad!" said Bois-Rose to Gayferos, "we have given you quite sufficient proofs of devotion, and now we must leave you for half or perhaps a whole day. We have some business in hand which requires three determined men; if this evening or to-morrow morning we are still alive, you shall see us return; if not, you know it will not be our fault. Here is water and dried meat, and twenty-four hours will soon pass."

It was not without regret that Gayferos consented to this separation; however, reassured by a new promise from the generous hunters, to whom he owed so much, he resigned himself to being left behind.

"I have one last word to say to you," said Bois-Rose. "If chance bring here any of the companions from whom you so unluckily separated, I exact from you, as the sole return for the service which we have rendered to you, that you will reveal to none of them our presence here. As for your own, you can account for it in any way you like."

Gayferos made the required promise, and they then took leave of him.

On the point of accomplishing one of his most ardent desires, that of enriching the child of his affection and adding immense treasures to his future fortune, Bois-Rose seemed to forget that it would raise an additional barrier between Fabian and himself.

Pepé, anxious to repair as far as possible the involuntary injury that he had caused to the Mediana family, walked along with an elastic step. Fabian alone did not seem happy, and after a quarter of an hour he stopped, saying that he needed rest. All three sat down on a little hillock, and Pepé, pointing to the mountains, cried, in a tone of gay reproach, "What! Don Fabian! does not the neighbourhood of those places, so fertile in gold, give new vigour to your limbs?"

"No," replied Fabian, "for I shall not go a step further in that direction till sunrise."

"Ah!" said Bois-Rose, "and why not?"

"Why? Because this is a cursed place—a place where he—whom before you I loved as a father—was assassinated; because a thousand dangers surround you, and I have already exposed you too much by making you espouse my cause."

"What are these dangers that we three together cannot brave? Can they be greater than what we have just passed through? And if it please Pepé and I to incur them for you, what then?"

"These dangers are of all kinds," replied Fabian, "why deceive oneself longer? Does not everything prove that Don Estevan knows also of the existence of the Golden Valley?"

"Well, and what do you conclude from that?"

"That three men cannot prevail against sixty."

"Listen, my child," replied Bois-Rose with some impatience, "it was before engaging in this enterprise that we should have made these reflections; now they are too late, and why do you not think to-day as you did yesterday?"

"Because yesterday I was blinded by passion; because affection has now taken its place; because I do not hope to-day what I hoped yesterday."

The contradictory passions which agitated his heart did not permit Fabian to explain more clearly to the Canadian the alternations of his wishes.

"Fabian," said Bois-Rose solemnly, "you have a holy but terrible duty to perform, and duty must be done; but who tells you that the expedition commanded by Don Estevan will take the same path as ourselves? And, if it does, so much the better; the murderer of your mother will fall into your hands."

"The guide conducting them," replied Fabian, seeking to hide his real sentiments, "can only be that miserable Cuchillo. Now, if I am not wrong, the valley must be known to him; in any case, we should await the return of daylight before entangling ourselves in a country we know nothing about, and in which these adventurers may prove enemies as formidable as the Indians. Do you not think so, Pepé?"

"Nearly all night, the wind has brought to our ears," replied he, "the sound of filing, which proves that the troop has been engaged with the Indians; it is not therefore probable that any one can be in advance of us. I must say that my opinion is, that we should without loss of time gain some place in the mountains where we may engage in a last inevitable struggle with our enemies; some well chosen spot where we can defend ourselves with a chance of success."

"It is this unequal struggle that I wish to avoid," replied Fabian, warmly. "As long as I could hope to overtake, before they readied Tubac, those whom Providence seemed to point out for my vengeance, and attack them while they were only five against three, I pursued them without reflection; as long as I could believe that this expedition had, like so many others, entered the desert only in search of some unknown spot, I followed them. But what has happened? After four days in which we took a different path, do we not find them near these mountains? Their aim is therefore the same as ours. Three men cannot fight against sixty; therefore God forbid that to further either my vengeance or my cupidity, I should sacrifice two generous friends whose lives are more precious to me than my own!"

"Child," cried Bois-Rose, "do you not see that every one is here for himself, and yet that our three interests are but one? When for the second time, God sent you to my arms, were we not already pursuing the man who was ruining your hopes, and had already assassinated your mother, and stolen your name? For ten years Pepé and I have been but one; the friends of one have been the friends of the other, and you are Pepé's son, because you are mine, Fabian my child; and thanks be to God that in serving our own cause we are also serving yours. Whatever happens, then we shall not take a step backwards."

"Besides," said Pepé, "do you count for nothing, Don Fabian, heaps of gold, and a whole life of abundance for an imaginary peril? for I repeat we must reach the valley first, and a day—an hour—in advance may enrich us forever; you see then that *we* are egotists trying to sacrifice *you* to our personal interest."

"Pepé is right," said Bois-Rose, "we want gold."

"What will you do with it?" asked Fabian, smiling.

"What will I do with it? the child asks what I will do with it!" cried Bois-Rose.

"Yes, I wish to know."

"What will I do with it?" replied the honest Canadian, whom this question embarrassed much, "parbleu—I will do—many things, I will give my rifle a golden barrel," cried he, triumphantly.

Pepé smiled and shrugged his shoulders.

"You laugh," said Bois-Rose. "Do you think that when you finish off an Apache, a Sioux, or a Pawnee with a blow of your knife, it would not be grand to say to him, 'Dog, the ball that broke your head came from a rifle of solid gold!' Few hunters can say as much."

"I agree to that," said Fabian; then added he seriously, "No, my friends! Don Estevan escapes my vengeance, and the gold that I believe would be mine escapes me also, for it is surrounded by soldiers. What matters? have I not still, if I should become ambitious, the name and fortunes of my forefathers to reclaim? Are there not in Spain tribunals which dispense justice to all? God will do the rest, but I will not madly expose two noble lives. I do not speak of mine; young as I am, I have drunk the cup of bitterness to the dregs. You have done enough, and your generous subterfuges cannot impose upon me."

So saying, Fabian held out his hands to the two hunters, who pressed them in an affectionate grasp. The Canadian looked silently for a minute at the noble face of him whom he was proud to call his son, and then said:

"Fabian, my child, all my life has been passed on the sea or in deserts, but I have preserved sufficient remembrance of cities and their customs to know that justice is rather sold than given. This gold we shall employ in making of you what you were intended to be; this gold, will smooth all the obstacles against which your rightful cause might break down. Pepé can tell you, like me, that we shall gladly expose our lives in the hope of restoring to you the property of your ancestors, and the illustrious name that you are so worthy to bear."

"Yes," said Pepé, "I have told you that the early part of my life was not such as I should wish. It was a little the fault of the Spanish Government, which never paid me for my services; still it is a weight upon my heart. Often, I think sadly of my past life, but God always pardons the repentant sinner, and gives him opportunity of repentance. That day has arrived; my pardon is near, and it is but justice that I should assist in restoring to you what I helped to take away."

"Let us go on then!" said Bois-Rose, "God has hitherto shown us our path and will continue to aid us. If you stay, Fabian, we shall go alone."

So saying, the Canadian rose, and throwing his rifle over his shoulder began his march. Fabian was forced to yield, and all proceeded towards the mountains.

Daylight had not yet quite appeared when a new actor advanced in his turn towards the same scenes. He came alone; his horse in its impetuous course made the sand fly under his feet, and the rider, who was no other than Cuchillo, showed symptoms on his sinister countenance of some secret terror. His flight might not have been unobserved even in the tumult of action, or some of the Indians might have noticed his desertion, and hence his fears. But Cuchillo was not a man to undertake a bold stroke without calculating the chances. As a hunter wishing to take the lion's whelps, throws him some bait to distract his attention, so Cuchillo had delivered to the lords of the desert his companions as a prey. He had calculated that the struggle would last a great part of the night, and that conquered or conquering, the adventurers would not dare, during the following day, to leave their intrenchments. He would therefore have long hours before him in which to seize on some of the treasures of the Golden Valley, with which he would afterwards return to the protection of his companions, and when they all reached the place he could still claim his share as soldier and as guide. Pretexts would not fail him for this second absence, but he had forgotten to calculate on Don Estevan's suspicions concerning him. To conclude his bargain with him he had been forced to give such a precise account of the situation of the valley that Don Estevan could scarcely miss the right road. After Cuchillo, followed by his horse, had glided out from the camp he had ridden straight towards the mountains, and cupidity, the most blinding of passions, had closed his eyes to the danger of his plan.

His heart palpitating with alternate hopes and fears, he had advanced rapidly, and only stopped occasionally to listen to the vague murmurs of the desert. Then recognising the groundlessness of his apprehensions, he had continued his road with renewed ardour.

Sometimes also the aspect of the places he had seen before, awakened gloomy souvenirs. On that hillock, he had rested with Marcos Arellanos; that nopal had furnished them with refreshing fruit; they had both contemplated with mysterious terror the strange aspect of the Misty Mountains, and his horse in its rapid course carried the murderer to the spot where his victim had fallen beneath his blows! Then to the fear of enemies succeeded that inspired by conscience, which while it often sleeps by day, awakes and resumes its empire during the night. The bushes—the thorny nopals—rose before him like accusing phantoms, opposing his advance with extended arms; a cold perspiration stood on his brow, but cupidity, stronger than fear, spurred him on towards the valley, and he began to laugh at his own apprehensions.

"Phantoms," said he, "are like alcaldes, who never address poor devils like me; but let me only get one or two arrobas of gold, and I shall have so many masses said for the soul of Arellanos, that he will be glad to have met his death in such generous hands."

He laughed at this quaint conceit, and then rode on quickly. In a few minutes he stopped and listened again, but heard no noise save the loud breathing of his horse.

"I am alone," thought he; "those brutes whom I have guided are fighting to give me leisure to despoil the sands of some of that precious gold. Who is to prevent me presently, when daylight appears, from picking up as much as I can carry without betraying my secret? This time, it will not be as when along with Arellanos; I shall not have to fly from the Indians: they are busy. Afterwards I can come back with such of my companions as escape the Apaches. How many will remain to partake with me? Oh! the thought of these treasures makes the blood boil in my veins. Is it not gold that gives glory, pleasure, and every good of this world? our priests say its power extends even beyond the tomb!"

While Cuchillo was advancing blindly to where his destiny led him, Don Estevan and Pedro Diaz were also on their way. Although the hills were but six leagues from the camp, yet, uncertain of the time of his absence, Don Estevan had left orders to his people to await his return. The two advanced silently, full of desire for the gold, but equally desirous of intercepting the traitor. Two hours' quick riding had produced no result. Thanks to his advance, Cuchillo was invisible; and the darkness would have hidden his track even from the eye of an Indian.

"There is no doubt," said Pedro Diaz, breaking silence, "that the knave must have profited by the confusion to fly towards the valley, and seize on a part of the treasures which he has sold to us."

"That is not what I fear most," said Don Estevan. "If Cuchillo has not exaggerated the riches of the place, there will be plenty left for all of us. But now so near attaining that for which I have crossed the desert—after having left a position envied by all, to brave the dangers of an expedition like this—a vague fear of failing agitates me. The desert is like the sea, abounding in pirates, and the soul of Cuchillo is full of treason: it seems to me that the villain will be fatal to us."

Suddenly Diaz dismounted, and picked up off the sand a dark object; it was a kind of valise, which Diaz at once recognised as belonging to Cuchillo.

"This shows you, Señor," said he, "that we are in the right path, and that the coming day will bring us into the presence of the traitor."

"It shall then be his last treason," said Don Estevan; and they now rode silently on with the certainty that Cuchillo was before them.

Strange chain of coincidences! When the sun appeared in the horizon, the different actors in this drama, apparently drawn together by accident, but in truth impelled onwards by the hand of God, had met in the most inaccessible part of the great American desert.

Chapter Forty Six
The Golden Valley

The darkness was no longer that of midnight—the outlines of the different objects began to be visible, and the peaks of the hills looked like domes or fantastic turrets in the half-light. Detached from the mass of the mountains, a rock in the form of a truncated cone towered up like an outwork. A cascade fell noisily from an adjacent hill into a deep gulf below, and in front of the rock a row of willows and cotton-trees indicated the neighbourhood of a stream. Then the immense plain of the delta formed by the two arms of the Rio Gila (which from east to west cuts for itself a double passage through the chain of the Misty Mountains) displayed itself in all its sombre majesty. Such were the striking points of the landscape which opened before the travellers.

Soon the blue light of morning replaced the darkness, and the summits of the hills one by one became visible. On the top of the rock two pines could now be seen, their bending stems and dark foliage extending over the abyss. At their foot the skeleton of a horse, held up by hidden fastenings, showed upon his whitened bones the savage ornaments with which he had been embellished, and fragments of the saddle still rested upon his back. The increasing light soon shone on more sinister emblems: on posts raised in different places, and human scalps floating on them. These hideous trophies indicated the burial-place of an Indian warrior. In fact a renowned chief reposed there; and his spirit overlooked, like the genius of plunder, those plains where his war-cry had so often resounded, and which he had ridden over on that battle-horse whose bones were whitening by his tomb. Birds of prey flew over his grave, uttering their shrill cries, as if they would awaken him who slept there forever, and whose cold hand would no longer prepare for them their bloody feasts.

A few minutes later the horizon became tinted with pale rose-coloured clouds, and soon after, like the first spark of a fire, a ray of sunlight struck like a golden arrow on the thick fog, and floods of light inundated the depths of the valley. Day had come in all its glory, but wreaths of vapour still hung capriciously on the leaves of the trees or clung around the trunks. Soon were displayed wild precipices, with falls of water foaming down their sides; then deep defiles, at the entrance of which fantastic offerings of Indian superstition were suspended.

Above the tomb of the Indian chief rose the spray of the cascade, in which was reflected the colours of the rainbow; and lastly, a valley was visible, closed on one side by peaked rocks, from which hung long draperies of verdure, and on the other by a lake, whose waters were half-hidden by the aquatic plants on its surface: this was the Golden Valley.

At the first glance the whole scene only offered the sombre features of a wild nature; but the scrutinising eye would soon have divined the treasures concealed there. Nothing betrayed the presence of living things in that deserted place, when the three hunters made their appearance on the spot.

"If the devil has an abode anywhere on the earth," said Pepé, pointing to the mountains, "it must surely be among those wild denies!

"But if it be true," continued he, "that it is gold which is the cause of most crimes, it is more probable that the old fellow has chosen the Golden Valley for his abode, which contains, according to you, Don Fabian, enough to ruin an entire generation."

"You are right," said Fabian, who looked pale and grave, "it was here perhaps that the unlucky Marcos Arellanos was assassinated. Ah! if this place could speak, I should know the name of him whom I have sworn to pursue: but the wind and the rain have effaced the traces of the victim as well as those of the murderer."

"Patience, my child!" replied Bois-Rose; "I have never in the course of a long life known crime to go unpunished. Often we recover the traces that were believed to have been long effaced, and even solitude sometimes raises its voice against the guilty. If the assassin be not dead, cupidity will doubtless bring him again to this place, and before long; for no doubt he is one of those in the Mexican camp. Now, Fabian, shall we wait for the enemy here, or shall we fill our pockets with gold and return?"

"I know not what to decide," replied Fabian; "I came here almost against my will. I obey your wishes, or else a will stronger than either yours or mine. I feel that an invisible hand impels me on—as it did on that evening when, scarcely knowing what I did, I came and sat down by your fire. Why should I, who do not know what to do with this gold, risk my life to obtain it? I know not. I know only that here I am, with a sad heart and a soul filled with cruel uncertainty."

"Man is but the plaything of Providence, it is true," said Bois-Rose; "but as for the sadness you feel, the aspect of these places sufficiently accounts for it; and as for—"

A hoarse cry, that scarcely appeared human, interrupted the Canadian. It seemed to come from the Indian tomb, as if it were an accusing voice against the invaders of this abode of the dead. The three hunters glanced simultaneously towards the tomb, but no living creature was visible there. The eye of one of the birds of prey, that were sailing above the rock, could alone have told where the cry came from. The imposing solemnity of the place, the bloody souvenirs evoked by it in Fabian's mind, and the superstitious ones in that of Pepé, joined to the strange and mysterious sound, inspired in both a feeling akin to terror. There was something so inexplicable in the sound, that for a moment they doubted having heard it.

"Is it really the voice of a man?" said Bois-Rose, "or only one of those singular echoes which resound in these mountains?"

"If it were a human voice," asked Fabian, "where did it come from? it seemed to be above us, and yet I see no one on the top of the hill!"

"God send," said Pepé, crossing himself, "that in these mountains which abound in inexplicable noises, and where lightning shines under a calm sky, we have only men to fight against! But if the fog contained a legion of devils—if the valley really contains, as you say, several years' income of the king of Spain, please, Señor Don Fabian, to recall your recollections, and tell us if we are still far off it."

Fabian threw a glance around him; the landscape was just what had been so minutely described to him.

"We must be close to the spot," said he, "for it should be at the foot of the tomb of the Indian chief—and these ornaments indicate that the rock is the tomb. We have no time to lose. You and Bois-Rose walk around the rock, while I go and examine those cotton-trees and willows."

"I am suspicious of everything in this mysterious place," said Bois-Rose; "that cry indicates the presence of a human being; and whether white or red, he is to be feared. Before we separate, let me examine the *sign*."

All three bent on the ground eyes accustomed to read there as in an open book. The prints of a man's feet were visible on the sand, and one of them had trodden down the plants, whose stems were still gently rising up again one after the other.

"What did I tell you?" cried Bois-Rose. "Here are the tracks of a white man's feet, and I swear it is not ten minutes since he was here. These footmarks lead towards yonder cotton-trees."

"In any case he is alone," suggested Fabian.

All three were advancing towards the trees, when Bois-Rose halted.

"Let me go first," said he; "this hedge may hide the enemy. But no, the man who has left these footprints has only pulled open the vines and glanced through—he has not gone further in that direction."

So saying, Bois-Rose, in his turn, pulled aside the branches and the climbing network which was interwoven with them, and after a short examination, which had no particular result, he retired and left the branches to reclose of themselves. He then tried to follow the tracks but further on the ground became stony, and all traces disappeared.

"Let us go round this conical rock," suggested Bois-Rose.

"Come, Pepé; Fabian will wait here for us."

The two hunters strode off, and Fabian remained alone and pensive. This Golden Valley, of whose possession he had dreamt at that time when his heart nourished sweet hopes, was now near to him. What had been a dream was now a reality, and still he was more unhappy than at the time when hopeful love caused him to scoff at poverty. It is thus that happiness flies just as we are about to seize it. Sometimes in the silence of the forest, the traveller lends a greedy ear to the notes of the mocking-bird, and advances with precaution towards the place where, hidden under the foliage, the bird of the solitudes utters its sweet song. Vain hope! he advances, and the singer flies, his voice still as distant and himself as invisible as ever! Thus man often hears in the distance voices which sing to him of happiness; seduced by their charm he rushes toward them; but they fly at his approach; and his whole life is passed in pursuing, without ever reaching, the happiness promised by these delusive sounds.

For Fabian, happiness lay no longer in the Golden Valley. It existed nowhere. No voice now sang for him; he had no aim to pursue; no flying but charming image which he hoped to overtake. He was in one of those moods that God in His mercy makes rare in our lives—during which all is dark, as when at sea the light that guides the sailor becomes suddenly obscured.

He advanced mechanically towards the thick row of trees that formed an almost impenetrable hedge before him, but scarcely had he made a passage for himself when he stopped motionless with surprise. The sunlight shone on the stones thick as those on a beach, and discovered innumerable glancing objects. Any other than a gold-seeker might have been deceived by these stones, which looked like vitrifications at the foot of a volcano; but the practised eye of Fabian instantly recognised the virgin gold under its clayey envelope, as it is brought down by the torrents from the gold-producing mountains. Before his eyes lay the richest treasure that was ever displayed to the view of man.

If the breeze could have brought to the ears of the young Count of Mediana the accents of Rosarita's voice, when she recalled him back to the hacienda, he would gladly have quitted all these treasures to run towards her. But the breeze was mute, and there is in gold so irresistible an attraction that Fabian, in spite of his sadness, was for the moment fascinated.

However, the soul of Fabian was not one to be intoxicated by success; and after a few minutes of this enthusiasm, he called his two companions. They came at his call.

"Have you found him?" said Pepé.

"The treasure, but not the man. See!" added he, pushing aside the trees.

"What! those shining stones!"

"Are pure gold—treasures which God has hidden during centuries."

"My God!" exclaimed Pepé.

And with ardent eyes fixed upon the mass of riches before him, the ex-carabinier fell upon his knees. Passions long kept under seemed to rush back into his heart; a complete transformation took place in him, and the sinister expression of his face recalled to mind the hour of crime, when twenty years before he had bargained for the price of blood.

"Now," said Fabian, looking sadly at the gold, as he thought that all these riches were not worth to him a smile or look from her who had disdained him, "I understand how these two rivers, in their annual rise, and by their torrents that descend from the Misty Mountains, covering this narrow valley, bring down gold with them; the position of this valley is perhaps unique in all the world."

But the Spaniard heard him not. Riches—which the rough lesson he had received, and the life of independence and the savage happiness he had enjoyed, had taught him during the last ten years to disdain—suddenly resumed their terrible influence over his soul.

"You could not have imagined, could you, Pepé?" continued Fabian, "that so much gold could be collected in one place? I, who have been so long a gold-seeker, could not have imagined it, even after all I had heard."

Pepé did not reply; his eye wandered eagerly over the blocks of gold, and cast a strange glance on Fabian and on Bois-Rose. The hitter, standing in his favourite attitude, his arm resting on his rifle, amidst all these treasures, looked only at what was dearest to him—the young man restored to him by heaven. Pepé had before him, on one side, his old companion in danger—in a hundred different battles they had uttered their war-cry together, like those brothers in arms in ancient chivalric times, who fought always under the same banner—who shared cold, hunger, and thirst together.

On the other side, the young man, partly orphaned by his crime—a crime which had occasioned him remorse through so many years—the love and sole thought of his only friend in the world; and the demon of cupidity at his heart effaced all these souvenirs, and he already began to think—

A shudder passed through his frame as strange thoughts crossed his mind. A struggle took place within him, a struggle of the feelings of youth with the more noble ones developed by the life of nature, where man seems brought near to God; but this struggle was short: the old outlaw disappeared, and there remained only the man purified by repentance and solitude. Still kneeling on the ground, Pepé had closed his eyes, and a furtive tear, unperceived by his companions, stole from his eyes, and rolled down his bronzed cheeks.

"Señor Don Fabian de Mediana!" cried he, starting up, "you are now a rich and powerful lord, for all this gold belongs to you alone."

So saying, he advanced and bowed respectfully to Fabian, who appeared somewhat surprised by the manner of his salutation.

"God forbid," cried Fabian, "that you, who have shared the peril, should not share the treasure. What do you say, Bois-Rose? do you not rejoice to become in your old age rich and powerful?"

But Bois-Rose, unmoved before all the riches, contented himself with shaking his head, while a smile of tenderness for Fabian testified to the only interest that he took in that marvellous spectacle!

"I think like Pepé," said he, after a pause, "what could I do with this gold that the world covets? If it has for us an inestimable value, it is because it is to belong to you; the possession of the least of these stones would take away in our eyes from the value of the service we have rendered you. But the time for action has arrived; for certainly we are not alone in these solitudes."

Pepé now began to pull aside the branches, but scarcely had he entered the valley when the sound of a gun was distinctly heard. In a moment his voice reassured his anxious comrades.

"It is the devil," cried he, "forbidding us to encroach on his domains; but at all events it is a devil whose aim is not infallible."

Before entering the valley Bois-Rose and Fabian raised their eyes to the top of the hill, whence the shot as well as the voice had proceeded. But the remains of the fog at that moment covered the top of the rock, and all three rushed simultaneously towards the isolated mass where they believed their enemy to be hidden. The sides, although steep, were covered with brushwood, which rendered them easier to climb; but it was a dangerous attempt, for the fog prevented them from seeing what enemies were above. Fabian wished to go first, but the vigorous arm of the Canadian held him back, and meanwhile Pepé was half-way towards the summit. Bois-Rose followed, begging Fabian to keep behind him.

Pepé mounted boldly, undismayed by the foes that might be concealed behind that mass of vapour, and soon disappeared under the mist. A cry of triumph soon warned his friends that he had arrived in safety. Both hastened to join him, but found no one on the rock except Pepé himself! Just as, disappointed at their want of success, they were preparing to descend again, a sudden gust of wind drove off the fog, and allowed them to see to a distance. To the right and left the plain presented the most complete picture of the desert in its dreary sadness. They beheld arid steppes over which whirled clouds of sand, a burnt and sterile ground, everywhere silence, everywhere solitude. At some distance off two men on horseback were seen advancing towards the rock, but at the distance at which they were, it was impossible to distinguish either their dress or the colour of their skin.

"Must we sustain a new siege here?" said Bois-Rose. "Are these white men or Indians?"

"White or red, they are enemies," said Pepé.

While the three friends bent down, so as not to be observed, a man, until then invisible, cautiously entered the lake. He lifted with care the floating leaves of the water lilies, and forming of them a shelter over its head, remained motionless, and the surface of the lake soon after appeared as if undisturbed. This man was Cuchillo, the jackal, who, led by his evil destiny, had ventured to hunt on the ground of the lion.

Chapter Forty Seven
The Punishment of Tantalus

Cuchillo, after reaching the mountains, had halted. He had not forgotten the appearance of the place, and his heart trembled with fear and joy. After a few minutes he looked around him more calmly. It was then dark, and when he arrived at the rock, the damp vapours from the lake enveloped with a thick veil both the valley and the tomb. The sound of the waterfall put an end to his uncertainties; he remembered that it fell into a gulf close by the golden placer.

He had dismounted his horse, and sat down to wait for daylight; but scarcely had he done so when he bounded up as though bitten by a serpent. A fatal chance had led him to sit down on the very spot where he had struck Marcos Arellanos, and quick as lightning, every detail of the mortal struggle passed through his mind. However this feeling of terror was of short duration.

In that part of America, superstition has not established its empire as in the old countries of Europe, where the evening mists give to objects fantastic aspects, and tend naturally to reflections upon the supernatural. From this arises the sombre poesy of the north, which has peopled our land with ghosts and phantoms. In the American solitude people fear the living more than the dead, and Cuchillo had too much to fear from men to waste many thoughts upon the ghost of Arellanos, and he had soon quite banished the thought from his mind.

Although he felt nearly certain that no one had seen him leave the camp, or had followed him, he resolved to climb the rock and look out over the desert. The two pines, whose sombre verdure crowned the summit, appeared marvellously fit to shelter him from the eyes of the Indians should any be near. As he advanced, however, he could not resist taking a glance at the valley; for a sudden fear took possession of his mind: was it still untouched as he had left it?

One glance reassured him. Nothing was changed in the valley; there were still the heaps of the shining metal.

The traveller, devoured with thirst in the sandy desert, does not more gladly catch sight of the oasis at whose waters he desires to drink than did Cuchillo the sight of the gold gleaming through the leaves of the trees.

Any other man would have hastened to seize as much of it as he could carry, and make off with his booty. But with Cuchillo, cupidity was a passion carried to its utmost limits; and before seizing it, the outlaw wished to feast his eyes on the treasure of which he had dreamed for two years, and for which he would not hesitate to sacrifice the lives of all his companions. After some moments of ecstatic contemplation, Cuchillo led his horse forward by the bridle, and having tied him to a tree, in a defile where the animal would be hidden from all eyes, he himself mounted the rock.

Arrived there, he looked around to assure himself that he was alone. He was soon satisfied, for at that moment neither of the other two parties were visible. Assured by the silence that reigned around, he looked towards the cascade. The water, which seemed as it fell to form a curve of running silver, opened at one place, and displayed a block of gold, sparkling in the rays of the sun. The most enormous cocoanut that ever hung on a tree did not surpass this block in size. Continually washed by the spray of the cascade, this gold appeared in all its brilliance, as if ready to escape from the silica which held it, and thus perhaps for centuries this king's ransom had hung menacingly over the abyss!

At the sight of this block, which looked as though it might be seized by stretching out his hands, a thrill of joy passed through Cuchillo's heart; and hanging over the precipice with extended arms, he gave utterance to the cry which had been heard by the three hunters below.

Soon, however, a spectacle, that Cuchillo was far from expecting to witness, drew from him another cry, but this time of rage. He had seen a man, possessor like himself of the secret of the valley, treading with profane foot on the treasure that he had believed wholly his. Bois-Rose and Fabian were hidden behind the trees; and thinking that Pepé was alone, Cuchillo had fired at him, without taking time for a proper aim, and thus Pepé had escaped the ball that whistled past him.

It would be impossible to paint his rage and stupefaction, when hidden behind the pine trees, he saw two men join Pepé, especially when in one of them he recognised the terrible hunter whom he had seen engaged with the tigers at Poza, and in the other, Fabian, who had already twice escaped his vengeance. A mortal fear chilled his heart; he almost fell to the ground. Must he again fly from that Golden Valley, from which fate seemed always to drive him?

Lucky for Cuchillo, the fog had hidden him from his enemies, and by the time they had reached the top he had descended on the opposite side—after having just caught a glance of Don Estevan and his companion in the distance. Here was a fresh subject of fear and surprise for Cuchillo who, gliding like a serpent along the rocks, hid himself, as we have seen, amid the leaves of the water lilies, to await the dénouement of this strange adventure. Hidden from all eyes, he held himself in readiness to profit by the approaching conflict between Don Estevan and Fabian, and a shudder of diabolical joy mingled with that caused by the gold; he was like the rapacious bird which awaits the issue of the battle to seize upon its prey. If the three hunters were victorious he had little he thought to fear from Fabian, who was still in his eyes Tiburcio Arellanos. The lower class of Mexicans think little of a blow with the dagger, and he hoped that the one he had given might be pardoned, if he were to throw the blame upon Don Estevan. If this last remained master of the field, he trusted to find some plausible excuse for his desertion. He decided therefore upon letting them begin the struggle, and then, at the decisive moment, should come to the assistance of the strongest.

While Cuchillo was endeavouring to console himself by these reasonings, Bois-Rose was able to distinguish the complexion of the newcomers.

"They are from the Mexican camp," said he.

"I foresaw," said Fabian, "that we should have the whole troop on our hands, and be caught like wild horses in a stockade."

"Hush!" said Bois-Rose, "and trust to me to protect you. Nothing yet shows that there are any others behind, and in any case we could not be better placed than on this rock; from here we might defy a whole tribe of savages. Besides, we do not yet know that they will stop here. Both of you crouch down. I shall watch them."

So saying, he lay flat down, hiding his head behind the stones which surrounded the top like turrets, but without losing sight of the horsemen. They began now to hear the sound of the horses' feet on the plain. The old hunter saw them stop and converse, but could not hear what they were saying.

"Why this halt, Diaz?" said Don Estevan, impatiently, "we have lost time enough already."

"Prudence exacts that we should look about us before proceeding. The knave may be hidden about here, as we have tracked him up to the rock; he may not be alone, and we have everything to fear from him."

Don Estevan made a gesture of disdain.

"Ah!" said Bois-Rose, in a low voice, "I recognise Don Estevan, or rather Don Antonio de Mediana, who is at last in our power."

"Don Antonio de Mediana! Is it possible? Are you sure?" cried Fabian.

"It is he, I tell you."

"Ah! now I see that it was the hand of God which brought me here. Shade of my mother, rejoice!" cried Fabian.

Pepé kept silence, but at the name of Don Antonio, hatred shone also in his glance. He raised his head, and his eye seemed to measure the distance between him and the object of his vengeance, but even the long rifle of Bois-Rose could scarcely reach them at such a range.

"Do not rise up, Pepé!" cautioned the Canadian; "you will be seen."

"Do you observe any others behind?" inquired Fabian.

"No one; from the point where the river divides to this place I see no living being; if," added he, after an instant's pause, "that black mass that I see floating on the river be only the trunk of a tree—but at any rate it is floating away from us."

"Never mind that," said Fabian, "describe to me the man who accompanies Don Antonio; perhaps I shall recognise him."

"He is tall and straight as a cane; and what a beautiful horse he rides!"

"A bay horse? and has he gold lace on his hat, and a fine face?"

"Precisely."

"It is Pedro Diaz. Now it would be a cowardice not to show ourselves, when heaven sends us Don Antonio almost alone."

"Patience," said Pepé; "I am as interested as you are in not letting him escape, but haste may ruin all. When one has waited for twenty years, one may easily wait a few minutes longer. Are you sure they are alone, Bois-Rose?"

"The sand whirls down there, but it is only the wind that is stirring it. They are alone, and now they stop and look about them."

So saying, Bois-Rose rose slowly, like the eagle who agitates before completely unfolding his wings—those powerful wings the rapid flight of which will soon bring him down to the plain.

"Señor Don Estevan," said Pedro Diaz, "I think we should return to the camp."

Don Antonio hesitated a moment. The counsel was good, but it was too late to follow it.

From the top of the rock the three hunters watched their every movement.

"It is time," said Bois-Rose.

"I must take Don Antonio alive," said Fabian. "Arrange that, and I care for nothing else."

Bois-Rose now rose to his fall height, and uttered a cry which struck on the ears of the new-comers. They uttered an exclamation of surprise, which surprise was still further increased at sight of the gigantic Canadian upon the rock.

"Who are you, and what do you want?" cried a voice, which Fabian recognised as that of Don Antonio.

"I shall tell you," replied the hunter; "it will recall to you a truth—never contested either in my country or in the desert—that the ground belongs to the first occupants; we were here before you, and are the sole masters of this place. We therefore wish one of you to retire with a good grace, and the other to surrender himself, that we may teach him a second law of the desert, 'blood for blood.'"

"It is some anchorite whose brain is turned by solitude," said Pedro Diaz; "I shall terminate the conference with a bullet from my rifle."

"No!" cried Don Estevan, stopping him, "let us see first how far this folly will go. And which of us is it, friend," continued he, with an ironical air, "to whom you wish to teach this law?"

"To you," cried Fabian, rising.

"What! you here!" cried Don Estevan with mingled rage and surprise.

Fabian bowed.

"And here am I, who have been following you for the last fortnight," said Pepé, "and who thanks God for the opportunity of paying off a debt of twenty years' standing."

"Who are you?" asked Don Estevan, trying to remember who it was, for years and difference of costume had altered the aspect of the old coast-guardsman.

"Pepé the Sleeper, who has not forgotten his residence at Ceuta."

At this name, which explained Fabian's words at the bridge of Salto de Agua, Don Estevan lost his air of contempt. A sudden presentiment seemed to warn him that his fortunes were waning, and he cast around him an anxious glance. The high rocks, which on one side shut in the valley, might protect him from the fire of his enemies; a short space only separated him from their foot, and prudence counselled him to fly there, but his pride forbade him.

"Well then!" cried he proudly after a pause, "revenge yourself on an enemy who disdains to fly."

"Have we not said that we wish to take you alive?" replied Pepé, coldly.

Chapter Forty Eight
The King-Maker a Captive

In the whole course of his adventurous life, Don Estevan had never been in such danger. The plain offered him no protection against the rifles of his enemies—two at least of whom had an infallible eye and steady aim—and who had also the advantage of an impregnable position, and turrets of rock behind which to intrench themselves. Don Estevan did not conceal from himself the extent of his danger; but neither did his courage give way.

"Let us have done with this trifling," cried the sonorous voice of Bois-Rose, whose generosity made him averse to profit by his advantages, and who scrupled always to shed blood if he could avoid it. "You have heard that we wish no harm to any but your chief, and you must make up your mind to let us take him. Retire then willingly, if you do not wish us to treat you as we intend to treat him."

"Never!" cried Diaz, "shall I commit such a cowardice? You are the first comers; so be it; we will yield the ground to you, but Don Estevan must be allowed to go with me."

"*We* refuse," cried Pepé; "we particularly want the man you call Don Estevan."

"Do not oppose the justice of God," added Fabian; "your cause is only that of man. We give you five minutes to reflect, after which our rifles and our good cause shall decide between us."

"You have but two minutes to decide," said Bois-Rose; "listen to me and avoid needless bloodshed."

Mediana kept silence and preserved his haughty air. Unshakable in his notions of chivalric honour, Pedro Diaz resolved to die with the chief, whose life he believed to be so precious to his country. He consulted Don Estevan by a look.

"Return to the camp," said the latter; "abandon to his fate a man henceforth useless to your cause, and come back to avenge my death."

Diaz was not to be moved, but gradually drew his horse close to Don Estevan, and when their knees touched, with his face still turned toward his enemies, he murmured, with scarcely a movement of his lips:

"Keep steady in your stirrups, have your horse ready, and let me act."

Don Estevan made signs with his hand as though to demand a truce; but he had taken a desperate determination.

"Bend down, Fabian; he is going to fire," cried Bois-Rose.

"Before my mother's murderer? Never!" cried Fabian. Quick as thought, the hand of the Canadian giant on his shoulder, forced him down. Don Estevan vainly sought for an aim for his double-barrelled piece. He could see nothing but the formidable rifle of Bois-Rose directed towards him, although in obedience to Fabian's wishes, Bois-Rose would not finish the combat by striking his foe to the ground.

With as much courage as agility, Diaz now jumped up behind Don Estevan on his horse, and throwing his arms around him to steady him after the shock, seized the bridle, turned the animal round, and galloped off, covering with his body, as with a buckler, the chief whose life he was willing to save at the expense of his own. While Fabian and Pepé rushed down the rock, at the risk of breaking their necks, Bois-Rose followed the movements of the horse glancing along the barrel of his rifle.

The two men appeared to make but one body: the back of the horse and the shoulders of Diaz were the only objects at which Bois-Rose could aim; only now and then the head of the animal was visible. To sacrifice Diaz would be a useless murder; and Don Estevan would still escape. A moment more and the fugitives would be out of range; but the Canadian was of that class of marksmen who lodge a ball in the eye of a beaver, that he may not injure its skin; and it was the horse he wished to aim at. For a single moment the head of the noble animal showed itself entirely—but that moment was sufficient; a shot was heard, and the two men and the death-stricken horse rolled over together on the ground.

Bruised by the violence of their fall, both men rose with difficulty; while, their poignards in their teeth, and their rifles in their hands, Fabian and Pepé advanced upon them. Bois-Rose followed with great gigantic strides, loading his rifle as he went. When he had finished, he again stopped.

Pedro Diaz, devoted to the last, rushed towards the gun which had fallen from Don Estevan's hands, picked it up, and returned it to him.

"Let us defend ourselves to the last!" cried he, drawing his long knife.

Don Estevan steadied himself and raised his piece, undecided for a moment whether to aim at Fabian or at Pepé; but Bois-Rose was watching, and a bullet from his rifle broke the weapon of the chief in his hands, just where the barrel joins the stock, and Don Estevan himself, losing his balance, fell forward on the sand.

"At last, after twenty years!" cried Pepé, rushing towards him, and placing his knee upon his breast.

Don Estevan vainly tried to resist; his arm, benumbed by the violence of the blow which had broken his gun, refused its service. In an instant Pepé had untied the woollen scarf which was wound several times round his body, and bound with it the limbs of his enemy. Diaz could offer no assistance, for he had himself to defend against the attacks of Fabian.

Fabian scarcely knew the Indian fighter; he had seen him only for a few hours at the Hacienda del Venado; but the generosity of his conduct had awakened in the heart of the young man a warm sympathy, and he wished to spare his life.

"Surrender, Diaz!" cried he, parrying a dagger blow slimed at him; but Diaz resolved not to yield, and for the few minutes during which Pepé was engaged in binding Don Estevan, there was a contest of skill and ability between him and Fabian. Too generous to use his rifle against a man who had but a dagger to defend himself with, Fabian tried only to disarm his adversary; but Diaz, blinded by rage, did not perceive the generous efforts of the young man, who, holding his rifle by the barrel, and using it as a club, tried to strike the arm which menaced him. But Fabian had to deal with an antagonist not less active and vigorous than himself. Bounding from right to left, Diaz avoided his blows, and just as Fabian believed he was about to succeed, he found himself striking in the air, and the knife menacing him afresh. Bois-Rose without waiting to reload, ran up to put an end to the struggle—in which Fabian's generosity placed him at a disadvantage—and Pepé, having fast bound his enemy, advanced also.

Thus menaced by three men, Diaz determined not to die without vengeance. He drew his arm back, and made a rapid thrust at Fabian; but the latter had been carefully watching the movement, and his rifle met the murdering weapon on its way. The dagger fell to the ground; and Pepé, seizing Diaz round the body just as Fabian struck him, cried, "Fool! must we kill you, then? If not, what shall we do with you?"

"What you have done to that noble gentleman," replied Diaz, pointing to Don Estevan.

"Do not ask to share his fate," said Pepé; "that man's days are numbered."

"Whatever his fate is to be, I wish to share it," cried Diaz, vainly trying to free himself. "I accept from you neither quarter nor mercy."

"Do not play with our anger!" said Pepé, whose passions were roused; "I am not in the habit of offering mercy twice."

"I know how to make him accept it," said Fabian, picking up the fallen knife. "Let him go, Pepé; with a man like Diaz, one can always come to terms."

Fabian's tone was so firm, that Pepé opened his arms and loosened the iron grasp in which the Mexican was bound.

"Here, Diaz," said Fabian, "take your weapon, and listen to me."

So saying, Fabian advanced and offered him his knife without any attempt at guarding himself. Diaz took the weapon, but his adversary had not presumed too far; at the heroic simplicity of Fabian his anger vanished on the instant.

"I listen," said he, flinging his knife to the ground.

"I knew it would be so," replied Fabian, with a smile. "You interposed unknowingly between crime and the just vengeance which pursued it. Do you know who is the man for whom you wish to expose your life? and who are those who have spared it? Do you know whether or not we have the right to demand from him, whom you doubtless know only as Don Estevan, a terrible account of the past? Reply honestly to the questions that I shall put to you, and then decide on which side justice lies."

Astonished at these words, Diaz listened in silence, and Fabian went on:

"If you had been born in a privileged class, heir to a great fortune; if a man had taken from you your fortune and your name, and reduced you to the rank of those who have to work for their daily bread, should you be the friend of that man?"

"No, I should be his enemy."

"If that man, to destroy the last souvenir of your birth, had murdered your mother, what would he deserve from you?"

"Blow for blow—blood for blood."

"If, after a long and difficult pursuit, fate had at last delivered the spoiler into your hands, what would you do?"

"I should think myself guilty towards God and man if I spared him."

"Well, then, Diaz," cried Fabian, "there is a man who has taken from me my name, my fortune, and murdered my mother; I have pursued this murderer and spoiler—fate has delivered him into my hands, and there he lies!"

A cloud passed over the eyes of Diaz at the sight of the chief whose doom was thus pronounced, for the sentiment of inexorable justice that God has implanted in the heart of man told him that Don Estevan merited his fate, if Fabian spoke truly. He sighed, but offered no reply.

While these events were taking place in the midst of the plain, the actors of the scene might have observed Cuchillo raise with precaution the leaves which covered his head, cast an eager glance on the Golden Valley, and then glide out of the lake. Covered with mud, and his garments streaming with water, they might have mistaken him for one of the evil spirits whom the Indians believed to dwell in these solitudes. But their attention was completely absorbed by what was taking place among themselves.

Chapter Forty Nine
The Two Medianas Face to Face

Pedro Diaz speedily roused himself from the deep depression and astonishment which had for a moment overpowered him.

"According to the rules of war, I am your prisoner," said he, raising his head, "and I am anxious to know your decision concerning me."

"You are free, Diaz," replied Fabian, "free without conditions."

"Not so! not so!" said the Canadian, quickly interrupting him. "We must, on the contrary, impose a rigorous condition upon your liberty."

"What is it?" asked the adventurer.

"You have now, in common with us," replied Bois-Rose, "become possessed of a secret which we have long since known. I have my reasons for wishing that the knowledge of this secret should expire with those whose evil destiny makes them acquainted with it. You only," added the Canadian, "will be an exception to the rule, because a brave man like yourself should be a slave to his word. I demand, then, before restoring you your liberty, a promise upon your honour, never to reveal to human being, the existence of the Golden Valley."

"I never indulged any hope in acquiring this treasure," replied the noble adventurer, in a melancholy tone, "beyond that of the freedom and aggrandisement of my country. The sad fate which threatens the man, to whom I looked for the realisation of my hopes, proves to me that in both cases I have entertained a delusive dream. Even should all the riches of the Golden Valley remain forever buried in these deserts, what would it avail me now? I swear then, and you may rely upon my honour, that I shall never reveal its existence to a living soul. I shall try to forget that I have ever, for an instant, beheld it."

"It is well," said Bois-Rose, "you are now free to go."

"Not yet, with your permission," replied the prisoner. "In all that has taken place, there is a mystery which I do not seek to penetrate—but—"

"Carramba! it is very simple," answered Pepé. "This young man," said he, pointing to Fabian—

"Not yet, Pepé," replied the latter solemnly, making a sign to the hunter to postpone his explanations. "In the court of justice which is about to be convened—in the presence of the Supreme Judge (Fabian pointed to heaven), by the accusation as well as the defence, all will become clear to Diaz, if he will remain a short while with us. In the desert, time is precious; and we must prepare ourselves, by meditation and silence, for the terrible deed which we are now compelled to accomplish."

"I am most anxious to obtain permission to stay. I do not know if this man be innocent or guilty; but, I do know that he is the chief whom I have freely chosen; and I will remain with him to the last, ready to defend him against you at the cost of my own life, if he is innocent—ready to bow before the sentence which condemns him, if he is guilty."

"Be it so," rejoined Fabian. "You shall hear and judge for yourself."

"This man is of noble birth," continued Diaz, sadly, "and he lies yonder in the dust, bound like the meanest criminal."

"Unloose him, Diaz!" replied Fabian, "but do not endeavour to shield him from the vengeance which a son must claim for his mother's murderer. Require from him a promise that he will not attempt to escape; we shall rely upon you in this matter."

"I pledge my honour that he will not do so," said the adventurer, "nor would I assist him in the attempt." And Diaz, as he said this, proceeded towards Don Estevan.

In the mean time Fabian, oppressed by sad and anxious thoughts, seated himself at some distance, and appeared to deplore his unfortunate victory.

Pepé turned away his head, and for a while stood as if attentively observing the mists as they floated above the crests of the mountains.

Bois-Rose reclined in his usual attitude of repose, while his eyes, expressive of deep anxiety, were centred upon the young man, and his noble physiognomy seemed to reflect the clouds which gathered upon the brow of his beloved protégé.

Meanwhile Diaz had rejoined the prostrate captive.

Who can guess how many conflicting thoughts crowded upon the mind of the Spanish nobleman, as he lay upon the ground? His expression retained as much pride as when in his more prosperous days he had imagined the possibility of conquering, and bestowing, a throne upon the deposed heir of the Spanish monarchy. At the sight of Diaz, who, he believed had abandoned his cause, an expression of deep melancholy came over his countenance.

"Do you come as an enemy, or a friend, Diaz?" said he. "Are you one of those who take a secret pleasure in contemplating the humiliation of the man whom, in the days of his prosperity, you, like others, would have flattered?"

"I am one of those who flatter only the fallen," replied Diaz, "and who are not offended by the bitterness of speech which is dictated by great misfortune."

As he uttered these words, which were confirmed by the dejection of his manner, Diaz hastened to remove the cords with which the captive's arms were bound.

"I have given my word that you will not endeavour to escape the fate, whatever it may be, which awaits you at the hands of these men, into whose power we have fallen by an unlucky chance. I believe you have not even thought of flight."

"And you are right, Diaz," replied Don Estevan; "but can you guess what fate these fellows have reserved for me?"

"They talk of a murder to be avenged, of an accusation, and a judgment."

"A judgment!" replied Don Antonio with a haughty and bitter smile, "they may assassinate, but they shall never judge me."

"In the former case, I shall die with you," said Diaz, simply, "in the latter—but of what use is it to speak of that which cannot be? you are innocent of the crime of which they accuse you?"

"I have a presentiment of the fate which awaits me," replied Don Estevan without answering the adventurer's interrogation. "A faithful subject will be lost to his king—Don Carlos the First. But you will carry on my work? you will restore the prosperity of Sonora. You will return to the Senator Tragaduros—he knows what he has to do, and you will support him?"

"Ah!" cried Diaz, sadly, "such a work cannot be attempted but by you. In your hands I might have proved a powerful instrument; without you I shall sink into insignificant obscurity. The hope of my country expires with you."

During this interval, Fabian and Bois-Rose had quitted the spot where the preceding scenes had so rapidly taken place. They had reached the base of the pyramid. It was there that the solemn assizes were to be held, in which Fabian and the Duke de Armada were about to act the parts of judge and criminal.

Pepé made a sign to Diaz; Don Estevan saw and understood it.

"It is not enough to have remained a prisoner," said Diaz, "you must meet your fate; the conquered must obey the conqueror—come!"

As Diaz ceased speaking, the Spanish nobleman, armed with the pride which never deserted him, approached the pyramid with a firm step. Pepé had rejoined his two companions.

Don Estevan's looks, as he advanced, displayed a dauntless composure equally removed from bravado or weakness—which won a glance of admiration from his three enemies—all of them excellent judges of courage.

Fabian rose and stepped forward to meet his noble prisoner. A few paces behind, Diaz also advanced—his head bowed low, and his mind oppressed by gloomy thoughts. Everything in the manner of the conquerors convinced him that, on this occasion, right would be on the side of power.

"My Lord of Mediana," said Fabian, as, with head uncovered, he paused a few steps in advance of the noble Spaniard who had approached him, "you perceive that I recognise you, and you also know who I am."

The Duke de Armada remained upright and motionless without responding to his nephew's courtesy.

"I am entitled to keep my head covered in the presence of the King of Spain; I shall use that privilege with you," he replied; "also I claim the right of remaining silent when I think proper, and shall now exercise that right if it please you."

Notwithstanding this haughty reply, the younger son of the Medianas could not but remember how he, a trembling and weeping child, had, twenty years before, in the castle of Elanchovi quailed beneath the glance of the man whom he now presumed to judge.

The timid eaglet had now become the eagle, which, in its turn, held the prey in its powerful talons.

The glances of the two Medianas crossed like two swords, and Diaz contemplated, with mingled astonishment and respect, the adopted son of the gambusino Arellanos, suddenly transformed and raised above the humble sphere in which he had for an instant known him.

The adventurer awaited the solution of this enigma. Fabian armed himself with a pride which equalled that of the Duke de Armada.

"As you will," said he, "yet it might be prudent to remember, that here the right claimed by power is not an empty boast."

"It is true," replied Don Antonio, who, notwithstanding his apparent resignation, trembled with rage and despair at the total failure of his hopes.

"I ought not to forget that you are doubtless inclined to profit by this right. I shall answer your question then when I tell you that I am aware of but one fact concerning you, which is that some demon has inspired you continually to cast some impediment in the way of the object I pursue—I know—"

Here rage stifled his utterance.

The impetuous young man listened with a changing countenance to the words uttered by the assassin of his mother, and whom he even now suspected was the murderer of his adopted father.

Truly it is the heroism of moderation, at which those who do not know the slight value attached to human life in the deserts, cannot be sufficiently astonished—for here law cannot touch the offender—but the short space of time which had elapsed since Fabian joined Bois-Rose was sufficient, under the gentle influence of the old hunter, to calm his feelings immeasurably.

He was no longer the young man whose fiery passions were the instruments of a vengeance to which he yielded blindly. He had learnt that power should go hand in hand with justice, and may often be combined with mercy.

This was the secret of a moderation, hitherto so opposed to his temperament. It was not, however, difficult to trace, in the changing expression of his countenance, the efforts he had been compelled to make to impose a restraint upon his anger.

On his side, the Spanish noble concealed his passion under the mask of silence.

"So then," resumed Fabian, "you know nothing more of me? You are not acquainted either with my name or rank? I am nothing more to you than what I seem?"

"An assassin, perhaps!" replied Mediana, turning his back to Fabian to show that he did not wish to reply to his question.

During the dialogue which had taken place between these two men of the same blood, and of equally unconquerable nature, the wood-rangers had remained at some distance.

"Approach," said Fabian to the ex-carabinier, "and say," added he, with forced calmness, "what you know of me to this man whose lips have dared to apply to me a name which he only deserves."

If any doubt could still have remained upon Don Estevan's mind with regard to the intentions of those into whose hands he had fallen, that doubt must have disappeared when he beheld the gloomy air with which Pepé came forward in obedience to Fabian's command.

The visible exertion he made to repress the rancorous feelings which the sight of the Spanish noble aroused in him, filled the latter with a sad presentiment.

A shudder passed through the frame of Don Estevan, but he did not lower his eyes, and by the aid of his invincible pride, he waited with apparent calmness until Pepé began to speak.

"Carramba!" exclaimed the latter in a tone which he tried in vain to render agreeable. "It was certainly worth while to send me to catch sea-fish upon the borders of the Mediterranean, so that, at the end of my journey, I might, three thousand leagues from Spain, fall in with the nephew whose mother you murdered. I don't know whether Don Fabian de Mediana is inclined to pardon you, but for my part," added he, striking the ground with the butt end of his rifle, "I have sworn that I will not do so."

Fabian directed a haughty glance towards Pepé, as though to command his submission; then addressing himself to the Spaniard:

"My Lord of Mediana, you are not now in the presence of assassins, but of judges, and Pepé will not forget it."

"Before judges!" cried Don Antonio; "my peers only possess the right of judgment, and I do not recognise as such a malefactor escaped from jail and a beggarly usurper who has assumed a title to which he has no right. I do not acknowledge here any other Mediana than myself, and have therefore no reply to make."

"Nevertheless I must constitute myself your judge," said Fabian, "yet believe me I shall be an impartial one, since I take as a witness that God whose sun shines upon us, when I swear that I no longer entertain any feelings of animosity or hatred against you."

There was so much truth in the manner with which Fabian pronounced these words, that, for an instant, Don Estevan's countenance lost its expression of gloomy defiance, and was even lit up by a ray of hope, for the Duke de Armada recollected that he stood face to face with the heir for whom, in his pride, he had once mourned. It was therefore in a less severe tone that he asked—

"Of what crime am I then accused?"

"You are about to hear," replied Fabian.

Chapter Fifty
Lynch Law

On the frontiers of the America there exists a terrible law, yet it is not this clause alone which renders it so—"Eye for eye, tooth for tooth, blood for blood." The application of this law is evident in all the ways of Providence, to those who observe the course of events here below. "He who kills by the sword shall perish by the sword," says the gospel.

But the law of the desert is terrible by reason of the majesty with which it is invested, or claims to be invested.

This law is terrible in common with all laws of blood, and the more so, since those who have recourse to it usurp a power which does not belong to them, inasmuch as the injured party constitutes himself judge of his own cause, and executes the sentence which he himself has pronounced.

Such is the so-called "Lynch law."

In the central parts of America, white men as well as Indians execute this law with cruel severity against each other. Civilised communities adopt it in a mitigated form as applied to capital punishment, but the untutored inhabitants of the desert continue to practise it with the same rigour which belonged to the first ages of mankind.

And may we not here make the remark, that the similitude of feeling on this point, between the white man and the savages, casts a stain upon the former which for his own honour he should endeavour to wipe out?

Society has provided laws for the protection of all men. The man who amongst us should assume the right of judgment, and take the law into his own hands, would thus violate it, and fall under the jurisdiction of those whom society has appointed to try, and to condemn.

We are not without a hope that at some future time, as civilisation advances, men will allow that they who deprive a culprit of that life which none can recall, commit an act of sacrilege in defiance of those divine laws which govern the universe and take precedence of all human decrees.

A time will come, we would fain believe, when our laws may spare the life of a guilty man, and suffer him to atone for his errors or his crimes by repentance. Such a law would respect the life which can never be restored; and while another exists which casts an irretrievable stain upon our honour, there would be a law of restoration capable of raising the man sanctified by repentance to the dignity which punishment would have prevented his attaining.

"There is more joy in heaven," says the gospel, "over a sinner who repents, than a righteous man made perfect." Why then are not human laws a counterpart of these divine decrees?

Now, however, liberty is the only boon which society confers upon him whose misfortunes or whose crimes have deprived him of it.

Misfortunes did we not say? Is there not in truth a law which assimilates the criminal with the upright though insolvent debtor, and compels him to the same fate in prison?

So much for this subject. Let us now return to the lynch law of the desert. It was before a tribunal without appeal, and in the presence of self-constituted judges, that Don Antonio de Mediana was about to appear. A court assembled in a city, with all its imposing adjuncts, could not have surpassed in solemnity the assizes which at this moment were convoked in the desert, where three men represented human justice armed with all its terrors!

We have described the singular and fantastic aspect presented by the spot, in which this scene was to be enacted. In truth, the sombre mountains, veiled in mist, the mysterious subterranean sounds, the long tufts of human hair agitated by every breath of wind, the skeleton of the Indian horse exposed to view, all combined to endue the place with a strange unearthly appearance in the eyes of the prisoner, so that he almost believed himself under the influence of some horrible dream.

One might have imagined himself suddenly transported into the middle ages, in the midst of some secret society, where previous to the admission of the candidate, were displayed all the terrors of the earth, as a means of proving his courage.

All this however was here a fearful reality.

Fabian pointed out to the Duke de Armada, one of the flat stones, resembling tombstones, which were strewed over the plain, and seated himself upon another so as to form with the Canadian and his companion a triangle, in which he occupied the most prominent position.

"It is not becoming for the criminal to sit in the presence of the judges," said the Spanish noble, with a bitter smile, "I shall therefore remain standing."

Fabian made no reply.

He waited until Diaz, the only disinterested witness in this court of justice, had chosen a convenient place.

The adventurer remained at some distance from the actors in the scene, yet sufficiently near to see and hear all that passed.

Fabian began:

"You are about to be told," said he, "of what crime you are accused. You are to look upon me as the judge who presides at your trial, and who will either condemn or acquit you."

Having thus spoken he paused to consider.

"It will first be necessary to establish the identity of the criminal. Are you in truth," he continued, "that Don Antonio, whom men here call the Count de Mediana?"

"No," replied the Spaniard in a firm voice.

"Who are you then?" continued Fabian, in a mingled tone of astonishment and regret, for he repudiated the idea that a Mediana would have recourse to a cowardly subterfuge.

"I *was* the Count de Mediana," replied the prisoner, with a haughty smile, "until by my sword I acquired other titles. At present I am known in Spain as the Duke de Armada. It is the name I shall transmit to the descendant of my line, whom I may choose as my adopted son."

The latter phrase, incidentally spoken by the prisoner, proved in the sequel his sole means of defence.

"Right," said Fabian, "the Duke de Armada shall hear of what crime Don Antonio de Mediana is accused. Speak Bois-Rose! tell us what you know, and nothing more."

The rough and energetic countenance of the gigantic descendant of the Norman race, as he stood motionless beside them, his carbine supported on his broad shoulder, was expressive of such calm integrity, that his appearance alone banished all idea of perjury. Bois-Rose drew himself up, slowly removed his fur cap, and in doing so discovered his fine open brow to the gaze of all.

"I will only speak of what I know," said he.

"On a foggy night, in the month of November, 1808, I was a sailor on board a French smuggling-vessel called the Albatros.

"We had landed according to a plan formed with the captain of the carabiniers of Elanchovi, on the coast of the Bay of Biscay. I will not relate to you," and here Pepé could not repress a smile, "how we were fired upon, and repulsed from the shore where we had landed as friends. It is sufficient for you to know that when we again reached our vessel, I was attracted by the screams of a child, which seemed to come from the depths of the ocean.

"These cries proceeded from a boat which had been abandoned.

"I pushed out towards it at the risk of my own life, since a brisk fire was opened upon our ship.

"In this boat I found a lady murdered, and lying in her blood. She was quite dead, and close to her was a little child who appeared to be dying.

"I picked up the child—that child is now the man before us; his name is Fabian.

"I took the child with me, and left the murdered lady in the boat. I do not know who committed the crime, and have nothing further to say."

As he finished speaking, Bois-Rose again covered his head, and seated himself in silence.

A mournful silence followed this declaration.

Fabian lowered his flashing eyes for an instant to the ground, then raised them, calm and cold, to the face of the ex-carabinier, whose turn had now come to speak.

Fabian was prepared to act his terrible part, and the countenance as well as the attitude of the young man, though clothed in rags, expressed the nobility which characterised an ancient race, as well as the collected coolness of a judge. He cast an authoritative glance towards Pepé, and the half savage trapper was compelled to submit to it in silence.

Pepé at length rose, and advanced a few paces, by his manner showing a determination only to utter that which his conscience approved.

"I understand you, Count Mediana," said he, addressing himself to Fabian, who alone in his eyes had the right to assume this title. "I will try to forget that the man here present is the same who caused me to spend so many long years among the refuse of mankind at Ceuta. When I appear before God He may require of me the words I have spoken, but I should again repeat them, nor regret that they had ever been uttered."

Fabian made a gesture of approbation.

"One night in the month of November, 1808," said he, "when I belonged to the Royal Carabiniers in the service of Spain, I was on duty upon the coast of Elanchovi, where three men disembarked from the open sea upon the beach.

"Our captain had sold to one of them the right of landing in a forbidden spot.

"I reproach myself with having been this man's accomplice, and receiving from him the price of culpable neglect of my duty.

"The following day it was discovered that the Countess Mediana and her young son had left the castle during the night.

"The Countess was murdered—the young Count was never seen again.

"A short time after, his uncle appeared at Elanchovi and claimed his nephew's fortune and titles. All was given up to him, and I, who believed that I had only sold my services to favour an intrigue or an affair of smuggling, found that I had been the accomplice of a murderer.

"I upbraided the present Count Mediana before witnesses, and accused him of this crime. Five years' imprisonment at Ceuta was the reward of my presumption.

"Here before another and more righteous tribunal, and in the presence of God who is my witness, I again accuse the man before me. I declare him to be the murderer of the Countess, and the usurper of her son's titles. He was one of the three men, who, during the night entered by escalade the chateau which Don Fabian's mother never again beheld.

"Let the murderer refute the charge. I have done."

"You hear him?" said Fabian, "what have you to say in your defence?"

A violent struggle between his conscience and his pride took place in Mediana's breast.

Pride however triumphed.

"Nothing," replied Don Antonio.

"Nothing!" answered Fabian, "but you do not perhaps know what a terrible duty I have to fulfil?"

"I can imagine it."

"And I," cried Fabian passionately, "shall not flinch in accomplishing it. Yet, though my mother's blood cries out for vengeance, should you refute the charge, I would bless you still. Swear to me then, in the name of Mediana, which we bear in common, by your honour and the salvation of your soul, that you are innocent, and I shall be too happy to believe you."

Then, oppressed with an intolerable anguish, Fabian awaited his reply.

But, gloomy and inflexible as the fallen archangel, Mediana was silent.

At this moment Diaz advanced towards the judges and the prisoner.

"I have listened," said he, "with the utmost attention to your accusation again Don Estevan de Arechiza, whom I also know to be the Duke de Armada; may I express my thoughts freely?"

"Speak!" said Fabian.

"One point seems to me doubtful. I do not know whether the crime you attribute to this noble cavalier was committed by him; but, admitting that to be the case, have you any right to condemn him? In accordance with the laws of our frontier, where no court may be held, it is only the nearest relatives of the victim who are entitled to claim the blood of the murderer.

"Don Tiburcio's youth was passed in this country. I knew him as the adopted son of Marcos Arellanos.

"Who can prove that Tiburcio Arellanos is the son of the murdered lady?

"How, after so many years, can it be possible for this hunter, formerly a sailor, to recognise in the midst of these solitudes, the young man, whom as a child he beheld only for an instant on a foggy night?"

"Answer, Bois-Rose," said Fabian, coldly.

The Canadian again rose.

"I ought, in the first place, to state," said the old hunter, "that it was not only for a few moments on a foggy night that I saw the child in question. During the space of two years, after having saved him from certain death, I kept him on board the vessel in which I was a sailor.

"The features of his son could not be more deeply impressed upon the memory of a father than those of that child were on mine.

"How then can you affirm that it is impossible I should recognise him?

"When you are travelling in the desert, where there is no beaten track, are you not guided by the course of streams, by the character of the trees, by the conformation of their trunks, by the growth of the moss which clothes them, and by the stars of heaven? and when at another season, or even twenty years afterwards, should the rains have swelled the streams, or the sun have dried them up, should the once naked trees be clothed with leaves, should their trunks have expanded, and moss covered their roots, even should the north star have changed its position in the heavens, and you again beheld it, would you not recognise both star and stream?"

"Doubtless," replied Diaz, "the man who has experience in the desert, is seldom deceived."

"When you meet a stranger in the forest, who answers you with the cry of a bird or the voice of an animal, which is to serve as a rallying signal to you or your friends, do you not immediately say, 'This man is one of us'?"

"Assuredly."

"Well, then; I recognise the child in the grown man, just as you recognise the small shrub in the tall tree; or the stream that once murmured softly in the roaring and swollen torrent of to-day. I know this child again by a mode of speech, which twenty years have scarcely altered."

"Is not this meeting a somewhat strange coincidence?" interrupted Diaz, now almost convinced of the Canadian's veracity.

"God," cried Bois-Rose, solemnly, "who commands the breeze to waft across the desert the fertilising seeds of the male palm to the female date-tree—God, who confides to the wind which destroys, to the devastating torrent, or to the bird of passage, the grain which is to be deposited a thousand miles from the plant that produced it—is he not also able to send upon the same path two human beings made in his image?"

Diaz was silent a moment; then having nothing more to advance in contradiction to the Canadian's truthful words whose honest manner of speech carried with it an irresistible conviction, he turned towards Pepé:

"Did you," said he, "also recognise in Arellanos' adopted child, the Countess de Mediana's son!"

"It would be impossible for any one who ever saw his mother long to mistake him. Enough! let the Duke de Armada contradict me."

Don Antonio, too proud to utter a falsehood, could not deny the truth without degrading himself in the eyes of his accusers, unless he destroyed the only means of defence to which his pride and the secret wish of his heart allowed him to have recourse.

"It is true," said he, "that this man is of my own blood. I cannot deny it without polluting my lips with a lie, and an untruth is the offspring of cowardice."

Diaz inclined his head, regained his seat, and was silent.

"You have heard," said Fabian, "that I am indeed the son of the woman, whom this man murdered; therefore I claim the right of avenging her. What then do the laws of the desert decree?"

"Eye for eye," said Bois-Rose.

"Tooth for tooth," added Pepé.

"Blood for blood," continued Fabian; "a death for a death!"

Then he rose, and addressing Don Antonio in measured accents, said: "You have shed blood and committed murder. It shall therefore be done to you as you have done to others. God commanded it to be so."

Fabian drew his poignard from its sheath. The sun was shedding his first rays upon the scene, and every object cast a long shadow upon the ground.

A bright flash shot from the naked blade which the younger Mediana held in his hand.

Fabian buried its point in the sand.

The shadow of the poignard far exceeded its length.

"The sun," he said, "shall determine how many moments you have to live. When the shadow disappears you shall appear before God, and my mother will be avenged."

A deathlike silence succeeded Fabian's last words, who, overcome with long suppressed emotions, fell, rather than seated himself upon the stone.

Bois-Rose and Pepé both retained their seats. The judges and the criminal were alike motionless.

Diaz perceived that all was over, but he did not wish, to take any part in the execution of the sentence.

He approached the Duke de Armada, knelt down before him, took his hand and raised it to his lips.

"I will pray for the salvation of your soul," said he in a low tone. "Do you release me from my oath?"

"Yes," replied Don Antonio, in a firm voice; "go, and may God bless you for your fidelity!"

The noble adventurer retired in silence.

His horse had remained at some short distance.

Diaz soon reached it, and holding the bridle in his hands, walked slowly towards the spot where the river forked.

In the mean time the sun followed its eternal course—the shadows gradually contracted—the black vultures flew in circles above the heads of the four actors in the terrible drama the last scene of which was now drawing near. From the depths of the Misty Mountains, shrouded in vapour, might be heard, at intervals, dull rumbling sounds, like thunder, followed by distant explosions.

Pale, but resigned, the unfortunate Count de Mediana remained standing. Buried in deep reverie, he did not appear to notice the continually decreasing shadow.

All exterior objects vanished from his sight. His thoughts were divided between the past which no longer concerned him, and the future he was about to enter.

However, pride still struggled within him, and he maintained an obstinate silence.

"My Lord Count," said Fabian, who was willing to try a last chance, "in five minutes the poignard will have ceased to cast a shadow."

"I have nothing to say of the past," replied Don Antonio. "I must now think only of the future of my race. Do not, therefore, misjudge the sense of the words I am about to speak. Whatever may be the form in which it may come, death has no power to terrify me."

"I am listening," said Fabian gently.

"You are very young, Fabian," continued Mediana, "and the thought of the blood that has been shed will therefore be so much the longer a burthen to you."

Fabian's countenance revealed the anguish of his feelings.

"Why then so soon pollute a life which is scarcely begun? Why refuse to follow a course which the unlooked-for favour of Providence opens to you? Here you are poor, and without connections. God restores you to your family, and, at the same moment, confers wealth upon you. The inheritance of your race has not been squandered by me. I have for twenty years borne the name of Mediana, at the head of the Spanish nobles, and I am ready to restore it to you with all the honours I have conferred upon it. Accept then a fortune which I joyfully restore to you, for the isolation of my life is burthensome to me; but do not purchase it by a crime, for which an imaginary act of justice cannot absolve you, and which you will repent to your last hour."

Fabian replied, "A judge who presides at his tribunal must not listen to the voice of nature. Supported by his conscience, and the service he renders to society, he may pity the criminal, though his duty requires that he shall condemn him. In this solitude, these two men and myself represent human justice. Refute the crime attributed to you, Don Antonio, and I shall be the happiest of us two; for though I shudder to accuse you, I cannot escape the fatal mission which heaven has imposed upon me."

"Consider well, Fabian, and remember that it not pardon, but oblivion, for which I sue. Thanks to that oblivion, it rests with you to become, in my adopted son, the princely heir of the house of Mediana. After my death my title will expire."

As he listened to these words the young man became deadly pale; but spurning in his heart the temptation held out to him, Fabian closed his ears to that voice which offered him so large a share of the riches of this world, as though he had but heard the light whispers of the breeze amid the foliage of the trees.

"Oh, Count Mediana, why did you kill my mother?" cried Fabian, covering his face with his hands; then, glancing towards the poignard planted in the sand, "My lord of Armada," he added, solemnly, "the poignard is without a shadow!"

Don Antonio trembled in spite of himself, as he then recalled the prophetic threat, which twenty years before the Countess de Mediana had compelled him to hear.

"Perhaps," she had said, "the God whom you blaspheme will ordain, that in the heart of a desert, untrodden by the foot of man, you shall find an accuser, a witness, a judge, and an executioner."

Accuser, witness, and judge were all before him, but who was to be the executioner? However, nothing was wanting for the accomplishment of the dreadful prophecy.

A noise of branches, suddenly torn apart, was heard at this moment.

The moment after, a man emerged from the brushwood, his habiliments dripping with water and soiled with mud. It was Cuchillo.

The bandit advanced with an air of imperturbable coolness, though he appeared to limp slightly.

Not one of the four men, so deeply absorbed in their own terrible reflections, showed any astonishment at his presence.

"Carramba! you expected me then?" he cried; "and yet I persisted in prolonging the most disagreeable bath I have ever taken, for fear of causing you all a surprise, for which my self-love might have suffered," (Cuchillo did not allude to his excursion in the mountains); "but the water of this lake is so icy that rather than perish with cold, I would have run a greater risk than meeting with old friends."

"Added to this I felt a wound in my leg reopen. It was received some time since, in fact, long ago, in my youth.

"Señor Don Estevan, Don Tiburcio, I am your very humble servant."

A profound silence succeeded these words. Cuchillo began to feel that he was acting the part of the hare, who takes refuge in the teeth of the hounds; but he endeavoured by a great show of assurance to make the best of a position which was more than precarious.

The old hunter alone glanced towards Fabian, as though to ask what motive this man, with his impudent and sinister manner, and his beard covered with greenish mud, could offer for thus intruding himself upon them.

"It is Cuchillo," said Fabian, answering Bois-Rose's look.

"Cuchillo, your unworthy servant," continued the bandit, "who has been a witness to your prowess, most worthy hunter of tigers. Decidedly," thought Cuchillo, "my presence, is not so obnoxious to them as I should have supposed."

Then feeling his assurance redoubled at the reception he had met with, which though cold and silent as that with which every new-comer is received in the house of death, still gave him courage to say, observing the severe expression on every face:

"Pardon me, gentlemen! I observe you have business in hand, and I am perhaps intruding; I will retire. There are moments when one does not like to be disturbed: I know it by experience."

Saying these words, Cuchillo showed his intention of crossing a second time the green inclosure of the valley of gold, when Bois-Rose's rough voice arrested him.

"Stay here, as you value the salvation of your soul, master Cuchillo," said the hunter.

"The giant may have heard of my intellectual resources," thought Cuchillo. "They have need of me. After all, I would rather go shares with them than get nothing; but without doubt this Golden Valley is bewitched. You allow, master hunter," he continued, addressing the Canadian, and feigning a surprise he did not feel at the aspect of his chief, "I have a—"

An imperious gesture from Fabian cut short Cuchillo's demand.

"Silence!" he said, "do not distract the last thought of a Christian who is about to die."

We have said that a poignard planted in the ground no longer cast a shadow.

"My lord of Mediana," added Fabian, "I ask you once again, by the name we bear, by your honour, and the salvation of your soul, are you innocent of my mother's murder?"

To this lofty interrogation, Don Antonio replied without relaxing his haughty demeanour—

"I have nothing to say, to my peers alone I allow the right of judgment. Let my fate and yours be accomplished."

"God sees and hears me," said Fabian. Then taking Cuchillo aside: "A solemn sentence has been passed upon this man," said he to him. "We, as the instruments of human justice in this desert, command you to be his executioner. The treasures contained in this valley will remunerate you for undertaking this terrible duty. May you never commit a more iniquitous act!"

"One cannot live through forty years without having a few little peccadilloes on one's conscience, Don Tiburcio. However, I shall not the less object to being an executioner; and I am proud to know that my talents are estimated at their real value. You promise, then, that all the gold of this valley shall be mine?"

"All—without excepting the smallest particle."

"Carramba! notwithstanding my well-known scruples, it is a good price, therefore I shall not hesitate; and if at the same time there is any other little favour you require of me, do not distress yourself—it shall be done cheaply."

That which has been previously said explains Cuchillo's unexpected appearance.

The outlaw, concealed upon the borders of the neighbouring lake, had escaped through the prologue which preceded the fearful drama in which he was about to perform a part. Taking all things into consideration, he saw that matters were turning out better than he had expected.

However he could not disguise from himself the fact that there was a certain amount of danger in his becoming the executioner of a man who was aware of all his crimes, and who could, by a single word, surrender him him to the implacable justice enforced in these solitudes.

He was aware that to gain the promised recompense, and to prevent Don Antonio from speaking, it would be necessary first to deceive him, and he found means to whisper in the ear of the prisoner—

"Fear nothing—I am on your side."

The spectators of this terrible scene maintained a profound silence, under a feeling of awe experienced by each of them.

A deep dejection of spirit had, in Don Fabian's case, succeeded the energetic exercise of his will, and his face, bowed towards the earth, was as pale and as livid as that of the man upon whom he had pronounced sentence of death.

Bois-Rose—whom the frequent dangers which belonged to the life of a sailor and a hunter, had rendered callous to the physical horror with which one man looks upon the destruction of his fellow—appeared completely absorbed in the contemplations of this young man, whom he loved as a son, and whose dejected attitude showed the depth of his grief.

Pepé, on his side, endeavoured to conceal under an impenetrable mask the tumultuous feeling resulting from his now satisfied vengeance. He, as well as his two companions, remained silent.

Cuchillo alone—whose sanguinary and vindictive nature would have led him to accept gratuitously the odious office of executor—could scarcely conceal his delight at the thoughts of the enormous sum he was to receive for the wicked service.

But in this case, for once in his life, Cuchillo was to assist in an apparently legal proceeding.

"Carramba!" he ejaculated, taking Pepé's carbine from him, and at the same time making a sign to Don Antonio; "this is an affair for which even the judge of Arispe himself would be sorry to grant me absolution."

He advanced towards Don Antonio.

Pale, but with flashing eyes; uncertain whether in Cuchillo he beheld a saviour or an executioner, Don Estevan did not stir.

"It was foretold that I should die in a desert; I am, what you are pleased to call, convicted and condemned. God has reserved for me the infinite disgrace of dying by the hand of this man. I forgive you, Fabian; but may not this bandit prove as fatal to your life, as he will be to that of your father's brother, as he was—"

A cry from Cuchillo—a cry of alarm, here interrupted the Duke de Armada.

"To arms! To arms! yonder come the Indians!" cried he.

Fabian, Bois-Rose, and Pepé rushed to seize their rifles.

Cuchillo took advantage of this short instant, and sprang towards Don Antonio. The latter with his neck stretched forward, was also examining the wide extent of the plain, when Cuchillo twice plunged the poignard into his throat.

The unfortunate Mediana fell to the ground, vomiting forth torrents of blood.

A smile relaxed Cuchillo's lips: Don Antonio had carried out of the world the secret which he dreaded.

Chapter Fifty One
The Judgment of God

An instant of stupor succeeded to the murder so suddenly accomplished. Don Antonio did not stir; Fabian seemed to forget that the bandit had only hastened the execution of the sentence which he himself had pronounced.

"Wretch!" cried he, rushing towards Cuchillo, with the barrel of his carbine in his hand, as though he did not deign to raise its butt against the executioner.

"There, there!" said Cuchillo, drawing back, whilst Pepé, more ready to acquit Don Antonio's murderer, interposed between them; "you are as quick and passionate as a fighting-cock, and ready every instant to sport your horns, like a young bull. The Indians are too busy elsewhere to trouble themselves about us. It was a stratagem of war, to enable me more speedily to render you the signal service required of me. Do not therefore be ungrateful; for, why not admit it? you were just now a nephew, most unsufferably encumbered with an uncle; you are noble, you are generous; you would have regretted all your life that you had not pardoned that uncle? By cutting the matter short for you, I have taken the remorse upon myself; and so the affair is ended."

"The rascal knows what he is about, undoubtedly," remarked the ex-carabinier.

"Yes," replied Cuchillo, evidently flattered, "I pride myself upon being no fool, and upon having some notion of the scruples of conscience. I have taken your doubts upon mine. When I take a fancy to people, I sacrifice myself for them. It is a fault of mine. When I saw, Don Tiburcio, that you had so generously pardoned me the blow—the scratch I inflicted upon you—I did my best to deserve it: the rest must be settled between me and my conscience."

"Ah!" sighed Fabian, "I hoped yet to have been able to pardon *him*."

"Why trouble yourself about it?" said the ex-carabinier. "Pardon your mother's murderer, Don Fabian! it would have been cowardice! To kill a man who cannot defend himself, is, I grant, almost a crime, even after five years' imprisonment. Our friend Cuchillo has saved us the embarrassment of choosing: that is his affair. What do you say, Bois-Rose?"

"With proofs such as those we possess, the tribunal of a city would have condemned the assassin to atone for his crime; and Indian justice could not have done less. It was God's will that you should be spared the necessity of shedding the blood of a white man. I say as you do, Pepé, it is Cuchillo's affair."

Fabian inclined his head, without speaking, in acquiescence to the old hunter's verdict—as though in his own heart he could not determine, amidst such conflicting thoughts, whether he ought to rejoice, or to grieve over this unexpected catastrophe.

Nevertheless, a shade of bitter regret overspread his countenance; but accustomed, as well as his two companions, to scenes of blood, he assented, though with a sigh, to their inexorable logic.

In the mean time, Cuchillo had regained all his audacity, things were turning out well for him.

He cast a glance of satisfied hatred upon the corpse of him who could never more speak, and muttered in a low voice:

"Why trouble one's self about human destiny?—for twenty years past, my life has depended upon nothing more than the absence of a tree."

Then addressing himself to Fabian:

"It is, then, agreed, that I have rendered you a great service. Ah! Don Tiburcio, you must resolve to remain in my debt. I think generously of furnishing you with the means of discharging it. There is immense wealth yonder; therefore it would not do for you to recall a promise given to him who, for your sake, was not afraid—for the first time, let me tell you—to come to an open rupture with his conscience."

Cuchillo, who, notwithstanding the promise Fabian had made—to satisfy his cupidity by the possession of the gold,—knew that to make a promise, and to keep one, are two different things. He waited the reply with anxiety.

"It is true; the price of blood is yours," said Fabian to the bandit.

Cuchillo assumed an indignant air.

"Well, you will be magnificently recompensed," continued the young man, contemptuously; "but it shall never be said that I shared it with you:— the gold of this place is yours."

"All?" cried Cuchillo, who could not believe his ears.

"Have I not said so?"

"You are mad!" exclaimed Pepé and Bois-Rose, simultaneously, "the fellow would have killed him for nothing!"

"You are a god!" cried Cuchillo; "and you estimate my scruples at their real value. What! all this gold?"

"All, including the smallest particle," answered Fabian, solemnly: "I shall have nothing in common with you—not even this gold."

And he made a sign to Cuchillo to leave the ground.

The bandit, instead of passing through the hedge of cotton-trees, took the road to the Misty Mountains, towards the spot where his horse was fastened.

A few minutes afterwards he returned with his serapé in his hand. He drew aside the interlacing branches which shut in the valley, and soon disappeared from Fabian's sight. The sun, in the midst of his course, poured down a flood of light, causing the gold spread over the surface of the valley to shoot forth innumerable rays.

A shudder passed though Cuchillo's veins, as he once more beheld it.

His heart beat quick at the sight of this mass of wealth. He resembled the tiger which falling upon a sheepfold cannot determine which victim to choose. He encompassed with a haggard glance the treasures spread at his feet; and little was wanting to induce him, in his transports of joy, to roll himself in these floods of gold.

Soon, however, restored to calmer thoughts, he spread his mantle on the sand; and as he saw the impossibility of carrying away all the riches exposed to his view, he cast around him a glance of observation.

In the meantime, Diaz, seated at some distance on the plain, had not lost a single detail of this melancholy scene.

He had seen Cuchillo suddenly appear, he had imagined the part he would be required to fulfil, he heard the bandit's cry of false alarm, and even the bloody catastrophe of the drama had not been unseen by him.

Until then he had remained motionless in his place, mourning over the death of his chief, and the hopes which that death had destroyed.

Cuchillo had disappeared from their sight, when the three hunters saw Diaz rise and approach them.

He advanced with slow steps, like the justice of God, whose instrument he was about to become.

His arm was passed through his horse's bridle; and his face, clouded by grief, was turned downwards.

The adventurer cast a look full of sadness upon the Duke de Armada lying in his blood; death had not effaced from that countenance its look of unalterable pride.

"I do not blame you," said he; "in your place I should have done the same thing. How much Indian blood have I also not spilt to satisfy my vengeance!"

"It is holy bread," interrupted Bois-Rose, passing his hand through his thick grey hair, and directing a sympathetic glance toward the adventurer. "Pepé and I can say that, for our part—"

"I do not blame you, friends, but I grieve because I have seen this man, of such noble courage, fall almost before my eyes; a man who held in his hand the destiny of Sonora. I grieve that the glory of my country expires with him."

"He was, as you say, a man of noble courage, but with a heart of stone. May God save his soul!"

A convulsive grief agitated Don Fabian's breast. Diaz continued the Duke de Armada's funeral oration.

"He and I had dreamed of the freedom of a noble province and days of splendour. Neither he, nor I, nor others, will ever now behold them shine. Ah! why was not I killed instead of him? No one would have known that I had ceased, to exist, and one champion less would not have compromised the cause we served; but the death of our chief ruins it forever. The treasure which is said to be accumulated here might have aided us in restoring Sonora; for you do not, perhaps, know that near to this spot—"

"We know it," interrupted Fabian.

"Well," continued Diaz, "I will think no more about this immense treasure. I have always preferred the life of an Indian, killed by my own hands, to a sack of gold dust."

This common feeling of hatred towards the Indians still further added to the sympathy which Bois-Rose had felt for the disinterestedness and courage shown by Diaz.

"We have failed at the onset," continued Diaz, in a tone of great bitterness, "and all this through the fault of a traitor whom I wish to deliver up to your justice—not because he deceived us, but because he has destroyed the instrument which God was willing to grant, in order to make my country a powerful kingdom."

"What do you say?" cried Fabian; "is it Cuchillo of whom you speak?"

"The traitor who twice attempted your life—the first time at the Hacienda del Venado, the second in the neighbouring forest—is the one who conducted us to this valley of gold."

"It was then Cuchillo who told you the secret. I was almost sure of it—but are you also certain?"

"As certain as I am that I shall one day appear before God. Poor Don Estevan related to me how the existence and position of the treasure became known to Cuchillo; it was in assassinating his associate who had first discovered it.

"And now if you decide that this man who has twice attempted your life deserves exemplary punishment, you have only to determine upon it."

As he finished these words, Pedro Diaz tightened his horse's girths, and prepared to depart.

"One word more!" cried Fabian, "has Cuchillo long possessed this grey horse, which, as you may be aware, has a habit of stumbling?"

"More than two years, from what I have heard."

This last scene had escaped the bandit's observation, the thicket of cotton-trees concealing it from his sight; besides, he was too much absorbed in the contemplation of his treasures to turn his eyes away from them.

Seated upon the sand, he was crouched down amidst the innumerable pieces of gold which surrounded him, and he had already begun to pile up upon his serapé all those he had chosen, when Diaz finished his terrible revelation.

"Ah! it is a fearful and fatal day," said Fabian, in whose mind the latter part of this revelation left no room for doubt. "What ought I do with this man? You, who both know what he has done with my adopted father, Pepé—Bois-Rose—advise me, for my strength and resolution are coming to an end. I have experienced too many emotions for one day."

"Does the vile wretch, who cut your father's throat, deserve more consideration than the noble gentleman, who murdered your mother, my son?" answered the Canadian, resolutely.

"Whether it be your adopted father or any others who have been his victims, this brigand is worthy of death," added Diaz, as he mounted upon his saddle, "and I abandon him to your justice."

"It is with regret that I see you depart," said Bois-Rose to the adventurer, "a man who like yourself is a bitter enemy to the Indians, would have been a companion whose society I should have appreciated."

"My duty recalls me to the camp, which I quitted under the influence of Don Estevan's unhappy star," replied the adventurer, "but there are two things I shall never forget; they are, the conduct of generous enemies; and the oath I have taken never to reveal to a living creature the existence of this Golden Valley."

As he finished these words, the loyal Diaz quickly withdrew, reflecting upon the means of reconciling his respect for his word, with the care and safety of the expedition entrusted to him by its leader, previous to his death.

The three friends speedily lost sight of him.

The sun shone out, and, glancing down from the Golden Valley, discovered Cuchillo, greedily bending over his treasures, and the three hunters holding council amongst themselves respecting him.

Fabian had listened in silence to Bois-Rose's advice, as well as that given by Diaz previous to his departure; and he only waited the counsel of the old carabinier.

"You have taken," said the latter, in his turn, "a vow, from which nothing ought to release you; the wife of Arellanos received it from you on her death-bed; you have her husband's murderer in your power; there is nothing here to deny it."

Then, observing a look of anxious indecision in Fabian's countenance, he added, with that bitter irony which formed a part of his character; "But after all, if this duty is so repugnant to you, I shall undertake it; for not having the least ill will against Cuchillo, I can bang him without a scruple. You will see, Fabian, that the knave will not testify any surprise at what I am going to tell him. Fellows who have such a face as Cuchillo's expect to be hung every day."

As he concluded this judicious reflection, Pepé approached the green hedge, which separated them from the outlaw.

The latter, unconscious of all that had taken place around him—dazzled, blinded, by the golden rays, which reflected the sun's light over the surface of the valley—had heard and seen nothing.

With fingers doubled up, he was busied rummaging amongst the sand with the eagerness of a famished jackal disinterring a corpse.

"Master Cuchillo! a word, if you please," cried Pepé, drawing aside the branches of the cotton shrubs; "Master Cuchillo!"

But Cuchillo did not hear.

It was only when he had been called three times that he turned around, and discovered his excited countenance to the carabinier—after having, by a spontaneous movement of suspicion, thrown a corner of his mantle over the gold he had collected.

"Master Cuchillo," resumed Pepé, "I heard you a little while ago give utterance to a philosophical maxim, which gave me the highest opinion of your character."

"Come!" said Cuchillo to himself, wiping the sweat from his forehead, "here is someone else who requires my services. These gentry are becoming imprudent, but, por Dios! they pay handsomely."

Then aloud:

"A philosophical maxim?" said he, throwing away disdainfully, a handful of sand, the contents of which would elsewhere have rejoiced a gold-seeker. "What is it? I utter many, and of the best kind; philosophy is my strong point."

Pepé, on one side of the hedge, resting upon his rifle, in a superb attitude of nonchalance, and the most imperturbable *sangfroid*, and Cuchillo, on the other side, with his head stretched across the green inclosure of the little valley, looked very much like two country neighbours, for the moment chatting familiarly together.

No one, on seeing them thus, would have suspected the terrible catastrophe which was to follow this pacific intercourse. The countenance of the ex-carabinier, only exhibited a gracious smile.

"You spoke truth," replied Pepé. "What signifies human destiny; for twenty years past you say you have owed your life to the absence of a tree?"

"It is true," affirmed Cuchillo, in an absent tone, "for a long time I preferred shrubs, but lately I have become reconciled to large trees."

"Indeed!"

"And yet it is still one of my favourite maxims, that a wise man must pass over many little inconveniences."

"True. And now I think of it," added Pepé, carelessly, "there are on the summit of yonder steep hill, two magnificent pine trees which project over the abyss, and which, twenty years ago, might have caused you very serious anxiety."

"I do not deny it; but at present I am as easy about it as if they were only cactus plants."

"Indeed!"

"Indeed!" repeated Cuchillo, with some impatience. "So then, you did me the honour to speak of me, and to what purpose?"

"Oh! a simple remark. My two companions and myself had some reasons for suspecting that amongst these mountains a certain valley of gold was to be found; but nevertheless, it was only after long seeking that we found it. You also know it now, and even better than ourselves, since unhesitatingly, and without losing an instant, you have appropriated to yourself, between what you call a heap and what you have already collected, carramba—enough to build a church to your patron saint."

Cuchillo, at the recollection of the imprudence he had been guilty of, and at this indirect attack, felt his legs give way under him.

"It is certainly my intention not to employ this gold to any other purpose than a godly one," said he, concealing his anguish as well as he could. "As to the knowledge of this wonderful valley, it is to—it is to chance that I owe it."

"Chance always comes to the assistance of virtue," replied Pepé, coldly. "Well, in your place, I should not, nevertheless, be without anxiety touching the vicinity of those two pine trees."

"What do you mean?" cried Cuchillo, turning pale.

"Nothing—unless this may prove to you one of those trifling inconveniences, about which you just now said a man should not trouble himself. Por Dios! you have enough booty to render a king jealous."

"But I acquired this gold legitimately—I committed no murder to obtain it. What I did was not worthless. The devil! I am not in the habit of killing for nothing," cried Cuchillo, exasperated, and who, mistaking the carabinier's intentions, saw only in his alarming innuendoes regret at his defrauded cupidity.

Like the sailor, who, overtaken by a storm, throws a part of his cargo overboard to save the rest, Cuchillo resolved with a sigh, to shun, by means of a sacrifice, the danger with which he was threatened.

"I again repeat to you," said he, in a low voice, "chance alone gave me a knowledge of this treasure; but I don't wish to be selfish. It is my intention to give you a share. Listen," he continued, "there is in a certain place, a block of gold of inestimable value; honest fellows should understand one another, and this block shall be yours. Ah! your share will be better than mine."

"I hope so," said Pepé; "and in what place have you reserved me my portion?"

"Up yonder!" said Cuchillo, indicating the summit of the pyramid.

"Up yonder, near the pine trees? Ah, master Cuchillo, how glad I am to find that you have not taken my foolish little joke amiss, and that these trees do not affect you any more than if they were cactus plants! Between ourselves, Don Tiburcio, whom you perceive to be deeply absorbed, is only regretting in reality the enormous sum he has given you, for a service which he could equally well have performed himself."

"An enormous sum! it was but a very fair price, and at any rate I should have lost it," cried Cuchillo, recovering all his habitual impudence of manner, on seeing the change that had taken place in the conduct and tone of the ex-carabinier.

"Agreed," continued the latter; "but in truth, he may have repented of the bargain; and I must avow that if he commanded me to blow your brains out, in order to get rid of you, I should be compelled to obey him. Allow me, then, to call him here so as to restore his confidence; or, better still, come and show me the portion, which your munificence destines for me. Afterwards we each go our own way; and notwithstanding all you have said about it, the share assigned to you will surpass all your expectations."

"Let us set off then," resumed Cuchillo, happy to see a negotiation—the probable result of which began to cause him serious uneasiness—terminate so satisfactorily for him and, casting a glance of passionate tenderness upon a heap of gold which he had piled up upon his wrapper, he set off towards the summit of the pyramid. He had scarcely reached it, when, upon Pepé's invitation, Fabian and Bois-Rose began to ascend the steep on the other side.

"No one can escape his fate," said Pepé to Fabian, "and I had already proved to you that the rascal would testify no astonishment. Be that as it may remember that you have sworn to avenge the death of your adopted father, and that in these deserts you ought to shame the justice of cities, where such crimes go unpunished. To show mercy towards such a knave is an outrage to society! Bois-Rose! I shall need the assistance of your arm."

The Canadian hunter, by a glance, interrogated him, for whom his blind devotion knew no bounds.

"Marcos Arellanos craved pardon and did not obtain it," said Fabian, no longer undecided, "and as this man did to others, so let it be done to him."

And these three inexorable men seated themselves solemnly upon the summit of the pyramid, where Cuchillo already awaited them. At sight of the severe aspect of those whom he had inwardly so many reasons to dread, Cuchillo felt all his apprehensions renewed. He endeavoured, however, to recover his assurance.

"Do you see," said he, pointing out behind the sheet of water, whose majestic torrent foamed beside them, "the spot where the block of gold sheds forth its dazzling rays?"

But the eyes of his judges did not turn in the direction he indicated. Fabian rose slowly; his look caused the blood to curdle in the veins of the outlaw.

"Cuchillo!" said he, "you saved me from dying of thirst, and you have not done this for one who is ungrateful. I have forgiven you the stab with which you wounded me at the Hacienda del Venado. I have pardoned another attempt you made near El Salto de Agua; also the shot which you only could have fired upon us from the summit of this pyramid. I might, in short, have forgiven every attempt you have made to take away a life you once saved; and with having pardoned you, I have even recompensed you, as a king does not recompense the executioner of his justice."

"I do not deny it; but this worthy hunter, who has informed me with a great deal of circumspection upon the delicate subject you wish to touch upon, ought also to inform you how reasonable he found me in the matter."

"I have forgiven you," continued Fabian, "but there is one crime, amongst others, from which your own conscience ought not to absolve you."

"There is a perfect understanding between my conscience and myself," resumed Cuchillo, with a graciously sinister smile, "but it seems to me that we are getting away from our subject."

"That friend whom you assassinated in such a cowardly manner—"

"Disputed with me the profits of a booty, and faith, the consumption of brandy was very considerable," interrupted Cuchillo. "But permit me—"

"Do not pretend to misunderstand me!" cried Fabian, irritated by the knave's impudence.

Cuchillo collected his thoughts.

"If you allude to Tio Tomas, it is an affair which was never very well understood, but—"

Fabian opened his lips to form a distinct accusation with reference to the assassination of Arellanos, when Pepé broke in—

"I should be curious," he said, "to learn the real facts concerning Tio Tomas: perhaps Master Cuchillo has not sufficient leisure to recollect himself, which would be a pity."

"I hold it necessary," continued Cuchillo, flattered at the compliment, "to prove that men own such a susceptible conscience as mine; here then are the facts—My friend Tio Tomas had a nephew impatient to inherit his uncle's fortune; I received a hundred dollars from the nephew to hasten the moment of his inheritance. It was very little for such a capital will.

"It was so little that I gave Tio Tomas warning, and received *two* hundred dollars to prevent his nephew becoming his heir. I committed a fault in— despatching the nephew without giving him warning, as I ought to have done, perhaps. It was then I felt how inconvenient a quarrelsome conscience like mine may become. I seized upon the only means of composition which was left me. The nephew's money was a continual remorse to me, and I resolved to get rid of it."

"Of the money?"

"Not so."

"And you despatched the uncle as well?" cried Pepé.

Cuchillo assented.

"From that time my conscience had but little to reproach me with. I had gained three hundred dollars by the most ingenious integrity."

Cuchillo was yet smiling, when Fabian exclaimed—

"Were you paid for assassinating Marcos Arellanos?"

At this astounding accusation a livid paleness overspread Cuchillo's features.

He could no longer disguise from himself the fate that awaited him.

The bandage which covered his eyes fell suddenly; and to the flattering delusions with which he had deceived himself succeeded a formidable reality.

"Marcos Arellanos!" he stammered out in a weak voice, "who told you that? I did not kill him!"

Fabian smiled bitterly.

"Who tells the shepherd," he cried, "where the den of the jaguar is to be found that devours his sheep?

"Who tells the vaquero where the horse that he pursues has taken refuge?

"To the Indian, the enemy he seeks?

"To the gold-seeker the ore, concealed by God?

"The surface of the lake only does not preserve the trace of the bird which flies over its waters, nor the form of the cloud which it reflects; but the earth, with its herbs and mosses, reveals to us sons of the desert, the print of the jaguar's foot as well as the horse's hoof and the Indian's track; do you not know it, even as I do?"

"I did not kill Arellanos," repeated the assassin.

"You did kill him; you cut his throat near to our common country; you threw his corpse into the river; the earth revealed it to me—since I noticed the defect in the horse you rode, as well as the wound in your leg, which you received in the struggle."

"Pardon, Don Tiburcio?" cried Cuchillo, overwhelmed by the sudden revelation of these facts, to which God alone had been witness. "Take back all the gold you gave me, but spare my life; and to show my gratitude, I will kill all your enemies everywhere, and always at a sign from you—for nothing—even my father, if you command me; but in the name of the all-powerful God, spare my life—spare me my life!" he continued, crawling forward and clutching at Fabian's knees.

"Arellanos also craved for mercy; did you listen to him?" said Fabian, turning away.

"But when I killed him, it was that I might possess all this gold myself. Now I restore it all for my life—what can you want more?" he continued, while he resisted Pepé's efforts, who was trying to prevent him from kissing Fabian's feet.

With features distorted by excess of terror, a whitish foam upon his lips, his eyes starting from his head, yet seeing nothing, Cuchillo still sued for mercy, as he endeavoured to crawl towards Fabian. He had by continued efforts reached the edge of the platform. Behind his head, the sheet of water fell foaming downwards.

"Mercy, mercy!" he cried, "in the name of your mother—for Doña Rosarita's sake, who loves you, for I know that she loves you—I heard—"

"What?" cried Fabian, in his turn rushing towards Cuchillo, but the question expired upon his lips.

Spurned along the earth by the carabinier's foot Cuchillo with head and arms stretched back was hurled into the abyss!

"What have you done, Pepé?" exclaimed Fabian.

"The wretch," said the ex-carabinier, "was not worth the cord which might have hung him, nor the bullet that would have sent him out of the world."

A piercing cry,—a cry which rose from the abyss—which drowned their voices and was heard above the roar of the cascade, caused Fabian to stretch his head forward and withdraw it again in horror. Hanging to the branches of a shrub which bent beneath his weight, and which scarce adhering to the sides of the rock, was fast giving way, Cuchillo hung over the abyss, howling forth his terror and anguish.

"Help!" he shouted, in a voice despairing as the damned. "Help! if you are human beings—help!"

The three friends exchanged a glance of unutterable meaning, as each one wiped the sweat from his brow.

Suddenly the bandit's voice grew faint, and amidst horrible bursts of laughter, like the shrieks of a lunatic, were heard the last inarticulate words that escaped his lips.

A moment after, and the noise of the cascade alone broke the silence of the desert. The abyss had swallowed up him whose life had been a long tissue of crime.

Chapter Fifty Two
The Man of the Red Kerchief

Six months have elapsed since the three hunters, without deigning to carry with them a single grain of the treasures of the valley of gold, directed their steps, following the course of the Rio Gila, to the plains of Texas. The rainy had succeeded to the dry season, without anything being known of their fate, or of the expedition commanded by Don Estevan de Arechiza.

Diaz was no more, having carried with him to the tomb the secret of the wonderful valley—and Gayferos had followed his three liberators. What had become of these intrepid hunters who had willingly encountered fatigues, privations and dangers, instead of returning to civilised life? Were they as rich and powerful as they might have been? Had the desert claimed these three noble spirits, as it has done so many others? Like the monk, who seeks in the silence of cloister forgetfulness of the world's vain show, had Fabian in the sublimity of solitude been able to forget the woman who loved him, and who secretly hoped for and expected his return?

What we are about to relate will answer these questions.

One sultry afternoon, two men, mounted and armed to the teeth, pursued the lonely road which leads from the utmost confines of the province of Sonora to the Presidio of Tubac. Their costume, the coarse equipment of their steeds, and the beauty of the latter, formed on the whole a striking contrast and seemed to indicate subalterns despatched by some rich proprietor, either to carry or to seek information.

The first was clothed in leather from head to foot, like the vaquero of some noble hacienda. The second, dark and bearded like a Moor, though less simply attired than his companion, did not appear to be of much greater consideration.

At the end of a journey of some days the white houses of the Presidio began to appear in the distance. The two cavaliers had probably exhausted every subject of conversation, for they trotted on in silence.

The scanty vegetation which covered the plains they were crossing was again becoming parched by the sun, after the winter rains; and the dry grass harboured innumerable grasshoppers whose shrill note was heard incessantly, mingled with the scorching breath of the south wind. The foliage of the Peruvian trees drooped languidly over the burning sand, like the willows upon the banks of a stream.

The two cavaliers arrived at the entrance of the Presidio just as the church clock sounded the evening *angelus*.

Tubac was then a village with two cross streets, its houses built of cement, with only a few windows in the front, as is the custom in places exposed to the sudden excursions of the Indians. Strong movable barriers, formed by trunks of trees, protected the four approaches to the village; and a piece of the artillery of the country, raised upon its carriage, was erected behind each of these barriers.

Previous to following the new-comers into the Presidio, we must relate an incident which, insignificant in itself, nevertheless acquired some importance in the heart of a solitary village of Tubac.

During the space of a fortnight a mysterious personage—inasmuch as he was unknown to the inhabitants of the Presidio—had frequently, and for a short time, appeared there. He was a man of about forty years of age, thin, but rough and vigorous in appearance, whose countenance seemed to tell of dangers overcome, but whose speech was as rare as his physiognomy was expressive. He replied shortly to any questions addressed to him; but, on the other hand, he asked a great many, and appeared particularly anxious to know what was passing at the Hacienda del Venado.

Some of the inhabitants of the Presidency knew the rich proprietor very well by repute, but few amongst them—or, one might rather say, none of them—were so thoroughly acquainted with Don Augustin Peña, as to be capable of answering the questions of the stranger.

Everybody in Tubac remembered the gold-seekers' expedition which had set out six months previously; and according to some vague replies given by the mysterious personage, it was suspected that he knew more upon the matter than he chose to reveal. He had, he pretended, encountered in the deserts of the Apache country, a troop commanded by Don Estevan in a very critical position, and he had reason for believing that they must have fought a last and terrible engagement with the Indians, from the result of which he augured no good.

The evening before the arrival of the two travellers, he had inquired what direction he ought to take to reach Don Augustin's house; and, above all, he had testified a great wish to learn whether Doña Rosarita was still unmarried.

The unknown always wore on his head a red checkered handkerchief, the folds of which hung down over his eyes; and in consequence of this head-dress he always went by the name of the "man with the red kerchief."

This being explained, let us now return to our two travellers.

The new-comers—whose arrival created some sensation—on entering the presidency, directed their steps towards one of the houses of the village, at the door of which sat a man, who was soothing his leisure hours by playing upon the guitar.

One of the cavaliers, addressing him, said—

"*Santas tardes*! my master; will you afford hospitality to two strangers for a day and a night?"

The musician rose and bowed courteously.

"Pray dismount, noble cavaliers," he answered, "this dwelling is at your service as long as you please to remain."

Such is the simple ceremonial of hospitality still in vogue in these distant countries.

The cavaliers dismounted from their horses, in the midst of an idle group who had collected around them, and who observed the two strangers with considerable curiosity—for in the Presidio of Tubac an arrival is a rare event.

The host silently assisted his guests to unsaddle their horses, but the more inquisitive of the crowd did not exercise so much discretion, and without scruple addressed a multitude of questions to the travellers.

"Good people," said one of the cavaliers, "let us first attend to our horses, and afterwards, when we have taken a mouthful of food, we shall have a chat. My comrade and myself have come here for that very purpose."

Thus saying, the bearded cavalier unfastened his gigantic spurs, threw them across his horse's saddle, which he deposited, together with its woollen covering carefully folded, in the piazza attached to the house.

The two strangers did not dwell long over their repast. They soon rejoined their host upon the threshold, and sat down beside him.

Their questioners had not yet departed from the house.

"I am the more inclined," resumed the bearded traveller, "to inform you all of the object of our visit to the Presidio, since we are sent by our master to ask you a few questions. Will that be agreeable to you?"

"Perfectly," replied several voices, "and first, may we know who your master is?"

"He is Don Augustin Peña; you are not without some knowledge of his name?"

"The proprietor of the great Hacienda del Venado—a man worth three millions! Who does not know him?" replied one of the bystanders.

"He is the same. This cavalier, whom you see, is a vaquero, entrusted with the care of the beasts of the hacienda; for myself, I am a major-domo attached to the service of the proprietor. Would you have the kindness, my dear friend, to give me a light for my cigar?" continued the bearded major-domo.

He paused to light his cigar of maize husk, and then resumed:

"Six months ago an expedition set out from here in search of gold dust. This expedition was headed by one named—let me see—*carrai*! I have heard him called by so many names that I cannot remember any!"

"Don Estevan Arechiza!" replied one of the interlocutors, "a Spaniard, and one such as we do not often see in this country; one who seemed, by his noble deportment and majestic countenance, to have commanded all his life."

"Don Estevan Arechiza: the very same," said the major-domo, "a man who as far exceeds all others in generosity as a gamester who has just won a fortune. But let me return to the expedition; about how many men composed it, do you guess?"

"More than eighty started out with it."

"More than a hundred," suggested another.

"You are mistaken—the number was not a hundred in all," interrupted a third.

"That matters little to Don Augustin, my master. It is far more important to know how many returned."

Upon this point also there were two different opinions.

"Not a single one," remarked a voice.

"Yes; there was one, and but one," continued another.

The major-domo rubbed his hands with an air of satisfaction.

"Good!" said he, "then at least one is saved, provided this gentleman, who declares that all the gold-seekers are not dead, be rightly informed, as I hope he is."

"Do you not think," said the last who had spoken, "that the man of the red handkerchief may not be one of those whose departure we witnessed six months ago? I would swear to it by the cross and Gospel."

"No! not so!" cried another, "that man never set foot in the Presidio before the other day."

"In any case," interrupted a third, "the man of the red handkerchief has doubtless something of interest in store for Don Augustin Peña, since he has so often inquired about him. With these gentlemen, he will probably be more communicative than with us."

"That will be just what we desire," resumed the major-domo.

"You must know, then, and I may without indiscretion inform you," continued he, "that Don Augustin Peña, whom God preserve, was the intimate friend of Señor Arechiza, and that he has had no news of him for six months past, which would be natural enough if he has been massacred by the Indians with all the rest. But my master is anxious for his return, that he may marry his daughter, Doña Rosarita, a beautiful and charming person, to the Senator Don Vicente Tragaduros. Months have elapsed, and since the hacienda is not on the main road from Arispe to Tubac, and that we cannot gain information from any one upon the subject of this deplorable expedition, Don Augustin determined upon sending us here to inquire about it. When he shall have established the fact that Don Estevan's return is impossible—and as young girls do not readily meet with Senators in the heart of the desert—nor do the latter often find there girls whose marriage portion is worth two hundred thousand piastres—"

"Carramba! that is a high figure."

"True, friend," continued the major-domo, "then the projected marriage will take place to the mutual satisfaction of all parties. Such is the object of our journey to Tubac. If, therefore, you can conduct me to him whom you describe as the sole survivor of this expedition, we shall perhaps learn from him what we wish to discover."

The conversation had reached this stage, when, at some distance from the house where it was taking place, a man was seen passing, with his head bent downwards.

"See!" said one of the party, pointing to the man in question; "there goes your sole survivor."

"In truth, it is a person whose conduct is sufficiently mysterious," added the host. "For some days past he has done nothing but come and go, from one place to another, without informing any one of the object of his journeyings."

Wood Rangers | 329

"If it please you, we shall question him?" proposed one.

"Hola! friend!" cried another of the party; "come this way; here is a gentleman who is anxious to see and speak with you."

The mysterious unknown approached at the summons.

"Señor cavalier," said the major-domo, courteously addressing him, "it is not to gratify an idle curiosity that I now address you; but the master whom I serve feels a natural anxiety at the disappearance of a friend, whose death he would greatly deplore. What do you know of Don Estevan de Arechiza?"

"Many things. But, pray what is the name of the master of whom you speak?"

"Don Augustin Peña—proprietor of the Hacienda del Venado."

A ray of joy lit up the countenance of the unknown.

"I am able," he said, "to furnish Don Augustin with all the information he may desire. How many days' journey is it from hence to the hacienda?"

"Three days' journey, with a good horse."

"I possess a capital one; and if you can wait for me until to-morrow evening, I shall accompany you, and communicate with Don Augustin in person."

"Be it so," answered the major-domo.

"Very well," added the man of the red handkerchief; "to-morrow at this same hour we will start, so that we may travel by night, and so escape the heat."

Saying this, he took his departure, when the major-domo remarked:

"It must be agreed, gentlemen, that nothing can exceed the complaisance of this cavalier of the red handkerchief."

The arrangement did not satisfy the bystanders, who were thoroughly disappointed; but their interest was renewed, on seeing the man of the red handkerchief pass by on horseback, and depart at full speed towards the north.

The unknown kept his promise: and on the day following he returned at the hour of the evening *angelus*.

Don Augustin's two envoys took leave of their host, assuring him of a kind welcome, if ever his affairs led him in the direction of the Hacienda del Venado. Even the poorest in this primitive country, would blush to receive any other reward for hospitality than sincere thanks, and a promise that they in their turn should receive it.

The three horsemen set off at full speed; the horse of the unknown equalled in strength and mettle those of Don Augustin's envoys. The journey was rapidly accomplished; and at dawn of the third day, they could trace in the distance the clock-tower of the Hacienda del Venado, and an hour afterwards they dismounted in the court-yard. Although it was at that early hour when the sun sheds its most enlivening rays, everything which surrounded this habitation bore the stamp of melancholy. One might have supposed that the gloomy nature of the inmates was reflected upon its exterior.

Doña Rosarita was dying of grief; and this filled the haciendado with the deepest anxiety. Don Augustin's daughter could not help the belief that Fabian yet lived. But why, then, had not Tiburcio, as she always called him, returned to the hacienda? Either he was dead, or he no longer loved her? It was this uncertainty that gave rise to Doña Rosarita's deep dejection.

Another source of anxiety to the haciendado, was the absence of all news from the Duke de Armada; and to this anxiety was added impatience. The projected marriage between Rosarita and the Senator had been devised by Don Estevan. Tragaduros had urged its fulfilment. Don Augustin had laid the proposal before his daughter, but she replied only by tears; and her father still hesitated.

However, at the expiration of six months, it was determined to put an end to the uncertainty by sending to the Presidio for information concerning the expedition commanded by Don Estevan. It was the last respite that poor Rosarita had ventured to demand.

The Senator had absented himself for some days from the hacienda, when the major-domo returned, and Don Augustin was informed of the arrival of a stranger who could remove his uncertainty. He ordered the stranger to be introduced into the chamber already known to the reader; and Doña Rosarita, who had been sent for, speedily joined her father.

In a few moments the stranger presented himself. A wide felt hat, to which on entering he raised his hand without removing it, shaded his face, upon which a keen anxiety was visible. From beneath the broad brim of his hat a red handkerchief fell so low upon his forehead as almost to conceal his eyebrows, and from beneath its shadow he gazed with a singular interest upon the pale countenance of the young girl.

Chapter Fifty Three
The Stranger's Story

Her head veiled by a silk scarf which partly concealed the luxuriant tresses of her dark hair as they fell in luxuriant clusters upon her bosom, Doña Rosarita's countenance gave evidence of long and secret suffering.

As she seated herself, a look of deep disquietude increased her paleness. It seemed as though the young girl feared the approach of a moment, in which she might be required to renounce those sweet dreams of the past, for the reality of a future she dared not contemplate.

When the stranger was also seated the haciendado addressed him.

"We are indebted to you, my friend," he said, "for travelling thus far to bring us news which I have been forewarned may prove of a very sad nature; nevertheless we must hear all. God's will be done!"

"My news is in truth sad; but as you say, it is necessary," and the stranger, laying a stress upon these last words, seemed to address himself more particularly to Doña Rosarita, "that you should hear all. I have been witness to many things yonder; and the desert does not conceal so many secrets as one might suppose."

The young girl trembled slightly, while she fixed upon the man of the red handkerchief, a deep and searching glance.

"Go on, friend," said she, in her melodious voice, "we shall have courage to hear all."

"What do you know of Don Estevan?" resumed the haciendado.

"He is dead, Señor."

A sigh of grief escaped Don Augustin, and he rested his head upon his hands.

"Who killed him?" he asked.

"I know not, but he is dead."

"And Pedro Diaz—that man of such noble and disinterested feeling?"

"He, like Don Estevan, is no more of this world."

"And his friends Cuchillo, Oroche, and Baraja?"

"Dead as well as Pedro Diaz, all dead except—but with your leave, Señor, I shall commence my narrative at an earlier period. It is necessary that you should know all."

"We shall listen to you patiently."

"I need not detail," resumed the narrator, "the dangers of every kind, nor the various combats in which we were engaged since our departure. Headed by a chief who inspired us with boundless confidence, we shared his perils cheerfully."

"Poor Don Estevan!" murmured the haciendado.

"During the last halt in which I was present, a report spread through the camp that we were in the vicinity of an immense treasure of gold. Cuchillo, our guide, deserted us; he was absent two days. It was doubtless God's will that I should be saved, since it inspired Don Estevan with the idea of sending me in search of him. He therefore commanded me to scour the country in the environs of the camp.

"I obeyed him, notwithstanding the danger of the mission, and went in search of our guide's footsteps. After some time I was fortunate enough to find his traces; when all at once I perceived in the distance a party of Apaches engaged in a hunt of wild horses. I turned my horse's head round as quickly as possible, but the ferocious yells which burst out on every side told me that I was discovered."

The stranger, in whom the reader has doubtless recognised Gayferos, the unfortunate man who had been scalped, paused an instant as though overcome by horrible recollections. Then in continuation, he related the manner in which he was captured by the Indians, his anguish when he thought of the torments they were preparing for him, the desperate struggle by which he kept up in his race against them with naked feet, and the inexpressible sufferings he endured.

"Seized by one of them," said he, "I was struck by a blow which felled me to the earth; then I felt the keen edge of a knife trace, as it were, a circle of fire around my head. I heard a gun fired, a ball hissed close to my ears, and I lost all consciousness. I cannot tell how many minutes passed thus. The sound of a second shot caused me to open my eyes, but the blood which covered my face blinded me; I raised my hand to my head, which felt both burning and frozen. My skull was bare, the Indian had torn off the hair with the scalp attached to it. In short, they had scalped me! That is the reason, Señor, that I now wear this red handkerchief both by day and by night."

During his recital, a cold perspiration covered the narrator's countenance. His two listeners shuddered with horror.

After a momentary pause, he continued:

"I ought perhaps to spare you, as well as myself, other sad details."

Gayferos then related to his auditors the unexpected assistance he had obtained from the three hunters who had taken refuge upon the little island, and was describing the moment in which Bois-Rose carried him off in the presence of the Indians, when this heroic action drew from Don Augustin's lips a cry of admiration.

"But there were then a score on this little island?" interrupted he.

"Reckoning the giant who carried me in his arms there were but three," continued the narrator.

"*Santa Virgen*! they were trusty men then—but continue."

The adventurer resumed:

"The companion of him who had carried me in his arms was a man of about the same age—that is, near five-and-forty. There was, besides, a young man, of a pale but proud countenance, a sparkling eye, and a sweet smile; by my faith, a handsome young man, Señorita; such a one as a father might with pride own as a son—such as a lady might be proud and happy to see at her feet. During a short interval of calm, which succeeded the horrible agonies I had suffered, I found time to question the preservers of my life concerning their names and occupation; but I could learn nothing from them except that they were hunters, and travelled for their own pleasure. That was not very probable, still I made no observation."

Doña Rosarita could not quite suppress a sigh: perhaps she expected to be reminded of a familiar name.

Gayferos continued the recital of various facts with which the reader is already acquainted.

"Alas, Señorita," he continued, "the poor young man was himself captured by the Indians, and his punishment was to avenge the death of their companions."

At this part of the narrative, Doña Rosarita's cheek became deadly pale.

"Well, and the young man," interrupted the haciendado, who was almost as much moved as the daughter, on hearing these sad events, "what became of him?"

Rosarita, who had remained silent as the narrator proceeded, returned by a look of tender acknowledgment, the solicitude her father testified for the young man, for whom in spite of herself, she felt so deep an interest.

"Three days and three nights were consumed in fearful anguish, relieved only by a feeble ray of hope. At length on the morning of the fourth day, we were able unawares to fall upon our sanguinary foes; and after a desperate struggle, the warlike giant succeeded in reconquering the youth, who, safe and sound, he again pressed to his heart, calling him his beloved child."

"Heaven be praised!" exclaimed the haciendado, with a sigh of relief.

Rosarita remained silent, but her colour suddenly returning, testified to the pleasure she experienced: while a joyous smile lit up her countenance on hearing the last words of the narrator.

"Continue!" said the haciendado; "but, in your recital, which is deeply interesting to a man who was himself during six months held captive by the Indians, I seek in vain for any details relative to poor Don Estevan's death."

"I am ignorant of them," continued Gayferos, "and I can only repeat the words spoken by the youngest of the three hunters, when I questioned him upon the subject."

"He is dead," said the young man to me, "you yourself are the last survivor of a numerous expedition; when you shall have returned to your own country—for," added he, with a sigh, "you have perhaps some one, who in grief numbers the days of your absence—they will question you concerning the fate of your chief, and the men he commanded. You will reply to them, that the men died fighting—as to their chief, that he was condemned by the justice of God, and that the divine sentence pronounced against him, was executed in the desert. Don Estevan Arechiza will never again return to his friends."

"Poor Don Estevan!" exclaimed the haciendado.

"And you could never learn the names of these brave, generous, and devoted men?" asked Doña Rosarita.

"Not at the moment," continued Gayferos; "only it appeared strange to me, that the youngest of the three hunters spoke to me of Don Estevan, Diaz, Oroche, and Baraja, as though he knew them perfectly."

A pang shot through Doña Rosarita's heart, her bosom heaved, her cheeks were dyed with a deep crimson, then became pale again as the flowers of the *datura*, but she still remained silent.

"I draw towards the close of my recital," continued Gayferos. "After having recovered the brave warrior's son from the Apaches, we journeyed towards the plains of Texas. I shall not relate to you all the dangers we encountered during six months of our wandering life, as hunters of the otter and the beaver, nevertheless, it had its charms; but there was one amongst us, who was far from finding this life agreeable. This was our young companion.

"When I saw him for the first time I was struck by the melancholy expression of his countenance, but afterwards, as we journeyed together, I noticed that this melancholy, instead of decreasing, seemed daily to augment. The old hunter, whom I believed to be his father (I know now that he is not), took every opportunity of calling his attention to the magnificence of the vast forest in which we lived, the imposing scenes of the desert, or the charm of the perils we encountered. They were vain efforts, for nothing could banish the grief that consumed him. He seemed only to forget it in the midst of the dangers he eagerly sought. One might have supposed that life to him was no more than a heavy burden which he desired to get rid of.

"Full of compassion for him, I often said to the old hunter—'Solitude is only suited to an advanced age, youth delights in activity, and in the presence of its equals. Let us return to our habitations.' But the giant only sighed without replying.

"Soon afterwards the manner of the two hunters, who loved their young companion as a son, became also saddened.

"One night while the young man and I were watching, I recalled a name which six months before he had uttered in his sleep. I then learned the secret of that grief which was slowly consuming him. He loved, and solitude had but increased a passion which he vainly sought to stifle."

Gayferos paused an instant to cast a searching glance upon the countenances of his auditors, especially upon that of Doña Rosarita. He appeared to take a secret pleasure in exciting the young girl by the recital of all the circumstances best calculated to touch the heart of a woman.

As a warrior and a hunter, the haciendado did not attempt to conceal the interest with which the stranger's narrative was inspiring him.

Rosarita, on the contrary, endeavoured, under a mask of studied coldness, to conceal the charm she experienced on listening to this romance of heart and action, whose most stirring pages were so considerately opened to her by the intelligent narrator.

But her heightened colour and the fire in her large dark eyes completely belied her efforts.

"Ah!" cried Don Augustin, "if these three brave men had been under Don Estevan's command, the fate of the expedition might have been far different."

"I am of the same opinion," replied Gayferos, "but God had ordained it otherwise. Meanwhile," he continued, "I felt a great longing again to see my native land, but gratitude required that I should conceal it. But the old warrior divined my thoughts, and one day addressed me on this subject.

"Too generous to suffer me alone to brave the dangers of my homeward journey, the giant hunter resolved to accompany me as far as Tubac. His companion did not oppose his resolution, and we set out for the frontier. The young man alone seemed, to follow us reluctantly in this direction.

"I shall not describe our fatigues and the various difficulties we surmounted, in the course of our long and perilous journey. I wish, however, to speak of one of our last encounters with the Indians.

"In order to reach the Presidio we were obliged to cross the chain of the Rocky Mountains. It was towards the approach of night that we found ourselves amongst their gloomy solitudes, and we were obliged to halt.

"This is a spot much frequented by the Indians, and we could not encamp without the greatest precaution.

"Nothing, as it seems to me, can better resemble the abode of condemned souls than these mountains, where we spent the night. At every moment strange sounds, which appeared to proceed from the cavities of the rocks, broke upon our ears. At one time it was a volcano, which rumbled with dull and heavy noise beneath us, or the distant roar of a cataract: sometimes resembling the howling of wolves or plaintive cries; and from time to time dreadful flashes of lightning tore aside the veil of mist which eternally covers these mountains.

"For fear of a surprise we had encamped upon a rock which projected, in the form of a table, above a wide open valley about fifty feet below us. The two elder hunters were asleep; the youngest alone kept watch. It was his turn, and as usual he had been compelled to insist upon it—for his companions seemed unwilling thus to allow him to share their toils.

"As for myself, sick and suffering, I was stretched upon the ground. After many vain efforts to obtain a little rest, at length I slept, when a frightful dream awoke me with a start.

"'Did you hear nothing?' I asked of the young man, in a low voice. 'Nothing,' he replied, 'except the rumbling of the subterranean volcanoes in the mountains.' 'Say, rather, that we are here in an accursed spot,' I continued, and then I related my dream to him.

"'It is, perhaps a warning,' he said gravely. 'I remember one night to have had just such a dream, when—'

"The young man paused. He had advanced to the edge of the rock. I crawled after him mechanically. The same object arrested our attention at the same moment.

"One of those spirits of darkness which might have inhabited such a spot, appeared suddenly to have acquired a visible form. It was a kind of phantom, with the head and skin of a wolf, but erect upon its legs like a human being. I made the sign of the cross, and murmured a prayer, but the phantom did not stir.

"'It is the devil,' I whispered.

"'It is an Indian,' replied the young man; 'there are his companions at some distance.'

"In short, our eyes, well practised in making out objects in the dark, could distinguish about twenty Indians, stretched upon the ground, and who, in truth, had no idea of our vicinity.

"Ah, Señorita!" added the narrator, addressing himself to Doña Rosarita, "it was one of those opportunities fraught with danger, which the poor young man sought with so much avidity; and your heart, like mine, would have been torn at beholding the sad joy which sparkled in his eyes; for the further we travelled in this direction the more his melancholy seemed to increase.

"'Let us wake our friends,' I suggested.

"'No; let me go alone. These two men have done enough for me. It is now my turn to run a risk for them and, if I die, I shall forget—'

"As he spoke these words the young man quitted me, made a détour, and I lost sight of him—without, however, ceasing to behold the frightful apparition which continued immovable in the same spot.

"All at once I saw another dusky shape, which rushed towards the phantom and seized it by the throat. The two forms grappled with one another. The struggle was short and noiseless, and one might have believed them two spirits. I prayed to God in behalf of the poor young man who thus exposed his life with so much indifference and intrepidity. A short time afterwards I saw him return; the blood was flowing over his face from a large wound on his head.

"'Oh, Heavens!' I cried; 'you are wounded.'

"'It is nothing,' he said; 'I will now wake our companions.'

"What do you think, Señorita?" continued the narrator. "Was not my dream a warning from God? A party of Indians, whom we had put to flight on the other side of the mountains—had followed our track in order to revenge the blood of their companions, which had been spilt upon the banks of the Gila—at the place where we had rescued the young man.

"But the Indians had to contend with terrible adversaries. Their sentinel was the phantom who had been killed by the courageous hunter before he had time to utter a cry of alarm, and the rest, surprised in their sleep, were nearly all stabbed; a few sought safety in flight.

"The night had not passed before this new exploit was accomplished.

"The tall hunter hastened to dress the wound of the young man, whom he loved as a son; and the latter, overcome with fatigue, stretched himself upon the ground and slept.

"In the mean time his two friends watched by his side to guide his sleep, whilst I in sadness contemplated his altered countenance, his reduced figure, and the bloodstained bandage with which his head was bound."

"Poor youth," interrupted Doña Rosarita, gently, "still so young, and yet compelled to lead a life of incessant danger. And his father, also, he must have trembled for the life of a beloved son?"

"Beloved, as you say, Señorita," continued the narrator.

"During a period of six months I was a daily witness to the infinite tenderness of this father for his child.

"The young man slept tranquilly, and his lips softly murmured a name—that of a woman—the same which had lately been revealed to me in his slumber."

Rosarita's dark eyes seemed to question the narrator, but her words expired upon her parted lips; she dared not utter the name her heart was whispering in her ears.

"But I encroach upon your time," continued Gayferos, without appearing to notice the young girl's agitation. "I draw towards the close of my narrative.

"The young man woke just as day began to dawn. 'Comrade,' said the giant to me, 'go down yonder and count the dead which these dogs have left behind them.'

"Eleven corpses stretched upon the ground," continued Gayferos, "and two captured horses, attested the victory of these intrepid hunters."

"Let all due honour be given to these formidable men," cried Don Augustin, with enthusiasm, whilst his daughter, clapping her little hands together, exclaimed, with sparkling eyes, and an enthusiasm which equalled that of her father—

"That is splendid! that is sublime! so young, and yet so brave."

Rosarita only lavished her praises upon the young unknown—though perhaps the acute perception which belongs to a woman, and which almost resembles a second sight, may have revealed to her his name.

The narrator seemed to appreciate the praises bestowed upon his friends.

"But did you not learn their names?" asked Doña Rosarita, timidly.

"The elder was called Bois-Rose, the second Pepé. As to the young man—"

Gayferos appeared vainly endeavouring to recall the name without remarking the anguish which was depicted in the young girl's agitated frame, and visible in her anxious eyes.

By the similarity of position between Tiburcio and the unknown, she could not doubt but that it was he; and the poor child was collecting all her strength to listen to his name, and not to utter, on hearing it, a cry of happiness and love.

"As to the young man," continued the narrator, "he was called Fabian."

At this name, which was unknown to the young girl, and which at once destroyed her pleasant delusions, she pressed her hand upon her heart, her lips became white, and the colour which hope had revived in her cheek faded away. She could only repeat mechanically.

"Fabian!"

At this moment the recital was interrupted by the entrance of a servant. The Chaplain begged the haciendado to come to him for an instant, upon some business he had to communicate to him.

Don Augustin quitted the apartment, saying that he should speedily return.

Gayferos and the young girl were now left alone; the former observed her some moments in silence, and with a delight he could scarcely conceal, saw that Rosarita trembled beneath the folds of her silk scarf. By a secret feeling the poor child divined that Gayferos had not yet finished. At length the latter said gently, "Fabian bore another name, Señorita; do you wish to hear it, while we are alone and without witnesses?"

Rosarita turned pale.

"Another name! oh, speak it?" she cried, in a trembling voice.

"He was long known as Tiburcio Arellanos."

A cry of joy escaped the young girl, who rose from her seat, and approaching the bearer of this good news, seized his hand.

"Thanks! thanks!" she exclaimed, "if my heart has not already spoken them."

Then she tottered across the chamber, and knelt at the feet of a Madonna, which, framed in gold, hung against the wall.

"Tiburcio Arellanos," continued the narrator, "is now Fabian, and Fabian is the last descendant of the Counts of Mediana—a noble and powerful Spanish family."

The young girl continued on her knees in prayer without appearing to listen to Gayferos' words.

"Immense possessions, a lofty name, titles and honours. All these he will lay at the feet of the woman who shall accept his hand."

The young girl continued her fervent prayer without turning her head.

"And, moreover," resumed the narrator, "the heart of Don Fabian de Mediana still retains a feeling which was dear to the heart of Tiburcio Arellanos."

Rosarita paused in her prayer.

"Tiburcio Arellanos will be here to-night."

This time the young girl no longer prayed. It was Tiburcio and not Fabian, Count of Mediana. Tiburcio, poor, and unknown, for whom she had wept. At the sound of this name, she listened. Honours, titles, wealth. What were they to her? Fabian lived, and loved her still, what more could she desire?

"If you will come to the breach in the wall, where, full of despair, he parted from you, you will find him there this very evening. Do you remember the place?"

"Oh! my God!" she murmured, softly, "do I not visit it every evening?"

And once more bending before the image of the Virgin, Rosarita resumed her interrupted prayer.

The adventurer contemplated for some instants this enthusiastic and beautiful creature, her scarf partly concealing her figure, her nude shoulders caressed by the long tresses of her dark hair, which fell in soft rings upon their surface; then without interrupting her devotion, he rose from his seat and silently fitted the chamber.

Chapter Fifty Four
The Return

When Don Augustin Peña returned, he found his daughter alone, and still kneeling; he waited until her prayer was finished. The news of Don Estevan's death so entirely occupied the haciendado's mind that he naturally attributed Doña Rosarita's pious action to another motive than the true one. He believed that she was offering up to Heaven a fervent prayer for the repose of his spirit, whose mysterious end they had just been made acquainted with.

"Every day," said he, "during the following year, the Chaplain will, by my orders, say a mass for Don Estevan's soul, for this man spake of the justice of God, which was accomplished in the desert. These words are serious, and the manner with which they were pronounced, leaves no doubt as to their veracity."

"May God pardon him!" replied Rosarita, rising from her knees, "and grant him the mercy he requires."

"May God pardon him!" repeated Don Augustin, earnestly, "the noble Don Estevan was no ordinary man, or rather, that you may now know it, Rosarita, Don Antonia de Mediana, who, in his lifetime, was Knight of the Grand Cross, and Duke de Armada."

"Mediana, did you say, my father?" cried the young girl, "what! he must then be his son?"

"Of whom do you speak?" asked Don Augustin, in astonishment, "Don Antonio was never married. What can you mean?"

"Nothing, my father, unless it be that your daughter is to-day very happy."

As she said these words, Doña Rosarita threw her arms round her father's neck, and leaning her head upon his breast burst into a passion of tears; but in these tears there was no bitterness, they flowed softly, like the dew which the American jasmine sheds in the morning from its purple flowers.

The haciendado, but little versed in the knowledge of the female heart, misconstrued the tears, which are sometimes a luxury to women; and he could conceive nothing of the happiness which was drawing them from his daughter's eyes.

He questioned her anew, but she contented herself with answering, while her lips were parted by a smile, and her eyes were still moist.

"To-morrow I shall tell you all, my father."

The good haciendado did indeed require the explanation of this mystery, when he was left in ignorance of the chief fact concerning it.

"We have another duty to fulfil," continued he; "the last wish expressed by Don Antonio, on parting from me, was that you should be united to the Senator Tragaduros. It will be in compliance with the request of one who is now no more, that this marriage should no longer be delayed. Do you see any obstacle to it, Rosarita?"

The young girl started at these words, which reminded her of the fatal engagement she had sought to banish from memory. Her bosom swelled, and her tears flowed afresh.

"Well," said the haciendado, smiling, "this is another proof of happiness, is it not?"

"Of happiness!" repeated Rosarita, bitterly. "Oh! no, no, my father!"

Don Augustin was now more puzzled than ever; for, as he himself alleged, his life had been spent more in studying the artifices of Indians, with whom he had long disputed his domain, than in diving into the hearts of women.

"Oh, my father!" cried Rosarita, "this marriage would now prove a sentence of death to your poor child!"

At this sudden declaration, which he had not expected, Don Augustin was quite stupefied, and it was with difficulty he subdued the anger to which it had given rise.

"What!" he cried with some warmth, "did you not yourself consent to this marriage only a month ago? Did you not agree that it should be consummated when we knew that Don Estevan could not return? He is dead; what then do you wish?"

"It is true, father; I did fix that period, but—"

"Well!"

"But I did not know that he still lived."

"Don Antonio de Mediana?"

"No; Don Fabian de Mediana," replied Rosarita, in a low voice.

"Don Fabian? who is this Fabian of whom you speak?"

"He whom we called Tiburcio Arellanos."

Don Augustin remained mute with surprise: his daughter took advantage of his silence.

"When I consented to this marriage," said she, "I believed that Don Fabian was forever lost to us. I did not know that he still loved me; and yet—consider whether I do not love you, my father; consider what a grievous sacrifice I made in my affection for you—I knew well—"

As she spoke these words—her eyes moist with tears, yet shining with their own sweet lustre—the poor girl approached, and, by a sudden impulse, threw herself upon her father's shoulder to hide her rising blushes.

"I knew then that I loved him only," she murmured.

"But of whom do you speak?"

"Of Tiburcio Arellanos—of the Count Fabian de Mediana—they are one and the same person."

"Of the Count Mediana?" repeated Don Augustin.

"Yes," cried Rosarita, passionately; "I still love in him Tiburcio Arellanos, however noble, powerful, and rich may be at this hour Count Fabian de Mediana."

Noble, powerful, and rich, are words that sound well in the ear of an ambitious father, when applied to a young man whom he loves and esteems, but whom he believes to be poor. Tiburcio Arellanos would have met with a refusal from Don Augustin—softened, it is true, by affectionate words—but had not Fabian de Mediana a better chance of success?

"Will you tell me how Tiburcio Arellanos can be Fabian de Mediana?" asked Don Augustin, with more curiosity than anger. "Who gave you this information?"

"You were not present at the close of the stranger's narrative," replied Doña Rosarita, "or you would have heard that the young companion of the two brave hunters whose dangers he nobly shared, was no other than Tiburcio Arellanos, now become the Count Fabian de Mediana. To this day I am ignorant of how, alone and wounded, he quitted the hacienda, and by what circumstances he found these unexpected protectors—or what relationship exists between Tiburcio and the Duke de Armada. But this man, who knows, will tell you."

"Let him be instantly sought," said Don Augustin, quickly; and he called an attendant to whom he gave the order.

Don Augustin awaited with the greatest impatience, the return of Gayferos; but they sought him in vain. He had disappeared. We shall presently explain the motive of his departure. Almost at the same moment in which the haciendado and his daughter were informed of it, another attendant entered to announce that Tragaduros was dismounting in the court-yard of the hacienda.

The coincidence of the Senator's return with the approaching arrival of Fabian, was one of those events in which chance, oftener than might be supposed, sports with the events of real life.

Rosarita, in order to secure an ally in her father, hastened to embrace him tenderly, and to testify her astonishment at a miracle, which had converted the adopted son of a gambusino into the heir of one of the most powerful families in Spain. After having launched this twofold dart against the Senator, the young girl vanished from the apartment, leaving her father alone.

Tragaduros entered like a man who feels that the announcement of his arrival is always welcome. His manner was that of a future kinsman, for he had obtained the father's promise and the daughter's consent, although that consent was only tacitly given. However, notwithstanding his self-satisfaction, and his confidence in the future, the Senator could not fail to remark the grave reserve of Don Augustin's manner. He thought himself at liberty to remark it.

"Don Estevan de Arechiza, the Duke of Armada, is no more," said the haciendado; "both you and I have lost a dear and noble friend."

"What, dead?" cried the Senator, hiding his face with an embroidered cambric handkerchief. "Poor Don Estevan! I do not think I shall ever be able to console myself."

His future, nevertheless, might not have been obscured by perpetual grief, for the regret he expressed was far from being in harmony with his most secret thoughts. While he acknowledged the many obligations he owed to Don Estevan, he could not help remembering that had he lived, he would have been compelled to spend in political intrigues the half of his wife's marriage portion; half a million of money he must thus have thrown to the dogs. It is true, he said to himself, I shall neither be a count, marquis, or duke of any kind, but to my thinking, half a million of money is worth more than a title, and will multiply my pleasures considerably. This fatal event will besides hasten the period of my marriage. Perhaps after all Don

Estevan's death is not a misfortune. "Poor Don Estevan," he continued aloud, "what an unexpected blow!"

Tragaduros had yet to learn that it might have been better for him had Don Estevan lived. We will leave him with the haciendado, and follow Gayferos—for perhaps the reader will be glad to hear from him again.

The adventurer had saddled his horse, and unseen by anybody had crossed the plain and again taken the road which led to the Presidio of Tubac.

The route which he followed for some time brought him in contact with few travellers, and when by chance some horseman appeared in the distance, Gayferos, as he passed him, exchanged an impatient salutation, but failed to recognise the one he sought.

The day was drawing towards a close, and it was at a late hour when Gayferos uttered a joyful exclamation on seeing three travellers advancing at a gallop.

These travellers were no others than the Canadian, Pepé, and Fabian de Mediana. The giant was mounted upon a strong mule, larger and more vigorous than the Mexican horses. Nevertheless this animal was somewhat out of proportion with the gigantic stature of the rider.

Fabian and Pepé rode two excellent coursers, which they had taken from the Indians.

The young man was greatly changed since the day when he arrived for the first time at the Hacienda del Venado.

Painful and indelible recollections had left their traces upon his pale and wasted cheeks, a few wrinkles furrowed his brow, though the brilliancy of his eye was heightened by the sorrowful reflection of the passion which consumed him. But perhaps in the eyes of a woman his pale and sickly appearance might render the young Count of Mediana still more handsome and interesting than was that of Tiburcio Arellanos.

Would not that countenance, ennobled by toil and travel, remind Doña Rosarita of the love for which she had every reason to feel proud and happy? Would it not tell of dangers overcome, and surround itself with a double halo of sacrifice and suffering?

As to the rough countenances of the hunters, sun, fatigue, and danger of every kind had left them unchanged. If the hot winds had bronzed their skin, six months more of the adventurous life to which they were accustomed left no trace upon their sunburnt features.

They testified no surprise on seeing the gambusino, but a lively curiosity was depicted in the glance of each. A look from Gayferos, however, soon satisfied them. That look doubtless assured them that all was as they wished. Fabian alone expressed some astonishment on seeing his old companion so near the Hacienda del Venado.

"Was if in order to precede us here that you came to take leave of us near Tubac?" asked Fabian.

"Doubtless—did I not tell you so?" replied Gayferos.

"I did not understand you thus," said Fabian, who, without seeming to attach much importance to that which was said or done around him, relapsed into the melancholy silence which had become habitual to him.

Gayferos turned his horse's head round, and the four travellers continued their journey in silence.

At the expiration of an hour, during which Gayferos and the Canadian only exchanged a few words in a low tone, and to which Fabian, always absorbed in thought, gave no attention, the recollections of a past, not very remote, crowded upon the memory of the three travellers. They were again crossing the plain which extends beyond El Salto de Agua, and a few minutes afterwards they reached the torrent itself which foams down perpetually between the rocks. A bridge, the same size as the former one, replaced that which had been precipitated into the gulf below by those men who now slept their last sleep in the valley of gold, the object of their ambition.

The Canadian here dismounted.

"Now, Fabian," said he, "here Don Estevan was found; the three bandits (I except, however, poor Diaz, the tenor of the Indians) were there. See, here are still the prints of your horse's hoofs—when he slipped from this rock, dragging you downwards in his fall. Ah! Fabian, my child, I can even now see the water foaming around you—even now hear the cry of anguish I uttered. What an impetuous young man you then were!"

"That I no longer am," said Fabian, smiling sadly.

"Oh, no! at the present time your manner is imbued with the firm stoicism of an Indian warrior who smiles at the tortures of the stake. In the midst of these scenes your face is calm, yet I am convinced the recollections they recall to you must be harrowing in the extreme; is it not so, Fabian?"

"You are mistaken, my father," replied Fabian; "my heart resembles this rock, where, though you say so, I no longer trace my horse's hoofs; and my memory is mute as the echo of your own voice, which you seem still to hear. When, before suffering me to return and live forever removed from the inhabitants of yonder deserts, you required as a last trial that I should again behold a spot which might recall old recollections, I told you those recollections no longer existed."

A tear dimmed the Canadian's eye, but he concealed it by turning his back to Fabian as he remounted his mule.

The travellers then crossed the bridge formed of the trunks of trees.

"Do you trace upon this moss which covers the ground the print of my horse's hoofs when I pursued Don Estevan and his troop?" asked Fabian of Bois-Rose. "No! the dead leaves of the past winter have obliterated them — the grass which sprung up after the rainy season has grown over them."

"Ah! if I raised the leaves, if I tore up the grass, I should again discover their traces, Fabian; and if I searched the depth of your heart—"

"You would find nothing, I tell you," interrupted Fabian with some impatience; "but I am mistaken," he added, gently, "you would find a reminiscence of childhood, one of those in which you are associated, my father."

"I believe it, Fabian, I believe it—you who have been the delight of my whole life; but I have told you that I will not accept your sacrifice until to-morrow at this hour, when you shall have seen all, even the breach in the old wall, over which you once sprung, wounded in body and spirit."

A shudder, like that of the condemned on seeing the last terrible instrument of torture, passed through Fabian's frame.

The travellers halted at length, in that part of the forest situated between the Salto de Agua and the hacienda, in the open space where Fabian had found in the Canadian and his comrade, friends whom God seemed to have sent to him from the extreme ends of the earth.

Now the shades of night no longer obscured the silent depths of the American forest—a silence in which there is something awful when the sun in its zenith sends forth burning rays like blades of crimson fire, when the flower of the lliana closes its chalice, when the stems of the grass drop languidly downwards, as though in search of nourishment, and the whole face of nature, silent and inanimate, appears buried in sleep. The distant roar of the cataract was the only sound which at this hour broke the stillness of the forest.

The travellers unsaddled, and having removed their horses' bridles, fastened them at some distance off. As they had travelled all night to escape the heat of the sun, they determined to take their siesta under the shade of the trees.

Gayferos was the first who fell asleep. His affection for Fabian was not disturbed by any fears for the future. Pepé was not long in following his example. The Canadian only and Fabian did not close their eyes.

"You are not sleeping, Fabian," said Bois-Rose, in a low voice.

"No, nor you. Why do you not take some rest, like our companions?"

"One cannot sleep, Fabian, in a spot consecrated by so many sacred memories," replied the old hunter. "This place is rendered holy to me. Was it not here that, by the intervention of a miracle, I again found you in the heart of this forest, after having lost you upon the wide ocean? I should be ungrateful to the Almighty if I could forget this—even to obtain the rest which He has appointed for us."

"I think as you do, my father, and listen to your words," replied the young Count.

"Thanks, Fabian; thanks also to that God who ordained that I should find you with a heart so noble and so loving. See! here are still the remains of the fire near which I sat; here are the brands, still black, though they have been washed by the rain of an entire season. Here is the tree against which I leant on the happiest evening of my life, since it restored you to me; for now that I can again call you my son, each day of my existence has been fraught with happiness, until I learnt what I should have understood, that my affection for you was not that to which the young heart aspires."

"Why so frequently allude to this subject, my father?" said Fabian, with that gentle submission which is more cutting than the bitterest reproach.

"As you will. Let us not again allude to that which may pain you; we shall speak of it after the trial to which I have submitted you."

The father and son—for we may indeed call them so—now maintained a long silence, listening only to the voices of nature. The sun approached the horizon, a light breeze sprung up and rustled among the leaves; already hopping from branch to branch, the birds resumed their song, the insects swarmed in the grass, and the lowing of cattle was heard in the distance. It was the denizens of the forest who welcomed the return of evening.

The two sleepers awoke.

After a short and substantial repast, of which Gayferos had brought the materials from the Hacienda del Venado, the four travellers awaited in calm meditation the hour of their great trial.

Some time passed away before the azure sky above the open clearing was overcast.

Gradually, however, the light of day diminished on the approach of twilight, and then myriads of stars shone in the firmament, like sparks sown by the sun as he quitted the horizon. At length, as on that evening to which so many recollections belonged, when Fabian, wounded, reached the wood-rangers by their fire, the moon illumined the summits of the trees and the glades of the forest.

"Can we light a fire?" inquired Pepé.

"Certainly; for it may chance that we shall spend the night here," replied Bois-Rose. "Is not this your desire, Fabian?"

"It matters little to me," replied the young man; "here or yonder, are we not always agreed?"

Fabian, as we have said, had long felt that the Canadian could not live, even with him, in the heart of towns, without yearning for the liberty and free air of the desert. He knew also that to live without him would be still more impossible for his comrade; and he had generously offered himself as a sacrifice to the affection of the old hunter.

Bois-Rose was aware of the full extent of the sacrifice, and the tear he had that morning shed by stealth, was one of gratitude. We shall by-and-by enter more fully into the Canadian's feelings.

The position of the stars indicated eleven o'clock.

"Go, my son," said Bois-Rose to Fabian. "When you have reached the spot where you parted from the woman who perhaps loved you, put your hand upon your heart. If you do not feel its pulses beat quicker, return, for you will then have overcome the past."

"I shall return, then," replied Fabian, in a tone of melancholy firmness: "memory is to me like the breath of the wind which passes by without resting, and leaves no trace."

He departed slowly. A fresh breeze tempered the hot exhalations which rose from the earth. A resplendent moon shone upon the landscape at the moment when Fabian, having quitted the shadow of the forest, reached the open space intervening between it and the wall inclosing the hacienda.

Until that moment he proceeded with a slow but firm step, but when, through the silver vapours of the night, he perceived the white wall with the breach in the centre partly visible, his pace slackened, and his knees trembled under him.

Did he dread his approaching defeat? for his conscience told him already that he would be vanquished—or was it rather those recollections which, now so painfully recalled, rose up before him like the floods of the sea?

There was a deep silence, and the night, but for a slight vapour, was clear. All at once Fabian halted and stood still like the dismayed traveller, who sees a phantom rise up in his path. A white and airy form appeared distinctly visible above the breach in the old wall. It resembled one of the fairies in the old legends of the north, which to the eye of the Scandinavian idolaters floated amidst vapours and mists. To the eye of Fabian it bore the angel form of his first and only love!

For one instant this lovely apparition appeared to Fabian to melt away; but his eyes deceived him, for in spite of himself they were obscured. The vision remained stationary. When he had strength to move, he advanced nearer, and still the vision did not disappear.

The young man's heart felt as if it would burst, for at this moment a horrible idea crossed his mind. He believed that what he saw was Rosarita's spirit, and he would rather a thousand times have known her living, though pitiless and disdainful, than behold her dead, though she appeared in the form of a gentle and benignant apparition.

A voice, whose sweet accents fell upon his ear like heavenly music, failed to dispel the illusion, though the voice spoke in human accents.

"Is it you, Tiburcio? I expected you."

Even the penetration of a spirit from the other world could not have divined that he would return from such a distance.

"Is it you, Rosarita?" cried Fabian, in a scarcely perceptible voice, "or a delusive vision which will quickly disappear?"

And Fabian stood motionless, fixed to the spot, so greatly did he fear that the beloved image would vanish from his sight.

"It is I," said the voice; "I am indeed here."

"O God! the trial will be more terrible than I dared to think," said Fabian, inwardly.

And he advanced a step forward, then paused; the poor young man did not entertain a hope.

"By what miracle of heaven do I find you here?" he cried.

"I come every evening, Tiburcio," replied the young girl.

This time Fabian began to tremble more with love than hope.

We have seen that Rosarita, in her last interview with Fabian, chose rather to run the risk of death than confess that she loved him. Since then she had suffered so much, she had shed so many tears, that now love was stronger than virgin purity.

A young girl may sometimes, by such courage, sanctify and enhance her modesty.

"Come nearer, Tiburcio," she said; "see! here is my hand."

Fabian rushed forward to her feet. He seized the hand she offered convulsively, but he tried in vain to speak.

The young girl looked down with anxious tenderness upon his face.

"Let me see if you are much changed, Tiburcio," she continued. "Ah! yes. Grief has left its traces on your brow, but honour has ennobled it. You are as brave as you are handsome, Tiburcio. I learned with pride that danger had never made your cheek turn pale."

"You heard, did you say?" cried Fabian; "but what have you heard?"

"All, Tiburcio; even to your most secret thoughts. I have heard all, even of your coming here this evening. Do you understand? and I am here!"

"Before I dare to comprehend, Rosarita,—for this time a mistake would kill me," continued Fabian, whose heart was stirred to its very depths by the young girl's words, and the tenderness of her manner, "will you answer one question, that is if I dare to ask it?"

"Dare, then, Tiburcio," said Rosarita, tenderly. "Ask what you wish. I came to-night to hear you—to deny you nothing."

"Listen," said the young Count: "six months ago I had to avenge my mother's death, and that of the man who had stood in my father's place, Marcos Arellanos; for if you know all, you know that I am no longer—"

"To me you are the same, Tiburcio; I never knew Don Fabian de Mediana."

"The wretch who was about to expiate his crime—the assassin of Marcos Arellanos, in short, Cuchillo—begged for his life. I had no power to grant it; when he cried, 'I ask it in the name of Doña Rosarita, who loves you, for I heard—,' the suppliant was upon the edge of a precipice. I would have pardoned him for love of you; when one of my companions precipitated him into the gulf below. A hundred times, in the silence of the night, I recalled that suppliant voice, and asked myself in anguish, What did he then hear? I ask it of you this evening, Rosarita."

"Once, once only, did my lips betray the secret of my heart. It was here, in this very spot, when you had quitted our dwelling. I will repeat to you what I then said."

The girl seemed to be collecting all her strength, before she dared tell the young man that she loved him, and that openly and passionately; then—her pure countenance shining with virgin innocence, which fears not, because it knows no ill, she turned towards Tiburcio.

"I have suffered too much," she said, "from one mistake, to allow of any other; it is thus, then, with my hands in yours, and my eyes meeting yours, that I repeat to you what I then said. You had fled from me, Tiburcio. I knew you were far away, and I thought God alone heard me when I cried: '*Come back, Tiburcio, come back! I love only you!*'"

Fabian, trembling with love and happiness, knelt humbly at the feet of this pure young girl, as he might have done before a Madonna, who had descended from her pedestal.

At this moment he was lost to all the world,—Bois-Rose, the past, the future—all were forgotten like a dream on awaking, and he cried in a broken voice:

"Rosarita! I am yours forever! I dedicate my future life to you only."

Rosarita uttered a faint cry. Fabian turned, and remained mute with astonishment.

Leaning quietly upon his long carbine, stood Bois-Rose, a few paces from them, contemplating, with a look of deep tenderness the two lovers.

It was the realisation of his dream in the isle of Rio Gila.

"Oh, my father!" cried Fabian sadly; "do you forgive me for suffering myself to be vanquished?"

"Who would not have been, in your place, my beloved Fabian?" said the Canadian, smiling.

"I have broken my oath, my father!" continued Fabian; "I had promised never to love any other but you. Pardon! pardon!"

"Child, who implores pardon, when it is I who should ask it?" said Bois-Rose; "you were more generous than I, Fabian. Never did a lioness snatch her cub from the hands of the hunters, and carry it to her den, with a more savage love than I dragged you from the habitations of men to hide you in the desert. I was happy, because all my affections were centred in you; and I believed that you might also be so. You did not murmur; you sacrificed, unhesitatingly, all the treasures of your youth—a thousand times more precious than those of the Golden Valley. I did not intend it should be so, and it is I who have been selfish, and not generous, for if you had died of grief, I should have died also."

"What do you mean?" cried Fabian.

"What I say, child. Who watched over your slumbers during long nights, to hear from your lips the secret wishes of your heart? It was I, who determined to accompany to this spot, Gayferos, whom at your intercession I saved from the hands of the Apaches. Who sent him to seek this beautiful and gracious lady, and learn if in her heart, she still treasured your memory? It was I still, my child, for your happiness is a thousand times more precious than mine. Who persuaded you to make this last trial? It was still I, my child, who knew that you must succumb to it. To-morrow I had said to you, I will accept your sacrifice; but Gayferos had even then read the most secret pages of this lady's heart. Why do you ask my pardon, when I tell you it is I, who should ask yours?"

The Canadian, as he finished these words, opened his arms to Fabian, who eagerly rushed into his embrace.

"Oh, my father," cried he, "so much happiness frightens me, for never was man happier than I."

"Grief will come when God wills it," said the Canadian, solemnly.

"But you, what will become of you?" asked Fabian, anxiously. "Your loss will be to me the only bitterness in my full cup of joy."

"As God wills, my child," answered the Canadian. "It is true, I cannot live in cities, but this dwelling, which will be yours, is on the borders of the desert. Does not infinity surround me here? I shall build with Pepé—Ho, Pepé," said the hunter in a loud voice, "come and ratify my promise."

Pepé and Gayferos came forward at the hunter's summons.

"I and Pepé," he continued, "will build a hut of the trunks and bark of trees upon the spot of ground where I found you again. We shall not always be at home, it is true, but perhaps some time hence should you wish to claim the name and fortune of your ancestors in Spain, you will find two friends ready to follow you to the end of the world. Come, my Fabian, I have no doubt that I shall be even happier than you, for I shall experience a double bliss in my happiness and yours."

But why dwell longer upon such scenes? happiness is so transitory and impalpable that it will not bear either analysis or description.

"There remains but one obstacle now," resumed the hunter. "This sweet lady's father."

"To-morrow he will expect his son," interrupted Rosarita, who stood by, listening with singular interest to the dialogue.

"Then let me bless mine," said the Canadian.

Fabian knelt before the hunter.

The latter removed his fur cap, and with moist eyes raised to the starry heavens, he said—

"Oh! my God! bless my son, and grant that his children may love him as he has been loved by old Bois-Rose."

The following day the illustrious Senator returned in sadness to Arispe.

"I was sure," he said, "that I should unceasingly mourn for poor Don Estevan. I might at least have possessed, besides my wife's marriage portion, a title of honour and half a million of money. It is certainly a great misfortune that poor Don Estevan is dead."

Sometime afterwards a hut made of the bark and trunks of trees was built in the forest glade so well-known to the reader. Often Fabian de Mediana, accompanied by Rosarita, to whom he was now united by the holy ties of marriage, performed a pilgrimage to the dwellers in the hut.

Perhaps at a later period one of those pilgrimages might be undertaken with the view of claiming the assistance of the two brave hunters in an expedition to the Golden Valley or to the coast of Spain; but that is a thing of the future. Let us for the present be content with saying, that if the happiness of this world is not a vain delusion, in truth it exists at the Hacienda del Venado, enjoyed by Fabian, Rosarita, and the brave *Wood-Rangers*—Pepé and Bois-Rose.